April Rising

April Rising
a novel
Corene Lemaître

Excerpt from *The Essential Kabbalah: the Heart of Jewish Mysticism* © 1995 by Daniel C. Matt, used by permission of HarperCollins *Publishers*. Scripture taken from the Holy Bible, New International Version R, © 1973, 1978, 1984, International Bible Society, used by permission of Zondervan Publishing House. Excerpt from "Jocko Homo," words and music by Mark Mothersbaugh © 1978, excerpt from "Through Being Cool," words and music by Mark Mothersbaugh and Gerald Casale © 1981 EMI Virgin Music Ltd. and Devo Music. All rights controlled and administered by EMI Virgin Songs, Inc. All rights reserved. International copyright secured. Used by permission.

First Carroll & Graf edition 1999

Carroll & Graf Publishers, Inc.
19 West 21st Street
New York, NY 10010-6805

Library of Congress Cataloging-in-Publication data is available.
ISBN: 0-7867-0654-6

Manufactured in the United States of America

To Andrew Kelly
Tree Riesener
Guy Lemaître
Todd Lemaître
with love

And to the memory of Bibi Jentoft-Nilsen

Acknowledgements

I would like to thank Nick Sayers, Susan Opie and David Marshall for making the first time so much fun.

I would also like to express my gratitude to Stephanie Cabot, Eugenie Furniss and Ruscha Fields for making it possible.

Thank you also to Susan Davis and Kay Sylvester.

1

It doesn't take me long to figure out that something is wrong. To begin with, my key doesn't turn in the lock. I try all the old tricks – rattling the doorknob, lifting the door half an inch off the ground – but same verdict. No entry. Access denied.

I'm being observed. Our next-door neighbour is giving me the evil eye. She doesn't look as though she recognizes me. I wonder how long it will be before she calls the police.

The lock has been changed. It's a good one, state of the art, the kind that could probably perform a citizen's arrest – more than could be said of the old lock, which had been more of a formality. Anyone could have broken in. No one ever had, of course. There is no crime in Philmont, or pain, or unhappiness, or anything resembling the usual range of human emotions. The streets are safe, divorce is rare and everyone has health insurance. The only thing likely to kill you is boredom.

Dragonlady is definitely on to me. She's exacting, believes in 'love thy neighbour' provided it's on her own terms. Keeps her lawn trimmed down to the regulation half inch, drives a station wagon, runs the Neighbourhood Watch. Still has that ash-blonde hair and those tilty tennis hips, the ones that remind me of a couple of cheese-slicers. Belongs to the local upper-middle-class militia, the Philmont Protective Association, a century-old society for the promotion of the status quo. My parents and she don't speak on account of the fact that they decline to cut the grass more frequently than once every two weeks. They pleaded not guilty on the grounds of having better things to do, but this was not accepted as an excuse. She crosses her arms, all hostile and DAR, ready to defend her own little patch of America.

Philmont is Utopia, an enclave regarded by its denizens as sanctuary in the midst of an increasingly hazardous country where sacred boundaries are being stretched, parameters violated every day. It has good schools, several churches. Some Methodists, many Presbyterians, a fair smattering of Quakers and a token Catholic or two. Nearby, a national park and a military academy where South American dictators send their sons. The local paper, *The Philmont Organ,* hard-pressed for significant copy, patiently covers church fairs, school board meetings, local politics, Society. The crime page is meagre. Petty vandalism in peripheral slums and the occasional DUI. Once in a blue moon, a flasher, for which many secretly prurient readers are grateful.

I wonder if one of the windows is open. I'm in luck. A benign smile to the neighbour and I'm swinging myself over the windowsill.

'Anybody home?' I yell. No answer.

They don't know I'm coming. My family, that is – my parents and two brothers, James and Matthew. I'd decided not to inform them. Give them a big surprise. But I'm regretting this already. Clearly, no one is home. A lavish welcome would have been nice, I find myself thinking.

I throw my bag at the bottom of the stairs and look around. Everything seems to be about the same. Same aloof furniture, same smell of wax and cleanliness. White walls, countless windows letting in sun, space, light, enlightenment. An umbrella stand full of carved canes that no one uses. A grand piano that no one plays. Peace and stillness reign as in a tiny, undisturbed kingdom too self-contained to require the ministrations of an interfering monarch.

But something is different.

I can't quite put my finger on it. It could be the fact that all the houseplants are missing – from the largest rubber tree to the smallest cutting gratuitously stolen by my mother from a garden shop. But there is something else. Something bigger, something I can't readily explain. A presence. A distinctive, tangible, bodily presence, one significant enough to have altered the air, the actual chemical composition of the household.

2

You can sense the addition and subtraction in a family – when someone arrives, when someone departs. Someone is here who wasn't here before. An otherworldly being has come out of orbit and landed on the surface of the Planet Harmony.

I'm apprehensive, but I'm also starving. Why face your fears when you can eat? So rather than investigate I head for the kitchen and open a few cupboard doors. The shelves are naked, stripped, completely bare of food. Even the really inedible food. Well, most of the food in our household is inedible, but there are always items on the shelves that defy description, that have been there for months, sometimes for years. Stiff little banana chips and leathery dried apricots. Boxes of textured soy protein and jars of withered brown rice. Wholemeal loaf heels that either grow mould or end up as some kind of bread pudding that no one is willing to eat. Tapioca mix with the instructions written in German. Fibre crackers. Stale bran cereal. Jars of no-sugar preserves. And in a sort of oubliette under the counter, packets of dandelion-leaf tea, forgotten because it's essentially undrinkable, and bags of home-grown herbs, never used because they all smell the same. The kitchen is immaculate, of course. We have a cleaner come in twice a week. The ethics of this were debated at length by my mother and my older brother James, James arguing that this was exploitative, my mother insisting that we were providing employment. The whole question was settled by the cleaner who said she had two kids in college and to mind their own damn business.

In the fridge I find a squeeze-bottle of spreadable cheese – orange, full of preservatives, the type that at one time would not have made it through the front door. I try a bit, squirting it directly into my mouth. It tastes like glue. Further investigation reveals a case, a whole *case*, full of diet soda. Diet soda, diet *anything*, is taboo in our house; my mother holds that dieting is symptomatic of a corrupt and decadent civilization more concerned with appearances than morality. One flavour, 'Fruit Frenzy'. I open a can and try a sip. Extraordinary. It's like chewing a whole packet of bubble gum, right down to the rubbery after-taste. Where did this stuff come from?

I'm getting a headache, the result of hunger and twelve hours of air travel. But try as I might, I can't relax. I feel edgy, like an

3

unwelcome guest in an off-season hotel. Something very weird is going on and I don't know what.

Then I hear music.

Thin and distant. Tinny pop music of the lowest variety, the kind you hear pounding out of cars charioteered by teenagers on their way to the Jersey shore with an illicit case of beer and no sunblock.

It's coming from upstairs.

No one in my family listens to pop music. My mother likes Mozart, my father Big Band, and James enjoys egghead music like Bartok. Even Matthew, my younger brother, hates pop music. He's a determinedly anti-social freak-geek who lives in the basement with his modem and his permanent smirk.

So whose is it?

Fee, fie, foe, fum, I think, creeping upstairs. Though uneasy, I am curious. Something tells me that the music, like the diet soda and the spreadable cheese, is a clue to what is going on and the sooner I come face to face with it, the better.

It's coming from my bedroom.

My bedroom. My *sanctum sanctorum*.

Righteous indignation conquers fear. I open the door.

Someone is sleeping in my bed.

In *my bed*.

Not only that, my room has been completely transformed.

My room, as I know it, no longer exists. It's gone. Just gone. My signature style. No more polished bare floorboards, Venetian blinds. No desk, no books, no Shaker-blue bedspread. All my stuff has disappeared. Everything has been replaced.

The effect is of a downmarket home furnishings showroom. At the windows, gauzy curtains, cheap and opalescent. On the floor, a fluffy lime-green rug like an oversized toilet-seat cover. On the bed, a pink bedspread made from the type of fabric that gives you a rash if it comes into direct contact with your skin. In lieu of the desk, a small vanity table, and in place of my prints of Kandinsky and Klee, three posters: the sun rising over a Bible quotation, a Christian pop singer, and a puppy and kitten curled up in the same basket. The room even smells different – a combination of scented deodorant and drugstore perfume. Another

4

person has taken my place, superimposed herself over me. I have been eradicated.

In the bed lies Goldilocks herself. Yes, Goldilocks – there is no doubt about it. As her back is to me all I can see is a fairly large form under the covers, a ribbon of nylon negligee and a great deal of long blonde hair. Her arm, draped across her side, is muscular yet oddly graceful. She snores, lightly.

I perch myself on a padded stool and stare. Extraordinary. She sort of heaves and relaxes, heaves and relaxes, peacefully, delicately, like a princess under a benevolent spell. Even more fascinating is the pile of chocolate-bar wrappers on the floor, about twenty of them. On top of the bedside table are yet more chocolate bars, piled high, an abundance of comfort and joy. There are Milky Ways and 5th Avenues, Baby Ruths and Nestlé Crunch, even a few of those Hershey's Miniatures you get at Halloween. Best of all, there are Peanut Chews, those stiff, nutty little rectangles that break your teeth and take your fillings out.

One of my all-time favourite movie scenes is the one in *Whatever Happened to Baby Jane* in which the starving Joan Crawford wolfs down a drawerful of chocolate. I am ravenous. The processed cheese has only whetted my appetite. A tidal wave of longing engulfs me as I survey these delicacies. I reach forward. I can't help myself. I want a Peanut Chew, just one. As my fingers close around it, the girl snorts and rolls over. Opens her eyes. Screams.

And continues to scream. I don't know what to do. I have no quarrel with this girl. I don't even know who she is. But I would like her to leave, as quickly as possible, so I stay and hold my ground. She's quite attractive when she screams, I note. Very pretty. A real damsel in distress sort of girl. Hm. Is she as helpless as she seems?

Suddenly she stops, gasping. Her nose is tiny and tip-tilted, her face round and vulnerable. A small hardness about the lips – a mere suggestion. 'Sorry,' she says. 'I was just making sure.'

'Of what?'

'That you were you, of course. I figured if you weren't, you would run away.'

I have no idea what she is talking about. '*Who* are *you*?' I ask.

'My name's April. Oh, it's embarrassing to meet people

unexpectedly like this. I'm not being very hospitable. You'll forgive me, won't you?' Her speaking voice is delicate, anachronistic, like a prim Midwestern schoolmarm. With a touch of the redneck, though. Just a touch. 'I bet I know who you are. You're Ellen.'

A confirmation might be misinterpreted as a friendly overture, so I look at her and say nothing – always the best tactic for getting the better of someone. I place my right ankle on my left knee. Jiggle my foot.

'We weren't expecting you,' she says gaily, as though discussing rain at an outdoor tea, 'but I know your parents are going to be thrilled you're home, just thrilled. I wish you'd called first – we could've thrown you a surprise party. Your mother just loves a celebration. And I bet she's missed you a bunch.'

Is it my imagination, or is she patronizing me? Her cosy attitude towards my parents, my home, towards *me*, is intolerable. 'Forgive me,' I say, 'but are you a long-lost relative nobody's told me about?'

'Oh, no.' She giggles. 'If that were the case, you'd think there would be a family resemblance – and you and I don't look a thing alike! I wish I was as thin as you . . . I'm your brother's girlfriend. James's girlfriend.'

James, or 'Spock' as he is fondly known, has never had a girlfriend, though not through lack of opportunity. He's tall and dark and has that alluring air of Vulcan reserve supposedly so enticing to women, but he's never allowed himself to succumb. He claims that emotion gets in the way of reason, of knowing right from wrong. He is obsessed with right and wrong. When I last saw him, he was working on his PhD. In ethics. And not having any fun. Now he's going out with Goldilocks here. *Why???*

'You have an awful lot of catching up to do,' she continues. 'On all the family news. You've missed a lot since you left for . . .'

'Europe.'

'That's right. You've been gone two whole years, after all.'

'Is he still at Berkeley?'

'Who, James? Oh, no. He quit. He's left all that behind.' This is said loftily, offhandedly, as though to discourage questions. 'He'll be awfully glad to see you. And I'm glad to see you, too – really glad. It'll be so nice to have someone my own age to

6

talk to. We're both twenty-three! I just know we're going to be great friends.'

I don't know what she's going on about. I'm still reeling from the shock. 'James has left Berkeley? But he seemed so happy there. Well, as happy as he ever is . . .'

'That's just it,' says April. 'He *wasn't* happy.'

I feel as though I am missing some crucial information. 'But he was so excited about living and studying in California. Something about needing to find himself. I mean, it took us by surprise at first, he'd been at Harvard for five years . . .'

'. . . and he hated that, too.' She smiles brightly, as though she's just demonstrated the solution to a tricky equation. 'Would you like a soda or something?'

'He did not hate Harvard.'

'Yes, he did.'

'No, he didn't.'

'Yes, he did.'

'No, he –' This is ridiculous. Better to try and establish a chain of events. 'Okay. So he went to Berkeley and failed to find himself. Then what?'

April's gaze hardens. 'He found me.'

Her tone is suddenly steely, veering towards the redneck. Reverting, rather. Regressing. Ah ha. So she isn't all sweetness and light after all. I am waiting for her to offer me my old room back. She isn't even making a move to get out of bed.

'Well,' I say. 'So. Where are my parents?'

'The supermarket. They should be home any minute now. Oh, about your room. I'll be out of here by tomorrow. Sorry about the imposition. I'll be moving in with your brother down the hall. Well, I guess you remember where your brother's room is.' She giggles again. 'I just wanted to redecorate it first. He's been sleeping on the downstairs couch while I put on the finishing touches. The paint's still drying.'

She speaks chattily, as though her role, her place in the family, is God-given and assumed. As though she's been here as long as I have. Has more right to be here than I do.

'We'll have lots of time to get to know each other,' she adds. 'I've heard so much about you.'

She does not elaborate. Still, I wait. I've no desire to be forthcoming myself. We stare at each other, eye to eye. Do I detect a flicker of hostility?

We are saved by a clattering downstairs. The arrival of my parents. My stomach shrinks and tightens. This is the moment I've been waiting for. My chance to make a grand entrance, show this blithe pretender what it's all about. I stand.

'It may be kind of a shock for them,' says April.

'That's the whole point,' I reply, and head for the stairs.

'Let *me*,' says April eagerly, and before I can stop her she is out of bed, wrapping a bathrobe around her body and bounding away, seizing the opportunity to be the bearer of glad tidings. I am left behind in mid-step, flabbergasted, infuriated. She has committed the worst possible sin. She has stolen my limelight.

I listen for whoops of pleasure and exclamations of delight. Mere silence reverberates. Then, a clearly audible, 'You're joking,' from my father.

'Did she say where she's been?' asks my mother. A gratifying touch of anxiety there.

'Yurrip,' says April, softening the 'r's, implying her own refinement, as though she'd been to Europe herself. 'I guess she's home for a visit. She didn't mention how long she'd be staying.'

'Just long enough to collect some money,' my father remarks. 'You know Ellen. Hello and goodbye.'

My indignation swells. They loved giving me money. Didn't they?

I wait to be welcomed and warmly embraced, interrogated with enthusiastic interest. But no one comes up the stairs. I try making noises, drop the usual hints. Until it becomes clear that doing so is pointless.

I hear laughter. My mother and father. Perhaps they are laughing at me. Maybe April has told a joke at my expense. Yes. She's a tricky one. This is almost certainly the case.

Thus war is declared. Saint April – the new family pet. God, I hate her. Presumptuous, patronizing, pretentious, poorly educated white-trash redneck bitch, too big for her britches. Tacky and vulgar. Dumb? Very possibly. But she is shrewd; she may turn out to be a more formidable foe than I think.

* * *

8

They march back and forth, bringing groceries in from the car. My mother and father, that is, who welcomed me, respectively, with, 'Hello, Ellen,' and, 'Those had better not be track marks on your arm, young lady.' The upholstery of their lives is tighter, brighter, than I remember, and there is a sense of renewal in the air, an irritating freshness from which I feel excluded.

My mother seems particularly focused. My memory of her is all static and interference, a fuzzy picture of exasperating conduct. Running after me with mittens, making me eat hot breakfasts. Trying to get my attention, getting in the way. Now, she is barely looking at me. She strides purposefully from car to cupboard, as though on a mission from God. Whatever has happened, she is no longer on automatic pilot, just going through the motions of everyday life.

'There's more in the car, Ellen,' she barks, all army sergeant. Very unusual for her, highly suspect. For all her liberal ravings, my mother has always maintained a veneer of calm. A rigid refusal to ruffle whatever the circumstances, as though determined to hold everything in. Once, in a fit of rare spite, my father accused her of being passive-aggressive. He later apologized, amending it to 'phlegmatic', but his exasperation exploded like an unexpected belch: 'God damn it, Julia, why can't you just get pissed off sometimes? Can't you just get angry?'

April is already off and running, of course, helping my parents to carry in the groceries like a fat Girl Scout. I wonder what exactly the arrangement is here. Is her stay temporary? Is she paying rent? Or is she plotting permanent residency and taking advantage of their generous nature? My first priority is to determine the facts. If April turns out to be a freeloader, then I have my work cut out for me. If not . . .

'Mom?' I say. 'Can I talk to you?'

'In a minute, Ellen. There are several more bags in the car.'

I consider dropping this hint to be in very poor taste. I've just arrived, and they expect me to carry groceries? 'It's about April,' I whisper urgently.

'Not now, Ellen.' She brushes past me pointedly. Philmont-wise, she's got the look. Reassuring shoulders, shiny hair. Straight nose at a perfect perpendicular to the mouth. In spite of her past of protest marches and peace pipes, she now looks, superficially, like the typical suburban housewife she never wanted to be. My father has disappeared, as he generally does when there are groceries to be unpacked. He always vanishes at key times. Like when his clients' verdicts are read out. Guilty. Not guilty. It's usually not guilty, as my father does a mean peroration, but apathy is his trademark. One way or the other, he just doesn't seem to care.

Just then April walks in, carrying two bags. 'My ears are burning,' she says cheerfully.

'We were just talking about you,' I reply.

'Uh oh.' She beams at me, then turns to my mother. 'Any more bags in the car, Mom?'

Mom???

'A few, dear.'

'I'll get them,' I say quickly, but April is already off and running.

I point in her direction. 'She's trying to make me look bad.'

'Don't be so paranoid, darling. She's just being helpful.'

'She's manipulating you and you don't even know it. You're being brainwashed.' I twirl one of my mother's neo-psychedelic refrigerator magnets in front of her face. 'Aaah, the evil Dr Mesmer.'

'Put that away, Ellen. You're being ridiculous.' She looks in the cupboards, at the groceries, everywhere but at me.

It all seems so unfair. I'd *meant* to bring the bags in; I am not getting credit for my good intentions. As for April, it is clear that she is trying to one-up me, sabotage me, displace me in my mother's affections. I am not thinking fast enough – this is the problem. I need to demonstrate that I am as devoted as this brown-nosing little goody-two-shoes.

But as I stand around trying to think of something to do, April bursts back in and starts unpacking the food. What emerges is America – an array of brand-name junk food, the existence of which my mother has previously refused to acknowledge. 'Mm, Ellio's Pizza. Yummy. And Diet Coke. And Doritos. And Miracle Whip. Did you get all this stuff for me?'

'Yes, dear, we want you to feel at home. I'm afraid this has always been a health-food household.'

'Yeah,' I say, looking on enviously. 'She never even let us eat white bread.'

April pulls a loaf out of a bag. 'Ooh. The mushy kind.'

'Ellen, stop staring.'

April pulls out Oreos, potato chips, chocolate milk mix, six TV dinners, individual pudding packs (the ones I'd always hoped to find in my lunchbox, only to be rudely shocked by packets of trail mix), hot dogs, fish fingers and a dozen flat sausages sandwiched between rubbery rolls, limp lettuce and squashed eggs. 'I can't believe it. All my favourites. This is so nice of you.'

'And the *pièce de résistance,*' says my mother, producing something from her totebag, 'Tastykakes.'

'Jelly Krimpets!'

'None other.'

April's cheeks are pink with shy delight, as though she is unaccustomed to anyone giving a damn about her. I sense a certain conceit around this – she slides too easily into being the apple of somebody's eye: I want treats, I want attention. Me, me.

'Is this the reason you cleared the shelves?' I am being sarcastic, but my mother's answer is frank, direct: 'Yes, Ellen. A fresh start. For all of us.'

I don't like the implications of this. A more direct approach is called for:

'By the way, Mom, where's my stuff?'

'What stuff, Ellen?'

'The stuff from my room. It appears to have gone missing.' The idea is to embarrass my mother, show April up for the interloper that she is. 'My bedspread, my books, my pictures, my desk –'

'In the guest room.' Her tone is firm, final.

'You mean the *Morgue?*'

'The guest room, Ellen. Well, for all we knew, you were never coming back. And April needed a place to sleep.'

The Morgue is the place we allegedly put guests, but it is in fact the junk room, where everything that is defunct, obsolete or best forgotten is consigned. You might say that it contains the whole history of our family, everything short of actual skeletons, a pageant of mortifications and events long blocked out. The

11

phoney foot in concrete one of my father's more dubious clients gave him before the 'not guilty' verdict was a sure thing. My mother's collection of paperweights made from genuine excrement encased in glass, bought in the Seventies from an Amsterdam street merchant. James's '*Requiescat in Pace*' box, which he made in ceramics for the ashes of his dead hamster Socrates (cremated in the backyard barbecue) when he was nine. The declaration Matthew issued through his computer to have his fourth grade teacher committed to the state mental institution. Two decades' worth of Halloween costumes: Helen of Troy (James in drag), Dr Terror (me), R2-D2 (Matthew), Castro (my mother), Henry VIII (my dad), Plato (James), the little Martian from the Warner Brothers cartoon (Matthew), Son of Sam (my dad again), Ghandi (Mom), Jesus (James – same costume, next year, modified), Benedict Arnold (Dad), Mother Angelica from the Eternal Word TV Network (me) and several shabby, grey, forgotten ghosts, all redolent of tricks or poisoned apples. This is the essence of my family: our beliefs, our creeds, our characters. Now all my belongings are there, too – a bad sign. I have been relegated to the Morgue. There is no doubt about it. Missing in action, presumed dead. *Requiescat in pace.*

2

I conk out due to jet lag, sleep for seventeen hours. Dream that I've turned into a giant radio and can't turn myself off. I wake up pounding myself on the side of the head; realize I'm lying in the Morgue and that what I'm hearing is the sound of the local military academy band bashing away at eight o'clock in the morning. I hear shouts and booms, a memory from childhood – it's all coming back to me now. I look out the window, observe a Stealth bomber fly over the house. After learning that they are covered with Teflon, I can't dismiss the image of a giant frying pan.

I go downstairs to find my parents already up and sipping coffee. My mother is neatly dressed in a skirt and blouse and is knitting. It's not a good idea to ask what she's making – she'll probably tell you it's a shroud. She keeps herself under control, by and large, but once in a while something slips out that indicates her general dissatisfaction with the universe. My father is wearing a sweatshirt he ordered from the National Public Radio catalogue; it reads, 'A good lawyer knows the law. A great lawyer knows the judge.' He's perusing the local paper. 'LandDevel Seeks Deal in Grosworthy Estate Controversy,' the headline states.

'Sleep well, Ellen?' my father cheerfully enquires. He knows perfectly well I've passed an unwholesome night.

'Sure have,' I say. 'Good morning, by the way.'

My mother murmurs greetings, pretends she's counting stitches, but you can't get anything past her so I know it's just a covert way of examining my humours, scrutinizing my character and general health. I know I ought to explain that the track marks on my arms are due to medical experiments, not drug

13

addiction, but I figure, let them wonder. Keep them hanging on a little longer.

'Coffee in the kitchen,' says my father. 'And one of those Entenmann's rings, but don't pick all the nuts off like you did last time.'

Last time? That was two years ago. They're acting like I haven't even been away. Is this a conspiracy the two of them have cooked up, a deliberate attempt to instil remorse? Well, it's not going to work. I will not be manipulated. It turns out the coffee is cold.

Where is James, my big brother, my idol, my main man? The one guy I could always depend on to adore me. When I got into fights he salvaged me, bandaging my wounds. When *The Empire Strikes Back* came out he took me, overriding my mother's objections to the patriarchal imagery. He let me try cigarettes and beer, while warning me of their dangers. Tried awkwardly, at my request, to clarify the facts of life. Explained at every turn the intricacies of morality – why sex without love is wrong and how carbon monoxide affects the ecosystem. He always put me first, was always on my side. So where is he now when I need him the most?

Straight answers from my parents are too much to hope for. They look up expectantly when I re-enter the living room. I nod politely and settle down with my coffee. Pick up a section of the local paper, the bulk of which my dad is hogging, and act as though everything is normal.

'Hey, Julia, listen to this,' my father says. ' "Local resident Eamon Grosworthy may be selling his historic two-hundred-acre estate to LandDevel Inc., a controversial 'planned community' corporation looking to construct further homes in Philmont. Nearby residents, concerned about a drop in their property values, are reported to be irate." What do you make of this guy?' My father backhands the paper, shakes his head with admiration. 'He's rich, crazy and he hates his neighbours. I think he and I would get along.'

My mother nods, continues to knit the history of the feminist revolution into her latest creation, a sweater which is looking more and more like a body bag.

'That case of mine is getting good coverage,' he continues. 'Uxoricide, embezzlement and an exotic dancer named Boom-

14

Boom. Mind-numbingly clichéd, huh? The man's guilty as hell.'

No one says anything. My father, undaunted, surveys his environment in search of fresh entertainment. He settles for me. Starts staring unapologetically, a big smile on his face. I try to ignore him, but I know it's only a matter of time. I am his chosen target. Here it comes, here it comes . . .

'Perusing the want ads, Ellen?'

I hurl the paper down, explode. 'Aren't you interested in how I am and where I've been?'

'No,' says my father.

'Now, Harry,' my mother admonishes.

'All right,' says my father. 'How are you and where have you been?'

I refuse to play their little games. 'I don't have to put up with this. I know what you're trying to do.'

They look at each other. 'Are we trying to do anything?' asks my dad.

'Not that I am aware of, dear,' my mother replies. They both turn to me, my mother projecting artificial concern, my father's brow furrowed in mock puzzlement.

Enough is enough. They think they can win. But they've underestimated the Grandmaster. 'I just want you to know that I'm really, really glad to be home,' I say, dripping with phoney sincerity.

'I'm pleased to hear that,' says my mother.

'So when are you going to get a job?' demands my dad.

I clear my throat. This is delicate ground. 'I'm afraid I don't follow.'

'Oh, you know,' he says. 'Home, job. Rent.'

My own parents are going to charge me rent?

'It's not *much* of a leap,' he continues.

My parents have never made me pay rent. Why should they? My dad makes six figures a year. This is an outrage, the final humiliation – particularly with Blondie upstairs living off the fat of the land. I must handle this diplomatically, though. It has to be said, I don't have much leverage. Until I acquire an advocate, I must act in my own defence, while taking care not to antagonize my opponent unduly.

'I'm going up to my room,' I announce, with dignity. 'Which

I trust has returned to being *my room*.' As I climb upstairs, I hear their murmured voices. But they're speaking too low for me to understand.

'James is so cute. I can hardly wait to see his head on my "tooth fairy" pillow.'

April is moving out of my room. Oh, yes. She destroyed and remade it. Now she is destroying it again. Creation and destruction, death and rebirth; the eternal cycle is taking place before my very eyes. She chats as she works, mouth moving, fabric flying, all tasks accomplished in a whirl of superhuman efficiency and domestic expertise.

'Where is James, incidentally?' I ask.

'Back at Berkeley,' she says, 'packing up his stuff. We left in kind of a hurry.' She folds two sheets simultaneously; anyone would swear she has four arms. 'I'll be out of here in no time, though we'll practically be roomies – after all, I'm only moving down the hall.'

A pile of brightly coloured bras dominates the mattress. The curtains, bedspread and toilet-seat rug have all been removed. The room is bare now – stripped, apologetic. She has thrown the windows open and a smell of roasting meat, rich and wholesome, drifts in from the neighbours' outdoor grill. A dog barks. A lawnmower hums. Four sets of church bells start to ring simultaneously.

April pauses briefly and sighs – a contented sound, rippling with pleasure. Suburbia has enveloped and remade, blessed and baptized her, initiated her into tranquillity and ease. But she won't acknowledge this. Oh, no. That would be to admit that she doesn't belong here, doesn't fit in. Which she doesn't. *Go away, go away.*

'I guess you'll be staying awhile, huh,' she says with forced cheerfulness, studying my face. 'Spending some time with your folks and all.'

'I don't know.' I refrain from further comment. She's pumping me for information and I am determined to give nothing away.

'I haven't seen my mom and dad for a year.' She drops her gaze, resumes her work – folding and flattening, smoothing and stacking. 'I dropped them a postcard to let them know where I was. I guess they'll be giving me a call soon.' She pauses, looks wistful. 'Though of course they're very busy. Hey, do you have any use for these curtain rings? I've got plenty.'

'What do your parents do for a living?' I ask.

'My dad's a mechanic.' Forced pride there – guarded, protective. 'My mom does some waitressing.' *Does some waitressing.* Not, *is a waitress.* Defensive. Doesn't want to talk about them. Why not? 'Hey, Ellen, you might want to watch out for that ivy coming in through the window. Reminds me of those horror comics I read when I was a kid. Do you remember? The ones with the vines that turn into snakes and strangle you? They gave me nightmares.'

I bet that's not all that gave you nightmares, April.

She chatters away, a patchwork monologue. A lifeguard she knows who was attacked by a small shark that worked its way into a public pool. A fellow 'Born Again' Christian who took a pre-marital vow of virginity only to discover on her wedding night that her husband had two sets of genitals. A bona fide miracle she'd witnessed in a shop-front church, where ten cans of food, donated for Christmas, turned into enough for every hungry family in town: 'They just kept coming out of the box. Peas and creamed corn. I swear.' She doesn't mention her family again.

I observe her as a scientist might study a laboratory animal. She has a funny, pointed little chin – delicate but just fractionally too sharp to be genteel. Cheeks like two scoops of butter pecan ice cream. Freckles, appropriate for a Midwestern gal, and small, slightly crooked doll-like teeth sunk gently into very pink gums. She flosses every night. I can sense it. This one looks out for herself.

'I thought I'd clear off one of James's shelves for my porcelain Jesus collection,' she says. 'He has *way* too many books – they take up an awful lot of space. I'm trying to convince him to box some of them up and put them in the basement.'

'Which ones did you have in mind?'

She wrinkles her nose. 'Philosophy.'

However distasteful she finds the subject, she clearly savours saying the word. It's the luxury of being able to reject something you thought you would never have the right to acknowledge as part of your world. April *likes* this new environment she has entered – the trappings of it, anyway. The landscape, the language. The way it looks and sounds. I can just imagine the sort of house she grew up in. Modern, split level, with wall-to-wall shag carpeting and a 'den'. Slightly run down, perhaps, neglected and bleak, with a rotting redwood patio and sliding doors that stick. Air conditioning that breaks down in August. A big, big TV. Several – one in the living room, one in the kitchen, one in each bedroom, a portable for the car . . .

Competition sizzles like an energy between us. Though our verbal exchanges are civilized, it is undeniably there. She may be the one in favour at the moment, but I have the power to make or break her. I am the enemy and she knows it.

'How long do you think *you'll* be visiting?' I ask.

She looks at once furtive and pitying and surprised. 'Didn't they tell you? Your parents said I could stay on for a while, until James and I have saved up enough to buy a place of our own.'

This is ludicrous. What kind of demented fairy tale is she living in? 'I hate to burst your bubble, April, but I think you might be in for a shock. Property is pretty expensive around here.' Our home is worth about half a mil – and that's regarded as affordable.

'I don't think that'll be a problem,' she says sweetly.

'You might be able to rent an apartment –'

'We want a house and we intend to buy.' She smiles condescendingly, as though clarifying something I really ought to have known.

'You're talking about a big downpayment,' I say.

'We'll save up. Jimmy's going to start applying for jobs.'

Jobs, huh. I can just imagine the type of 'job' she has in mind for him. A trade, like her father. He'd be lucky to get that. She doesn't seem to realize how few jobs are open to a guy with a philosophy degree. 'And what about you?' I ask. 'Do you plan to start looking for work?'

'Of course,' April says, a little too quickly. I am deeply suspicious. There is something of the soap-watching, chocolate-devouring housewife about her – the kind who holds a telephone in one hand and jerks off her wage-slave husband with the other.

'I'm going to check the local paper tomorrow, see what's available.'

'*The Philmont Organ.*'

'What?'

'The local paper. *The Philmont Organ*. That's what it's called.'

'Oh.' She laughs breathlessly, as though amused at this example of small-town eccentricity – in spite of the fact that where *she* comes from, near relations mount each other. 'Well, I'm sure I'll be able to find something.'

Paying what – minimum wage? How can she be so unconcerned? Then the obvious explanation dawns on me. She fully anticipates that my parents will provide the downpayment. This wench without a pedigree is expecting Mom and Dad to cough up. Of course. *That's* what she has in mind.

'Eventually, I'll need a job with paid maternity leave –' she continues.

'Presumably a long, long way in the future,' I remark.

'Not necessarily.' She smiles tightly. *Piss off, Ellen.*

These words are as loud in my mind as if she'd shouted them. It's strange, very strange – April and I seem to have a connection. I can almost hear her thinking. Conversations without words. Soulmates. Psychic connection. Sisters under the skin. How is it that I feel that I know her so well?

'I presume you've acquainted my mother with your plans to make her a gramma.' My mother is vehemently against early marriage and parenthood. Claims it's doomed from the start and can rattle off several dozen sets of statistics to prove it. 'If not, you really ought to tell her. Seriously. She'll be thrilled.'

'Do you think?' Violently hopeful, can't believe I'm confiding . . .

'Sure. She's a mom, too, you know.'

. . . advising her, helping her out . . .

'That's true.' She digests this. 'So you think she'd approve?'

'You bet. I'd let her know – the sooner, the better.'

'Well, I sure would like to.' Her self-doubt returns, like a slap of paint down the side of her face. 'Ellen, could I ask you a question? Do you think she likes me? Your mom, I mean?' Fishing for compliments. 'She and I get along really well – we've had some great talks since I got here. But sometimes, you know,

19

people *like* you until they realize you're going to be sticking around. Then they change. I know I don't have a giant brain like her, and we don't have much in common, but do you . . . do you think . . .'

Do you think she thinks I'm good enough?

I pause, look away. Deny external validation. 'I wouldn't worry about it, April. My mother likes all kinds of people. We had a Vietnamese refugee stay with us for a while. Couldn't speak a word of English, but they got along really well. She taught him grammar and vocabulary and he showed her how to make model cars out of Coke cans. I think they still correspond.'

It does the trick. April looks devastated. The same status as a homeless immigrant?

'I guess you're looking forward to spending some time with her,' she says in a small voice. Polite. 'Your mom.'

'Very much so.' I hadn't thought about it, actually.

'She says the two of you are inseparable.'

Hardly. I couldn't wait to leave home, and once I did, I never looked back. Opportunities came up and I took them. Friends invited me for holidays and I accepted. One time I returned at Christmas break, only to have to inform her that I'd made other plans, would be leaving the next morning for Vermont. Her face. White with panic. The present thrust forward. My irritated response. Telling her that I didn't want to have to carry it. To give it to me when I returned. In July.

'We're very close,' I say. Then lightly, casually: 'What else has she said about me?'

She beams, freezes up. 'Oh, lots of things.' Her turn now to withhold gratification. Then she sighs, loses interest in anything beyond immediate concerns. 'I sure am going to miss this room. I've really enjoyed staying here. Last place I lived was New Mexico. Hot. Cockroaches like you would not believe.' She shudders. 'They just dropped off the walls. I had to move my bed into the middle of the room.'

'How did you end up in New Mexico?'

'My job took me there. I used to do Herbals.'

Herbals? What on earth is an Herbal? She is proving more and more bizarre. My mother is into herbs, but she uses them for cooking – and for witchcraft, which is quite respectable in

20

Philmont provided you are a member of a registered coven and are, preferably, a graduate of Bryn Mawr. I have a feeling that this is not what April is referring to.

'HerbElixir, the Fat Fixer,' she explains. There she goes, mind-reading again – it's making me really nervous. 'You know, that bottled water that helps you lose weight.'

Ah ha. A kind of witchcraft, after all. The phoney, hocus-pocus kind. My mother will love this. 'That stuff is supposed to be a rip-off. They did an exposé on TV.'

'It's *not* a rip-off.' I am surprised by her vehemence. 'It comes in a squirt bottle and all you do is say to yourself, "I'm slim, I'm slim, I'm lean and trim, I'm fighting fat and I'm going to win." Then you spray it all over your body –' she demonstrates, miming '– top to bottom and it works. It's like a miracle. I've seen the results.'

'I have to say, the empirical evidence seems a *little* flimsy . . .'

April flushes. 'Well, I guess you've never been desperate to change your life. Do you know, a lot of fat people – especially poor ones – think they *deserve* to be heavy? That it's their fate to be overweight and unhealthy? My job was to persuade them that they had as much right to be thin as anyone else.'

'So you were a con artist.' I am testing the waters.

'I was a *dietary consultant*.'

'Okay, okay – it's just unusual, that's all.'

'Well, how many careers do you think are open to someone without a college degree?'

So she hadn't been to college. Well, I ought to have guessed. It's funny – she seems fairly bright, pretty quick on the uptake. I briefly wonder what she would have been like had she been educated.

I try to imagine her marketing the alleged powers of HerbElixir in the New Mexico heat. Climbing out of a deathtrap car, trudging into another hostile hotel lobby, proselytizing to a group of wary fatties. Dancing, demonstrating, selling the Elixir of Life. Shiva down on his luck, bottles in all four hands. It's quite a picture. Makes me glad I've never done a day's work myself. I'd always wondered if my abstention was unwise but now it strikes me as a sensible decision.

She is smiling grimly. Her face is harsher; the hardness of her mouth has spread. 'I suppose you're wondering why I didn't use it on myself. I guess I believed in the Elixir, but not in me.' She draws a forearm over her face as though wiping off the sweat, the toil, the anguish and desert dust. 'I ended up in California selling the stuff. No one in New Mexico seemed to have any money, so I went to LA. But I hadn't figured on everyone being thin already. I ended up sleeping in my car, eating out of restaurant dumpsters. I don't know what I would have done if I hadn't met James. He rescued me.'

I really don't want to hear any more. I just don't want to know. One, she's winning the sympathy vote, which is not part of the plan. Two, I'm beginning to like her. In spite of everything.

'Look. I'm sure you can get a better job around here.' Well, what am I supposed to say? This girl has eaten out of garbage cans. 'James has a lot of friends – maybe one of them could set you up with something. As for James, academia pays pretty well, and I have a feeling he'll be getting back to his PhD once he realizes how much he misses it –'

'I've *met* his *friends*,' April says sarcastically. This statement is apparently self-explanatory. She scoops up the last few items to be transported to James's bedroom. 'And I *think* I *told* you, he's given up his PhD. He doesn't want to do that. Never has. Can't you people just accept that?'

Right. That's it. She had her chance and she blew it. My dislike bubbles up, like rice on the boil, black scum rising to the top. 'Well, what *exactly* is he going to do for a living then?'

'I don't know. But he's so smart, he'll be able to take his pick. Unlike me.' Another grim smile and she disappears behind his door, shutting it firmly in my face.

I have been dismissed. At least now I know what I am up against. I have been enlightened as to her intentions, her methods, her general character. But however well I arm myself, she has the greater ammunition. Is cunning and clever. A trickster, a peddler of the phoney Elixir of Life.

Clearly, I am going to need all the help I can get. So there is only one thing to do. Enlist allies.

Matthew. The Technological Antichrist and my kid brother. He's one of the new breed, tore out of the womb all wired up and ready to race down the information superhighway: 'Never mind cutting the cord, Doctor, make sure the power's shut off at the socket. This one's dangerous.' He lives in the basement, which is dominated by a large computer, and is fitted out like Mission Control. His creed is ruthless logic and relentless truth. To be perfectly honest, we're all slightly afraid of him – not the least because we don't know what the hell he's doing down there. He's a little too together for his age – just a little – and in possession of a preternatural calm. Nothing wrong with that, of course – quite the contrary. It's just a bit unnerving in an eleven-year-old boy.

I make my way down to his lair and immediately want to turn back. It's dark. The half-windows have been covered with aluminium foil. The sources of light – German, sinister – look as though they will give you a nasty electric shock if you try to turn them on. The only illumination comes from the large computer screen which at the moment is swimming with a strange screen-saver. Tadpoles? No, not tadpoles. They are white. Like spermatozoa. Surely not . . .

My mother once asked him why he wouldn't sleep in his bedroom. He explained: 'Because it has teddy-bear wallpaper. Because it's next to your room and I need my privacy. Because it sucks.' She had stumbled away, crying.

Something draws me to the screen. I approach with caution and tap 'Enter'. One word appears.

'Doktorlogik'.

Doktorlogik. My little brother is Doktorlogik. It has a nasty Nazi quasi-sexual ring to it. This is the boy I played blocks with as a child. What a sweet kid he had been. Small for his age and trusting. I had been nice to him by and large, though once when I was babysitting I locked him in a dark room and forgot about him for about twelve hours. I look around. Where is he?

Bravely, I tap the 'Enter' key again. Another word appears on the screen: 'Destroy'. Several names follow, one of which I recognize. It's the name of a boy who tied Matthew's wrists to his ankles and hung him upside down inside a locker when he was seven.

'*Greetings,*' says a voice. An electronic one. I jump.

'Matthew? Where are you?'

23

'*I'm in here.*'

'In the computer?'

'*Affirmative.*'

I am mighty confused. 'Cut it out, Matthew. This isn't funny.'

'Relax.' My little brother appears out of the shadows. Only his face is visible, as he has taken to dressing entirely in black. 'It was only me talking through the speakers. Thought I'd give you a good scare.'

He's hell-bent on revenge, clearly. 'Hiya, Undead. Did you miss me?'

'We thought you *were* dead.'

'No such luck. I see you haven't turned into a normal person yet.'

'Quite the contrary. You're the one who hasn't managed to evolve into a higher life form.'

'Why the black? You look like a demented cat burglar.'

'I'm in mourning for reality. It's obsolete. Everything is virtual now.'

'Wrong, my friend. This, *this* is reality.' I grab his head and give him a noogie; with satisfaction I feel my knuckle digging into his skull. 'Stick this in your disk drive, loser.'

'Hey.' He squirms out of my grasp. 'Cut that out.'

'Do I get put on the Hit List now?' I indicate the screen.

Matthew looks embarrassed. 'I'm not really going to destroy them.'

'No?'

'"Destroy" is a metaphor.'

I do not make further enquires. Funnily enough, I am almost glad to see him. I feel that he and I are on the same wavelength. Everyone else in the house has gone completely around the bend – except maybe Dad, who tries to disassociate himself from the rest of us, anyway. 'Say, do you ever bring friends back here?'

'All my friends are online.'

'Speaking of friends . . .'

'April. You want to know how to get rid of her.'

My little brother. He has everything figured. 'Don't be ridiculous. I've only just met the girl.'

'Ellen, I know you. You don't like her. You're emitting what you might call *hate* vibes.'

I'm going to have to play this carefully. 'It's not that I don't like her. I just don't feel she's good for James.'

'In other words . . .' He assumes the manner of a beady-eyed psychiatrist. 'You feel *threatened* by her.'

'No, no, no. I'm just concerned –' I stress the word '– *concerned* that she's taking advantage of him. You know, milking him for all he's worth.' Including his sperm. 'I feel it's my duty to look out for him.'

'How altruistic of you.'

I am gratified by this response until I realize he is being sarcastic. 'Look, Soapscum, can't you get it through your head that I am simply trying to help?'

'Ellen, I have never known you to "simply help" anyone. You're the ultimate ethical egoist. You act strictly in your own self-interest.'

'Okay, let me ask you this. Do you seriously think she's making him happy?'

He smirks. 'Are you kidding? He finally has a sex life. Believe me, at this point, there is no *way* you can oust her. Do you know what he says to her every night? "Show me the light, April – take me to Jesus."'

'You are one sick bastard.'

'You think that's bad? You haven't heard the half of it. I could tell you all *kinds* of things . . .'

The boy definitely has the information. 'What are you talking about?'

'Let's just say that she and I have had a couple of heart-to-hearts.'

'She's been *down* here?' I have seriously underestimated her.

'Sure. She likes my steady supply of "Fruit Frenzy".' He indicates a brand-new vending machine in one corner.

'Where the hell did you get that?'

Matthew lays a hand on his computer. 'Right here.'

'So she isn't scared of you, like everyone else?'

'If so, she's hiding it real well.'

Oh, boy. She's one up on me and I've only just got here.

'Also,' he says, 'she loves me.'

'She *loves* you?'

'Yes.'

25

'And you don't *mind*?'

'No.'

'Well, hell, I *love* you.'

'Yes,' he says pointedly, 'but you haven't been around.'

Not that again.

'Also, you shut me in a dark room when I was five.'

'It was an accident.'

'For twelve hours.'

'Okay. I'm sorry.'

'You *forgot* me.'

'I made a mistake, for God's sake. I'm only human.'

'Computers don't make mistakes. That's what I like about them. They're trustworthy. They're my *friends*. If I say destroy, they destroy.'

'Boy, that's some criteria. Forgive me if I say I'm glad I don't qualify. Now, are you going to help me get rid of her or not?'

'*Negative.*'

He's turning back into his own technology. It is best to leave before he starts to mess with my head. 'Fine. Now I know where your loyalties lie. But just remember . . .' I raise my finger, try to think of a threat. 'Just remember . . .'

'Give it up, sis'. We both know which one of us is high-fiving the palm of God in this power relationship.'

I cannot believe this. 'You're eleven years old. Shouldn't you be out saving the environment or something?'

He sits down in the chair, which also looks vaguely German, and whirls himself around. 'I could save the whole planet from here.'

'Then why don't you?'

'How do you know I'm not?' He puts his fingertips together. 'How do you know things wouldn't be a whole lot worse if I wasn't sitting in this chair?' He bristles; his eyes glitter. 'Or better?'

My mother manages to look normal and insane at the same time. Once you become aware of this, it's quite something to observe. She acts the model mother and wife, but there is something deviant in her personality that manifests itself in a patina of artificial glossiness and a thoughtful, slightly mad look in her eyes consistent with the contemplation of some unspeakable act. It is as though there is something boiling beneath the surface, something powerful, something waiting for the right moment to burst out. Something almost *physical* – akin to the stomach-dwelling co-dependent in *Alien*. She doesn't cultivate it. I don't think she can help it. It's just there. The family time bomb.

Perhaps now would be an appropriate time to detail one of my mother's peculiarities of behaviour, a phenomenon we call her 'practicals'. We consider it an outlet, something that keeps her from exploding, and live in hope that someday she'll explain. It reflects a tendency to deliberately antagonize people – in the most genteel possible way, of course. Serving dinner and embedding tiny spiders in the Jell-O. Entertaining guests and dropping plastic eyeballs in their drinks. Stitching a minute '666' to her collar where it isn't visible at first glance. Leaving ghoulish books by the toilet. It's as though she is making a statement, though nobody is sure what it is. But we humour her and try to take them in stride, until such day as the code is revealed.

She's bustling around. 'There's a cake in the oven, Ellen. I'd appreciate it if you kept an eye on it.'

You wouldn't want to eat my mother's cakes unless you knew her really well. 'Is it carrot?'

'No. Chocolate.'

My mother has never made a chocolate cake in her life. She doesn't even bake with sugar, for Chrissakes. 'Look,' I say. 'What is going on around here?'

'Whatever do you mean?' She ceases her constant, pointed activity and turns to me, all butter-wouldn't-melt and faux-naive.

'Please don't treat me like I'm stupid, Mother. If I've done something wrong, couldn't you just yell at me like a normal parent?' I've been trying to get her to yell at me for years. She uses a more effective approach – acting as though nothing is wrong, which always ends with me offering to place my head under the tyres of a car.

To my surprise, she straightens up and looks straight at me – for the first time, really, since my arrival. 'You've missed a few things while you were gone.'

Here it comes. The guilt trip. Well, at least I would get it over with. 'Like what?'

'Well, Matthew almost got expelled. He hacked into the school computer.'

'Did he try to change his grades?'

'Like any other child? Of course not. No, he formed a Philmont Middle School Anti-Authoritarian League and tried to plant evidence that the principal favoured the legalization of marijuana.'

'Quite right, too. How did he get out of it?'

'*I* got him out of it. It wasn't easy. I had to resort to blackmail. It seems that his own son has been banged up for drug use since he was twelve. Thank God. Then your father almost lost his job.'

'Dad? But he's one of the best defence attorneys in the state. He could have got Carlos the Jackal off the hook.'

'Ellen, your father walked into the senior partner's office and told him that he hated his job and to please fire him. He begged to be fired. He said he couldn't quit, that he didn't have the *chutzpah*, so would he please fire him so that he could live out the rest of his life with a minimum of torment.'

'Wow.'

'Fortunately, his boss called me and we had a chat and forced him to take a vacation and accept a raise.'

'So all's well that ends well.' I still don't see what the big deal is.

'Also –'

'What?'

'Your grandmother is dead.'

'Gramma's dead?'

'Yes.'

'But . . . you *wanted* her to die. We all hated her. Remember? I mean, if I'd known I would have sent a card. "Congratulations" or something like that.'

'Ellen –'

'I know I've missed some family news, but forgive me if I don't consider that I've missed anything *terribly* important.'

'You're absolutely right, Ellen, nothing remotely important. I had my womb removed, did you know?'

What is she trying to tell me? I wish she'd just come out with it. I look down, then away. Feel very uncomfortable. This is not what I came home for.

'Look,' I say. 'I figured the odds were that everything would be all right here. Everything's always fine. Nothing ever goes wrong.'

'Did it ever occur to you to give us a call? Or that it might have been nice to send a postcard?'

'But I did. From Prague. I didn't have a stamp but I figured they'd just reverse the postage. Didn't you get it?'

'No.'

'Oh.'

Then silence. I am hoping for a torpedo of reproach. But no such luck. I give up. It's pointless. My mother travels far beyond normal moral frontiers; she's on a completely different ethical prairie altogether. Child of the Sixties with a Calvinist bent. She thinks the Dalai Lama has shortcomings.

'Look,' I say, 'about April. Is she paying any rent, or what?'

'No, she isn't paying rent because she doesn't have any money. A bit like, well, you. As soon as she procures employment, I have no doubt she will contribute.'

'Oh, really? She doesn't seem too enthusiastic about getting a job, let me tell you. In fact, I've just found out one or two things about her that I think you'll find really interesting. Do you know what she was doing for a living over in the Land of Fruits and Nuts? Selling HerbElixir. That rip-off concoction that's supposed to help you lose weight.'

'So? That's nothing to be ashamed of. I gather some people swear by it.'

Hey. No fair. My mother is changing the rules. 'Whatever happened to dieting being symptomatic of a decadent and overly appearance-orientated society? I thought it was meant to precede the fall of civilization. I thought the whole diet industry was supposed to be corrupt.'

'She says it works and I believe her.'

'*Why?*'

'Because I want to.'

Boy, does she fight dirty. Whatever happened to my mother,

the rationalist? 'Well, it's thanks to her that James has dropped out of Berkeley and is planning some kind of crazy career change. God knows what he'll end up as if she has her way. I don't know about you, but I don't intend to allow it to happen.'

'To tell you the truth, Ellen, you're the last person who has any right to interfere.'

So that's the thanks I get. 'All right, but don't blame me for the consequences if you stand by and do nothing.'

My mother is silent – a sure sign that she can't refute the point. She looks hard at me for a moment. I pursue my advantage.

'Also,' I continue, 'she talks too much.'

'I beg your pardon?'

'She talks too much. It's really annoying. She's getting on my nerves and she's going to start getting on your nerves, too. Just you wait – "Hell is other people".' One of my mother's favourite expressions. 'Remember?'

'Ellen, I don't know how long she's going to be with us but by God as long as she is living under this roof you are going to be friendly and civil to her or I will demonstrate the most extreme and uncompromising example of tough love you have ever witnessed. Street. You. Out on. Do you understand?'

I say nothing. She is behaving very oddly. I wonder if she is remotely glad to see me.

'Can I have some money?' It's worth a try. 'Just a loan, I mean.'

'Absolutely not.' She puts on her jacket. Prepares to go out. 'Not until you tell me what you plan to do next. I want to know what you intend to do with your life, Ellen. When you come to me with a plan for your future, we'll talk hard cash. Until then, *nada*.'

And she is gone.

Later, I wander into her private room. Her study, where she reads and listens to music. And stares into space, which she'll do for hours, silent and bemused, mulling over . . . well, nobody knows.

Her desk is covered with objects. A voodoo doll of our local Republican congressman, into which she sticks macramé pins. A piece of carved ivory, seething with rats, which apparently represent good fortune but remind me of the horror movie *Ben*,

30

which used to give me bad dreams. A small sign that reads, 'Abandon hope', which she made herself in a ceramics class. There is a picture of James and April, one of Matthew (in his pyjamas, holding a hand to the camera; he hasn't allowed himself to be photographed since a friend of his got arrested by the FBI) and one of Dad. There is no picture of me.

3

Philmont. The land of opportunities. It's quite a place, actually – contains just about everything you need. In fact, it isn't necessary to leave town to take care of your basic requirements if you don't want to, and those who live there seldom do. A few, armed with newspapers and thermal coffee mugs, commute to Philadelphia, taking the Philmont Local into Center City, a sleek, silent journey through abundance and prosperity, terminating in the birthplace of American democracy and a good monthly pay cheque. Others pass their days in suburban real estate offices, local colleges and shops, only having to step out of bed to enter their world. The men all work – unemployment happens elsewhere. For the women, choices vary. Many spawn, place ads for nannies and return to medicine and the law. Others, more traditional, bake cookies and keep house, relinquishing financial independence for the rewards of being a stay-at-home wife.

The town itself looks pretty much the same – a relief, considering the upheavals at home. I pass the offices of the local newspaper, *The Philmont Organ*, that mighty powerhouse of reportage. And the gift shop, a respectable establishment that refuses to stock dirty birthday cards. The ladies' clothing boutique, the windows of which display cocktail dresses, woolly suits and cotton lingerie against a background of what look like artefacts from someone's recent arctic expedition. The shoe repair shop where they always seem to know your name – even if they've never met you before. The mens' shop with the peeling signs reading 'London Fog' and 'Arrow Shirts'. The Art Deco movie theatre, where clocks fall off walls and doors lock behind you with no explanation save the occasional appearance of a man named 'Xavier' who glares at you and then disappears. The antique store, which never seems to be open, and the local barber, whose windows are perpetually fogged. I peer closely into the window of the ladies' boutique – they've mocked up a bookshelf behind the polar bear's head. *Practical Lovemaking*, reads one title. *Happily Ever After and Other Myths*, reads another.

Various other establishments, a lot of trees. The whole town reeks of family values and Victoriana. No one admits to unacceptable desires, even if such things exist. There is a conspiracy of silence.

I'm almost enjoying the trip down Memory Lane, wallowing in a kind of twisted nostalgia, but what I really need to do is sit down and consider my position, figure out a systematic plan. Then I spot the local pizza parlour. The perfect venue for my rumination. I have to be careful not to get too comfortable, the greatest short-term danger I face. The problem with suburbia is that it grows on you, like a deadly fungus. Philmont, the magic mushroom you can't eat. Not so much because it will make you shrink as because it will make you disappear altogether.

'One anchovy slice, please,' I say to the boy behind the counter. Well, actually, he's more than a boy. He's a *guy* – a cute one. He heats my food, hands me my change. Doesn't give me a second glance.

Nothing unusual in that, actually. My love life has always been lacking. I don't have charms that soothe or a face that launches, so it's not exactly 'Hello, sailor'. And of those few men who look at me twice, very few are willing to man the battle stations. But seriously. I've always had to tolerate fumblings, close encounters of the lowest kind. Sometimes I think I'll get there in the end, but how many noxious ordeals will it take?

I settle down at a table and start to eat, sucking on strings of cheese. I am looking forward to James's return. He's always been more than just a big brother.

'Hey, hey, hey.'

I should have known better than to think I wouldn't be disturbed. My dad strides in, looking, as always, like a caricature of himself. He's a crack defence attorney, grooms himself to fit the role, only he really does regard it as a role and goes out of his way to look like a TV sitcom version of a lawyer. His nose points ahead like an accusing finger. His mouth is the kind that seems perpetually on the go. His hair, parted unnecessarily far to the side, falls across his scalp like a bad hand of cards. His face is permanently set in an expression of sardonic glee, which he exacerbates by wiggling his left eyebrow. To complete the look, he pairs well-cut conservative suits with loud ties, frequently in plaid or purple. 'Well, why shouldn't I?' he once said. He's Harry Kaplan. He can get away with it. The judges know him, the defendants don't care, so why shouldn't he have a little fun? Most of the time, when someone points out his incongruous neckwear, he pretends not to know what they're talking about and fixes them with . . . the *eyebrow*.

He seats himself. 'Ellen. What a coincidence.' It's not, of course. He'll have followed me from home. Determined to make my life hell.

'Shouldn't you be at work?' I say.

He laughs, a long, loud laugh, twisting around in his chair in the direction of the other customers as though sharing the joke. He doesn't answer the question. To my surprise, he's wearing his yarmulke, which ordinarily he keeps in his underwear drawer, bringing it out only when he goes to visit relatives – and sometimes not even then.

'What's with the beanie, Dad?'

'It covers up my bald spot.' Throws his head back. Cackles.

My dad has never been religious. My ritual-obsessed mother used to encourage him to keep in touch with his roots, providing matzoth at Passover, bringing out a menorah in December. She went so far as to offer to have James circumcised, a suggestion that made even my father turn pale. Eventually, she gave up, gave in to his indifference. A lapsed Protestant troubled by a patriarchal god, she understood his desire to distance himself from the religion of his childhood, but worried that he was doing so for the wrong reasons. To deny certain things – about himself, not his faith. To avoid coming to terms with who he was. Thus it is a big surprise to see him flaunting his skullcap. It sits jauntily on his head, a bit like a fez. I decide not to make further enquiries.

'So, how's business?' I say. 'Defend any innocent men lately?'

'That's for me to know and you to find out.'

34

I wish he'd cut it with the one-liners. I need some hard cash, and he's being evasive.

'This is a great place,' he says, looking around with an air of appraisal. 'You got some good jobs going there behind the counter.'

'Dad, I know my showing up was a surprise and all, but –'

'Was talking to a client of mine the other day. A guy whose millionaire father insisted he work his way to the top. Wouldn't give him an easy break. And you know what? That boy became a millionaire himself. Granted, he did it by embezzling from his own dad, but it obviously taught him a sense of responsibility. I think it's really important to have a sense of responsibility, Ellen, don't you?'

'Sure is. Say, Dad, I could really use a loan.'

He smiles. Opens his briefcase. 'I was hoping you'd say that.' This is too good to be true. I am in luck. He's going to hand me a large wad of bills, just like he always did when I was about to return to college after my summer break.

But no money manifests itself. Instead, he slams down a copy of *The Philmont Organ*. Of all things. He leans back in his chair, hands behind his head, as though he's about to have a frank heart-to-heart with one of his clients.

'You know, Ellen, it's a tough old world out there.'

I nod. This is the prelude to giving me money. Part of the ritual.

'Things don't always turn out the way you expect,' he continues.

Hurry up.

'Sometimes you have to face the fact that life holds some unpleasant surprises. That you've got to Hustle when you'd rather be doing the Cakewalk.'

'All right, Dad,' I say. 'I know what you're leading up to. Ellen-you've-been-away-for-two-years-you-don't-have-a-job-what-are-you-going-to-do-with-your-life.'

'Close,' he says, 'although those weren't the exact words I was going to use. You decide against grad school. Okay. A well-thought-out, mature choice. You go to Europe. Fine. A lot of young people do. You resolve to stay for a while and live like a bum. Good. Shows initiative. We don't hear from you for two

35

years. No problem. We don't know where you are, what you've been doing or even if you're still alive, but that's okay. Then out of the blue, you come home and it turns out you haven't even *considered* getting a job. Terrific. Your mother and I are absolutely delighted that you have no work experience and no practical means of making a living. We think that's great. But what do you say . . .' He leans forward. 'What do you say – just for the hell of it – to trying the old-fashioned route of *working?*'

My head hits the back of the wall. I am stunned. 'I suppose you have something specific in mind.'

My dad grins broadly and indicates *The Philmont Organ*. 'Well, I was just thinking, seeing as we spent a small fortune sending you to Columbia . . .'

'So that I'd know my way around campus when I went to collect my Pulitzer Prize –'

'. . . and you *claim* to want to be a journalist . . .'

'Well, I do, *eventually* –'

'. . . that it might be an idea to try . . . *writing an article*. For the local paper. As a start. To cut your teeth on, I mean. Well? What do you think?'

'I can't imagine anything more humiliating,' I say. 'I'd rather die that contribute to that ill-written reactionary glad-rag.'

He leans back again, pleased. Folds his hands on the table. 'Good. I was hoping you'd say that. We have a deal, then. You write an article for *The Philmont Organ* and upon publication I will personally give you three thousand dollars in crisp new bills to return to Europe or do whatever you want with. No catch, no strings, no conditions.'

Well, what can I say? My father has made me an offer I cannot refuse.

He shuts his briefcase, gets up to leave. Pauses, as though he's remembered a choice tidbit he thought I might appreciate. 'Want to hear something funny, Ellen? Heard a remark the other day. Woman said there were too many Jews in the neighbourhood. And you know what? There's only one. Me.'

He gives me a comic salute the way he did when I was a kid. Trudges out, head bowed, as though listening to some private death march. For a moment, he's somebody other than the Lawyer. Yarmulke or no, the back of his head looks sad. I remem-

36

ber seeing him at a party once, standing with a group of his colleagues, glass in hand, trying to pretend he was having a good time. Heard the forced laughter, saw the look of despair. I could tell he wanted to be anywhere but there. I can still picture him, trapped and struggling, swallowing his anguish, trying to resuscitate his soul. For a moment, I wish he would turn around, come back, though I am not sure what I would say to him if he did.

I am hoping to avoid another confrontation with my mother, but no such luck. I am lying on the sofa in the living room when she comes bustling in, her arms full of bags, having obviously completed yet another nefarious little shopping expedition. She appears to have bought plants, houseplants to replace the ones that have gone missing (I am still awaiting an explanation for their disappearance), and an ocean of arts and crafts paraphernalia. Twine. Bits of gold and silver. Beads. Sequins. Glue.

'Hello, Mother,' I say.

She does not reply, but begins unloading the houseplants. A small spiky tree like malevolent bonsai stabs her in the face as she lifts it out. 'Careful,' I say. 'That one's out to get you.'

'Where is April?' she asks.

'I've no idea. Why?'

'Because these are for her.' She indicates the baubles as she unloads seedlings, one by one. 'I trust you'll help me look after these plants, by the way. They'll need water. Conversation. Nourishment.'

'You bought her presents? Why don't I get a present?'

'These are not presents,' she tells me. 'I am investing in her new business. She is going to make jewellery.'

'She's a rip-off artist, Mom.'

'She's a skilled craftswoman. Trained with the Abudabu Indians, an obscure tribe of Native Americans who incorporate spirituality and some say magic into every piece they make. Didn't she tell you? She's such a modest little thing.' Now I *know* she is trying to rile me. Isn't she? 'We must do everything we can to encourage her. She doesn't believe in herself.'

'Well, what about me? Don't I need encouragement?'

'Don't be ludicrous, Ellen. And stop feeling sorry for yourself. Why don't you give her a hand? Teach her some bookkeeping?'

'I don't know anything about bookkeeping.'

'Don't you?' She looks directly at me; she's getting into the habit of doing this and I'm not sure I like it. 'Well, why don't you learn?'

'Because I'm a journalist, that's why.'

She continues to look at me, seriously, as though evaluating this statement. 'No, you're not,' she decides, and continues to unpack.

'How many of those did you steal, Mother?'

She ignores me.

'Just out of curiosity,' I say, 'what happened to all the original houseplants?'

'They died.'

'How?'

'Ellen, your father hasn't been well.'

I fail to make the connection. 'I'm sorry?'

'Ellen, he murdered them. He took them out on the front lawn, dumped them out of their pots and went over them several times with a lawnmower. He used to mow down my plants accidentally on occasion, but this time he did it on purpose. I wish I knew why. We never really talked about it. We haven't really talked in a long, long time.'

She pauses. If she's hoping for a response from me, she can forget it. Then, to herself, she says, 'Perhaps this is all there is. This is it. This is all there will ever be.'

I don't want to know. My parents' sordid marital problems are none of my concern. As for my father murdering houseplants, this is no more or less ruthless than anything else he does. He has an aggressive streak. He is a lawyer, after all.

'Hey, guys, what's all this stuff?'

April has materialized, clad in pink overalls, with matching ribbons in her hair. She tries to peer into one of the bags. My mother anticipates her. Out they pour, the glittering baubles. 'Wow,' breathes April, as though presented with the riches of Aladdin's Cave. 'You raided Kraft Korner.' Examines the contents with the delight of a child more accustomed to finding cruel jokes in her Christmas stocking than toys and candy. More exclamations follow, some from April and some from my mother, who is acting as though she has never seen the stuff before in her life.

'Now you can start up your business, April,' proclaims my mother, in her Go Forth and Conquer voice.

'I sure can,' says April. 'Thank you so much. You don't know what this means to me. Oh, Ellen, you've got to come upstairs and help me set up my new workshop. Your mother says I can use the library.'

The illiterate guttersnipe. I refuse to participate in dismantling my own home. 'Thanks,' I say, 'but I've got to help *Mom* unpack the rest of her shopping.'

'You go ahead, Ellen.' She doesn't miss a trick, my mother. 'There isn't much. Just a few prickly pears and a couple of things I bought for dinner tonight.'

'Is it going to be *boeuf bourguignon*?' I ask. This is my traditional homecoming dish. 'Or veal?'

'We no longer eat veal in this household,' my mother informs me. 'How would you like to be boxed up in a crate and fed nothing but milk? You should know better, Ellen.'

'I have an idea,' says April. 'Why don't I make dinner tonight?'

'*You*?' I say.

'I'll make chilli,' she decides. 'Chilli and cornbread and salad.'

'Why, April, that sounds lovely,' says my mother. 'But please don't feel you have to.'

'*Have* to? I *want* to. After all you've done for me . . .' She indicates the beads and buckles and nauseating little bows. '. . . it's the least I can do. Besides, it'll be my way of welcoming Ellen back.'

The sanctimonious little hypocrite. Who the hell does she think she is?

'Well, it will certainly be nice not to have to make dinner for a change,' says my mother. 'It will be a real treat. Thank you, April. How considerate of you.'

My objections to April are myriad, but primarily, it's simply that she's beloved by all. Try as I might, I cannot see the appeal, but I'm afraid to point out that she's a fraud. She projects perfection without being perfect. Entrances people until they are blind to her faults. *I* was the centre of my parents' universe until the Golden Girl showed up and, unreasonable though this might seem, I don't appreciate the Copernican assertion that the planets

39

revolve around the sun. I'm not a huge fan of heliacal rhythm – to my mind, dawn is the worst time of day. But now I find myself in a position where I don't have any choice but to submit to Ra and worship until such time as I can contrive the ultimate solar eclipse.

In the meantime, I am expected to be supportive of her repulsive little dinner party and act as though it's the best thing that's ever happened to me. There is a festive atmosphere in the house. Her 'feast' is being treated as an event. With a glad heart, I note that she is handling it badly. I catch a glimpse of her in the kitchen, making frantic preparations and looking rather scared. My mother has put a lace tablecloth on the dining-room table along with the silver cutlery and the best bittersweet-patterned china. I feel very left out.

As far as dinner is concerned, there are two saving graces. The first is that my napkin ring, my very own napkin ring, is at my usual place at the table. A gift from James, who brought it back from Japan where he'd gone with his fellow child geniuses on a class trip when he was sixteen. It is ivory and shows a dolphin and a shark locked in mortal combat. It is hard to say which is winning, the dolphin or the shark. I cherish it and allow no one else to use it.

The second is the fact that there will be wine at dinner. We all enjoy the occasional bottle (except for Matthew, who prefers some kind of nerdy bug juice) and there is always something exceptional at anything vaguely celebratory. James champions this. He pretends not to be a wine snob but is in fact obsessed, and several years ago single-handedly dug a cellar in the back garden after Matthew took over the basement. In light of my return, I assume that he will provide a particularly special bottle.

'We'll be dressing,' says my mother as she passes me on the stairs. By this she means that we will all have to put on 'something nice' to wear. Whether we like it or not.

'What should I wear?'

'Something nice.'

'I don't have anything nice.'

'Borrow something from April, then.' She continues downstairs, looking conspicuously busy.

40

All I have are two pairs of trousers (spandex, too tight, and linen, dirty), several shirts with frayed cuffs and an old cotton tennis sweater a male friend of mine left behind. Which means that I will look shabby and horrible while everyone else looks 'nice' and I will catch some serious flak from my mother, whose good books and cheque book I need to get into ASAP.

I hate this. I hate having to dress up. It's at times like this that I wish I were from a normal family, where you don't even eat at the same table. I am surveying the tattered remains of my clothes when I hear a soft voice at my bedroom door.

'Ellen?' says April. 'Can I talk to you?' She is standing before me in a shiny nylon slip, looking vulnerable and rather cold. 'I need your advice.'

Hm. Does she mean it? Or is she trying to get on my good side by appealing to my expertise in order to lull me into a false sense of security? She is wily. I have to be careful. Unwillingly, I follow her to the room she now shares with my beloved older brother.

I am in for a shock. James's Spartan quarters, so much like my own, have been transformed. Gone are the desk, the straight-backed chair, the iron bedframe and the plain white walls. April has done more than just redecorate. She has turned my brother's bedroom into her warped and Biblical idea of Paradise. Her filmy curtains frame the windows, where they float like flimsy clouds. One wall has been painted light blue to resemble a sky, complete with rainbow and bright yellow sun. Silk and plastic flowers adorn the bedframe, while the comforter itself is a Noah's Ark nightmare, a menagerie of pigs, bunnies, bears, giraffes – even a llama or two. His shelves are now taken up with the aforementioned porcelain Jesus collection, which is in itself extraordinary – a display of Christs of all shapes and sizes, cherubic and roguish, haloed and hung, right down to what is probably a pretty accurate Middle Eastern version with dark skin and big gnarled feet. James's books and papers are not in evidence. They have been 'disappeared'. I do not like this at all.

'Well, what do you think?' asks April.

'It's . . . different,' I say. 'How does James feel about it?'

'He loves it,' she says. 'I showed it to him just before he left. He had tears in his eyes.'

I'll bet he did. 'I like the way you put a smiley face on the sun.'

'Thanks. So does he. You know, Ellen, he's denied himself a lot. Stuff that other people take for granted.' She sits down on the edge of the bed. The crinkles crease the animals' faces, making it look as though they are smiling. 'Did you know that he'd never been on a romantic picnic, until he met me? That was how I got the idea for this room. I'd planned a picnic one day, for just the two of us, but it rained, so I thought, why don't we have it in here? And then I thought, why not make every day a picnic?'

Why not, indeed? Because it's a very corny idea?

'I wanted to bring the whole world inside, make him a gift of it,' she says. 'All he's ever done is work – even in California, where most people go to have fun. He never went to the beach. I don't think he even noticed the sky. That's why I put it over there –' she points to the light blue wall '– right where he could see it. Now he's got *two* skies. One inside, one outside. He's got a spare sky.'

I feel very strange inside, as though an old friend has boarded a train before I've had a chance to say goodbye. 'I practically grew up in this room. It's looked the same way for years.'

'You won't miss it, will you?' She sounds anxious. 'It was a nice room but it's better now, it really is. Just like the new Jimmy. Oh, he's still the same old Jimmy but he's happier now, much happier. He's finally doing what he wants to do.'

'And what is that, exactly?'

'I told you,' she says loftily, 'he's looking for a job.' There is a note of triumph in her voice that I do not like at all.

'I'll be interested to hear more about this,' I say. 'From him.'

'Well, don't be too surprised if he doesn't want to talk about it yet. It's all very new and he only wants to confide in *me*.'

As though suddenly aware that she is antagonizing me – an unwise strategy – April softens. 'Thanks for listening, Ellen. This isn't the reason I asked you down here, actually. I don't know what I should wear for dinner tonight and I wondered if you could give me some advice.'

So that's it. Whatever her secret intention, she is trying to get her head around my mother's absurd and unreasonable custom. 'Look, you really don't have to dress up. This is just a thing of my mother's. She's always trying to get us to dress for dinner because she likes a sense of occasion. I think she also sees it as some kind of bonding ritual for the whole family. It drives us all nuts.'

'But I think it's great,' she says. 'I wish my family had done stuff like that.'

'You don't understand. Believe me, you don't understand. One time, she insisted that we all dress up for Christmas Eve. Matthew showed up in army fatigues. She made him go down and put on a dinner jacket. We had company and he refused to come out of the basement. James and my father took his side. I took Mom's because she was giving me money and I didn't have any choice. We all had a big fight, and after a while, she forced everyone to sing Christmas carols and recount their favourite holiday memory. I think she enjoyed the whole thing. The guests were scared to leave.'

'My family fights sometimes. My mom and dad, that is.'

No doubt this is bait and she's hoping I'll bite, but I have priorities other than April's dysfunctional family. Anyway, I don't want her trying to make me feel all sorry for her again. She's too good at it. I veer away from the topic.

'Look, *I'm* not dressing up,' I say. 'I'll pay the price but it will be worth it to prove a point. Sometimes you have to stand up for what you believe in. Anyway, I have nothing to wear.'

'But you can borrow something of mine!'

I refrain from pointing out that we are entirely different sizes and shapes – she large, with a lot of stuff on top, me small, except for my nose and feet.

But in her enthusiasm, she throws open the closet. James's clothes have been pushed to one side. 'I have plenty of stuff. I know I'm bigger than you, but some of these things are supposed to be baggy. Like this.' She pulls out a fuzzy white sweater, clearly acrylic, with a daisy-shaped decal on one shoulder. 'Or this.' A red knit dress with batwing sleeves and a cowlneck collar. 'I guess it's kind of Seventies, huh. Used to be my mom's. Hey, what about this?' A leopard-print blouse with a couple of plastic eyes staring out at the front. 'It's more for going out, really, but I think it would do. Your mom would get a kick out of it. She's such an adventurous person.'

Is she? I can't say I've ever noticed.

'I thought I might wear this.' April holds up a badly cut pastel pink skirt and jacket that I imagine will be singularly unflattering. 'If you think it's okay.'

'That's perfect,' I say. 'That outfit is gorgeous. It's just the thing.'

Her relief is evident. 'Great. But what about you?'

I pick up the leopard-print blouse. 'Maybe I'll wear this.' It won't look so bad with my spandex leggings. In fact, it will help me make a grand entrance, and that's important. Also, if April is going to dress up, I had better dress up, too. I don't want her one-upping me again. 'Thanks.'

As usual, she looks pleased to have been of some service, to have been able to help. 'Jimmy should be here in an hour or so. He's going to be really, really glad you're home.'

'I hope so,' I reply. 'It's funny to think of him leaving Berkeley. Did he go out there alone?'

'No. He took a couple of friends of his.' She looks uncomfortable.

'Why didn't you go, too?'

'I told him it was either them or me.' Hot under the collar, self-righteous, self-pitying: 'Well, I'd planned a nice little trip for us together, and he decides to go and invite them along . . . Oh, Ellen, now that you're here, maybe you can help me talk some sense into him. Persuade him to spend more time at home. He'll listen to you.'

He certainly will. 'I'll do my best.'

I can hardly wait to see him. My welcome will be made formal at dinner, I am sure, once James is there to take the lead. He will propose a toast to me – he always does – and my mother and father will follow. Soon, I'll have regained my rightful position and everything will be back to normal. April is about to learn, the hard way, that this family revolves around me.

Dinner, I presume, will be a fairly predictable affair. Matthew will eat in the basement – my mother gave up trying to make him sit at the table long ago. James will pour the wine, lecturing us on the vintage as he does so, the only irritating habit he has. My mother will introduce a topic of conversation such as civil rights, Marxist economics or peasant uprisings in the fourteenth century and make us all talk about it, and my father will treat the whole event like the farce that it is. At least, I hope this is what will happen. I don't want any more unpleasant surprises.

I dress and comb my hair which frizzes out and makes me look like a fuzzy toy that's been through the wash. Evening falls, the temperature drops. The sky turns purple and I shiver. My legs feel like someone's stretched them out and let them snap back several times. James should be home any minute.

'Hahahahahahahaha.' Laughter is travelling via the forced air heating system that carries sound all over the house. Whose is it? Nobody laughs around here. 'Hahahahahahahaha.'

It is April.

I lunge for the grate, pressing my ear to the ornamental iron until it forms an indentation on the side of my face. 'Hahahaha-hahahaha.'

I recognize my father's voice, punctuated with periodic bouts of April's laughter. Instantly, and with a kind of sick dread, I realize what is going on. My father is cracking jokes and April is laughing at them. April has discovered his Achilles heel, his weak spot, the one thing he cannot resist – someone who laughs at his jokes. Somehow, she has clued into this and is pursuing her advantage.

It wouldn't have been so transparent had his jokes actually been funny. There's nothing wrong with his comic timing. It's just that his sense of humour dates back thirty years: 'Take my wife – please' etc. Very dubious. Everyone tells him to get a new repertoire but he simply won't listen – he insists the oldies are goodies. All his life, I think, he's been hoping to find someone who will laugh at his jokes, and clearly, at last, he has.

Goddamn her, she's done it again. Now she's won over my father. She is gaining territory rapidly. First, she seduces my older brother. Then she endears herself to my mother, who proceeds to forsake me. Now she's tricked my father – my *father*, of all people – into thinking she's the cat's PJs. She's even softened up that bastion of evil, Matthew. There is even the possibility – the awful, very real possibility – that she will manage to convert me. Why not? It's worked on everybody else. I will have to be on my guard.

*   *   *

45

Music greets me as I make my way downstairs. Lounge lizard type stuff, the kind you would expect to find in the cheesier variety of nightclub. I catch sight of my father, microphone in hand. Uh oh.

'Hello, ladies and germs.' He is still in his work clothes but has donned a turban and several Hawaiian leis. April sits in front of him, laughing her head off. Periodically, he stops and laughs along with her; he is one of those people who has no problem laughing at his own jokes. My mother is hiding around the corner – even she is laughing. I don't understand. They are the same old jokes. She has always hated them.

'A man comes home and finds his best friend in bed with his wife. He says, "I have to, Larry, but you?"'

Hysteria. You would have thought he was Johnny Carson. April is helpless with mirth and my mother is clutching her sides. Oh, God. I am going to have to laugh, too. It's laugh or be the party pooper. I can't let April make me look bad.

Try as I might, I can think of nothing funny, nothing that would produce a reasonably authentic chuckle. I consider going 'ha ha ha' sort of mechanically and making light of it, but under the circumstances I suspect it won't wash. There is only one thing to do. Hide. Play for time, keep an eye on things. Wait for the right moment to appear. I duck behind one of the new plants, a large one with big thick tentacles, and start taking mental notes.

'But you haven't heard the best one yet.' My father convulses, then pats the air with his hand as though trying to quiet an audience of thousands. 'This guy named Artie goes to the Mob and says he wants to be a hit man. The Godfather says, so you wanna be a hit man? Then go to the Acme, knock off these four guys and I'll give you a dollar. So he does. And do you know what the headlines said the next day?'

'I give up,' say my mother and April in unison.

'Artie chokes four for a dollar at Acme!'

They roar. April roars, my mother roars, my father roars. I fail to see the humour and start to wonder if there is something wrong with me.

'Where's Ellen?' says my father, when they have managed to calm down.

'Goodness knows. She's always late. You know how she is. We

46

may have to start without her.' My mother comes out from behind the corner, wiping her eyes. My father actually goes up to her and puts an arm around her waist, something I've never seen him do, ever.

She reacts with surprise, trepidation, then delight, and puts a tentative hand on his shoulder. He takes her other hand in his and starts to scoot her around the room with a semi-comic flair, pausing every so often to tilt her backwards, lower her almost to the floor. He is in his element. She is astonished and thrilled. I am outraged, confused. Wait. Halt. Stop the proceedings. *Tell me what is going on.*

My mother and father have always had a good relationship. 'Good' in the sense that they never hold hands or anything nauseating like that. They read the *New York Times* together in the morning. They discuss politics and the plumbing repairs. They never do anything romantic, but I have always considered that a strength. It never occurred to me that something might be wrong until James drew her tie-knotting technique to my attention.

'Have you ever noticed anything funny about the way she knots his tie?' he said.

'No. Why?'

'Well, it's kind of like she wants to strangle him.'

'*What?*'

'Oh, I don't mean literally. It's more like she's trying to get his attention. Say, Ellen, do you think they still . . .'

'Still what?'

'You know.'

'No, I don't.'

'Oh, well. Forget it.'

In later years, when I figured out what he was talking about, I was deeply grateful that he hadn't pursued the subject. But from time to time, I wonder why they bother staying married. My father works long hours, comes home sardonic and hassled. My mother knits mutinous sweaters and mourns her diminished capacity for rebellion. Apart from brittle chats about his sister Eileen/her cousin Alexander/foreign policy in China/the latest public spending cuts, they don't seem to have a whole lot to say to one another. So why live under the same roof?

47

But now they are dancing. My father spins my mother around a few times, like someone on TV.

I am beginning to feel seriously excluded. I'd better make my move before things get out of hand. I rise slowly from behind the plant, parting it in the middle. Point to my leopard-print blouse, utter fake roaring sounds. My mother and father stop short. April blushes. Looks decidedly guilty, like a trainee enchantress caught casting a spell.

'Ellen,' says my mother. 'We were just about to send out a search party. What an interesting outfit.'

April, I note, looks pretty in her little pink suit. Not like an oversized ice-cream cone at all.

There is a knock at the door. My mother and father exchange looks.

'James,' says April.

He enters, hair wild, arms long, eyes bright, and hands April a large bunch of flowers. It is nothing like the perfunctory nosegay my father brings my mother the first Friday of each month. Rather, it resembles some monstrous wedding bouquet, the kind you might encounter in the South Bronx (walking down the street, smoking a cigarette). A bundle of daisies, yellow roses and carnations sprayed with adhesive and sprinkled with gold glitter. April, of course, is delighted.

James plants kisses all over her butter pecan cheeks. She gazes at him adoringly as he soaks up her dime-store radiance. My first reaction is alarm. He's looking really peculiar. While still gorgeous – build of a rower, alabaster skin, eyes like liquid demerara – his hair is all out of control and, in an attempt to loosen up, no doubt, he is wearing his own unique version of hippie clothes: a sort of white tunic, embroidered with silver, over jeans and tall black boots. His idea of sartorial counter-culture. It's all sufficiently Starship Enterprise, I suppose, the kind of thing Spock might wear to a wedding, but this is a man who has never worn anything more subversive than a cotton tee-shirt. He looks kind of happy, I have to admit. Beatific. All right – he's grinning like a Moonie.

Oh, April, you don't know how lucky you are. He only wants you because you ensnared him, cast your net, a second-rate mermaid in a plastic seashell bra. And of course, because he has nothing to compare you to, no point of reference. Except me.

As mentioned earlier, James has never had a girlfriend. The history of his love life is an odd one, very odd. His sex drive is alive and well – his books on the female nude outnumber all the others – but, to my knowledge, he's never actually *had sex*. It's not for want of offers. Women throw themselves at him, but he always makes excuses for their behaviour. A girl who took one look at him and backed her car into a building was apparently just trying to park. Another, who called him twice a day for twelve months, just needed someone to talk to. When questioned – or rather cornered – he explains that human passions interfere with moral decision-making mechanisms. Then he starts going on about Plato. Sometimes I think he's waiting for the right girl to come along. Other times, I think he's just afraid.

But he's always had me – to talk to, to confide in. To reassure him that his paper on the Stoics *would* be the best in the class. Sometimes, I'd even fall asleep next to him. And wake up to find myself safely tucked up in my own bed.

His greeting is enthusiastic enough: 'Ellen! Little sis'! I don't believe my eyes.' But his mind seems to be elsewhere.

'Just thought it was about time to come home,' I say, and go up to him for my hug. Over his shoulder I catch a glimpse of April, smiling impatiently, possessive. I give him a light kiss on the lips. Her face darkens.

'Well.' He draws his head back, looks down at me, surprised but obviously pleased. 'You're looking well, Ellen. Doesn't she look great?'

'She sure does,' April says, all at once extraordinarily house-wifey. She wrenches his arm away from me and hangs on to him coyly. 'Food's almost ready, honey. Did you have a good time in Berkeley?'

'Sure did.' He grins. 'The apartment's all cleaned up. Gave most of my stuff to the Salvation Army. I didn't think it would take as long as it did. I'd hoped to be back sooner.'

She smiles, all tolerant and I-told-you-so. 'It's a special supper tonight. A "welcome home" party for Ellen.'

'Well, I can't think of any better excuse,' he says, reaching out to ruffle my hair. April looks really taken aback. Excellent. I resolve to cuddle James as much as possible. Snuggle, kiss, caress, fondle. Whatever it takes.

'Looks like we love the same man, April,' I say jokingly. She can't handle this. Holds the bouquet up to her chest like a crucifix. Get thee behind me.

But once again, I have underestimated her. She sits him down and starts talking about his prostate gland. Whoa. She must know my aversion to medical intimacies. I head for the kitchen, seeking shelter, only to encounter my parents embracing passionately. Now, there is nothing more revolting than seeing your parents kiss; but to see them kissing enthusiastically, unapologetically *right in front of you* is intolerable. They don't even have the decency to stop. They just sort of mumble, 'Hello, Ellen,' out of the corners of their glued-together mouths and carry on. What could have triggered this unseemly display? It has to be April's doing. Everyone is acting out of character.

I decide to exercise my ancient right to sanctuary and head for the basement, where I hope I won't be forced to witness some unpredictable obscenity. Matthew, I assume, is proceeding as usual, ignoring everyone completely and refusing to participate in all the family fun. However, he appears to be putting on a suit. He looks up matter-of-factly as if to say, 'What did you expect?'

'What the hell are you doing?' I hiss.

He shrugs. 'The family is a delicate web of relationships. An intricate network of filaments, tenuous and mutually dependent.'

April. I should have known. 'How much is she paying you?'

'We made a deal: she babysits, she turns a blind eye and doesn't force me to go outside and interface with my peer group. I get to stay in the basement and Mom gets told I went out for some fresh air.'

'And what does she get?'

'Nothing.'

'What do you mean, nothing?'

'She doesn't want anything. She's just being nice.' He affects a mock-California accent: 'She's, like, a *rilly, rilly nice person, mon.*'

The little bastard. I have to follow him upstairs.

My mother is flabbergasted. 'Matthew?'

'Himom.' He says it as one word. 'Hiya, Dad.' He goes and takes his place at the dining-room table.

My mother stares after him as though at an apparition. Seems about to faint; my father steadies her from behind. 'Oh, my God,' she says. 'We're going to have a family dinner.' He has to help her into her chair.

Then, as natural as anything, April slides into my place at the table, between my mother and James.

Who's been sitting in my chair?

This is too much. She has been sleeping in my bed, littering the house with strange brands of porridge, and now she is sitting in my chair. It's *my* chair, my special chair. In fact, the only other chair is the Broken Chair, the one with the wobbly legs that my father has been promising to fix for years.

'There's nowhere for me to sit,' I say loudly.

'Sit over there,' says my mother absently.

'That chair's broken.'

'Then get one from the kitchen. And while you're out there, why don't you dish out the chilli?' She places her napkin on her lap and reaches for the salad tongs. 'My, this looks good.'

'Look what I got!' April picks up my napkin ring – *my* napkin ring – as though it is some kind of party favour. I snatch it out of her hand and stomp out to the kitchen, leaving April open-mouthed, and ladle out the chilli, which looks and smells disgustingly good. I can't quite believe that *I'm* waiting on *her*. Enough is enough. There is no way I am going to eat her food. I fling a piece of cheese on a plate for myself.

The kitchen chair has the disadvantage of making me a foot shorter than everyone else. I am forced to listen to everyone praise April's pitiful efforts.

'You'll have to show me how to make chilli, dear.' My mother still looks all dazed from her five-minute honeymoon. 'Aren't you having any, Ellen?'

'Thank you,' I say primly, 'but I have become a vegetarian.'

Five spoons hit china.

'*You?*' says Matthew.

'All you eat is meat,' says James.

'Not any more. I no longer pollute my body with corpse flesh. You think I'm going to eat a cadaver?'

51

'Tell me,' says my father, sensing the opening for a good argument, 'is this for health or ethical reasons?'

'Ethical,' I decide. Why not? I figure while I'm at it, I might as well take the moral high ground.

My father leans towards me. 'Bullshit.'

'Language, dear,' remonstrates my mother.

'It's not *my* fault you're hell-bent on the destruction of the ecosystem,' I say. 'I see animals as our friends and I firmly refuse to eat friends.'

'Good thing,' says Matthew, 'considering you don't have any.'

'Hey, I empathize,' says James, chewing concentratedly. 'I would have a hard time eating something I loved.'

I picture a giant roast April.

'Of course, in certain civilizations,' says my mother, 'to eat someone was to honour him.'

'Or her,' I say. My mother the feminist glares; she does not like being caught out.

'The problem with the ethical stance,' says my father, with the slightly detached air of someone accustomed to winning, 'is that if you don't kill these beasts and serve them up for dinner . . .' He places a croûton on the table and, with relish, smashes it. 'You take away their *raison d'être*. They become obsolete.'

'The tablecloth, dear,' says my mother.

April is looking confused. 'I wish I'd known, Ellen. I'd have fixed you something else.'

'That's all right,' I say nobly, indicating the cheese on my plate, a slice of overripe Camembert. 'I'll make do with this.'

April wrinkles her nose. 'It sure does smell.'

'Oh, don't you like aged cheese, April?' I start scooping it into my mouth. 'I'm sorry, I forgot – you prefer the kind that comes out of a bottle. Stilton is my favourite, actually. Ripe, unpasteurized, with a really good blue mould running through it. And the older, the better. You know what they say – if it isn't crawling with maggots, it isn't ready to eat.'

April is turning green around the gills. James looks undecided as to whether to agree with me or grab a bucket.

'Speaking of cheese,' I say, 'where's the wine?'

James and my mother exchange glances.

'Chilli, cheese, you can't go wrong with a good robust red,'

I continue. 'Well, James? Aren't you going to do the honours?'

'Ellen –' He shifts, nervously.

'Five minutes in the kitchen, Ellen.' In one swift motion, my mother puts her napkin on the table and exits stage left, her usual subtle signal for wanting to speak to you privately. I peevishly follow. What now?

'Ellen, April doesn't drink. Everyone, absolutely everyone, in her family is an alcoholic except her. She comes from a long line of substance abusers. So, for the duration of her stay, there are to be no wines at dinner and nothing stronger than aspirin in the medicine cabinet.'

'But this is absurd. She can't be that sensitive.'

'We don't want to trigger painful memories. Now, we have a wonderful substitute.' Takes two bottles out of the fridge and holds them in front of my face.

'*Grape* juice?'

'Still and sparkling.'

'For God's sake – is *she* an alcoholic?'

'No.'

'So she's a recovering non-alcoholic.'

'Don't be sarcastic, Ellen. Carry those, would you?'

There is worse to come.

'Do you know what just occurred to me?' asks my mother, after we have seated ourselves. 'We haven't said grace.'

'Saying grace' is another one of my mother's embarrassing habits. It means saying a few 'meaningful' words at dinner. She bullies us into taking turns. My father enrages her by treating it flippantly and expressing gratitude for the country's madmen and criminals (his legal clients). James tries too hard to be fair and multi-cultural by taking about ten minutes to offer thanks to the many gods of the world's various faiths, throwing in ancient Latin and Hebrew prayers. Matthew . . . well, he's never at the dinner table. I generally mumble something generic.

'April,' says my mother, 'it is traditional in our household for one of us to say a few words before dinner. They do not have to be of religious origin, although of course religious references are perfectly acceptable.'

'Praise be to Satan,' says my father.

'The basic object,' my mother continues, 'is to give everyone

53

some food for thought. As this is our first full family dinner since your arrival, perhaps you would like to do the honours.'

'Me?' April blushes.

'Yes. James tells me that you've been "Born Again". Feel free to mention Jesus.'

I can tell that April does not feel comfortable with being in the spotlight. She rises, then looks embarrassed, as though fearful she's done the wrong thing. Her suit looks tight and strained from holding in her bulk. 'I just want to say –' Her voice cracks. She clears her throat.

'I'd just like to say how grateful I am and how lucky I feel to be here. Family has always been really important to me and for the past few weeks I have felt just like part of this wonderful family. I was a complete stranger but you took me in, gave me food to eat and a bed to sleep in. Made me feel like anything was possible after years of nothing but despair. I know first-hand how love works now and if I have anything to thank Jesus for, it's for showing me that people like you exist.'

She sinks back in her chair. Lowers her eyes. 'Amen.'

James rises abruptly, almost angrily. 'My turn.'

He looks so regal, standing there like a space-age diplomat about to deliver a declaration of universal harmony, that I tremble with pride and . . . and . . . Has he ever looked quite so divine? I try to remain calm. Here it comes, I say to myself. My welcome-home speech.

'I don't think I'm the only one present who is glad for the opportunity to officially welcome a certain person,' James begins.

A bit wordy, but not a bad start.

'She is a woman for whom the world is a miracle, who looks upon each day as a fresh adventure. She faces adversity with courage and rises to every new challenge with a spirit that we would all do well to emulate. She has revived my sense of wonder and shown me how to live. I don't know how I survived the past couple of years without her. She is the food of life itself.' He raises his glass of grape juice. 'To April.'

Has there ever been a time when you felt like mowing down a roomful of people with an Uzi? This is how I feel. My parents are busily toasting April, who naturally bursts into tears. Once more, I have been passed over, ignored. But do I show my feelings? Of course not. I grin cheerily, raise my glass to her, am very brave, etc. But I need to get my own back. I require a small dose of revenge. Just to tide me over. I decide to introduce some general conversation.

'April,' I say, 'what does your family do for fun?'

She turns white. Thought she might. Something tells me that they're not the sort of family that has much fun.

'I just thought you might want to share some of *your* family's traditions with *us*,' I suggest.

'Well . . .' She pauses. I wonder if this will occasion another bout of weeping. 'My mother . . . she likes to do leatherwork. She burns designs in things. Made herself a pair of chaps.' Stops. Is trying to think of something, some tiny thing they do *together*. 'And my dad . . . he enjoys meditation. Likes to think about things. For hours, sometimes.' Her eyes glaze over, as though beholding a vision she'd rather not see. 'When we're together, we eat . . . we watch TV . . . we play games. Board games. Checkers. Cards. Parcheesi.'

I wonder how much of this is true. It must be at least partly true (I can't imagine making up something as humiliating as leatherwork) but I detect a large degree of fabrication. Should I press further? Back her into a corner? Reveal her for the inbred redneck fraudster that she is?

'Sometimes we go places,' she continues, in a funny flat tone of voice as though even she doesn't believe it. 'In the truck. My dad's truck. We have picnics and go to ball games and things.'

Uncomfortable silence. James looks sad. So does my mother. My plan has backfired. This has gone badly wrong.

'Mom makes us go places,' states Matthew matter-of-factly.

'That's not fair, Matthew,' says my mother. 'Nobody has to go.'

'We *have* to,' he informs April.

'He's right,' I say, hoping to get Matthew on my side.

'Vile slander. Lies,' says my mother.

'Art museums, botanic gardens, historical graveyards, public monuments . . .' Matthew drones. 'Washington's House, Liberty Bell, Independence Hall, Valley Forge Park . . .'

'Be fair,' says James. 'You haven't hated *all* of them. Remember the medical museum, where they had all those pickled body parts and the Siamese twins in a jar?'

55

'Yeah, that was cool,' he admits.

'Let's go somewhere,' says April suddenly. 'All of us. Together. As a family.'

My mother's face lights up. 'Of course! April, that is an excellent idea. It's high time we took a family excursion. I can think of several lovely destinations right off the top of my head but I would like to consult my file. Matthew, run up and get me my file. *Now.*'

Matthew goes off, dragging one foot, left shoulder lifted hunchback-style.

Once more, I've been trumped. April has done it again. She's hit upon my mother's essential weakness – family excursions. Tedious familial bonding experiences in which we are periodically forced to participate. Even Matthew can't get out of them. Not only that, you have to pretend to enjoy them or you suffer. She knows perfectly well that we hate them, but it doesn't make any difference – the penalties for insufficient enthusiasm are severe.

Matthew returns and hands her a thick file. She puts on her wire-framed spectacles (yes, spectacles; like Benjamin Franklin). 'Now. Let's see. I notice that we haven't been to Independence Hall for a while.'

'I've been ten times,' I say.

Matthew raises his hand. 'Eight.'

'Fourteen,' says James, 'including that time I applied to be a National Historic Park Ranger.'

'All right, then . . .' She rifles through her papers some more. 'The Liberty Bell.'

'*No,*' my father screams.

'How about Edgar Allen Poe House?' suggests James.

'Too scary,' says April, giggling.

'Too *boring*,' says Matthew.

'I know,' says my mother. 'The art museum. The Philadelphia Museum of Art.' She takes off her spectacles, a sure sign that the subject is no longer up for discussion. The matter is closed.

Well, we are doomed. My mother hands out a study sheet on the museum in order that we might refresh our memories as to its general layout and contents. I grimace and look around for mutual commiseration, but to my irritation everyone looks as though they are quite looking forward to another trip to the art museum. Even my father is refraining from his usual smirk.

April. She has managed to beguile all of them. My homecoming has been disregarded. I am going to have to employ drastic measures. She needs to be put in her place.

I'll git you yet, Saint April. Fasten your seat belt.

4

I awake early the next day to the sound of James yodelling in the shower, something he'd picked up in Switzerland on yet another class trip. Sunlight is muscling its way in through my Venetian blinds. My eyes hurt. My mouth is dry. My hands and feet feel strangely detached from the rest of my body. After the 'family dinner' I'd ended up getting very drunk on my own with an illicit bottle of Jack Daniels, in the back garden where there was no danger of offending April's delicate sensibilities. James had declined to join me, preferring to stay inside where my mother was forcing everyone to play a game of charades.

James is in top form: 'Yodeleheeyodeleheeyodele-hee-hoo.' It's actually kind of sexy. Ridiculous as it is, it's hard to resist. He's always been able to do anything and do it well. At school, he'd juggled the dual presidencies of the debating team and the honour society. In his spare time, he'd written letters on behalf of prisoners of conscience and circulated petitions for the benefit of obscure species of fish. Along the way he'd mastered calligraphy, fencing, first aid, safe-cracking, sleight-of-hand, the ukelele, the harpsichord, the didgeridoo, ballroom dancing, abseiling, karate kick-boxing, ventriloquism, mime, funambulism, firewalking, the finer points of Mandarin and, ultimately, yodelling. He'd even been captain of an entirely fictitious rugby team designed to give eggheads an interscholastic sports credit on their university applications. He's very, very good at everything and there is something very attractive about that.

Just how good is he in bed? I have to wonder. I can't *help* it. April may be on the receiving end of something spectacular and I think I have the right to know. I can't exactly ask her, but surely it is logical to conclude from James's expertise in other areas that April is reaping certain benefits that give her added inducement to stick around. Unwillingly, I find myself craving detail. Who makes the first move? Who climbs on top? I can't stop thinking about it – try as I might – though I recognize the sick and lurid nature of my speculation. James and April. April and James. Black and white, chalk and cheese, wrapped together like a big yin-yang ball.

What does he *see* in her? This is what I cannot figure out. Okay, she's pretty, but mostly she's run-of-the-mill. Maybe that's it – she's completely unthreatening. He can't handle the notion of an equal. Perhaps he's afraid that a highbrow, well-born type would reject him, and thus he has set his sights low. That would explain his lack of interest in the others – it was a subconscious fear of being spurned. What I ought to do is find him a mistress, to build up his confidence a little. A temptress, a Messalina, a high-class free-agent sort of girl . . .

I think I'm on to something.

My hangover is getting worse. I feel as though my head is being dragged around by forceps. I stumble downstairs just as James is exiting the bathroom.

'Hello, Ellen, you're looking particularly fetching today.' He hardly even glances at me. He wears a towel covered with smiley faces and is grinning from ear to ear. Uh oh. Cloud Nine Syndrome. Seeing him half-naked reminds me how good his legs and shoulders are. One of the grinning circles is centred right over his dick.

I've got to work my way back into his confidence. 'Hey, big brother, what say you and I –'

'Sorry, Ellen, I'm in a hurry. I've got an appointment. We'll have a good talk later, I promise. No hot water, by the way,' he sings, and disappears.

Bastard. As if that were not bad enough, I am greeted in the kitchen by the sight of April sitting at the table watching television and spreading jelly doughnuts with Cool Whip, that ersatz whipped cream billed as 'non-dairy topping'. She hasn't bothered to turn off the portable stereo, which is tuned into the National Public Radio station my mother keeps on day and night to ward

59

off burglars (very effective). The TV screen shows two people with perfect hair lifting their faces to each other in chiselled misunderstanding.

'It's the new morning soap,' says April cheerfully. '"Endless Eternity". Comes on at nine a.m. every day. Sit down and I'll fill you in.'

Boy, is she breaking the rules. In our house, you do not watch television in the kitchen and you certainly never watch it first thing in the morning. As for soaps, well, if you crave junk television, you watch something that could pass for edifying like a documentary on UFOs or bleeding statues in remote Italian villages.

'No thanks,' I say, but she doesn't seem to hear me. Without taking her eyes from the screen, she presses a doughnut into her little-girl mouth and moves towards the kitchen counter. 'I'll pour you some coffee. James says you like it black.'

A veiled reference to my hangover, no doubt. I eye her warily, following her ever-surprisingly graceful and competent movements. I note that she is using my childhood frog-mug, the one with fake slime running down the side. It has a crack that I am certain wasn't there before as well as a sticky pink mouth-mark. She is wearing a short yellow terry-cloth robe and tiny high-heeled marabou-topped red slippers of the type you see only in the tackier variety of lingerie shop. She must be a size three.

She catches me staring and giggles. 'Aren't they a scream? I was lucky to find them, actually. I have a hard time finding shoes that are small enough to fit my feet.' Those tiny, tiny feet. Kill, kill.

She places the coffee in front of me, in a gas station mug that I assume is a memento of her time in California. 'Let this be the day you discover the Real You,' it reads in balloon letters. The rim is so thick, I can hardly get my lips around it. Coffee dribbles down my chin.

'Oops,' says April.

It tastes like someone has dabbled a brown crayon in it. 'I can't drink this,' I say. 'It's too bland.'

She reaches over and plops a lump of Cool Whip into my cup. 'There. Doughnut?'

The soap opera draws her attention back to the screen. She

turns up the sound and sits there like the queen of the kitchen, stuffing doughnuts into her mouth. Annoyingly, she keeps wiggling and jiggling those tiny feet.

'Are you familiar with the ancient Chinese practice of footbinding?' I ask loudly, over the combined noise of the radio and TV.

'Can't hear you,' she shouts.

'Footbinding.'

'Bookbinding?'

'FOOTBINDING.'

She turns abruptly and stares at me. Clicks off the television.

'Footbinding,' I repeat. 'Ancient Chinese custom of the upper and middle classes. Girls' feet were tightly bound with bandages, a practice which resulted in extreme pain, infection, the dropping off of toes and, ultimately, ridiculously tiny feet that were considered, for some reason, attractive.'

April's face grows pale. She stops chewing.

'It was not uncommon,' I continue, 'for the toenails to grow into the soles of the feet. They would wear tiny decorative slippers designed to cover up the blood and pus –'

'Ellen, this is making me kind of sick.'

' – which would show off the deformed feet to their very best advantage. It was rumoured to affect the female genitals –'

'Ellen.'

' – and enhance the enjoyment of the sexual act. For the guy, anyway. Isn't that just typical?'

'Ellen.'

'Kind of a raw deal for the woman, but big feet, no husband. That's patriarchy for you. Interesting, because the modern high-heeled shoe has its foundations in the same barbaric practice. The object is to cripple women, restrict their movements and keep them from running away. Which is why *I* –' I look pointedly at her feet ' – don't wear high heels. And neither should you.'

She looks puzzled. 'What difference does it make if I wear them or not?'

'They're *symbolic* –' I make a point of sounding exaggeratedly patient here ' – of the oppression of women.'

She frowns. 'So what?'

'What do you mean, *so what?*'

'Well, what does that have to do with me?'

Ouch. Excellent. All I have to do is get that on tape and play it back to my feminist mother.

'That reminds me,' she says, and fumbles around in her pocket for something. A tube, which she places in front of me. 'I got it free at the mall with these slipper-things. It's for you.'

A tube of cherry-scented foot-scuffing cream. The label shows a foot with flakes of skin falling away under the attentions of a slender hand.

'Thanks.'

'No problem. I thought we could have a girls' night in. Exfoliate our feet and give each other pedicures.'

She just doesn't quit, does she? 'Not tonight, thanks, April – I buffed my feet last week. Hey, do you know what James is up to today?'

'Um, yes. He's taking the cats to the vet.'

Ah, the cats. I neglected to mention the cats. Brother and sister. Purebred Burmese and as inbred as they come. They would have been at it all the time had we not done something about their private parts.

'You've met Cleopatra and Igor, then.'

'Sure have,' she says. 'They're really sweet.'

Like hell. Igor has muscular shoulders and likes to draw blood. He'll wait on the ledge above your door – for hours, if necessary – and jump on your head, claws fully extended. Cleopatra's right eye looks like it's filled with brown glue; she likes to wipe it clean on your leg. If you cross her, she'll bunch up her neck at a ninety-degree angle and affect a limp that can last for days.

'They slept on my bed last night,' she adds.

The last time they'd climbed on my bed had been to throw up on it.

April sighs. 'James sure keeps busy. Feels like I've hardly seen him lately.' A suggestion of self-pity crosses her face. Then she brightens. 'After the vet, he's got some kind of appointment. He won't tell me what it is, but he's says I'm going to like it.'

Uh oh. I do not like the sound of this. I wonder how I can intercept this little errand. Lock him up, maybe? Shut him in the basement with Matthew?

The radio is still on, broadcasting an interview with a socially conscious folk singer who'd wed the ex-conductor of the New

York Philharmonic. Her voice is twangy and implies the necessity for a constant defence of their union. 'It's a marriage of true minds, really. The differences are only in people's heads. Once they get to know us . . .'

April squirms. 'God, this stuff is so boring.' She turns the dial until she hits some anodyne pop music and assumes a maddening look of superiority. 'Don't tell her I said so, Ellen, but sometimes I think your mom's a little weird.'

'James?'

'Not now, Ellen.' He is on his way out the door, swathed in the same bizarre sense of purpose that I'd noticed in my mother upon arrival. He is no longer wearing his silver-and-white tunic but is dressed in a suit and tie. 'Wish me luck.' Peck. Peck. A kiss on both cheeks. And he is gone.

I am bereft. That was my chance, and I blew it. Why does he keep disappearing? I run out of the house, but he's already vanished – perhaps he's been beamed up by Scottie. More likely, he's been picked up by one of his friends and is en route to wherever he is going. James seldom drives (it pollutes the air) but for some reason he doesn't mind car pooling.

James's best friends are a rum bunch. They've known each other since elementary school and have stuck together through all the minor adversities that plague people who are both financially well-off and highly educated. There is Zero, the scientist. Physicist, actually. Now ensconced in a research department where they wheel their meals in on trays. And Kermit, a shy computer expert who has some kind of skin disease and needs to be kept moist. Then there is Frederick.

Observing Frederick is a bit like seeing a statue come to life. At first, you don't believe that anyone could be that handsome. Then he turns his head, just a fraction of an inch, and looks at you. And you freeze.

Imagine a blond cobra with cheekbones. A snake who charms but won't allow himself to be charmed. Who tempts but is incapable of being tempted.

And who has a reputation for being very good in bed.

Frederick is a bit of a mystery, even to James. He's a fun guy

63

(apparently) but secretive. For instance, nobody really knows what he does for a living. His parents are rich and he travels all around the world helping them out with whatever it is they do to stay rich, but no one has ever been able to get him to divulge *exactly what he does*. Drug dealing? International arms smuggling? It seems unlikely – James would never hang out with such a guy – but who knows. The key to his bedroom performance remains an enigma, too. When questioned, his victims generally shake their heads and say, 'I can't explain.' They never seem to recover. Nor, they claim, do they want to.

As a child, I'd had a crush on him. I'd had crushes on all my brother's friends, one after the other (even Zero), but Frederick had always been special. He always took notice of me, singled me out for special attention. Would tie my shoelaces together and try to make me walk. Would tickle me mercilessly, even spank me now and then. That's a good word to describe Frederick: merciless. Even towards nine-year-old girls. He gave me a full and frank account of his sexual activities one day, explaining them in great detail through a series of illustrated texts – the *Kama Sutra*, a Victorian sex manual and a brand new copy of *Hustler*. And he gave me my first kiss, on my eleventh birthday. On the cheek? Oh, no. That was not Frederick's style. I grew up and left town, but I never forgot him. Next to James, he was my idea of the perfect man. Sometimes I think Frederick is James's dark side, a golden-haired devil to his angel of light. Other times, I think he's simply the blessed oblivion into which you want to fall, the place where you allow yourself to be destroyed.

It doesn't seem fair that April has a boyfriend while I have none. The last person I'd been with was a medical student. Piers. Two inches shorter than me and depraved. *Huge* collection of old medical textbooks, the kind with those black-and-white photos of deformed bodies and festering private parts. British medical students – I couldn't even begin to describe their idea of a party game. They are twisted, completely twisted. I gather it's how they unwind. So, surgical masks and two of his friends. It was kind of fun but . . . not *sexually*. It was more of a novelty, if you know what I mean, living proof of the peculiarities of foreigners. I met him at the St Thomas Pharmaceutical Research Centre, where I was allowing myself to be subjected to various tests in an effort to raise funds for my plane ticket home. I could have contacted my mother and father and asked them to wire me money but after two years of silence I didn't think they'd react too kindly to a phone call and anyway, that would have ruined the surprise.

I had very much hoped that they'd be glad to see me. Europe had proved disappointing. To be frank, I'd had a rotten time. I spent most of my money right away, then decided, unwisely, to pursue my travels nonetheless. The problem with having no cash is that you tend to make a virtue of necessity and end up doing things you would not otherwise consider. Sleeping on the Metro and attempting to persuade the Paris police that you're doing research for a BBC documentary. Trying to explain to the head of a men-only Italian *collegio* that you're (one) a boy and (two) Catholic. Dating a Hungarian who looks like he could buy you a good dinner but who ends up asking to try on your underwear. I'd concluded that the Grand Tour wasn't all it was cracked up to be and had longed to be home. To where I knew I would be safe and comfortable. To where I felt valued and . . .

Loved?

Discouraged, I turn indoors and make my way upstairs. I can hear my mother chatting gently with April. It hurts.

I have two challenges. One, locating an appropriate siren. Two, writing the article for *The Philmont Organ*. You wouldn't think either would pose much of a problem. A cute girl, a little plagiarism . . . No. I am not going to take that route. No more doing things the easy way. It always backfires. I have to make things happen and I have to do it right – with as little effort as possible, of course.

There are several ways I could go about obtaining a seductress to captivate James. The most logical would be to hire someone. Recruit a local college girl and pay her when I sell my article, or find a drama student who's willing to go the extra mile. The difficulty lies in there being no margin of error. I have to find just the right person. If it doesn't work the first time, there won't be a second chance. I need someone who can do the job for sure.

As for the article, I have to admit, I don't have a whole lot of

65

ideas. A piece for the local paper means local colour and, as far as I'm concerned, there is none. How can I write about a place I've no interest in whatsoever? Yet this is what I have to do. My dad would call it 'being a professional' but I consider it unreasonable and inhumane. I decide that the best approach would be to find my old typewriter and set it up. That would be a good start.

It occurs to me that I am all alone on the third floor. This would be a perfect opportunity to snoop. James is out, April is downstairs. It seems too good a chance to pass up. If anyone should catch me, I can explain that I am trying to track down the tools of my trade. Maybe the solution to my problems is just an arm's length away. Who knows what discoveries I will make.

It looks as though April has allowed James to put some of his books back, though not the philosophical tomes. I note two or three of the coffee-table variety ones that April probably regards as decorative. A book on Leonardo da Vinci. One on Native American culture. A volume of fifteenth-century Flemish art. A Bible, not surprisingly. And a photo album – a rather old-fashioned one, like something a grandmother might have left behind. It's April's.

The first photograph shows three people and a dog. The caption beneath it reads, 'Mom, Dad, me & Innertube. Summer.'

This is a younger April, hopeful but strained, conscious that this is one of the few moments they'll ever have together. The father seems slow, wary, quietly grateful for any good thing. The mother's face is puzzled, hard. A cautious smile, as though she can't quite believe she's being photographed. The dog is large, lean, looks like he ought to be wearing a necktie. Is sitting up straight. Proud to be part of the family.

'Beach.' A downmarket beach, the kind where the sky, sand and water are all a dull grey. The mother in a one-piece bathing suit that sags down her thighs, laughing as though laughter is an unaccustomed activity. The dog, big-boned, is loping behind, shyly pleased to be included in the fun.

'Lunch.' April preparing sandwiches. Kneeling in front of a plastic picnic basket as her father awkwardly pretends to throw sand on the food. Like he knows he's supposed to be having a good time and is trying to demonstrate good faith. Learn how.

There are a couple of others. One of the parents, posing duti-
fully as though for a shotgun wedding, and one of April, waving,
arm lifted high, as though trying in vain to pull all the elusive
strings of her universe together, tie them up in one everlasting
bundle.

What's most pathetic is that most of the album is empty. I
sense a kind of terror in the pages. Where are the shots of her
friends? Of birthdays, relatives and reunions? I turn over page
after blank black page, every sheet a sort of cry for help. I shudder,
put it back on the shelf. Is despair contagious, like plague? Quite
frankly, I don't like sharing a house with her. There should be
a rule of quarantine. She ought to be kept in isolation, boarded
up in a shed. God have mercy on this girl.

In a drawer, a few bits of plastic jewellery – her own efforts,
presumably. A tiny crucifix and some plastic trinkets, the kind of
toys you get out of gumball machines. A few fuzzy hair elastics.
Old sales receipts. Bits of half-eaten candy. Lint, fluff, deliberately
retained. As though even the most worthless possessions have
value.

If I was hoping for something incriminating, it isn't there. I'm
not quite sure what I was expecting. A satin G-string and a thick
wad of bills? An address book full of sinister names like 'Bugsy'
and 'Jake the Hacksaw'? Whatever secrets she has, she's hidden
them well. Clearly, I am wasting my time.

I locate my typewriter, a monstrously heavy old IBM. My legs
buckle trying to lift it. I stagger and drop it. It crashes to the
floor.

'Everything all right up there?' my mother calls.

'Just fine,' I yell. And crumple, sobbing, to the side of my
machine.

'Oh, April, they're beautiful.'

I've walked in on my mother and April having a tête-à-tête
and an aggravating little tea party with the chocolate cake my
mother has baked. As I enter, my mother looks up.

'April was just showing me some of her jewellery designs,' she
says. 'They are absolutely remarkable. You might want to take a
look.' She is wearing a necklace of delicate terracotta beads. When
I examine them more closely, they turn out to be made of plastic,

67

but it doesn't seem to matter. They transform her whole face. She looks radiant. 'I feel like a whole different person,' she says, and smiles at April, who looks gratified.

I try to recall some special moments between me and my mother. I rack my brains but I can't think of one. Just briefly, I cringe at the nightmare of rejection she must have endured. Talking to me as she watered the plants, only to discover I'd left the room. Preparing lunch for two, hoping I'd join her, only to hear me say I wasn't hungry. Asking me if I wanted to talk about boys and . . . things, only to be informed that I knew everything I needed to know about fornication.

Christ, why hadn't I taken the hint? No wonder she couldn't care less about me now. She has a *new* daughter, an amiable one, a sucker for hot food and advice. Well, at least I'm self-sufficient – that must count for something, surely. Isn't she proud of me, of the way I turned out?

'The first thing I did,' says April, 'was make presents for everybody. This is for you, Ellen. Ellen? Earth to Ellen.'

I hadn't *meant* to hurt my mother. What had she wanted from me, anyway?

'El-len,' says April, in a sing-song voice. I realize that she is trying to get my attention. She is holding out a necklace, dangling it like a coy matador teasing a uninterested bull. 'James told me you liked black. I bet it'll look really pretty on you.'

As though anything would. At the moment, my appearance leaves something – *many* things – to be desired. My skin is grey and my hair is breaking off. Months of seedy living have taken their toll. I wouldn't give a damn but I've caught myself thinking about Frederick. A lot. I have to be honest: *all the time*. Chances are that he's forgotten me completely. After all, he hasn't seen me for years. This could actually work in my favour, of course – I'm no longer 'James's kid sister'. It might be fun to show Frederick my new self, my grown-up self. I wonder what he'd make of it. Not much, I suspect, unless I upgrade my image. This is the insurmountable problem.

'Thanks,' I say lifelessly, accepting the necklace. It's a choker made up of flat black plastic discs. I hold it up to my throat and look in the mirror. To my surprise, I have metamorphosed. I look fabulous – and I am frank about my looks. My hair shimmers and my skin looks clear. Even the dread proboscis looks sexy. I don't ask questions. I don't want to know how this came about. All that matters is that I am transformed.

I don't even mind complimenting her. 'It's not bad. Not bad at all. I think I could get some use out of this.'

April beams. 'Good. Now you'll be able to impress *you-know-who*.'

I drop my arms, unable to hide my alarm. 'What are you talking about?'

'Oh, you know.' She looks sly. 'That guy.'

'What guy?'

She leans forward on her arms. 'I *know* you have a crush on some guy, Ellen Kaplan. You can't fool me. I can tell.'

Is it *completely impossible* to have any privacy around here? It's that psychic streak of hers, rearing its ugly head. I wonder if she knows it's Frederick. I hope not. The very idea of him is obscene and I don't want her thinking I'm some kind of perv. I am about to reply in the negative when James arrives, bursting in through the door like a character in a bad Western.

'I have gainful employment,' he shouts. 'A job, people. I got a job.'

You have to understand that the notion of a job is completely new to James. He's never had one. Why should he get a job, with half a dozen fellowships breathing down his neck? April shrieks and jumps up and down. He picks her up and whirls her around – I am surprised he can even lift her. In a funny way, they go well together: he, tall and dark and slim, she, short and blonde and fat. My mother just sits there, stunned. This has clearly taken her by surprise. She must have believed, deep down inside, that he would end up back at Berkeley. Serves her right for not encouraging my intervention.

'What kind of job?' my mother asks.

He stands before her proudly. 'I am going to be a sanitation man.'

'A *garbage guy*?' squeals April.

'A trash collector,' I grimly affirm.

'You mean . . .' My mother is aghast. 'You're going to ride around the neighbourhood in one of those trucks? *Our neighbourhood?*'

69

'Lots of neighbourhoods,' he says cheerfully. 'Just think of all the things I'll get to see. All the people I'll meet – many of whom I would not encounter in the normal course of events. *This* is what I went out to California hoping to find. Life experience.'

'I thought you went out to find yourself,' I say. 'Well, as long as you found something. More cake, anyone?'

My mother appears to be going into shock. She's frozen in position like a rusty wind-up doll. 'James, dear, is this temporary?'

'Nope,' he says. 'Career move.'

She thinks he's joking, starts to laugh. Stops when she realizes he means it. This is a fitting punishment, it really is. Now she knows how we feel when she pulls one of her 'practicals'.

'You can't be serious,' she protests.

'Oh, I am,' he says. 'I'm very serious. Want to see?' He whips out a pair of coveralls.

'You're not going to wear that,' she says.

'Oh, yes, I am. I might even get a tattoo.'

Gingerly, she fingers them, as though they are already covered with grime. 'I think you should take those back where they came from.'

'Oh, but look, Mom.' I grab them. 'They're very practical – zippers, water-resistant, detachable lining for the winter . . .'

'I absolutely forbid you to go through with this,' she orders.

'But it's so *non-conformist*,' I enthuse. 'It's just the sort of job an ex-hippie like you would do, in the absence of a flair for Apple Macs. I would have thought you'd be delighted, Mother. Personally, I can hardly wait to tell Dad.'

This is the best thing that's happened to me since arriving home. James is on the road to ruin and it's *unarguably* April's fault. All I have to do is put my feet up and wait for my mother to see the light.

'Ellen's right, Mother,' says James. 'Funny how your liberal principles fly out the window when it concerns your own son. Don't you remember what you used to tell me? All jobs have equal value.'

'Is this, by any chance,' says my mother, 'some kind of deferred teenage rebellion? A delayed reaction to your father and I threatening to divorce when you were seven?'

70

'You threatened to divorce?' I say. 'Why didn't somebody tell me? I could have gotten *years* of mileage out of that.'

'But why are you so upset?' asks April.

My mother shakes her head, jerkily, as though trying to shake off a cobweb. 'I don't know. I don't know.'

April kneels beside her and takes hold of her arm. 'All he wants is to be happy,' she says softly. 'It's important to go with your gut instinct sometimes. I know it doesn't pay very much, but he really needs a change. Maybe he'll decide to try something different later on, but this is right for right now.' She continues, more boldly. 'I think it's time you gave some thought to what *you* want to do. Sometimes you seem so sad. Perhaps it's time you made some decisions. We want you to be happy, too.'

My mother looks at her as though she can't quite remember who she is, then lays a hand on her hair and strokes it a little bit. I remember that gesture. She used to do that to me.

'April is right,' she says to James. 'That's the important thing. Happiness.' As though she's known very little of it. Magnanimously: 'You have my blessing.'

'So how much does it pay?' I ask.

'That doesn't matter,' April snaps, as though I've ruined a special moment.

'Tell us how it happened, dear,' suggests my mother, who has completely regained her composure.

'Well,' says James, 'it was the darnedest thing. I checked the classifieds in *The Philmont Organ*. I was equally unqualified for everything, so in the end it was kind of an arbitrary choice. I just put on a suit and typed up my résumé. It didn't take long, seeing as I have no employment history. The interviewer, Mr Tribbage, wasn't too impressed with my degrees, but he liked my attire. It seems he only hires people who turn up in suits. He approves of people who honour their profession. He's a bit idiosyncratic that way, apparently.'

'Apparently,' I say.

'Very intelligent man,' says James. 'We spent some time discussing the metaphysical aspects of the job.'

'You talked metaphysics?'

'Of course. Being, truth and knowledge.'

'It's garbage collecting, James.'

71

'Yes, Ellen. Surely you can appreciate all the potential points for discussion. I brought up eudemonics. He thought I was a Satanist! Can you imagine?'

Does he have any idea what this is going to do to his sex appeal? If only he knew all the trouble I was going to on his behalf. I don't care if he wants to play 'garbage guy' for a little while. What I'm worried about is the effect this will have on the *femme fatale* I'm trying to line up for him. I didn't need this little added complication.

'Then we went for a ride on the truck,' he continues, 'which is *great* fun – you must try it sometime – and I was suddenly struck by a feeling of destiny, as though I were riding along on a great chariot and that my role was to put everything in its proper place. There's nothing wrong with garbage, you know. It's not dirty or disgusting. Like anything, it just needs to be nudged along to its ultimate destiny.'

'As landfill,' I say.

He pays no attention to me. 'Properly disposed of, it can play a vital part in the ecosystem. If I play my cards right, they might even let me go into recycling. I tell you, Mother, I finally felt that I was doing something real, something useful. My co-workers are very nice, incidentally. Fascinating people. Amazing how they live from pay cheque to pay cheque.'

My brother has finally discovered the existence of wage-slaves.

'My boss has already invited me and April to dinner. Their friendliness is outstanding. Completely different from academia, where simple human relations are inevitably impeded by professional competition. I've decided I'm a huge fan of the notion of Fate. Maybe the Greeks were right all along. Maybe I should find myself an oracle to consult on a regular basis. Thank you, don't mind if I do.'

April is feeding him bites of cake. My mother collects the cups and walks towards the kitchen. I follow. Maybe I can get her to give me a hug. I sure could use one.

'Mom?'

She turns as though expecting a torrent of objection. 'Yes, Ellen, I know, it's crazy, but I think just this once I'm going to try to go with the flow. Maybe he *wasn't* happy at Berkeley. I know Barnard drove me up the wall.'

Later, my father comes home. I hear him at the door. 'Thirty thousand dollars a year,' he roars. James's college tuition. 'Garbage guy? *Dead* guy.'

'He had scholarships, dear. Remember?'

'Thirty thousand dollars a year.'

He continues to rant, so there is still hope. But he'll probably catch the happiness bug, too. Then, once again, I'll be left out in the cold, when the one pressing her nose to the window should be April. I can't get the picture of her and my mother out of my head, and every time I remember it, I feel my heart turn a little blacker. Jealousy is roasting me from the inside out and I'm becoming internally charred.

I've got to take action, walk the walk. I need money and money is power. I'll work on my article, make it the best it can be. Then, if all else fails, I can buy her out, pay her off, present her with a one-way ticket to hell.

5

The Philmont Organ. Not exactly the *New York Times*. Still, I'd read of a regional newspaper reporter who had won a Pulitzer Prize for uncovering a medical scandal involving a drug called Alphatriptoline that apparently causes people to walk in their sleep. The citizens of the town of Smoky Fort, North Carolina, a small village surrounded by mountains, had been secretly chosen as a test-group in the Fifties by the US government; it seems they had been experimented upon for decades. They hadn't been particularly grateful for the intervention – people had been sleep-walking for years and they just thought it was normal. The point is, the journalist collected her award and went on to fame and fortune, so maybe Dad's idea isn't such a bad one after all.

All I have to do is persuade the editor to let me cover a story, which shouldn't be difficult – after all, we're talking about a small suburban weekly. They will probably welcome my offer, particularly when they discover that I am willing to write for free.

It's a tenacious little paper, actually. Has been around for over a century, during which time it has reported on the small-scale effects of several large-scale wars, detailed the comings and goings of various residents, outlined many re-zoning proposals and covered numerous local elections. The lead stories generally revolve around tracts of land being sold off for development, parking problems and the school system going over-budget. It has a Society page, a Business page, a Sports page, a thick Real Estate section. An Editorial page with opinions crammed in beside each other like battery hens. It struggles valiantly to serve

74

the community, but one is left with the feeling that it secretly hungers for controversy, like a small man no one suspects of being capable of daring. Its motto? – 'Think of the *Organ* as *your Organ*.' Its circulation? Falling.

I grew up with this paper. Seldom read it, though I regularly skimmed the front page for scandalous headlines (very rare). It's ironic that it now has the power to make or break me, but I think we'll be able to do business. One measly article and three thousand dollars will be mine, all mine. Surely it will be a cinch.

I wake up feeling fresh and optimistic, for the first time in months. I recognize the smell of cut grass and fresh bread baking. All is well. In fact, it seems as though nothing could go wrong. On the landing, Cleopatra and Igor are giving each other baths, rather than planning an assault on me, which is what they usually do when I come home. Downstairs, no April in sight, only James, looking rumpled and attractive. He does not look up but I attribute this to the fact that he is engrossed in his favourite breakfast activity, reading the cereal box. Morning is the best time for reflection, he says, as one's head is clear and it is easy to meditate upon new ideas.

'Listen to this one, Ellen: "My mind is my own church." What do you think?'

One of James's tiny quirks. He craves more erudite reading than that which is normally featured on your average package of Frosted Flakes, so he copies out quotes from books and pastes them on the box.

'I don't know, James. It's seven o'clock in the morning.'

'Guess who said it.'

'I have no idea.'

'Go on, guess.'

I sigh. 'Plato.'

'Don't be silly. Guess again.'

'Aristotle.'

'Nope. You're not trying.'

'I give up. Just tell me.'

'Thomas Paine. *Loser*. I have to say, little sis', that was *pathetic*.'

'I'm not the one who spends hours doctoring boxes of Captain Crunch.'

'These are Coco Puffs.' He chews with relish.

Well, that's one thing he and April have in common – their love of junk food. I pick up the box. 'How long do these things take you, anyway?'

'Days, sometimes weeks. I like to get them right. Sometimes I have to write to people, asking them to verify the wording or the source. Do you know, I got a personal letter from Noam Chomsky the other day? Nice guy.'

'Have you ever tried writing to Aristotle? Or Socrates?'

'Don't be silly, Ellen.'

'Well, who knows? Maybe there's someone out there answering their mail.'

James says nothing, but continues to shovel mounds of soggy brown sugary sludge into his mouth. A piece of puffed rice sticks to his cheek like a beauty mark. Now is the time to strike, I think.

'So,' I say casually. 'When are you and April getting married?'

He chokes on his cereal. 'Excuse me?'

'Hitched. You know. Wedding. Tux and a white limo. Tin cans. Eternity.'

He shrugs. 'I hadn't really thought about it. Hey, have you read this one? "Atheism is a non-prophet organization."'

'Mm hm. You do know she's interested in having a baby, don't you?'

'I didn't, actually. What about this one – "It is the test of a good religion whether you can joke about it." Gilbert K. Chesterton. I'd say he was right on the money, wouldn't you?'

He's being evasive. I decide to try another tactic. 'By the way, big brother, congratulations on your new job. It's quite a step up, rising academic star to trash collector.' I am leaning over his shoulder. An aroma of cinnamon man-smell rises up from a nice couple of square inches right below his jawline. I take advantage of his close proximity. Start rubbing his shoulders.

But, unusually, he seems uncomfortable. Takes one of my hands, pats it, lets it go. 'Thanks, sis'.' A few years ago he would have been hauling me on to his lap. Holding me upside down and engaging me in a variety of other torments.

'Will you be home late?' I ask. 'Should I put dinner on?'

'You know you can't cook, Ellen. Anyway, I expect April will have taken care of that.'

'Trying to give you a taste of marital bliss, I suppose.'

He twists around, looks up at me with a quizzical grin. 'What is all this about marriage, Ellen?'

Make him paranoid. 'Well, it's fairly obvious.'

'What is?'

'That she's waiting for you to propose.'

He looks at me as though he's been told he's about to be buried alive. Then he laughs, turns back to his food. 'Oh, Ellen, you disappoint me. I never thought you'd turn out to be like other girls. Sighing over engagement rings, begging to be a bridesmaid. Seeing a wedding in every relationship . . .'

I don't seem to be getting through to him. 'I'm serious, big brother. I get the impression she's into it. Remember, she hails from a part of the country where it's normal to marry young.' At about the age of twelve.

But he continues to look amused, as though he's decided I'm mad but harmless. 'It's a bit early in the morning for this kind of thing, little sis'.'

I nod at the box. 'But not for *that* sort of thing.'

He doesn't answer. Continues to eat. Won't look me in the eye.

Dearest James. If only he knew which one of us was deluded. He's always been there for me, now I'm going to be there for him – regardless of how often he dismisses my concerns as mere invention. He's always been so good – too good to be true. It's rather strange, now that I think about it. Could he be psychotic? A sex-crazed maniac waiting to strike? I suppose anything's possible. Poor guy. I blame it on our parents. They're bound to have had something to do with his complete inability to form an emotional bond with anyone other than me.

I try rubbing his shoulders again. This time, he lets me. I sense the beginning of a return to our former rapport. I must work on making my influence felt, in order to prevent him from doing anything foolish.

'Hey,' I say. 'Is this a theme box?'

Sometimes he does cereal boxes in themes: love, death, the existence of God, vice versus virtue, politics, free will . . . including quotations both pro and con, in order to keep it balanced and represent all points of view.

'You bet,' he says. 'This one is on religion. I thought it might set April's mind at ease. She seems to think I'm some sort of heathen, just because I haven't been "Born Again". Look – I've got Billy Graham on the other side.'

It is reassuring to hear him speak semi-facetiously of April. So he hasn't been totally brainwashed, after all. 'Did you tell her about the time Mom tried to get us to attend one of her pagan ceremonies?'

'No.' He smiles reminiscently. 'I thought I'd have to wear a funny white robe, but Mom said no, just wear your usual clothes. And then we had to go out to the Zone One playing field and practise prancing around those pseudo-prehistoric stone columns put up by the Township with leftover rock from where they ploughed down those houses and rooted everything up for the new expressway.'

'Zonehenge.'

'That's it.'

'And you flat-out refused to go,' I continue, 'because you thought all your friends' mothers were going to be there, standing around naked. You wouldn't let her take me, either.'

'I remember.'

'Thanks for standing up for me.'

'No problem. Those were the days, eh?'

'They certainly were.'

We fall silent. After a few moments, he says, 'Actually, the thought of all those mothers standing around naked was terribly exciting. Especially Frederick's – she was gorgeous. It's just that I knew Mom would be there, too, and that would've been really embarrassing.'

This is the opening I've been waiting for. 'Is Frederick around, by the way?' I ask offhandedly.

'Oh, probably. You know Freddie. He might be in town. Why?'

'Just wondering,' I say. 'Is he still living in the same house?'

'That post-modern architectural monstrosity with the iron gate and the ex-marine security guards? He is, but you won't get past the Rottweilers. I'd wait until he stops by.'

'Did I tell you?' I am suddenly longing to impress him. 'I'm going to pay the local paper a visit today.'

'You don't say?' I can see the corner of his teasing smile. 'Well, best of luck. They should get a real kick out of you.'

Great. Not even James believes in me. 'Lie down and I'll do your lower vertebrae.'

'Thanks, Ellen, but I've got to get going. The world's refuse awaits. It's my first day of work and I don't want to be late.' He gives my hand a squeeze (is it my imagination or does he hold it a bit longer than usual?) then rises to zip himself into his coveralls. He pauses. 'You know, Ellen, I feel as though I've reached some kind of turning point. This could be my big chance to make a contribution to humanity.' He resumes his preparations for the day, executing a few T'ai Chi moves and slipping a corned beef sandwich and a couple of bananas into his pocket. 'Who knows, maybe garbage is my mission. Perhaps untold vistas of environmental transformation lie ahead. It's a start, anyway. And yes, I will miss you.' A kiss on the cheek and he is gone.

Oh, big brother. Crackpot or no, how will I ever find anyone to compare with you?

I try to get into the shower. The door is shut. April. I can tell by the smell. She is using one of those professional salon shampoos, the scent of which makes you want to run screaming into the street. I bang on the door. 'April, are you going to be long? I only ask because I have a job interview.'

She pokes her head out. Her hair is flattened, covered with cream, like a bastardized water-nymph, sloppy with sea-foam. 'Ooh, that's great. You and Jimmy are such whiz kids. I won't be a sec'.'

Then something barks.

April looks guilty.

My mother enters. 'Ellen, what did I tell you about barking?'

We hear it again, a kind of pitiful yap-yap-yapping. April is shaking from the bottom up. A battle is taking place around her ankles. A dog appears, a small shaggy mutt with dirty white fur and pleading eyes.

'Yap-yap-yap,' it says, staring imploringly at my mother. Then it turns around, takes a running jump and hurls itself at April, a homesick puppy hoping to die in the arms of the mother country.

'I was just about to scrub her,' says April, picking her up. 'She followed me home.'

Sure she did. The dog pants pathetically. I am struck by the resemblance between the two. Half-entreatingly, half-defiantly, as though addressing a hostile crowd, April makes her case: 'She's very thin under all this fur. She's homeless. She has nowhere to go.'

I marvel at this. One of the most affluent neighbourhoods in America and April has managed to find a starving mongrel.

My mother looks regretful. 'We can't, April. The cats. They wouldn't get along.'

'They would eat her,' I add.

'I bet they'd get along just fine,' says April. 'Look.'

Cleopatra and Igor have appeared, lured, no doubt, by the smell of strange beast. April sits the dog down in front of them.

'I call her Puddles,' she informs us.

The three of them sit still for a moment and look at each other – Puddles humble, the cats disdainful. Then they have a good sniff around and walk off together, Puddles trailing along behind.

'See?' April is triumphant.

'That thing has fleas,' I say.

'We'll get some powder,' says my mother. 'And shots and a dog tag.'

'Oh, thank you,' cries April joyfully. 'You won't regret it, I promise. She seems very sweet-natured. I have a dog back home named "Innertube" – I called him that because I saved him from drowning. He was an unwanted puppy and they put him in a sack . . . I dove in and pulled him out. You have no idea how much I miss him. My mom and dad said they'd take care of him until I could collect him, though. Bet they'll miss him when I do.'

I wonder if her mother and father miss her.

My mother looks funny, as though she wants to say something but is weighing her tact against her better judgement. Finally she says, 'You can give your parents a call whenever you like, April. Our treat. I'm sure they'd be delighted to hear from you.'

April looks down. 'Thanks. I will. I just keep forgetting.'

'They haven't called you, have they?' My mother watches her face closely. 'Do they have our number?'

'Um, I'm not sure. I may have forgotten to give it to them.' Poor April. She's such a bad liar. It's perfectly obvious that they just haven't bothered to telephone. In spite of her protestations of family togetherness, they clearly have no intention of getting in touch. She sighs. 'I sure do miss Innertube.'

'April, please feel free to make arrangements to collect him. I'm sure we can accommodate another dog.' My mother speaks intently, as though trying to convince April that she is not alone.

'Mom, have you forgotten about my dog phobia?' I demand.

She looks at me blankly. 'What dog phobia?'

'Oh, you remember. My *dog phobia*.'

'That was a long time ago, Ellen.'

'It's still painful.'

'I'm sure it is, dear –'

'I hate dogs,' I inform April.

'But,' my mother continues, 'I'm sure you will get over it. In the meantime, we must endeavour to make Puddles feel at home.'

Puddles (what kind of a name is that) comes shuffling back in, with a considerably lighter step. Puts her paws on my shinbone and gazes up at me. I withdraw my leg. She stumbles.

'Careful,' my mother admonishes. I scowl at her. Judas.

But Puddles is not to be put off. Sturdily, she gets up and pursues me. Wherever I go, she follows. Whatever I do, she watches. I get the impression I could give her a swift kick up the rump and still she would persevere.

'She likes you,' says my mother, as though this is a totally inexplicable phenomenon.

It rapidly becomes evident that not only is this unknown canine going to make herself at home, but I am going to be the one she follows around. God knows why – I make my repugnance clear – but she continues to gaze at me adoringly. April is pleased about this and ties a pink bow between the mutt's ears. I despair.

Puddles is, in fact, the only member of the household who seems to be taking any interest in me. It's really degrading. I stomp around for a while, trying to put her off (no such luck), then go back upstairs to dress. She trails me everywhere, even to the bathroom. As I sit on the toilet, I can hear her snuffling at the door, desperate to get in. I can't pee when someone is listening. I will her to go away.

'Yap-yap-yap.' Her meaning is clear: I'm here to stay.

The situation is getting all out of control. I need to get into April's head, under her skin, winkle out unpleasant points about her character. I decide to invite her to walk along with me when I go to see the editor of *The Philmont Organ*.

She responds eagerly. 'I'd love to. In fact, I have an errand of my own to run. Your mom thinks maybe I can get the local gift shop to carry some of my jewellery.'

They won't know what's hit them. Half an hour later I scream, *'April going into town now wanna come?'*

She comes bounding downstairs in her little pink suit, carefully ironed, wearing a pair of high-heeled pumps. She has piled her hair on top of her head like a self-deluded Cinderella who's arrived too early for the ball and she carries, to my surprise, a rather nice beige sample case. She lifts it up.

'Present from your mom,' she says, then smiles and does a twirl. 'How do I look?'

Awful. 'You look great.'

I've locked Puddles in the Morgue. It's hard to listen to her pitiful whimpering, but kind of fun, too. We set off.

'So, today you start your career as a reporter, huh, Ellen,' says April.

Ellen Kaplan, Cub Reporter. I am struck by a vision of myself, midget-sized, with notebook, cigarette and porkpie hat, a cheese-burger stain on my lapel. 'Something like that.'

'Do you enjoy writing?'

'I hate it.'

'Have you had lots of articles published?'

'No.'

'Jimmy told me your high-school paper published a whole bunch of your stuff.'

'Yes, but that doesn't count.'

'Sure it does!' She bounces along beside me. 'They wouldn't have printed it unless it was good, right?'

'Dunno,' I mumble.

'And he said your high-school paper won lots of prizes.'

The paper had, but I hadn't. I'd worked under that notorious student editor, Tyler Spee. My crush on him had been my initial motivation for joining – that and the free pizza they gave out at every meeting. But it wasn't long before I was learning the tricks of the trade, and discovering that I enjoyed them. I got a kick out of snooping, liked seeing my name in print. In the end, Tyler was just an excuse. After all, I could have joined the school jazz band, headed by Jet 'Give me a Little Sizzling Saxophone Action' Jolssen. But hot lips couldn't compare to hot lead, and in the end, journalism won out. I foresaw notoriety and kudos, adventure and travel. I felt I'd found my true calling. Problem was, I wasn't a very good writer, which was a bit of a stumbling block.

'I would have loved to write,' says April wistfully.

She knows not what she says. *Probe, Ellen, probe,* Tyler had ranted. Those words come back to haunt me. And, 'Ellen, you can barely type, let alone write.' The first of many insults. People told me he only did it because he cared, but I think he had sadistic tendencies. Which is fine for the bedroom, if you like that sort of thing, but it didn't do a whole lot for my composition.

'I admire your ambition,' April continues.

I'm going to work for a paper with a circulation lower than my SAT score. This is ambition? My shoulders slump. Christ. What am I doing with my life?

'So,' I say dully. 'When did you first learn to make jewellery?'

'When I was a girl scout.'

Of course. Suddenly, I can see her as a big fat Brownie. It's funny – I wouldn't have immediately identified her as a 'joiner'. She gives the impression of being someone who is always on the edge of the group, wanting to join in, but unwelcome. 'Did you like it?'

'I loved it,' she enthuses. 'I collected lots of badges. Well, to be perfectly honest, I never made it past Juniors –'

'Why not?'

She looks away. I glimpse a small ashamed smile. 'Oh. Well, it's hard to explain. My mom gets a bit crazy sometimes and . . . can't cope. She wasn't able to pick me up after the meetings.'

Wasn't able. Because she was drunk. And April, too shy to ask a friend for a ride.

'I have to admit, I was kind of disappointed, because I was

becoming really popular. Everyone wanted a necklace – I could design them with their names. For a while, everyone liked me a lot. Then they kind of forgot about me.'

April's brief insight into what it's like to be accepted. I could tell her that peer endorsement is overrated but I don't want her thinking that I *like* her or anything. I've got to cut to the nitty gritty. 'Saw James this morning,' I say. 'Getting ready for work.'

'So did I.'

'Sure hope he likes it. Collecting trash.'

'Uh huh.'

'I can't help but think he'll change his mind about all this, go back to research.'

'No. I told you. He's given all that up.' Stubbornness moves over her face like clouds shadowing the sun.

'April, I'm not convinced that he *wanted* to give it up. You don't spend years doing something you don't enjoy.'

'You do if you have a super-exaggerated sense of duty like Jimmy.'

If anything is super-exaggerated, it's her. 'What do you mean, duty?'

'I mean your parents really wanted him to become an academic, so he did.'

I think this over. To be fair, there is probably *some* truth to it. I remember my mother's reaction to his Harvard acceptance: 'Just think, darling, you can stay there for*ever* and *ever* and *ever* . . .' And my father, grinning and opening his chequebook: 'How many zeros, son? Just name a figure.'

'I'm right, aren't I,' says April.

'Well . . . they only wanted him to do it because they thought *he* wanted to do it.'

'I hate to say it but they were wrong. He didn't.'

'Okay, but you're not going to tell me he doesn't love to read.' I am thinking of the disappearance of his books. 'He's always been a book lover –'

'Ellen, I don't want him *reading* his life away.' She pronounces the word 'reading' with utter contempt. Looks mildly disdainful, as though privy to a more fundamental knowledge. 'There are too many other more important things in life. So I told him not to.'

This is too much. I can't control myself any longer. 'April, aren't you being kind of a fascist?'

She glances sideways at me – furtive, alarmed. Clearly she had not anticipated confrontation. 'What do you mean?'

'For God's sake, April, you can't order him not to read books. It's pathetic and anyway I don't think he'll . . . obey.'

'But he will.' She sounds surprised. 'He promised.'

'April, you're depriving him of something he loves.'

'He loves *me*,' she snaps. Then simmers down, as though she's remembered the need to cultivate my friendship. 'He was spending so *much* time reading, that's all. Hours every day. Between that and visiting people he knows . . .'

'. . . you felt neglected.'

'Sort of. It wasn't just that, though. I'm not sure I *like* his friends. I don't think they're a good influence.'

This is preposterous. 'April, correct me if I'm wrong, but would I be right in thinking that you have a little bit of difficulty getting along with them?'

She looks shamefaced, then defiant. 'Yes. But you don't know what it was like!' She stops in the middle of the sidewalk and turns to face me – earnest, serious. 'The first time I met them, I mean. We'd only just arrived, we'd barely settled in, and the first thing he does is call them up and arrange to see them. It was like he couldn't wait to get away from me.'

'Did he offer to take you along?'

'Well . . . yes.'

'So what's the problem?'

She snuffles – a bit like Puddles, actually. 'I don't know. I guess I didn't want him to go with or without me. So I kind of got upset.'

Oh, no. I can just picture the scenario: James tries to go off and see his buddies, and April bursts into tears. The queen of emotional blackmail. 'Then what happened?' I ask.

'I went with him, in the end.'

'And?'

'Oh, Ellen, it was awful.' Wobbly face. About to cry. I nudge her and we resume walking. 'I can't begin to tell you how hard it was. Frederick was there –'

Frederick.

'– you know, that horrible boy who looks like a Nazi, and that yucky boy Zero –'

'Oh, for goodness' sake, April, Zero's a good guy. He's harmless.'

'Ellen, he asked me what I did for a living, and when I told him I sold HerbElixir, he looked at me like I was insane.'

'Zero looks at everyone as though they're insane. He talks to himself. His socks don't match. He's a theoretical physicist.'

'He was looking down on me.'

'April, you take things too personally. Let me ask you this: while you were talking to him, was he fiddling with the waistband of his underpants?'

'Yes. Inside his shorts.'

'Well, that means he likes you.'

'I just thought he was a pervert.'

'He is. But when he fiddles with his waistband, that means he likes you. Trust me.'

'Well, what about Frederick, then?' she demands. 'He was *really* looking down on me. I could tell by the tone of his voice. He sounded like the villain in one of those old horror films – "Dracula" or something. Dragging out each word extra long.'

'April, he was *patronizing* you. He meant it as a compliment. Most girls consider it a turn-on.'

'You mean . . . it *excites* them?'

'Sure.'

She is looking totally confused. 'So he was coming on to me?'

Whoa. 'I wouldn't go that far. But it certainly doesn't mean he was looking down on you.'

'There was another guy there. Just briefly. A real brain. Didn't say a word to me. Looks like a frog.'

'Kermit. Yes. Computer scientist. He kind of lurks around. Started college when he was nine, child genius sort of thing. It's made him very shy.'

April sags, overwhelmed by explanations. 'All the same, I don't think they wanted me around.'

'Relax,' I say. 'You just don't know how to read the signals.'

Don't think for a moment that my motives are altruistic. My objective is to make her fearfulness seem foolish. The more pressure she comes under to see his friends, the more of a strain she will feel. Until she cracks.

She digests this. 'What does he need them for, anyway? Aren't I enough?'

'April, no one is ever enough. Don't you see? If you're going to be happy together, you need independent lives. *Very* independent. In fact, the more time you spend apart, the better.'

'What do you mean?'

'I mean, familiarity breeds contempt. You don't want him to become contemptuous of you, do you?'

She looks troubled. 'No.'

'And you know what they say – if you love someone, set him free.'

April nods in reluctant agreement. 'I know what you're saying is right, Ellen. I mean, maybe I am kind of clingy.' She hesitates. 'It's just that I'm so afraid of losing him, you know? Sometimes I wonder what he sees in me.'

We walk along silently for a few moments. Her heels sink into the ground as we cross a strip of grass. She grabs my arm.

'Oops,' I say.

'There's something else,' she says abruptly. 'Ellen, I have to talk to you about this. It's important.' Takes a deep breath, as though about to confide a terrible secret. 'Do you know a girl named Courtney?'

Sure I do. Who doesn't? Courtney Huffington, Philmont's quality tramp. Half John Singer Sargent, half man-eating slut. Upper-crust and very sexually active. 'Hm. Doesn't ring a bell. Who is she?'

'Zero's cousin. She went to Benetton.'

'Bennington.'

'Huh?'

'Bennington. Not Benetton. Bennington is an expensive private college for spoiled dilettantes. Benetton is a clothes shop.'

'Oh. Well, anyway, she's really pretty and intelligent. She was there the day I met his friends, and I think she may have been coming on to him.'

'What was she doing?'

'The usual things. Paying a lot of attention to him, fluttering her eyelashes . . .'

'Do people really do that?'

'What?'

'Flutter their eyelashes.'

'*She* did.'

'Was he responding?'

'I don't . . . think so.'

'What do you mean, you don't *think* so?'

'Well, it's really hard to tell. I mean, I don't *think* he was, but then maybe I just couldn't read the signals. And then I got all spazzy and mad at him but couldn't tell him why, because then he'd think I was jealous. Do you think I'm too possessive?'

I hardly hear her. Fireworks are going off in my head. Courtney. Of course. Why didn't I think of this before?

'Ellen?' April tugs at my arm. 'Ellen? Are you listening?'

'Huh? Oh.'

'I hate to ask, but could you do me a favour?'

'Sure,' I say expansively. 'Anything.'

'Seeing as you and he are so close and all, I wonder if you could sort of ask him about Courtney. Find out whether or not he likes her. Likes her *that way*.' She screws her mouth up meaningfully. 'But try not to let him know that I want to know. That part's really important because I don't want him to think I'm insecure. Girls like Courtney are pure confidence. I have to convince him I'm as good as her. I guess I'm asking you to spy on your own brother, Ellen, but there's no one else I can turn to. I can't stop thinking about it. I don't know what else to do.'

'Well . . .' I pause. Look reluctant. Relent with a nod. 'Okay, I'll try. I've been meaning to have a heart-to-heart with him, and I guess I could arrange for that to come up in conversation.'

We've reached the centre of town and the offices of *The Philmont Organ*. The moment of parting can no longer be delayed. Yet April seems curiously reluctant to be on her way. I can just make out the gift-shop window, filled with cut-crystal candlesticks, enamelled fountain pens, and music boxes with pop-up twirling ballerinas.

'Oh, I almost forgot – I have a present for you,' she says, and pulls something out of her sample case, balancing it on her knee. 'I was carrying this when I met James. It brought me luck. Maybe it will bring you luck, too.'

It is a plastic representation of the Son of God. I pull the string in its back. 'Jesus loves you,' it groans.

'It glows in the dark,' she adds.

'Thanks. I don't know what to say.'

'Ellen?' April says. 'How long will this meeting of yours take?' How long, O Lord, how long? 'I've no idea.'

'Because if you're not too tired afterwards, maybe we could have some fun. Just the two of us. Go roller-skating, maybe, or bowling.'

'Yeah. Maybe.'

'Great,' she says, beaming. To my embarrassment and dismay, she hugs me. Throws both arms around me and squeezes. 'Thank you, Ellen, for helping me out.' And if she has ever been insincere, I would be willing to swear that at this moment she has never meant anything more.

I present myself at *The Philmont Organ*. A pretty typical small-town newspaper office except for the giant duck sitting in the corner. A wooden duck, vividly painted, with a frightening grin, the kind you'd expect to find on a demonic marionette. It's big enough to fit a person inside. A twelve-year-old, perhaps. Like, say, the one sitting in front of me, at a desk with his feet up. He looks up in an unfriendly manner.

'I'd like to see the editor, please.'

He appears to be sewing. A computer twitches and jerks beside him, almost as though it is writing its own copy. 'Concerning what?'

'Tell him I went to Columbia and that I need a job.'

He puts his sewing down and goes out. Comes back. 'He says, "Go away".'

I pause. 'Tell him I'll work for free.'

'He still says no.'

'You haven't even told him yet.'

'He and I have a very close psychic connection.'

He wears baggy trousers and thick-soled pointy-toed shoes upholstered in fake tiger skin. His hair is slicked back and his whole face culminates in his nose, which is prominent. His eyes duck behind it, shrewd soldiers in a trench. He's not going to let me get away with anything.

Casually, I lean over the desk that separates us. Feign a polite interest. 'What are you sewing?'

He holds it up. A small drawstring bag. 'For export,' he says. 'We live in an age of poison and toxins. Diseases and fatal viruses. Live defensively.'

'Posy bags?'

'For a bunch of loonies living in Australia. Some cult convinced that we're heading towards the next plague. These things have to be made by underage Cytrons.'

'What's a Cytron?' If I distract him, maybe I can make a dash for the editor's door.

'Don't know, but apparently I am one. The money's pretty good. I'd recommend you for a posting but you don't look like a Cytron.'

'Don't I?'

'No. It seems that the world is divided into Cytrons and Gonatrons and you are definitely a Gonatron.'

The term has a pejorative ring to it. A tape is playing in the background. Mexican mariachi music. 'Are you sure that's not just a sewing project for your mandatory home ec' class?'

He stands, leans over, puts his face close to mine; I can feel the lengthy line of his nose. His breath a bowl of fruit punch balanced on a dung heap. 'Go away.'

'You go to Philmont Middle School, don't you.'

'Fuck off.'

'This is some kind of internship, isn't it. Work-study. My kid brother did that. Matthew. Matthew Kaplan. For a computer programming firm. He hacked into head office files and assigned himself a salary. Six months went by before they noticed.'

'Matthew Kaplan's your brother? *The* Matthew?'

'The one and only.'

For a moment, he looks impressed, and I figure I'm in with a chance. Then he snarls:

'You shut him in a dark room when he was five.'

'I know. I'm sorry. Look, could I have a word with the editor? Just a sort of an info-view?'

'Forget it.' He leaps over the desk and starts to push me bodily out of the office. He *looks* a bit like Matthew, actually – his evil double, future lord of the print media.

'Okay,' I say, playing for time. 'Okay. Here's what we'll do. You let me in to see him and I'll . . . I'll . . .'

'Let her in, Myron,' someone shouts from the back.

I smirk. *'Myron.'*

His nose lengthens, swells. 'Let's get one thing straight, *Columbia*. I'm his *protégé*. That means I get *privileges*. So if there's any job going, I get it.'

'You? You're not even old enough to sweep chimneys.'

'I'm waiting,' bellows the Voice from Hell.

Matthew scowls. I have earned a permanent enemy. He has to let me through and he doesn't like it one bit.

'Thanks,' I say, maintaining eye contact until I've almost left the room. As I pass through the door marked 'Editor', unfortunately, I trip over the threshold and stumble.

He is sitting in a chair, one of those unmanageable swively office chairs that are liable to shoot off in the wrong direction if you're not careful. He has a leg stretched out in front of him. One leg. He has only one leg.

'I was in 'Nam,' he explains. 'My tentmate went insane and cut it off at the hip. Can't say I blame him.'

The office is antediluvian. Not a computer in sight. A manual typewriter as large as an upright piano. Cheap metal shelves crammed with peeling reference books. A worn, dark green carpet, covered with great black stains. An angled lamp looming like the head of the Loch Ness Monster. Wooden rulers and gutted staplers. Phone numbers written on the wall behind his head.

'I'll come straight to the point,' I say. 'I need a job. I want to do one assignment, just one, to gain some experience.'

He smiles – pleasantly, affably. Looks as though he *might*, just might, have a metal plate inside his skull.

'Do you know the story of the "Philmont Duck"?' he asks. 'You probably saw it on your way in. You may find this hard to believe, but *The Philmont Organ* was not always the success it is today. It was the town's first newspaper, and in the beginning reaction was guarded, to say the least.' He thumbs a portrait on the wall, an old photograph of a bespeckled man in a stiff collar. 'Elijah Doppelganger. Editor and founder. He was determined

91

to make it work. Imagine Philmont back then. No income tax. Old money. No one would let him through their front door. What good is a paper if there's nothing to print? He had to win them over. So what did he do?' Accents the air with a raised finger. 'Smart guy. He built that giant duck, hollowed it out, and stuck his son inside. Little Ichabod, or "Icky". A charming but malnourished fellow. Then he wheeled him to a local society ball, left him at the gates, and told him not to come home until he got the story. Needless to say, the fascinated guests dragged in the duck and got the surprise of their lives – mainly that its occupant had almost suffocated. The debs took him to heart, the "Night of the Duck" became an annual event, and the paper acquired some much-needed credibility. Sales shot up. And that's all that matters. Now *that* was an editor of genius.'

'Very interesting,' I say.

'Ever since, it has been traditional to keep the "Philmont Duck" on the premises. Which is why *The Philmont Organ* is sometimes known as *The Philmont Duck* or just *The Duck*.'

'Gee.'

'Over time, it has come to represent everything we stand for, being wooden, hollow, and largely deceptive. Tell me,' he says, 'why should I take you on?'

'Because if you let me do one story, you'll never hear from me again. If you don't, you'll never see the back of me.'

The editor looks hard at me for a long moment. Heaves himself up in his chair and cracks his spine as though I've given him a backache. 'Okay. But let's get one thing straight. There are three rules. Firstly, our mission is to dig up the truth. We love America and America is truth – or so says my boss, though he's a Republican and a jackal-begetting liar. Secondly, don't *ever* accuse a colleague of being drunk, even in jest. Because chances are it's probably true and we don't like to draw attention to the fact.'

'What's the third rule?'

'The third rule is, I don't exist. If you get into trouble, I don't want to know. Have you read *Oliver Twist*? Recall Fagin's instructions: if you get caught, don't come running to me. Understand?'

I nod.

'Good. Observe all usual reporter ethics, unless I say otherwise.

Now, let's see what kind of a story we can come up with for you.' With a mighty shove of his foot, he hurls himself clear across the room to a dented olive-green filing cabinet, from which multi-coloured shades of translucent paper protrude. Takes out a file. 'Let's see. How about following up a lead on bat dung in the Presbyterian belfry?'

'Pass.'

'Okay.' He opens another folder. 'How about a story on six unidentified baby skeletons recently found in an attic? Everyone loves those. You'd have to sneak into the local history archives and probably lower yourself down a well.'

'I'd rather not.'

'No? Pity. Because that really would have been good.' He squints at some more papers. I notice that they don't seem to bear any relation to what he is talking about. In fact, they appear to be covered with cartoons and small doodles, several of which look decidedly pornographic. 'How about a human interest story on organ transplants? Seems a local entrepreneur has been shipping them in direct from China. I gather it's hard to get a hold of a good set of heart and lungs and those political prisoners are proving a rich source. Think you could cover that?'

'If you don't mind my saying so . . .'

'Hit me.'

'This doesn't sound at all like the *Organ* I know.'

He shrugs. 'You've got to move with the times. Readers around here are sick of small-town news. Straight reportage won't satisfy their ravenous appetites any more. They want to be in touch with the mysterious. They need to believe that the extraordinary is taking place right on their own front doorsteps, that their lives aren't as banal as they think. They want irony and instruction. Meaning and significance. *They want weird*. As a newspaper, it's our duty to give it to them. And if that means unearthing old skeletons, exposing the local trade in body parts, and pointing out that the Lord's creations are crapping on his own temple, then *that's what we do*.' He cracks his spine again. 'Also, rumour has it that another local paper is about to be launched for the first time in one hundred and twenty years. Full colour, lots of money behind it. Some joker has spotted a gap in the marketplace for a paper that people actually want to read.

93

So we've got to find an angle, a way back into people's hearts. We need another Duck. And I want *you* to get me that Duck. Well? What do you say?'

'Um . . . well . . .'

'What is it?'

'I'd like a story that will give me a reasonable shot at a Pulitzer Prize.'

The editor thinks a minute, then slaps his leg, or rather the space where his leg would have been if he'd had a leg, and says, 'I've got it. A hot lead. You'll love this. The Grosworthy Estate.'

'The Grosworthy Estate?'

'Yeah. You know, that big tract of land about a mile east, owned by Eamon Grosworthy. Steel magnate and local kook. I can't get anyone else to do it. You game?'

'What's the peg?'

'Find out whether or not he's going to sell to LandDevel Inc. They're buying up every bit of property they can in the area – and getting away with it. Do you remember that public park, they one they built for handicapped children? They bought that. And the arboretum to the south of Reynolds Road, the one all the kids use to do their leaf collections? They bought that, too.'

'But how are they getting away with it?'

He smiles. 'Friends on the Zoning Hearing Board? Who knows. The thing is, Grosworthy's neighbours are up in arms because they're worried about a drop in their property values. Have you ever seen a LandDevel Home? It looks like a . . . well, a piece of shit, frankly. So I think they're going to make trouble. This is a potentially explosive story that concerns a very weird guy. And weird is good. We like weird. Repeat after me: weird is good.'

'Weird is good.'

'Bring me this grail, O Young and Unworthy One, and I think I can guarantee you a front-page byline.'

It sounds simple enough. 'Why hasn't anyone else been willing to cover this?'

'Because he keeps a selection of fully loaded firearms in his house. And because he discourages visitors. Especially journalists.'

'So he's . . . eccentric.'

'He's a loon.'

'I have a question.'

'Shoot.'

'Exactly how likely is it that I will be killed?'

'I'd say a sixty-forty chance, odds in your favour.'

'I'd like a different assignment, please.'

'No can do.' He folds his hands over his stomach. Swings himself from side to side in his chair; he *enjoys* making other people's lives hell.

'Why me?' I ask. Maybe he thinks I've got what it takes.

'Because you're expendable,' he says.

'Is that it?'

'Yes.'

'Permission to ask one more question, sir,' I say.

'Yes? Go ahead.'

'Do you love America?'

He leans forward, very close, a bit like Myron. Takes a deep breath.

'I *hate* it.'

After this, there seems to be nothing more to say. He has given me a virtually impossible assignment and there doesn't seem to be any chance of changing his mind.

'My-*ron*,' he bellows. Myron comes running in with a wheelchair. He's quite the little henchman. 'Take me around the corner or I'll beat you.' Turns to me. 'You know, I like to think that Myron embodies the spirit of little Icky.'

'Incidentally, whatever happened to little Icky?' I ask.

'He sought his fortune in the West Indies. Got eaten by cannibals.'

'Watch out – he's a *maniac*,' Myron mouths. Is this a gesture of solidarity or is he trying to frighten me off? Probably the latter. The dulcet tones of Tyler Spee come back to me with rule number one: trust nobody. No one tips off a journalist without a reason – not even another journalist.

The editor doesn't really beat him, surely?

'I really appreciate this,' I call out. 'I won't let you down.' His back is to me; he gives me a Queen Elizabeth from the wrist. Myron strains and grimaces. As they exit, I notice that he walks with a slight limp. It might just be the thick-soled shoes, one of which is thicker than the other. It might not.

Well, I got what I came for. I ought to be thrilled. For the first time in years, I've succeeded at something. And career-wise, isn't this what I wanted? One of those 'hot leads' Tyler was always telling me about?

An old expression comes to mind: be careful what you ask for . . .

. . . for you will surely get it.

Hell, I might as well give it a shot. I've got nothing left to lose. For better or worse, I am entering the danger zone. I will undoubtedly fail.

6

'The Fate of the Grosworthy Estate.'

At least the page is no longer blank. I have set up my old IBM. It gives the impression of having swelled to the point where it takes up my entire bedroom but I am fully aware that this is simply the consequence of my paranoia. I am almost afraid to touch it at first. Suspect it might burn me or something. No such luck, of course. It's aching to be used – a couple of pokes and it's lurching along like the Frankenstein monster taking its first few tentative steps.

I can hear the voice of Tyler Spee: '*Write*, Ellen – don't regurgitate.' I stare at the sullied white paper. I've assassinated it. My language is destitute. What is it they say? Just open a vein.

This is ridiculous. Writing an article isn't that big a deal. Just do it, Ellen, I tell myself, and begin:

'It has been confirmed that prominent local resident Eamon Grosworthy will be selling his extensive estate to LandDevel Inc. Construction of a new housing project is scheduled to begin later this year.'

Then I insert a second sheet and type:

'It has been confirmed that prominent local resident Eamon Grosworthy will *not* be selling his extensive estate to LandDevel Inc.'

My reasoning is simple. Either he's selling or he's not. So I am going to write two articles, one stating that he *is* and one stating that he *isn't*. Then all I will have to do is find a couple of sources and confirm my facts. Tyler Spee used to give me a little pep talk on this subject. It went something like this:

'*Two* sources, *two*, you idiot – and one should preferably be

97

the horse's mouth.' He never seemed to have much faith in me: 'If I scoured the world I couldn't find a more useless, feeble, pathetic excuse for a so-called journalist than you. You're *inert*, Ellen. I could use you to prop open the door. Do you realize that?'

He had a way with words, did Tyler. Apparently even my shorthand was deformed.

'Buildings are to be constructed in a manner that will destroy the elegance and natural beauty for which Philmont is noted.'

I stop. Bite my hands. The tone is too tabloid. But hadn't the editor implied that he needed to spice things up a bit around the *Organ*? I stare at the paper some more. Wonder if there's any way to get the article to write itself.

It occurs to me that there is.

Matthew doesn't want me to get rid of April. Fine. But I don't see why he shouldn't be willing to help me come up with some decent copy. It's no skin off his nose. Besides, as my kid brother, he owes me, just for letting him exist. I've been *way* too tolerant. I figure he can look a few things up on the Internet, shift the sentences around and the deed is as good as done. He won't do it gratis but I'll just ask him to name his price. Then I'll collect three grand from Dadsville, pay up, and get out of town. After playing Cupid to James and Courtney, of course.

Matthew is seated at his terminal, as usual, bonding with his technology and consuming a meatball sandwich. This is interesting. I've often wondered what he eats. He never seems to use the kitchen. Occasionally, a man comes to the door with a hot wrapped package for him. It might be fast-food delivery. It might not. I've heard human livers steam when they're torn out. He's biting into his food pretty ferociously, actually. I wonder how he's going to react when he learns I need a favour.

'Thought you might find your way back down here,' he says, his food a mobile lump in his cheek. 'What is it this time?'

'What do you mean, "What is it this time?"' I say. 'Maybe I don't want anything. Maybe I've just come down to say hello.'

'And the Pope smokes dope.'

He's pissing me off and loving it. I need to divert him, change the subject. Polite enquiries are called for. I nod at the computer.

'How's Deep Blue, by the way? Still suffering from a massive superiority complex?'

'What, like you? Just tell me what you want – besides a life, I mean. Temporary residence on Mount Olympus? A trip back to the Stone Age in a time machine? The first I can probably manage but only for a couple of days. You'll have to talk to Zero about the latter. The Stone Age would suit you. I think you'd fit right in. Then again, I understand the greater deities really know how to party. You'd be just in time for the annual Zeus-a-thon.'

'All right, Matthew. That's enough.'

'Not interested? I'd have thought Zeus would be right up your alley. The kind of guy you could really relate to. Being a giant egotist and all.'

'Talk about egotistical. You're the self-proclaimed master of the universe.'

He continues as though I haven't spoken. 'So what's it to be? A fake job recommendation? Money?' He finishes his sandwich. Starts picking his teeth. 'I'd better warn you, I can only come up with counterfeit at the moment. Nobody's into the real thing any more. Though I might be able to loan you a twenty.'

'All right, all right,' I say. 'You win. I give up. I seek information, brother o' mine. For an article I'm writing for *The Philmont Organ*. I'm researching a man named Grosworthy. Eamon Grosworthy. Any chance you've heard of him?'

Matthew nods. 'Made his money in steel. Hates his neighbours.'

'So they say.'

'Shoots people for fun.'

'Oh, for goodness' sake, Matthew, we don't know that that's true.' I know it's true. I can already see the white line around my body.

'They say his entire household is a catacomb,' he continues. 'He has his dead friends exhumed, strips the bodies, sets them up in his living room, and calls it social life.'

'That's just a rumour, Matthew. Be serious.'

'I am being serious. Do you know what you're getting yourself into? I'd be worried, but I know perfectly well you don't have the guts to follow through.'

'Just look him up on the Web, would you? I stand to make a

lot of money off this and I'll give you ten per cent if you help me out.'

'You mean, if I do the work for you.'

'If you *assist* me. But don't think you'll be getting more than –'

'Relax, sis'. I don't take money from charity cases.' Puts his fingers to his keyboard. The maestro at work. Pauses. Looks up. 'God, you are so easy to rile.' Proceeds.

A house comes up on the screen. Large, made of stone. 'Nice, eh? Dates back to the Revolutionary War. Note the artillery positioned at the windows.' Another picture, this time of the grounds. 'He loves nature. The place is practically a conservation area. Rare species of birds. Plants. Even a wildcat or two. Well, those escaped from a zoo but they go there to feed. Completely docile, once they set foot in his domain. They say a unicorn wanders around, looking for a virgin's lap to lay its head in.'

'It must be getting tired.'

'And this is the man himself.' A photograph of a guy in his sixties. Thinning white hair brushed over a largish head. Grim mouth. Sad eyes. 'Deceptively puny-looking guy. Could take on an elephant and win. He's obsessed with war, of course.' Text rolls up on the screen. 'Fought in Korea. Wanted to study anthropology but his family forced him into a military career. American bluebloods. Always a hazard.' A shot of Korea. 'Became very interested in Oriental culture. Didn't appreciate having to blow up the natives. Pretty wholesale stuff, the slaughter. Children, the elderly – anyone wearing white pyjamas was a target. It screwed him up. That and the deaths of the men he fought with, including his best friend, Monty. Did you know that Vietnam was a direct result of Korea? Didn't have to happen. Just an attempt to salvage some American military pride.'

'The editor of the local paper was in Vietnam.'

'I know. Old "One-Legged Willie". He's almost as well-known as Grosworthy, though it has to be said, it's more of a cult following. Anyway, Grosworthy can't stop thinking about his slain comrades. Never recovered from the fact that they died and he didn't. How much do you know about the Korean War, Ellen?' I stare at him blankly. He takes another stab. 'Korea? Peninsular country in east-central Asia?' He pauses. '"M*A*S*H"?'

With relief, I feel the recognition factor kick in. 'I had a crush on Alan Alda.'

'That's kind of a tenuous connection but you have a reference point, at least. Four million dead. Mostly Korean, mostly civilian. Not surprisingly, Grosworthy ended up hating his own country. And I don't have to tell you, Ellen, that if you reject your own country, you end up rejecting a part of yourself. This is who and what you're dealing with. Know anything about jellied petrol bombs?'

I squirm. Feel guilty. Tyler Spee had cited the work of various war correspondents but I hadn't been listening.

'Anyway,' Matthew continues, 'the North Korean government is still holding on to the remains of some of his pals, and he's determined to get them back. He's been pulling some strings.'

'Heartstrings?'

'Purse strings. The guy's worth millions. Was so disillusioned with life that he decided to get rich – which is a pretty smart decision, when you think about it. Had a good record in community service a couple of decades ago. Funded a bunch of homeless shelters and generally helped the underdog. His neighbours went ballistic when he wanted to set up a little rehab centre in his house, start importing drug addicts from the inner city. So they made a fuss. He fought back. And it's been battle lines ever since.'

'Sounds like a pretty good guy to me.'

'Yeah. Except that he claims he sees ghosts and drives around his estate in an old jeep hollering orders at them, taking pot shots at anyone who gets in his way. Which no one ever does, of course, apart from kamikaze reporters like yourself. He keeps a full security force on the premises. Claims the CIA are out to get him.'

'Does he ever venture out into the real world?'

'Sure. In disguise. Gets the idea occasionally that he's the archangel Gabriel, Messenger of God. Tools around town handing out messages from the dead to complete strangers: "Marion is fine – she says you've got to have the boil lanced." "Your father would like you to know that he likes the new tattoo." Scary thing is, they generally turn out to be true.'

'Does he ever stop for a cup of coffee?'

'No, but he does hang out at the public library.'

'The public library?'

'Yes, Ellen. Big building? Lots of books? He's intelligent and highly knowledgeable in the field of anthropology. Claims he's had plenty of opportunity to study the follies of humankind. Also, I think he picks up women there.'

So this is the infamous Grosworthy. A harmless old man who waves a gun around once in a while. So what? So does half of America. 'Thanks, Matt-man. I really appreciate this.'

'Don't mention it.'

'The thing is, I have to find out if he's going to sell his estate to LandDevel Inc.'

'Sacrifice his nature reserve? Not likely. And it's not as though he needs the money. Why would he want to do that?'

'Nobody knows. *Duh*. That's the news peg.'

Matthew considers this. 'There's more to this than meets the eye. Anti-establishment pro-conservationist rich misanthrope willing to sell to rapacious land developers? It doesn't add up.'

He is beginning to sound like a bad detective novel. '*I* don't know,' I say. 'That's why I have to talk to him.'

'Well, good luck.'

'What do you mean, "Good luck"?'

'I mean, something tells me he isn't going to take kindly to you marching up to his front door.'

'Well, that's why *I'm* the investigative journalist and you're the lame kid brother. I intend to track him down.' What am I saying? I have no intention of approaching this man. 'Just look up LandDevel for me and that'll be it.'

Matthew sighs, turns back to his computer. 'You know, I shouldn't be making this so easy for you.'

'Relax. You'll get your cut.'

'Ellen, I don't need a cut. I make more money than Dad.'

More pictures appear on the screen. A house. Or rather, a sort of two-storey garden shed. There's a sad little driveway to one side and a single brave tree. 'That's a typical LandDevel Starter Home.'

'Looks like you could practically put it together yourself.'

'You could. It's not the house that draws the crowds, it's the location. People want to be able to say "I live in Philmont". Reap all the benefits of having "a good address". Status. Prestige.

The final stage of the American Dream. And Grosworthy knows it.'

'You'd think he'd despise people that shallow.'

'I guess he hates his neighbours more. He's the kind of guy who *enjoys* getting even. Retaliation is his *raison d'être*. He puts out a newsletter, *Revenge Weekly*. Ten thousand subscribers. And growing.'

The screen goes blank. Matthew taps a few more keys. Bangs his mouse around a bit. 'That's funny. Something seems to have happened to the visuals.' He scrolls up a bit. Images appear to be dissolving. He frowns. 'Hope this isn't some sort of virus.' He experiments. 'Nope. Other sites seem to be okay.' Leans back in his chair, baffled. 'Huh.'

'I never thought I'd live to see the great Matthew Kaplan stumped.'

'Look, I think you're on to something hot, Ellen. There's clearly some kind of cover-up going on. I'd get moving on this, and fast.'

The private-eye patois is starting to get on my nerves. Especially as Matthew is beginning to invest it with a certain irony which I think is directed at me. 'So what do you suggest I do?'

'*I* don't know, Ellen. You're the . . .' He pauses. Makes as if to burp. '*"Investigative journalist".*'

'You have the superior intellect, Matthew – I acknowledge that. So help me out here.'

'Well, you could try the public library. Look up LandDevel in *The Readers' Guide to Periodical Literature*. Who knows – you might even run into Grosworthy. Keep an eye out for an old guy in a bad suit. You'll have to be really observant, though. He'll blend in with the rest of the impoverished individuals who go there to seek shelter and warmth.'

'Impoverishment? In Philmont? There isn't any.'

'You don't know your own home town, Ellen. There's plenty of impoverishment right under your nose. Spiritual. Emotional. Financial. Aesthetic. Try visiting the LandDevel project by Willow Avenue sometime. It's so impoverished, tumbleweeds roll across the lawns.'

'Speaking of impoverishment, could you loan me some money?'

He pulls out a few bills. Hands them to me. 'Keep it.'

'Thanks,' I say. Realize I'm quite touched by this gesture. 'Have Mom and Dad said anything about me, by the way?'

'Uh huh.'

'You going to tell me?'

'Nope.'

Fair enough. I'm not that curious. Time enough for all that. I turn to go. Turn back. 'Matthew? What exactly is a "Zeus-a-thon"?'

He shrugs. 'Beats me. I read about it in this magazine, *Naked Greek Gods.* Go figure.'

I manage to get some gear together. Notebook, for my second-rate shorthand. Pen – the only one I can find, one of those plastic ballpoints that runs out of ink when you need it the most. My camera? Sitting in a pawnshop in East Germany. I rummage around for my old tape recorder but it seems to have gone astray. I'll look for it later. Better to get moving.

The Readers' Guide to Periodical Literature is a helpful but very heavy series of volumes that never fails to irritate me – the small print, the whispery paper. The volume I need is being used at the moment by an obtuse-looking boy of about seventeen with bewildered eyes and quivering cheeks who might well require several hours just to achieve one small task. I settle myself in a carrel to wait. Take my shoes off. Amuse myself by tearing up the bits of scrap paper they leave lying around for people who forget to bring notebooks. Chew a spitball and shoot it into the 'L's. Neatly write a small obscenity on the desk in Gothic letter-ing. I try tapping on the side of the carrel, hoping to annoy the person sitting next to me, but she doesn't seem to mind. In fact, she starts tapping back, using a sophisticated jazz rhythm.

I stick my neck out to see how Chubby Cheeks is getting on. He is nowhere in sight. A small monkey has taken his place and is calmly tearing a page out of *The Readers' Guide.* Horrified, I stare. Am I seeing things? The creature peeks brightly around and is gone. I examine my fellow patrons. Surely I was not the only witness?

I wasn't. The monkey has made a profound impact on old Chubby Cheeks, who has resurfaced and is tearing out multiple sheets and stuffing them in his pockets – probably the most exciting thing he's ever done in his life. I run to the volume, push him out of the way, check the page the monkey's taken and, lo and behold, it is the very one I need. Someone is trying to prevent my enquiries but my lust for truth has kicked in. This setback has only served to raise my journalistic hackles. I suddenly feel invincible. Nothing and no one is going to get in my way.

Could there be a version on disk? The place is littered with computers. The librarians are standing around, all blasé and cyberpunk. They look the same as ever – woolly jackets, stiff hair – but they've got more attitude than they used to and I'm not sure this is a good thing. I go up to the counter. Librarians scare me, generally – that patronizing, slightly irritated quality of theirs. I always have trouble approaching them. One of them is speaking to a colleague.

'Hung,' she says, 'like my Aunt Mary's washing.'

'You're kidding.'

'You would not believe.'

I clear my throat. 'Excuse me –'

'One moment,' she says to me coolly. Turns back to her associate. 'I thought I was hallucinating.'

'I need to use the computer,' I announce loudly. *The Readers' Guide to Periodical Literature.*'

She points – one long red fingernail, an authoritative cuff. 'Over there.'

The computer, unfortunately, seems to be malfunctioning. Every attempt to bring up the necessary reference results in a blank screen. After entering 'LandDevel' about twelve times I am ready to abandon ship. I pause. Moodily contemplate failure.

'I suck,' I whisper to myself.

A message appears: 'Better luck next time, Ellen.'

I stare at the monitor for a moment. Is this really happening?

I type in, 'LandDevel is a corrupt organization and I'm going to bring it down.'

It throws up, 'You and whose army?'

This is too much. I punch in angrily: 'I'm going to find you.'

Is it my imagination or do I hear a tinkle of electronic laughter? The word 'Error' starts flashing and the machine starts making

105

beeping noises. The librarian looks over angrily. *'What's going on there?'*

'I don't know,' I say helplessly. The computer seems to be disintegrating. The letters are falling to the bottom of the screen. A chunk of plastic drops off the side. A small trace of smoke is rising from the circuitry at the back. The woman marches over.

'Now look what you've done,' she snaps. Calls back over her shoulder: 'Can you believe this?' To me: 'You're wasting tax-payers' dollars.'

'I . . . I'm sorry,' I stammer.

She presses her lips together and shakes her head. Clicks her tongue. 'Like I don't have better things to do.'

Time to make a clean getaway. Better for all concerned. I back away towards the check-out desk, where a whole group of librarians have gathered.

'Rumour has it that he's very good in bed,' one of them says.

The others concur:

'He would be.'

'I love rich men.'

'Me, too. And I love a man with a mind.'

'He's very well-endowed, apparently.'

'Short men often are.'

'My husband's short and bald and he's huge. But not like this guy.'

'It would be interesting to do a study. Size of genitals relative to height. But he's not *that* short, is he? Probably just a touch of osteoporosis.'

They all seem to be taking a genuine clinical interest in the subject. A couple of them are comparing written notes. I can't stand it any longer. 'Who are you talking about?' I ask the one nearest to me, an African American dressed like Lauren Bacall.

As though I'm very stupid, she replies, 'Why, Eamon Groswor-thy, of course. Comes in here almost every week.'

Frantically, I scan the area. Survey various armchairs.

'He's gone,' she says with satisfaction. 'You missed him.'

I run out the door, but too late. If he was ever there, like the monkey, he's vanished. I'm frustrated, exhausted, and I know more than I'll ever need to know about short, bald men. Search for truth or no, I want to go home.

106

On the way out, I spot a flyer on the bulletin board:

'LandDevel Threat. Save Our Community. Special Emergency Meeting for Residents of North Philmont.' It's tomorrow night. What incredible luck. I take note of the location and time.

So, I've made progress after all. Today I'm only a partial failure. I think I can live with that.

'Lunchtime,' April trills as I walk though the door. She is standing in front of me wearing a flowered apron and holding a frying pan. 'I was hoping you might be back in time. I'm making flapjacks.'

'For lunch?'

'Sure. Sometimes we had them three times a day back home. Mom would buy a big bag of buckwheat and we'd cook it up. For a treat, we'd have bacon. Except I always hated eating strips of little fried piggies.'

Actually, it smells kind of good. I'm really hungry. I'd made up my mind to accept no favours from her but surely a pancake or two wouldn't hurt. I put my notebook down, drag a hand through my hair. Smiling, she hands me a cup of coffee.

'Nice and strong,' she says, 'just the way you like it.'

I am dumbfounded. No wonder James likes her so much. She has the gift of anticipating one's every need. It is deceptive, of course – she is totally self-serving. 'Ulterior Motive' is her middle name. It's good Java, though, I have to admit. I wonder if she can operate a cappuccino machine.

'So how was your day?' she asks. I am half-tempted to confide in her, if for no other reason than the fact that she is there. That's what she has a talent for – *being* there. Perhaps that's why James likes her so much. It's not *much* of a gift. But then again, it's more than I have, and maybe it's more important to James than anyone ever realized. Looking back, Dad was always busy, my mother – with the best of intentions, of course – left him to his own devices, Matthew was living in Virtual World and I . . . well, *I'd* been there for him. Hadn't I?

April's set a place at the kitchen table for me, with a little vase of wildflowers in the centre. I touch the plate. It's warm. There's my napkin ring, and it looks as though the linen has been washed and ironed. I guess this is more like what I'd imagined, or what I would have imagined had I been able to get my head around

107

the notion of a person like April showing up. She's very acceptable in her capacity as domestic. It might even be pleasant to have her around for another week or so.

She sits across from me as I eat. 'You still haven't told me how your day was,' she says teasingly.

'Shitty,' I say. She doesn't flinch, just gazes steadily. And, to my very great surprise, I find myself talking.

I don't tell her everything. I edit out the particulars. After all, knowledge is power. But I tell her about LandDevel and the Residents' Association. My quest for facts and my lack of success. Chin in hand, she takes everything in. The quality of her listening is extraordinary. As I talk, she is completely present, totally absorbed in what I am saying. When I am finished, she frowns. Looks thoughtful, then sly. 'I have an idea. Let's go there.'

'Where?'

'LandDevel. The Willow Avenue development.'

'You're joking.'

'Well, why not? You can get your facts, and I can look at some houses. I understand they have a "Show Home".' She is taking off her apron. Pinning up her hair. 'I saw one of their ads in the paper. I think it might be just within our budget.'

'You don't mean to tell me you'd actually consider *buying* one of those things.'

'Sure I would. They have something called a "Starter Home". The idea is you don't stay there for long, just a couple years, while you save up for something better. Me and Jimmy don't want to move far away.'

'Why don't you stay here?' I don't want her to move across town. I want her to go back where she came from. And in order to accomplish this, I need to retain her within my jurisdiction for the time being.

She looks away. 'Just trust me.'

I wouldn't trust her as far as I could hurl a sofa. 'Look, April, I have reason to believe that LandDevel are on to me. Don't ask me how, but they are. If I go, they'll get wind of it and then it's curtains for me.' That damned jargon. It's like a disease.

'Then go in disguise.'

'Don't be ridiculous.'

108

'No, think about it. We'll dress you up as a boy. You can go as my husband.'

'Are you nuts?'

'But it's a great idea. Then you'll be incognito and *I'll* have a husband and everyone knows they take you more seriously if you're married.'

'Why not get James to go with you?'

'I sort of want to . . . take him by surprise.' She looks uncomfortable. 'I don't think he likes LandDevel-style houses. But if I can *persuade* him . . .'

'I see.'

This is good, actually. When James – who dreams of an Elizabethan cottage in the English countryside – learns that April wants to live in a LandDevel Starter Home, he might stop short in his tracks. 'All right,' I say magnanimously. 'You win.'

She looks so happy that I almost feel bad. 'Wait,' she says. 'I know what would make it perfect. The finishing touch.' She runs out, rushes back in again with Puddles under her arm. Sees my expression. Stops short. 'It'll make it more authentic,' she adds, as though stating a reasonable case.

Puddles eyes me balefully. 'Fine,' I sigh. 'Bring her along.'

Puddles relaxes. Luxuriates in the withdrawal of rejection. April thrusts her at me: 'The guy always carries the dog.'

'She won't wee on my arm, will she?'

'Only if you tell her you're a tree.' April examines me critically. 'You know, Ellen, we could almost give you sideburns.'

'Great idea,' I say. Bitch. 'Let's go.'

There it stands, in all its glory. The Starter Home Show Home.

'Oh,' breathes April. 'I love it. It's so peaceful. Jimmy and I could be happy here. Oh, look, Ellen – sorry, Edgar – it has such character.'

She must be joking. A shy house that knows it's flimsy, it begs to be forgiven. Small garage, gravel walk. A window with one striped awning like a single lowered eyelid. I have to admit, there's a kind of order, a simplicity and cleanliness about the place. I can almost see the appeal. A dwelling like that has no history and thus no painful memories that might penetrate the lives of its early occupants. The estate itself, however, is stark.

Though relatively small, it gives the impression of a vast, barren plain. Matthew was right about the tumbleweeds – they are very much there in spirit. The horizon is low and the ground is hard. It's dotted with houses like pimples of varying sizes. They've managed to poke a tree into the soil here and there but most of them seem to be trying to claw their way out again. It feels several degrees colder than Philmont proper. Worst of all, a sinister cloud hangs over the place, a sort of haze that smells like gasoline. 'Chumley Mansions' reads the sign out front (one of those pseudo-English names – very embarrassing). 'A LandDevel Company – For Phamily, For Philmont, Phorever.'

April surveys the area, tries to look cheerful. 'I guess they haven't finished landscaping, huh.'

'No. They've been working on containing the toxic gases.'

April dismisses my concern with a wave of her hand. She seems eager, almost anxious, to find a home of her own. But why?

I can't believe that Grosworthy would allow this to happen to his land. Not if he loves it the way he's supposed to. Someday, every inch of open space will have been bought up – all the old mansions, the woods, the farms – and then, will Philmont still be Philmont?

Not that I care.

Puddles is squirming. I'm worried about getting dog hairs all over my suit. It's interesting, the things men have to contend with. I like this suit, actually. It's one of James's, a sort of strange orange-and-green checkered wool number he picked up in London in a fit of sartorial daring. It's a bit big for me but stylish. I'd thought about stuffing a sock down my underwear for added authenticity but decided against it.

'You make a great guy, Ellen,' says April.

'Thanks. Shall we go inside?'

I am hoping there will be someone to interview there. A salesperson whose brains I can pick. Unfortunately, there is a deserted look about the place, a sense that the appointed representative has already defected. I wish I could ditch April – she is a bit of a liability, if only because she keeps hanging on to my arm and calling me 'honey'.

Inside, the house is eerie – almost as though it's been abandoned before ever being bought. There is carpeting on the floor, in a shade I can only describe as the infamous 'Burnt Sienna'. There are three tiny rooms downstairs – living room, dining room and kitchen – and two upstairs.

'For couples with brats,' I remark. April says nothing.

A sort of office has been set up in what would be the dining room. In one corner sits a desk, a telephone, a lamp. I pick up the phone. The line is dead. I can't help but feel as though we're being watched.

'Well, what do you think, Ellen?' April asks.

'It's stunning,' I say.

'It could be, couldn't it?' she says. 'Or cosy, anyway.'

Puddles seems to like it. She is running around, staking out her territory. Growling, attacking imaginary adversaries. Or maybe not so imaginary – the place reminds me of one of those stories you see on TV about poltergeists who terrorize the inhabitants of modern split-level homes.

I lean against a wall, look out the window. April joins me. The atmosphere is so grey. A feeling of desolation comes over me. I think of April's painted blue sky. It seems representative of the way she has to live – improvising, making do, pretending things are better than they are. I enter her universe for a moment, try to imagine a life of constant striving.

'How did you get into selling HerbElixir?' I ask curiously.

'Got recommended by a friend,' said April. 'She knew I needed a job. I'm not qualified for much, but I work hard and I'm very good with people. Went out to New Mexico where they needed reps. Or "consultants".' She giggles. 'The whole thing came as a bit of a shock, to tell you the truth. They'd led me to believe that it was something kind of . . .'

'Special.'

She giggles again – embarrassed, this time. 'Yeah. Promised me a company car and everything. I'd counted on that. Drove my own out there and it almost fell apart. Turned out you didn't get the car until you'd sold a certain amount of Elixir. *A lot*. Had to find my own place to live, too. I had about twenty dollars left by the time I arrived.'

'Twenty dollars?'

'Well, I only started out with sixty. I wouldn't have even had that if my parents hadn't helped me out.'

'They let you leave home with only sixty dollars?'

'You don't understand, Ellen. It was more than they could afford. Fact is, I almost left without it. I was pulling out of the driveway and they came running after me.'

How much had my parents given me over the years? Thousands, easily. And we're talking pocket money. 'So where did you sleep?'

'In my car.'

This could be some kind of sob story, of course, designed to invite sympathy. But her recounting is matter-of-fact, as though it hadn't been any big deal.

'Didn't you want to go to college?' I ask.

'Sure. Kept trying to save up. But my parents needed help. My dad got sick and my mom kept losing her job.'

'What do you think you would have studied?'

April doesn't answer immediately. Then she drops her head to one side with a half-joking smile and says, tentatively, 'Journalism?'

It's my turn to be silent. This is too much. She actually believes she could handle a career in the media? My original assessment of her as 'presumptuous' had been correct. I think she detects my utter disgust because she blushes and moves quickly away.

But this discovery continues to niggle at me. I can't get it out of my head. Journalist. How preposterous. Surely she knows she would be unsuited to the job. The level of intelligence and commitment required are . . . not to mention the education . . .

I think back to the scene in the kitchen. How I talked. And how she listened.

How she listened.

It hits me with the force of a cannon. Tyler Spee's words: 'Ellen, you couldn't pry open an oyster that's dying to spit its pearl out. Nobody wants to open up to you. People find you really off-putting, do you know that? Don't you know that personality is part of the job?'

One like April's, he meant. She doesn't even have to try.

I shake myself. Why am I dwelling on this? What I need to do is carry on with getting what I came for. I go over to the desk, start opening drawers. April has wandered off into another room. Absorbed in my search, I fail to notice Puddles sniffing around and pulling back a corner of the Burnt Sienna carpet. By the time I look up, she's dragged something out and seems very excited.

At first I think it must be a dead animal, but it's an envelope, large and brown. Inside is a list of names and some photographs. Full colour. I examine them. And can hardly believe what I've found.

'Hey, April.' In my elation, I momentarily forget my animosity. When she appears, I note with surprise that she's been crying.

'Have you discovered something?' she asks eagerly. Trying to pretend her eyes aren't red.

Why is she so upset? I am suddenly desperate for something to offer her – not because I like her, of course, simply because demonstrations of strong feeling unsettle me. But I have no present, no necklace, no glow-in-the-dark Christ. I panic, thrust the packet at her. 'Get a load of these.'

Slowly, cautiously, as though she's not quite sure what to expect, she takes them, looks them over. Starts to laugh. 'Oh, Ellen. These are great.'

And they are. Candid snapshots of a group of friends. Very candid. The occasion is clearly a Thanksgiving Day celebration, complete with Pilgrims and a turkey. Except that the pilgrims are wearing nothing but hats and the turkey is a trussed naked man who looks like he's having the time of his life. Lavish piles of food adorn a long wooden table. It's clearly taking place in a somebody's substantial old home.

'Are you familiar with the notion of wife-swapping, April?'

'I've heard of it.'

There are more. One of an Indian pinning down a Pilgrim with a blunderbuss – nice reversal of history there. Another of a cheerful-looking woman in full period costume, a man kneeling beneath her skirt. Two men in grinning tug-of-war mode, each pulling an arm of a lady in a feather headdress, ash-blonde hair above and below. I have to admit, she's gone to a lot of trouble. She deserves a certain amount of respect.

'Thanksgiving is a very special day, isn't it,' I say.

'It certainly is.'

The men are all good-looking in that smug I-work-at-J.P. Morgan kind of way. The women are attractive and trim, with the light all-over tan that denotes a discreet holiday to a private beach. I'd put them all at about forty-five, the age at which they say you start to seek a little extra excitement.

'But who are they?' April asks.

'Well, presumably, the people on this piece of paper. Which appears to be . . .' I examine it. '. . . the membership list of the North Philmont Residents' Association!'

We grab hands and start jumping around the room. I almost forget that I don't like her. It's hard not to respond when someone's happy for you. Even if you know she's . . .

For a moment, I cannot think of one bad thing about April.

I feel like someone's pushed me off a cliff while I wasn't looking. I grope around for my dislike, clutch it to my heart. Every fibre inside me is screaming 'give in' but I can't bring myself to do so. She's nudged me out of my own family and I'm supposed to admit defeat? And the journalism thing. Jesus, how did she expect me to react? What did she think I was going to do? Offer to *help* her?

Soon I'll have nothing left to call my own. She'll have taken everything. If I am to be squeezed out, all right. But I'm not going down without a fight.

'But what could the photographs mean?' April asks. We're driving home. Or rather, I'm driving and she's trying to keep a wiggling Puddles from flying out the window.

'Well, presumably LandDevel were planning to blackmail local residents into letting them go ahead with their plans.'

'Could the people really stop them?'

'Probably not. But they could delay things by making a stink, buy enough time to sell their houses. Zoning disputes can drag on for years, and I suspect LandDevel are in a hurry. The term "fly-by-night" comes to mind.'

'But who does the land belong to?'

'A guy named Grosworthy. Eamon Grosworthy.'

At the mention of his name, she starts flapping her arms around. Puddles tumbles into the back seat. 'But I *know* him.'

'Everyone knows him.' I consider the librarians. 'Demented rich men get a reputation really quickly.'

'But I –'

114

I cut her short. Hurt her feelings for the second time that day. 'Look. I know all I need to know about Grosworthy. I've already done my research.'

'I was just thinking it might be a good idea to interview him.'

I can't believe she is actually trying to tell me how to do my job. Yet something in my brain prickles unpleasantly – the feeling that she is right.

'Do you think?' I say.

'Sure. You know what they say – don't anticipate an angle. Go into a story with an open mind. Get all the information you can and *then* draw your conclusions.'

Oh, is that what they say? Christ. She's as bad as Tyler Spee.

'I don't think so,' I say. 'I personally consider this conclusive proof that he's planning to sell.'

'I guess you're right.' She looks crestfallen, then brightens up. 'Hey, Ellen, if you need any help –'

'I won't.' I know I'm being short with her. But enough is enough – she's begging for scraps. And I don't like the implication that I don't know what I'm doing. She opens her mouth to speak again, hesitates, shuts it. Seems disappointed rather than hurt. I take the opportunity to change the subject. 'So, are you still thinking of buying a LandDevel Home?'

She turns her head to the window. Rests it against the glass. 'I guess not,' she says. And falls silent.

April asks to be dropped off at the local Christian book store. I head home, Puddles riding shotgun, intending to relax and enjoy a little peace. But the moment I set foot inside the door, my hopes are shattered. Something is wrong. I hear shouting.

My parents seldom yell. In fact, they never yell. To them, extreme displays of emotion are anathema. But now my father is bellowing as though he's been bottling it up for years. This must, in some way, be April's doing. It couldn't have happened before. She's upset the applecart. The systems are breaking down. Everything is out of control.

He is standing in the middle of his office, looking up. In a ragged voice, with his own twisted version of a smile contorting his features, he roars:

'*Yahweh sucks.*'

Yahweh? Who the hell is Yahweh?

'Yahweh is a big fat bully. I hate you, Yahweh – do you hear me?'

I have ducked into the Morgue in order to monitor developments. He's really going all out. He's screaming at the top of his lungs, and it sounds as though he's throwing things around.

'Yahweh, Yahweh, Yahweh,' he chants, as though repetition of the word will strip it of all meaning. 'Come and get me, Big Fella. Hit me with your best shot. Just you and me, together. Let's see what you're *really* made of.'

'Harry, be quiet.' My mother's voice – calm and rational. 'Harry, calm down and listen to me.'

'Yah, Yah, Yah, Yah.'

'Harry, shut up.'

He subsides, panting. I stick my head out, just a little. Hunched over, hair damp, he resembles the guy in the anti-war films who goes berserk and ends up ploughing down multiple civilians with a machine gun. He is struggling with the window. Gets it open. Yanks out a drawer of his filing cabinet and starts throwing its contents at the sky: *'Have one on me, Big Guy.'* This is truly a man on the edge. He appears to be attempting to destroy the tangible parts of his universe, the physical components that constitute his life. Files. Papers. Photographs of us. One object is almost too heavy to lift. An iron football that used to belong to my mother's dad. He heaves it up; it ricochets off the wall.

'Harry, what on earth are you doing?'

'I hate You,' he yells, rotating his face to the sky. Turns to my mother. *'And I hate you.'*

She goes up to him and grips his arms. Speaks sharply. 'Get a hold of yourself, Harry. This is totally unnecessary.'

He shakes her off. She grabs him again: 'You've got to listen to me, Harry.' He ignores her, pushes her away. She hurls herself forward and tackles him; this time he cannot get rid of her. Ends up wearing her on his shoulders like some kind of prizefighter's mantle as he bucks and spins around in the middle of the room.

'I don't understand,' says my mother. 'You kissed me –'

'Get off my *back*.'

'Please say you don't hate me,' pleads my mother, gasping.

116

'I don't just hate you,' he roars. 'I hate *Him, too.*'

'But you're an atheist, Harry.'

'Not any more, baby.' He throws her off. Starts chucking things out the window again. 'From now on, *I'm* going to have someone to blame. Celestial accountability. Whoo-ee, I'm loving it, man, I'm loving it.'

My mother is near hysterical. *'Stop it, Harry, stop it. The children, Harry. Do it for the children.'*

'I *am* doing it for the children. This is their legacy. Let them have the full knowledge of it in all its glory. *They're all going to end up like me.'*

'You're doing this to hurt me, aren't you?' says my mother. 'You're doing this to punish me.'

My father continues, exultant: 'Let them know me for who I really am. A pathetic, miserable, craven, vile, contemptible, abominable, despicable –'

He stops, exhausted. For a moment, I think everything is going be all right. That reason will prevail.

He turns to her, says, 'It's over. I want a divorce.'

'All right,' my mother replies calmly.

'Well, that's that, then,' he says.

'Yes. That's that.'

I draw my head back in. I can't quite believe what I've just heard. Then I hear a blow struck. A yelp of pain from my dad.

'If you think I'm going to let you give up on your marriage, your self, your life, you're wrong,' my mother says. I hear another blow. 'I love you, you bastard.' Her voice is hoarse, as though she's been dragging herself through the desert for many years. 'You bastard. You bastard.' Continues to say this, choking and gasping, as though it is a mantra, something that will help and protect her. 'You bastard. You bastard. You bastard. You bastard.' I hear more evidence of violence. Chairs being thrown down. Bookcases toppling. What is going on in there? I hope they haven't killed each other. Then silence. I'm not too reassured. Good sign? Bad sign? Could go either way.

'I'm disgusting,' I hear my father whisper. 'I'm disgusting.'

'No, you're not,' my mother says.

I peek out again. See my father lifting his face. The dead

117

volcanoes of his eyes. 'Take a good look at me, Julia. Look hard. *What do you see?*

He crumples. Starts sobbing. I have never seen him cry. He folds himself into my mother's arms, ducks his head into her reassuring shoulder like a terrified extraterrestrial. She rocks him back and forth. I don't remember her ever cuddling me that way, but then I can't recall ever needing to be cuddled. Maybe this is what she's been looking for all these years. A soul to nourish. A life to save. Someone who can admit to needing to be held.

They crouch there for a while, hunched on the floor – my father no longer sardonic and hellbent on victory, my mother mutinous and dissatisfied no more. They look down into the pit into which their lives have collapsed, and hold each other tighter.

'If He took everything away,' my father whispers, 'I could love Him so much more.' My mother nods. He tries to pull away, as though undeserving of her grace. 'I wish He'd speak to me. I want it to be over.' He is shaking. She draws him back. Continues to hush him. Strokes his head.

What does he regret? Everything?

After a while he says, 'You know, I'd love to defend an innocent man.'

'I know.'

'If you have enough money, you get off. It's as simple as that.'

'So I gather.'

'Colleague asked me to help out with a new case yesterday,' he says. 'Defending a guy who beat up a twelve-year-old boy – or "kike" as the client put it. I found myself saying, "Sure, Hartman, just leave the brief on my desk." You know what the worst thing was? It wasn't the first time.'

They've papered over the cracks for years, but the structure has finally crumbled from within. Now there's no going back, which some would say was a good thing, but going forward is a different matter. Oh, April, we were fine until you came along. You should have left us alone. Now my parents have to learn to walk and talk and see and think and *feel* and they can't handle it. They're almost *fifty*, for goodness' sake. It wasn't fair to give them the option.

'What do we do now?' says my father.

'I don't know.'

118

More silence.

'What do you think is out there, Julia? Anything?' he asks, as though they are gazing at the stars.

'I've never thought so,' she says. 'But I'm prepared to change my mind.'

'Incidentally, have I ever told you that I love you?'

'Yes. Once.'

He looks surprised. 'I did?'

'You put a message in a fortune cookie. I caught you trying to shove it in with the tip of a kebab skewer.'

'Afraid to say it.'

'So it would seem.'

'Was that all it said?'

'No. It also said, "Marry me".'

'I didn't *ask* you? In person? My God, I was such a *wuss*.'

'I still have it,' she says, smiling.

'No.'

'I do. In my jewellery box. In that locket you gave me for Christmas one year.'

'You mean, the year I didn't get you a toaster?' he says.

'Or an electric can opener or a microwave? Yes.'

'Boy.' He looks pretty impressed with himself.

As for me, I'm beginning to lose the sensation in my legs. I try to shift around a bit, but every time I move, the floor creaks. I'm tired and I have to go to the bathroom. I wonder how long they're going to be.

'You used to be so romantic, Harry.' My mother is in full reminiscence mode. 'Remember that trip to my parents' summer home? Where you rowed me around the little lake?'

'And your father stood on the shore, threatening to drown me? Sure, I remember.'

'They didn't want me to marry a Jew.'

'Mine didn't want me to marry a *shiksa*.' He laughs, teeth bared, a real mouth-of-hell roar. Affects a Hispanic accent. *Too bad, honey.*'

'They got used to the idea eventually,' says my mother.

'Yeah. Too bad it meant disowning us,' says Dad. 'It would have been nice for the kids to get to know their grandparents.'

'There was my mother.'

'Yes. There was your mother.'

Silence again. Then they both start to giggle.

'Do you remember when we met?' says my father.

'Yes. It was at Gerry's party.'

'That guy with the hairy chest was after you.'

'No, that was you,' she says.

'It was a costume party. He'd told everyone to come dressed as an aspect of democracy.'

'He was such a pretentious bastard.'

'You came as the Statue of Liberty,' he says.

'And you came as yourself.'

'Well, I was studying law, wasn't I? What could be more appropriate?'

At this point I am twisting around, trying to get some feeling back in my legs. I hope they don't start to talk about the first time they *did it* or anything. Because that really would be disgusting.

'Undressing the Statue of Liberty was incredibly erotic.'

Oh, no.

'You were very adept,' my mother says, 'at taking my clothes off.'

'Well, it was basically a toga and a spiky hat, wasn't it?'

Great. This marvellous transformation of their relationship is taking place and I'm stuck in the Morgue. I take one step forward and almost topple over. I try squatting down. Pretty soon I've cut off the blood flow to my feet.

'Liberty. Belle.' My father is sounding all mushy. My mother responds with some funny little murmuring noises. 'I haven't called you that for years, have I? My Belle.'

So that was it. And all the while I'd thought he was just getting her name wrong.

'You know,' he says, 'when I first learned that James was giving up on his PhD, I was really angry. Even when he told me he'd been unhappy. I said to myself, what right does he have to be happy? *I'm* not happy. Is anybody happy? But then I got to thinking, Buddhists are happy and . . . well, I couldn't think of anybody else.'

'Buddhists aren't happy, dear. They try to free themselves from desire in an attempt to achieve –'

120

'Nirvana. Yes, I know, Belle, but let me tell you, from where I'm standing, Nirvana looks pretty damned blissful to me. I got to thinking that happiness, maybe, is normal and the *abnormal* state is misery. And that my chance was gone. It was too late for me. I'd made my choices and I'd missed out on something wonderful. And all for nothing.'

'What a waste,' says my mother dreamily. 'I wish you'd told me.'

'So do I. There are so many things I wish I'd told you. But I hardly knew them myself. I don't even know who I am.'

'Is that why you're wearing the yarmulke?'

'Yeah. I thought . . . this is going to sound insane. I thought it would help me discover my true identity. Help me discover something more, well, *spiritual*. Hell, all I've ever done is work, Belle, like my father before me. I saw that as my destiny. But that isn't what life is all about, is it? It's about love . . . and fun and *beauty* and . . . I don't know. But good things. I'm sure God didn't intend it to be soul-destroying – if there *is* a god, and I'm beginning to think there is. Look at this.' Clumsily, urgently, tears a book out of his pocket. Shows it to my mother.

'The *Kabbalah*,' she notes.

'Kind of a Jewish Buddhism. It's great. Listen to this: "Now you, my child, strive to see supernal light, for I have brought you into a vast ocean. Be careful! Keep your soul from gazing and your mind from conceiving, lest you drown. Strive to see, yet escape drowning. Your soul will see the divine light – actually cleave to it – while dwelling in her palace." I've no idea what it means but isn't it beautiful, Belle? Isn't that what life is all about?'

'Quit your job,' says my mother. 'Quit. Your. Job.'

'But you –'

'I want us to cut our losses. We're being offered a second chance. Let's take it.'

'I can't –'

'Do it. Get the hell out of that place. You never have to go back.'

'My boss –'

'Tell him to go stuff himself.'

My father gazes at her in wonder as though witnessing the

121

rebirth of a star. 'This is what I'm going to live for from now on,' he says. 'Life, the pursuit of happiness and the Liberty Belle.'

She blushes. Good God. Like April. 'Oh, Harry.'

'I've neglected you,' he says. 'I'm going to start paying you a lot of attention. Do you think you can get used to that?'

'Oh, I think so.'

And what about me? I can't believe this. Do they have any idea how they've neglected me?

'Will you talk to me in future about what you want?' he asks.

'Yes. But I want a lot, Harry. Impossible things.'

'Nothing is impossible,' he says. Starts pacing around. 'Belle, I feel like I could move mountains right now. I could conquer the world.'

'Do you think you could you get Matthew to come upstairs now and then?'

He roars with laughter again. 'Are you kidding? With pleasure. I'm sick of that supercilious little brat monopolizing the basement. I'm going to make him come out and do some yardwork. What else do you want?'

'I want to go back to college and finish my degree.'

'You got it. I'll write you a cheque. Anything else?'

'I want Ellen to sit down and talk to me.'

He stops short. 'Now *that's* a tall order.'

Oh, I get it. Any lack of communication is *my* fault. This is all down to me.

'Why do you think she came home?' says my mother. 'Just to get money?'

'Of course not.' He doesn't sound as though even he believes this. 'Well, it was partly to get money. But there were other reasons. I'm not altogether sure what they are . . .'

They are being very hard on me, while I have been incredibly tolerant. Damn that April. The Stepford Daughter. I suppose they'd prefer someone big and blue-collar and 'born again' . . .

'It's just that she doesn't seem to care about anyone but herself,' he says. 'I hate to say this, Belle, but she might be a lost cause. That article I tried to get her to write? It's not going to happen.'

'I don't understand,' my mother says. 'I tried to make the right decisions, tried to raise her well . . .'

'Maybe we raised her *too* well – never criticized her, never gave her anything but positive reinforcement.'

'I just wanted her to be able to achieve her dreams. The problem is, she doesn't seem to have any.'

'The problem is, she's lazy, spoiled and megalomaniacal.'

'Sometimes,' says my mother, 'I get the feeling she doesn't like me.'

'I get the impression,' my father remarks, 'that Ellen doesn't like anybody.'

'She likes James.'

'Yes, she likes James.' His tone is ambiguous.

'They were awfully close as children,' says my mother. 'She kept saying she wanted to marry him.'

'Yes. She used to shanghai him into those mock-wedding ceremonies. Used to worry me, I have to admit.'

'It's nice that they got along.'

'Yes, but it's also nice that he *finally* has a girlfriend.'

'There is nothing wrong with waiting.'

'Belle, it's not *normal* to be celibate. Not for a healthy young man with no visible hang-ups. I'm glad he finally has a better half. Speaking of which, what do you think of April?'

'Well, I think she's harmless enough.' Harmless? That's rich. My mother wrinkles her brow, as though considering all the data she has gathered over the past few weeks. 'As long as they don't get married and start a family too quickly . . .'

'I hope they're being careful,' says my dad.

'Oh, I'm sure they are.'

'Are you? We weren't. Careful, that is.'

There is nothing she can say to this. Except, 'It was a nice wedding.'

'Very nice. A bit rushed, but nice.'

They meditate on this for a few moments.

'Well, time to break up the party,' says my dad.

'I suppose so,' says my mother, regretfully.

They rise. For a moment, I think they're going to shake hands, as though they've concluded negotiations. But my dad gives her a kiss, a bit like the one that took place in the kitchen. Yuck. I take the opportunity to slip out.

*   *   *

123

In my bedroom, I examine the sheet of paper on which I've started my article. Someone has written 'could do better' in the margin in green ink.

I look to my window and think I see the shadow of a monkey.

No, it had to be James. His idea of a practical joke. Either that or April, trying to undermine my confidence. I lift it off the typewriter and examine it. Yes, this is just the sort of thing James would have pulled on me when I was a kid. Isn't it?

I wad it up and throw it away, then pick it out of the trash and smooth it out again. Green ink. Very peculiar. James refuses to use anything but black or blue.

Well, it's clear that the family gap into which I might have wedged myself is beginning to close. If I'm going to act, I have to move fast. I can't stave off a sense of panic, a feeling that I'm being left behind. I've been judged without benefit of trial by jury. If only I'd been allowed to state my case. Well, I'll show them. Then they'll be sorry. Bet they'll miss me when I'm gone.

7

I don't want to go see him – Grosworthy, that is – but I can't rid myself of the niggling feeling that *April* would. It would be the wrong decision entirely, of course. Totally unnecessary legwork. But still . . .

I can't help but think that, were April in my position, she would be succeeding where I am failing. There is an unnerving intelligence about her, a sort of instinctive ability to get results. It's not as though she has any kind of an intellect, of course, it's just that . . . well, she knows how to make things happen, which seems to be more than I am able to do.

I can't give in to this. I've got to fight it, be proactive – prove to her and to everyone else that I am as capable of succeeding as anybody. I know I can do it, but sometimes I feel as though I'm in one of those horror films where one character is slowly superseded by another. April will end up taking my place, will claim to be the 'real' Ellen Kaplan. She may even start to look like me. I should just accept that I'm doomed.

The photographs were a plus, but what I told April is wrong. They do not constitute conclusive proof. But the truth may be only a phone call away. Why don't I call LandDevel? The incident in the library was no doubt a fluke, a high-tech prank planted by a junior jokester like Matthew. I call Information. No such number, apparently. 'LandDevel?' says the operator, as though I were asking for the telephone number of the moon.

Then I have an idea. I run to the living room and leaf through the *Organ* until I find an ad for LandDevel. It shows a house much like the one we looked at, but they've airbrushed it and added a phoney landscape filled with flowers and trees. It lists a toll-free hotline.

I pick up the phone, decide to pose as a would-be buyer. Dial. Wait.

'Welcome to the world of LandDevel Homes.'

It's a recording. I should have figured. Really corny voice. I sigh. Might as well hear the pitch. If I stay on the line, maybe I'll get to talk to a real person, and then I can make my enquiries.

'We'd like you to come on down and check out a Show Home in our latest planned community, Chumley Mansions, located in prestigious Philmont. We're very excited about this development and we know you will be, too.'

This is really tedious. 'Look, chumps,' I say. 'I know you're listening. I want to talk to you.' Yes, it's ridiculous, but I'm getting impatient. And I'm trying not to throttle the phone.

'Our business is *your future*.'

'What's wrong?' I taunt. 'Are you afraid of me?'

'Ten thousand satisfied customers can't be wrong.'

'So,' I say, 'how *do* you feel about destroying a conservation area?' They can't hear me, but I'm practising – it would be a good question to pose. 'Don't ask the obvious,' Tyler Spee used to say. Generally followed by, 'You idiot.'

'. . . ten thousand marital aids, raw-action movies, and *erotic magazines*. Everything the discerning shopper desires. So, come on down to the Sex Supermarket, New Jersey's finest Adult Entertainment Outlet, located on Route 301 across from the Blossom Hill Mall . . .'

The *Sex Supermarket*? For goodness' sake. I hold the phone a foot away from my face and look into the earpiece as though I might be able to see the speaker. Suddenly, I am disconnected. I immediately call back, and get someone speaking Punjabi.

Could this be more than just a bad case of crossed wires? I recall the words of Tyler Spee: 'If you can't get the interview, *that's the story*. That person has something to hide.'

'Okay,' I mutter. 'You want to do this the hard way? Fine by me.'

I'm going to go for it. Head for the horse's mouth.

*   *   *

126

The Grosworthy Estate gives the impression of being a place only the blessed can enter. How else could you account for so much natural beauty? It's Eden, the real thing, as opposed to April's manufactured one, but like Heaven (and Harvard) you have to have certain qualifications to get in, and I suspect only the pure in heart need apply.

Over the high stone walls, I catch a glimpse of trees. To my surprise, the iron gates open as I approach, as though I've uttered a magic password.

I thought I knew what to expect, but nothing had prepared me for this. The grass is lush and green without that Astroturf look that comes of dousing it with weed-killing chemicals. The air is fresh and perfumed with the scent of wildflowers. The trees look as though they've been there for centuries. Will LandDevel chop them down, I wonder, or build around them? They'll have to axe a good few to make space for the houses and give it that LandDevel 'look'.

Shortly thereafter, however, the landscape begins to change, as though I've suddenly stepped through the looking glass. It's a different place altogether. I find myself driving through acres of smoking, ashen land, like the aftermath of trench warfare. I pass rows and rows of bizarre topiary, bushes trimmed into the shape of tanks and cannons. A skeleton is positioned behind one of them, as though getting ready to fire. An animal runs into my path, what looks like a small fox; it stands still for a moment, as though evaluating me, then calmly moves on. My first inclination is to turn around and go home, as everything I've been told is turning out to be disconcertingly true. But then I hear April's voice: '. . . it might be a good idea to interview him.' And I decide to follow through.

The house itself is pretty impressive – you can imagine George Washington expressing an interest in it from a real estate point of view. Grosworthy obviously suffers from some kind of warped patriotism. American flags, stained and tattered, hang from every window, and cracked busts of every president of the United States adorn pedestals on the lawn, where they are clearly used for target practice. A smallish man in too-large khaki shorts, a tank top, a pith helmet and black shoes and socks is balancing an apple on top of the head of Harry S. Truman. He backs up and raises a gun. Takes careful aim.

127

'Excuse me,' I shout. 'Excuse me? Ellen Kaplan of *The Phil-mont Organ* here. Hate to disturb you, but I wonder if I could ask you a couple of questions.'

The figure turns and looks straight at me. Swings the gun around and fires.

It's a surprisingly narrow driveway. I've never reversed so fast in my life. My greatest immediate fear is that the gates will be shut and locked, but to my great relief, they're open. I exit, break the speed limit, get as far away as possible as fast as I can. A few miles down the road, I pull over. If my hands weren't shaking, I'd put them together and say a prayer of thanksgiving for having had the great good sense not to get out of the car. I sit there for a while, trying to calm down.

Well, I didn't get the interview. Tyler Spee would not be very impressed. I bet April would have gotten it. Nobody would fire a shot at her – not with a face like that. Yet again, I have failed. Maybe it's a sign that I should just give up. Yes, it's time to throw in the towel. This story and this career are not worth risking my life for.

I drive to the offices of *The Philmont Organ*. I intend to do what I have to do with dignity. I burst in, present myself at the front desk. Myron, who is reading a comic book, looks up with a sneer.

'I give up,' I say cheerfully. 'I quit.'

He rolls his eyes. 'You'd better come with me.'

The offices are larger than I thought they would be. We go up and down some stairs, then through a corridor lined with doors, the kind with that ancient gilt lettering you only encounter in buildings that haven't yet been hit by profiteers. Myron's head bobs along in front of me.

'We rent out a few offices,' explains Myron. 'Helps out with the bills – keeps us from going under. Back in the Twenties, this place was booming, but then the Depression hit and things haven't been the same since.'

Come to think of it, Myron looks a bit Depression-era; today he's flopping around in plus-fours. We pass a door that reads 'Arthur J.R. Scullin, Mortician' – the occupant is just moving in. Myron shrugs. 'They've contracted out the printing to a firm upstate. We have to do something with the back room.'

I appreciate the guided tour but wonder where he's taking me. Finally, he all but throws me into a basement. 'Used to be the county jail,' he says, and shuts the door. I hear the sound of a key being turned.

I find myself in a large room.

This is the home of the archives, clearly. They are not, however, stored with much respect. Reams of newspapers dating back to 1890 are haphazardly stacked and in some cases strewn across the floor. There is a sign on the door: 'No Smoking'. Below that, another, larger sign: 'Positively No Smoking'. On top of one of the piles, an improvised ashtray full of butts and a plastic lighter.

On a table sit an old blue typewriter and an adding machine, along with sundry other items. Two bottles, one labelled 'aspirin' and the other, 'pain reliever'. A dusty, wadded-up piece of gauze and what looks like a green garden hose. Pieces of typesetting equipment. Rolls of water-damaged paper. A yellow apron. A plastic pen caddy *covered* in ink. A high metal stool, an enormous hole-punch, and quite a new-looking radio. The floor is covered with maroon carpet on to which the walls are flaking. There are great chunks of metal everywhere and what appears to be a bicycle chain hanging from the ceiling.

The entire building is permeated with a feeling of doom and despair. There is a stomping of feet above my head and every so often what sounds like a stampede, as though the staff are running from one side of the room to another, trying to keep the *Titanic* from tipping over. Every once in a while, I hear a hoot or the sound of hollow laughter. 'Fire,' someone shouts, in a voice of bitter gladness.

I feel like an animal that knows it's headed for the abattoir. I figure I'd better start looking for a way out. I try a door at the back. It opens into a large room that contains the glorious remains of a printing press. They are already moving the coffins in. A bespectacled man, face pinched with woe, has climbed on top of the press and is clutching it: *'I won't let them take you.'* I shut the door. Look around for refreshment. The closest I can find is a bottle of old cola and several mugs filled with blackened, solidified liquid and buboes of mould.

'You again.'

I turn. The editor stands before me. He gets around pretty

well, for a monoped – I didn't even hear him come in. He's propped up on a sort of cane, à la Fred Astaire, and he's wearing what look like his old combat fatigues.

I hear a moan from the printing room.

'Don't mind him. He's been in there for days.' He seats himself on the tall metal stool. Crosses his arms. 'So. I hear you want out.'

'Yes,' I say, 'and if you don't let me out of this room right now, I'll scream.'

'Not so fast,' he says. 'I'll let you go. As soon as you tell me why.'

'I went to his estate and he took a pot shot at me.'

'Uh huh. Now tell me the real reason.'

This is outrageous. 'But it's true. You know what he's like – you told me so yourself.'

The editor shuts his eyes, smiles, does a Stevie Wonder from the waist. 'Columbia, Columbia, I believe you, but you're not telling the whole truth. You're not being honest with me – or yourself. Come on. Level with me.'

He continues to say, 'Come on,' as though coaxing a timorous puppy to come out of a hole.

I try to look as though I am thinking hard. 'I'm not altogether sure this is something the public needs to know. I mean, so what if he does sell? No one gives a damn but his neighbours, who are probably a bunch of jerks. Property gets developed all the time.' I am starting to babble. 'Besides, LandDevel builds tasteful homes. Sure, they look like downmarket mausoleums *now*, but it's architecture that will endure –'

'Fine,' he says. As though he's lost interest.

'You can't stop progress,' I add.

'Okay.' He is all but filing his nails.

'So I'm withdrawing from the assignment and, in fact, the whole profession. Not because I want to, you understand, it's just that –'

'No problem. Now, go and bullshit someone else. Stop wasting my time.' He hops over to the door. Holds it open for me.

The real reason is none of his business. Some would say that I am searching for excuses. Looking back, I'd always wanted results without doing the work, and not infrequently I'd gotten away with it. At college, I'd partied, had scraped by with C's, dismissing the diagnosis of Head-Sand Syndrome. Had tried not to care when awards were handed out and I didn't even receive a booby prize. I told myself that living for the present was the right thing to do, only to discover that the present turns into the future pretty quickly, and if you haven't stored anything up, you find yourself in a serious grasshopper-ant situation. I recall classmates walking into jobs at the *New York Times*. I'd purchased a one-way ticket to Flat-on-My-Face. And here I am, still trying to stand and still falling, in spite of all the miles travelled.

'I don't have all day,' says the editor.

But my feet aren't moving.

'Go on, what are you waiting for?' he says.

Now is my chance to give it one last try. To prove – to *myself* – that I can do it. The door is open but I'm not leaving, not yet, not until I've made one last attempt to jump the hurdle. I look up at the editor sullenly.

'You do realize he was probably firing a blank,' he says. 'Even he couldn't escape a murder charge.'

'I suppose.'

'And I might have been exaggerating a *little* when I said the odds were sixty-forty,' he continues. 'I'd says they were seventy-thirty, tops. Now, do you want to carry on?'

I shuffle. 'I guess so.'

'Good,' he says, pleased. 'Bear in mind that there may be more to this story than meets the eye. I gave you a lead, but that's all it is – a lead. We don't know the truth yet. The truth could be anything.'

'Next you'll be telling me it's "out there".'

He sits down on the stool again. 'Have you ever worked with a sympathetic editor?'

'No.'

'Good. Hopefully, you never will. Do you know why I treat Myron the way I do?'

'No.'

'Because I care.'

It's Tyler Spee all over again. I don't need this. I prepare to leave.

'Honour your profession,' he says. 'This may be just a small-town paper but it's our lifeline to integrity.' He points at me. 'And you know you want it. You are *desperate* to do a good job. Your bravado doesn't fool me, Columbia.'

'In other words, get the Duck.'

'Get the Duck. *Don't return without the Duck.*'

At this point, Myron rushes in with the wheelchair, scoops up the editor, and they are away like a newly-wed couple.

'Oh, and Ellen?' he says.

'What?'

'Don't forget – it's the journey, not the destination that's important.' He and Myron exit, laughing hysterically. I am left standing there like a fool, alone with the realization that I am in it for the duration.

I bang back in through the door, wondering if April might be there to make me another lunch. No such luck. I encounter my mother, sitting on the sofa, as though she has been waiting there for a long time – twenty years or so. I think of Rip Van Winkle, awakening after his long sleep. Wonder what madness he would have suffered if he'd been conscious, merely frozen in place.

'Hi,' I say.

'Hello,' she replies. She's knitting, but fooling no one.

There is an awkwardness in the air. 'What are you making?' I ask lamely.

She holds up the garment. 'A sweater.'

'For whom?'

'For April.'

It's pink and soft. I can't help but feel an ache, yet I know perfectly well that everything she ever knitted for me ended up lying at the bottom of my closet. April will wear hers proudly, I know. Will tell everyone that 'Mom' made it just for her.

I clear my throat. 'Looks pretty,' I say, like someone just learning the art of civilized conversation.

'Thank you,' she says. Makes as though to put the garment down, hesitates. 'So, how's it going?'

I am surprised to hear her use the vernacular of youth. I used to get mildly reprimanded for using it myself. 'Fine. How's it going with you?'

'Fine.'

More uncomfortable silence. She has a funny look on her face, as though she wants to ask me a question but hasn't decided whether or not this is a good idea. Her patina of protective glossiness is gone. Her forehead, usually artificially smooth, is crinkled, as though with concern. Her smile is half there, half not, and her eyes lack their usual certainty.

'Are you enjoying being at home?' she asks.

'Um . . . sure.' I can't bear it any longer. She seems to want to talk, but clearly can't think of anything to say. Not my problem. I turn my attention to yesterday's newspaper.

Then . . .

'Ellen?' she says. 'Do you like your name?'

I look up. My *name*? 'Sure.' She seems to be expecting something more. 'Well,' I go on, 'I've never really thought about it. It's a good name.' What on earth does she want? 'It's served its purpose.'

'I've often wondered if we shouldn't have given you a more . . . *special* name.'

Like what? John Lennon Lotus Blossom Living-in-a-Commune Kaplan? 'Look, don't browbeat yourself. The kids with unusual names all got beaten up at one point or another. One guy was called Hector. Can you imagine going through life with a name like Hector? He really got harassed.' I feel a twinge of guilt. I'd been one of the tormentors. Well, anyone with a name like Hector deserves it . . .

'I was worried that it might be a bit ordinary,' she says.

Well, Mom, there's no one more 'ordinary' than me. I'm trying to come to terms with it. I speculate briefly – if I'd had a different name, would I have had a different life? 'Ellen suits me,' I said. 'Ellen is the name I deserve.'

'Actually, I considered calling you Theodosia.'

Theodosia? Sounds too much like euthanasia.

'Or Christabel,' she continues. 'But your father thought they were a bit much.'

'He was right.' Jesus. Christabel?

'Ellen, you don't hate me, do you?' she asks abruptly.

For goodness' sake. Where does she come up with this stuff? 'Of course not.'

133

She attempts a laugh. Sweating, I wonder how to change the subject.

'I always felt that we neglected you a bit, as a child,' she says.

Neglected me? They hadn't neglected me enough. I wish they'd neglected me more. My mother, always hovering, teaching me about blue and yellow using Van Gogh's 'Starry Night'. My father saying hopefully, 'Hey, Ellen, you want to hear about this sizzling case I'm handling?' I spent most of my early life hiding behind furniture.

'You didn't, Mom, really. Don't worry about it.'

'I often regret,' she says, 'not having played with you more as a child.'

Those tedious games of blocks, the hours spent over the erector set, like she wanted to turn me into some kind of architect. Then there was the Lego. Mind-numbing. She played with me all the time – I was always wandering away. What is she talking about?

'Maybe,' she says, 'we shouldn't have given you all those gender-neutral toys.'

Now, that *hadn't* been a mistake. If there is anything I hate more than Lego, it's Barbie dolls, with their long blonde hair and their stupid little feet. Or plastic babies that leak water if you feed them a bottle. Why is changing diapers considered terrific entertainment for a child? This is something adults pay other people to do.

'I hope you understand,' she says, 'that we were only trying to do the right thing.' Looks at me carefully, as though trying to gauge my reaction. Doesn't know, of course, that I'd overheard her uncharitable words yesterday, and that I know what she really thinks of me.

'Sure, I do,' I say. Neutral face and tone. 'Look how well I turned out.'

My mother bursts into tears. Oh, no – she's cracked. It was bound to happen sooner or later. I put down my newspaper. Study the carpet.

'Mom, don't cry,' I say. 'It's fine. Everything's fine.'

She wipes her eyes. 'Is it?' She sounds bewildered.

I decide a calm, professional approach is in order. 'Look, if you're worried about whether I harbour any deep-seated resentments towards you, I don't. My childhood was flawless, absolutely fantastic, and I have no bad memories whatsoever. Now, stop worrying.'

I would have thought that this would do the trick, but she's sitting on the edge of her chair, as though hoping against hope that I'll say something more. I guess I look a little impatient, because she smiles brightly and states that she'd better be getting on with things. Then leaves the room quickly.

I am suddenly flooded with anguish. I feel as though she's died. She's still there – I could run after her – but I lack the courage. What if she rejected me as I've just rejected her? I've been pushing her away for years.

Come back, I silently plead, *give me one last chance*. Why can't I say these words out loud? Why is it so hard?

For the first time in my life, I feel an irreversible sense of loss.

And a wave of shame.

James's room is cool and shadowy. I had forgotten the peculiar quality of afternoon here. Everything slows down, like it's been drugged with molasses. He must have finished work early, as he appears to be taking an afternoon nap. April, to my amazement and relief, isn't there.

He looks quite alluring, lying in bed with a book across his chest. I hate to say it, but sometimes he's more appealing with his mouth shut. Lately, he's been as elusive and unpredictable as light bouncing off walls. I am determined to pin him down now.

I reach under the sheet, carefully, so as not to wake him. Grope around. Find my target. Wiggle my fingers. He shrieks. Jumps a mile.

'*What the hell do you think you're doing,*' he gasps, backing away.

'Hello, this is your wake-up call,' I say. 'What's wrong, big brother? No more garbage to metamorphose for the day? No glorious vistas of transformation?'

He stares at me uncomprehendingly for a moment, as though my very existence completely baffles him. '*Are you crazy?*'

'Oh, come on, James, I used to come in here all the time, when I was a kid. You were always glad to see me then.' When a guy wakes up, he generally has a hard-on. Well, okay, I *know*

135

this is true – first hand, so to speak. And when a guy is sexually aroused, he is very easy to manipulate. But I can't take advantage of this. Can I?

'Just thought I'd stop by and say hello.' I wedge myself on to the pillow beside his head, draw my knees up, and look down at him. 'We haven't exactly had a chance for one of our heart-to-hearts, have we?'

I move to tickle him again. He raises an arm, recoils. 'You stay *away* from me.'

'I've missed you, that's all.'

'Are you completely psychotic? You almost gave me a heart attack.' He examines me more closely. Peers into my face. 'Is there something in particular you want to talk about?'

Many things, James. 'No, not really.'

'You're not . . . in trouble or anything?'

'No.'

'Not on the run from the French Foreign Legion?'

'No.'

'Because I know you, Ellen.'

'I know.'

'You can't fool me.'

'Sure.'

'And I want you to know that I'm here for you. You do know that, don't you?'

'Sure.' I lie down fully. Relax with my hands behind my head – on *April's* side of the bed. His scent almost overwhelms me. She's manipulative, I want to shout. She's looking out for number one. You're going to be collecting garbage for the rest of your life.

He punches my shoulder. Cocks his head at me. Like I'm a chip off the old . . . 'Remember when I used to call you El-El?'

For Christ's sake. He's not going to start going on about El-El. 'James . . .'

'Yes?'

'I've been worried. About you.'

There is a split-second of silence before he answers. 'In what sense?'

'You know what sense.' I can tell he knows what I'm talking

about – he looks really troubled. 'April. Are you in love with her?'

'Eros. Interesting concept. Plato stressed the value of rising above earthly love –'

'James.'

'– the purpose being to develop a strong moral character. By practising a non-particular kind of love it is possible to reconcile love and reason –'

'James, your Spockness is showing.'

'It is important to think in terms of values, not passion. Strong feelings undermine self-control and interfere with the ability to do the right thing –'

'Answer the question.'

'Yes. Yes, I love her. I've loved her from the moment I laid eyes on her.' The way he says it, I know he means it. 'I'm in the grip of something that scares the hell out of me, Ellen. It's like a fever and I don't know what to do.'

I detect a note of panic. For a moment, I think he's started to cry – he has a very strong feminine side, my brother. Great sensitivity. But no, he's only rubbing his brow. Tormented. Undecided. A bit Hamlet. A bit . . . human.

Where the hell is Spock? 'James. You're letting your emotions get the better of you. You're not used to that. Of *course* you're going haywire. But I'm sure between the two of us, we can –'

'I love her.'

All his pain, all the years of loneliness come through in this cry, as though silver arrows have pierced the armour of this already wounded knight. 'If I had one wish,' he says, 'I would wish away her love for me. I'm not good enough for her. I don't deserve her. I'm afraid of screwing it up, Ellen. I don't know how to love.'

What can I say? Neither do I. I can't coach him, talk him through it – even if I wanted to and I *don't*. 'What do you see in her?' The question slips out perfectly naturally.

'If you'd ever been in love, Ellen, you'd know that was a very silly question.'

I explode. 'For God's sake, Jimmy Jams, she's using you. Don't you see? She recognized you for the sucker you were, latched on to you, made you feel *responsible* for her . . . I can just *hear* her

137

. . . it's a textbook case of opportunism gone wild. It's time you started thinking rationally again, big brother. She's got you by the ears.'

I face him defiantly, expecting a rebuke. But he just laughs. Relaxes. Takes one of my hands in his.

'Ellen, when I first met April, she was taking shelter at the bus station. There's a kind of wilderness in LA, a wasteland of poverty and desperation, tucked away where the rich don't have to look at it. That's where I came across her.'

'What were you doing there?'

'I was on my way back from a community centre where I'd gone to see about working as a volunteer. Soon discovered that they don't have much use for philosophers. They looked at me as though I had wires coming out of my brain. Didn't even like the idea of letting me dish out soup. It was humiliating, Ellen. I'd never been rejected before, and I couldn't help but feel that it was all my own fault. The result of severe moral shortcomings, some deep flaw of character.'

'What was she doing? Just sitting?'

'Yes. Looking terrified. Some joker was trying to convince her there was an eleventh Commandment: "Thou shalt not refuse liquor." Wine maketh glad the heart and all that. He was hassling her to take a swig of something, and you know April. She's so gentle. She was trying to figure out how to refuse.'

She attracts weirdos, all right. Look at Puddles. 'Did you think she was pretty?'

'Yes.'

'Sexually attractive?'

'Very.'

'James . . .'

'Yes, Ellen?'

'I hate to put it like this, but . . . do you think it's possible . . .' How can I ask my own brother about his sex life? 'Do you think it's possible that . . . because you haven't had much *experience* . . .'

'That I was attracted to her because of her non-threatening sexual availability? No. You can set your mind at ease about that, Ellen. I'd had plenty of opportunities to have sex, you know. Truth be told, I was dying to have sex – you might say it was

138

my one unrealized ambition. I mean, I'd aimed high before, but let me tell you, getting into Harvard was a piece of cake compared with –'

'I get the picture.' I'm not sure I want to hear this, actually.

'I got a blow job once.'

'Did you?' Politely. Shut up, James.

'At a St Valentine's Day dance at the country club. A beautiful girl. Very wealthy. She just grabbed me and sucked me off. Then she looked at me as though I was supposed to . . . *do* something and I had no idea what. I panicked. Ran back inside. People talk about how hard the first time is for girls, but it's hard for guys, too. No one tells us what to do – they just expect us to be experts. I was only fifteen. And this girl . . . it was clear she'd done this kind of thing before – *many* times – and that she expected something special in return. Cunnilingus or intercourse, one or the other. And I had *no* clue –'

That's it. I've heard enough. I'd craved answers but had not expected things to go so far. Also, I'm very squeamish about matters physical – the result, I think, of being experimented upon. Anything remotely biological and it's curtains. 'Look, James, maybe we've discovered the deep-seated psychological reason for your previous sexual reticence. Maybe you're afraid of girls of your own, uh, class.'

'No, Ellen. I'm sorry. I'm afraid of my own feelings, not nymphomaniacal debutantes.'

'I appreciate what you're saying but maybe we should just test my theory. How about this girl Courtney?' Subtle, Ellen. *Very* smooth.

'Ah, yes. The lovely Courtney.' I detect his smile.

'Yeah. Zero's cousin.'

'Bennington graduate and certified man-eater.'

'Something like that.'

'She's not really my type, Ellen.'

Not yet, maybe. 'Just thought I'd better check. I'm only looking out for your best interests.'

'I'm very grateful, Ellen.'

He's being facetious, the bastard. 'Where is April, anyway?'

'At a prayer meeting. She's been attending a local church she likes – "The House of Fishes and Loaves". Evangelical but not too flaky. It's good, gets her out of the house. She ought to have pursuits of her own. She seems to think that if we don't do everything together . . .'

'You'll abandon her.'

'Precisely. I don't quite know how to reassure her.'

Now is my chance. With a needle, Ellen. 'How would you feel if she decided to have a baby?'

'She wouldn't do anything so foolish.' He seems confident of this.

'Wouldn't she?'

James looks at me narrowly for a moment, then turns to the window as though hoping to find solace in the slender ray of sun fighting its way through. 'I'd love to be a dad. But Ellen, that scares me more than anything.'

'Why?'

'Because I'd fail,' he says simply.

Well, maybe he would. It's easy to fail. Look at me, look at James – one unemployed hack and one emotional cripple. And most would say that my parents did a *good* job.

'You're probably right,' I say cheerfully.

'Ellen?' he asks. 'I need a favour.'

Something tells me I'm not going to like this. 'What?'

'I'm meeting up with Frederick and Zero tomorrow at the local café, and I was wondering if . . .'

'I'll do it.'

'You don't even know what I'm going to ask you.'

Doesn't matter – if Frederick's involved, I'm in. 'Okay, what?'

'I was hoping maybe you'd come along and give April some moral support. You know, make her feel at ease, boost her confidence a little. Something happens to her when we go out with my friends. She freezes up, hardly says a word. If she'd just relax and be herself . . .'

Oh, no. I'm being given chaperoning duties. I don't believe this.

'She really likes you,' he continues, 'and I think she rather admires you. She couldn't stop talking about you the other day – about how savvy you are and what a good journalist you're going to make . . .'

I'll bet she did. Boy, is she crafty. Keep your enemies closer . . .

'I'm pleased at how well the two of you have hit it off,' he says. 'Initially, I wasn't sure if you would get along. Let's face it – you don't have much in common. And, as you probably know, Ellen, you're a bit of an acquired taste.' He punches me again, playfully. I stare at him. 'I talked about you a lot, I have to admit. I think I might have scared her. But she went from finding you rather intimidating to referring to you as the sister she never had. So I'm recruiting you.' He claps me on the shoulder. 'You in?'

'Do I have any choice?'

'Excellent. I knew I could count on you. It's the Café Olympus on Roland Avenue. You'll see it – it's hard to miss. Be there at three.'

'Fine.' I hope he's not going to make me promise.

'Oh, and Ellen? '

'Yeah?'

'Promise me you won't let me down.'

'Have I ever let you down?'

'Just promise. Put your hand on mine like you did when we were kids and swear.'

I am in too deep to refuse. I do as he says. Mumble, 'Promise.'

Suddenly, an idea comes to me in a great blinding flash. I will call up that dork Zero and get him to bring his cousin Courtney along. James claims he doesn't like her, but I suspect it's just a question of exposure. All that is required is to get the dosage right: not too much, not too little. Like radiation. Enough to cure but not kill.

I am not sure how the North Philmont Residents' Association will feel about a member of the press showing up on its front doorstep. It's almost dark by the time I get there. I find myself driving through a neighbourhood where I spent a lot of time as a teenager. The houses are huge and, by and large, predate *The Philmont Organ*. They are made of stone, clapboard, stucco and brick — massive, solid and idiosyncratic. They stand like great ships, windows open and blazing, porches stretched across the front like long and elegant arms. Each has a carriage house in back large enough to comfortably accommodate a family of four. Seeing the place, I think I understand what may be going through their heads. They're not just fighting for their land. They're fighting for the right to separate themselves from the nouveaus, the parvenus, the relocs and wannabes. It's us versus them. The final showdown. The last stand.

I locate the right residence. It emits a golden glow. The cars outside are all Mercedes and BMWs, though I spy a red Porsche as I pull up. 'YALE LAW' reads the licence plate.

The house has a Christmas-party feel about it, as though it is anticipating something other than the usual agenda. I'd thought about calling in advance, but had decided to take advantage of the element of surprise. The door is opened by a woman I *think* might be the mother of one of my old classmates. I don't look too closely.

'*Philmont Organ* here.' I should have thought to bring a press card. She's staring at me like I'm a nut. 'We're following the LandDevel story very closely and I wondered if I could sit in on your meeting.'

I'm in luck. She smiles graciously and opens the door a little wider. 'We'd be delighted,' she says. 'You've no idea what we've been through. Right this way.'

I am led into a vast expanse of living room, all hardwood floors and period features. High ceilings, big fireplace. Antique furniture, French doors. People are sitting around, chatting. I am offered a glass of iced tea.

'It's an old tradition,' she explains. 'No alcohol. In tribute to the Victorian gentlemen who founded the Association.'

Uh huh. Here's betting they get sauced afterwards. I can see bottles of alcohol lined up along the hand-carved bar, an old man in a white jacket at the ready. The woman explains that I am from the local paper, and response is generally favourable. So far, I am pretty pleased with myself. Clearly the power of the press opens all kinds of doors.

'Nice to see *someone* taking this seriously,' a man remarks. 'We asked a representative from LandDevel to come and explain himself, but he didn't show up.'

I'm not surprised. The guy looks like he pulls people's fingernails out for fun. Members continue to trickle in. Peculiarly, they each throw their car keys into a basket by the door. One of them yawns and asks if there is any coffee going.

A tall blond man, who appears to be the leader, is wielding a

gavel and trying to get everyone to come to order. I think he's
the man with the blunderbuss. A great strapping self-righteous
fellow with just the suggestion of a stomach. You can imagine
him reacting badly when he looks at his middle in the mirror –
it's probably the only time during the course of the day that he's
forced to own up to an imperfection. His hair ripples back from
a patrician forehead. Square jaw and firm, well-shaped nose. Good
provider, that one. Bet he makes his wife – *all* the wives – very
happy. And probably some of the husbands, too. He turns
around. *Nice* ass; even the corduroy can't hide it.

He bangs the gavel against the mantelpiece. 'I'd like to thank
you all for coming. As you know, this is an emergency session
of the North Philmont Residents' Association. I understand we
have a journalist present.'

Everyone looks over at me. I grin cheesily, wave.

'We all know what the problem is.' Nods and angry muttering
from the floor. 'Grosworthy – with no regard for his neighbours – is threatening to sell to rapacious land developers who
will destroy what is currently a beautiful natural area. I won't
pretend that our concern is solely ecological in nature, but
I think we all agree that, at this point, strong action is called
for. We need to decide, once and for all, what we are going
to do.'

'Torch his house,' says Fingernail Man. 'Set it on fire. I know
someone who will do it for almost nothing.'

This suggestion is greeted with enthusiasm.

'That's the great thing about the tighter immigration laws,'
someone says. 'You can get foreigners to do almost *anything* for
a pittance.'

'They're absolutely desperate.'

'It's a pity, really.'

'We'd be acting in the public service. These people have to
eat.'

There are murmurs of agreement. 'Thank you,' says Blunderbuss. 'Any *practical* suggestions?'

A hand goes up. 'Why don't we bump him off?'

This, apparently, is a more acceptable proposition. Even
Blunderbuss thinks so. 'I like it. Might be more discreet.' He
turns to Fingernail Man. 'Would your contact be willing to –'

I don't quite believe I'm hearing this. Are they really suggesting . . . no. This has to be a joke. A moment later he starts banging his gavel again, having seemingly come to his senses.

'Order, order. You forget we have a member of the press here. We were just joking – right, everybody?' They look disgruntled. 'We intend our actions to be dignified but effective. All we want to do is make our feelings clear.'

Another hand goes up. 'I say we dump a daily load of manure at his front gates.'

'No good. He'll only use it for fertilizer. Anything else?'

'Does he have children or any living relatives?' someone asks.

'Kidnapping is out, Charlie. Last meeting, remember?'

A woman in a tartan suit and pearls rises. 'How about blackmail? Could we dig up some dirt?'

'I don't know. Men like that cover their tracks pretty well,' he says. 'Also, remember this man is a decorated veteran. If we try to make *him* look bad, *we* look bad. None of us here has ever been so fortunate as to serve our country in war, so we'd automatically be denied the sympathy vote. We just don't qualify for the PR.'

Suddenly, it all strikes me as very funny. They're talking about blackmail when dirty photographs of all of them are lying in an envelope in my bedroom, just aching to be downloaded on to the Internet. I suddenly recall what they look like naked. And start to laugh.

Blunderbuss looks over at me with the self-assurance of centuries of good genes. 'So you think this is funny, do you? How would you feel if it were *your* home?'

This makes it worse. I almost fall off my chair. He starts towards me angrily. I head for the door. Stop. Look back briefly. Listen.

'Well, I'm stumped,' says Fingernail Man. 'Let's eat.'

Blunderbuss has already forgotten my existence. *Bang*: 'Meeting adjourned.' He tosses the gavel to one side. Makes a beeline for the basket of keys.

They certainly lose interest quickly. Talk about a short attention span. These people have one thing on their minds. They race for the liquor, start cramming food into each other's mouths. The elderly bartender has disappeared. Fingernail Man walks past me; he's already rolled up his sleeves. Someone gets out a video camera. I exit to the sound of Greek dancing music.

Outside, I find a sheet of paper stuck under my windshield wiper: 'Ellen, you're not trying.'

Green ink. I shiver, look around. I'm beginning to feel genuinely unsafe. Once more, I've failed. I have a feeling I may have just had my last laugh.

Later that night, I hear noises coming from James's room. Little hoots and groans. I assume the worst and put a glass to the wall. Don't want to, but I feel I need to keep tabs. To my surprise, fornication doesn't seem to be the order of the day. In fact, they are reading bits of the Bible out loud to each other. James is doing some old prophet in a funny voice and April is giggling.

How happy she sounds. I consider the Courtney plan. Tomorrow it will all be over. I feel chilled, culpable, almost like an executioner. Momentarily cannot bear the thought of what lies ahead.

Why not just welcome her in? Why not?

Because she makes me feel inadequate.

Because her very presence is implied criticism.

Because I can't live with the fact that everyone loves her more than me.

Because she gets all the attention.

And because she always gets her own way.

This time, *I* am going to win. And then my world will go back to being mine. Things will be the way they were before, and I will be able to start all over again. It will be *my* rebirth. I know I can do it, if I can just get her out of the way.

'"How beautiful you are, my darling."' James is speaking. '"Oh, how beautiful! Your eyes behind your veil are doves."'

I can picture that, actually. April, eyes flirtatious above a veil. All at once, it dawns on me. He is seducing her with the Song of Songs.

'"How delightful is your love, my sister, my bride! How much more pleasing is your love than wine, and the fragrance of your perfume than any spice!"'

I can hardly bear to listen.

If only someone would say things like that to me.

145

' "My lover is radiant and ruddy," ' says April, ' "outstanding among ten thousand." '

Silence. Then she explodes with laughter.

For a moment, I mourn the friendship that might have been. It's almost a pity she's got to go.

8

'Is this it?' says April.

'Must be,' I reply.

Before us stands a high-tech Parthenon, all mock-marble and chrome, on a slight hill surrounded by as yet unlandscaped grounds. The Café Olympus. It used to be a parking lot. Rose out of a sea of dirt to become the local hot spot. Twenty kinds of cappuccino, as many types of milk, a selection of foreign newspapers, exotic sandwiches and cakes. A couple of years ago, this would have been unheard of. I can remember when black coffee constituted living on the edge.

In my absence, Philmont has become habitable, even cosmopolitan, which is annoying. What was the point of having left in the first place? If I'd known, I wouldn't have gone to so much trouble. I haven't even been away that long. But then they say that one day in outer space equals twenty years on earth, and that the price you pay for the great adventure, the close-up view of a distant galaxy, is the possibility that you will return home to find that your children are older than you are, your spouse has been frozen in a cryogenic tank and the earth has been covered by a big plastic bubble intended to obviate the need for an ozone layer.

'Are you ready?' asks April timidly.

'Sure am,' I say grimly. 'Let's go in, shall we?'

We are engulfed by the aroma of ground coffee as soon as we step through the door. The scent alone is enough to induce a caffeine high. Zero is already there. I spot him in a corner, engaged in a lively conversation with the sugar bowl. Catching sight of us, he rises and I greet him: 'What's up, Zero?'

'Certainly not my penis. Long time no see, Ellen. Looking good.' Lonely guy, Zero, but eternally hopeful. Learned the art of small talk out of a mail-order guide advertised in the back of a comic book. 'I see you've brought James's babe along. That's swell.' He offers his hand to April, who shakes it reluctantly as though fearful of catching some unpleasant disease.

As I'd mentioned to April, Zero is a bit of a pervert. The nicest possible type of pervert, but a pervert nevertheless. He's a good guy, just sexually frustrated – and hell, who isn't? He is skinny, with glasses that engulf his nostrils and brown hair cut in a bowl. Summer and winter, he wears two or three holey cardigans and sandals. He stares at people for long periods without explanation, laughs at unexpected times for no reason at all, trips over things that aren't there, and generally inhabits a completely different world from the rest of us, a parallel universe where the impossible is possible and different rules apply.

'Hey, hey, hey,' he says, moving his fists around in the air enthusiastically. I take this to mean, 'Sit down and I'll get you a coffee.' You have to kind of get the hang of interpreting what he is saying – he comes out with all kinds of incomprehensible stuff. April looks confused. I push her into a chair as Zero goes dancing off in his sandals like a jubilant Hermes. It's hard to keep him sitting – he's always jumping around as though something incredibly exciting is about to happen. Like he expects the world to explode into a sea of atoms at any moment.

'Don't mind Zero,' I say. 'His parents didn't love him. He was raised by a microwave.'

'Ellen?' whispers April, dry-mouthed, clearly intimidated by the sophisticated atmosphere. 'I want to go home.'

'Don't be silly,' I say heartily. She's not wiggling out of this. Actually, I can't say I feel terribly comfortable myself. The place is too cool. You almost expect people to whip out black berets and break into a round of finger-snapping. This is not like Philmont at all. There are at least eight people in the corner writing poetry and the rest seem to be engaged in an attempt to become one with the universe. A man chews a Danish and breathes in through his nose like some kind of swami. A girl inhales the steam of a latte as though trying to enter a trance. The barista is booking a folk singer . . . It's official. Philmont has changed. Or has it always been this way? Are people simply no longer willing to pretend?

Zero, bless his heart, has beaten everyone to it. Nirvana, that is. At least, he's already well on his way. He comes bobbing back, bearing a tray of elaborate coffee, one dark soda and a plate of fashionable rock-hard cookies.

'Did you know,' he says, 'that introducing the right variables into the behavioural constant increases the likelihood of improbable events?'

This is exactly what I'm talking about – he just comes out with this stuff. 'Zero, *be cool.*'

April looks doubtfully into her coffee. 'What is this?'

'It's a latte,' he says. 'I thought you'd enjoy it.'

For some reason, she seems to find this vaguely insulting, as though Zero has patronized her in some way. Granted, it looks a bit like a chocolate sundae, a beverage fit for a child, but he was only trying to be nice. She glances over crossly at my drink, a regular cappuccino. Zero takes the opportunity to survey his environment.

'That woman over there isn't wearing a bra,' he remarks. 'Of course, Hawking claims that the outcome is never a foregone conclusion. You never *know* what's going to happen. All the equations in the world can't foretell events.'

'Tell that to the local soothsayer,' I say. 'You know, Zero, there are decent people out there trying to make a living predicting the future. Intellectual scum like you deprive them of their livelihood.'

'I guess you don't believe in that stuff, huh, Zero,' ventures April in a small voice. 'Fortune tellers and stuff.' Poor girl. No idea what to say to him.

'No,' he says, 'but then, what the hell do I know? She's cute.' His eyes follow a woman out the door.

I look over at April to see if she seems shocked. She doesn't. Quite the opposite. She actually looks a little more at ease. 'James says the key to discovery is a sense of wonder and an open mind.'

'He is so right,' says Zero. 'I *love* the guy – though we had a tremendous argument about fatalism versus free will the other day. We've always seen eye to eye but he's developing an alarming

149

theory of determinism. Must be your influence,' he says, nudging April playfully in the ribs.

'Science never made sense to me,' says April.

He clamps his lips together and clutches his ribcage, as though trying to contain his mirth. Bursts out with: *'Me neither,'* and laughs. April joins in.

'I always just thought I was stupid,' says April. 'The teacher never took the time to explain things very well. It wasn't his fault. He had about forty students and there weren't enough Bunsen burners.'

'You're not stupid,' he says, as though he senses she needs to hear this.

'I'm not?' She sounds perplexed.

'Of course not,' he says. 'On some level, all things make sense. You just have to get off on the right floor. And take it from me, the elevator doesn't always work.'

I'd been counting on him to unsettle her, but they are getting on like a house on fire. He's staring at her intently, which generally has the effect of unnerving people completely, but oddly, she doesn't seem to mind. Uh, oh. He and April seem to have forged some kind of bond. She nods, as though she understands him – which is more than I do.

'You mean,' she says slowly, 'it's okay if I don't "get it" right away?'

'Sure. In the beginning, Einstein didn't know what the hell was going down. Understanding is preceded by *not* understanding. An initial degree of non-comprehension is necessary for enlightenment later on.'

Oh, God. Not only is my plan backfiring, as usual, but I have to listen to Zero talk Zen Science.

'So it's kind of like faith,' says April. 'You believe before you *believe.*'

He slams the table with his open palm. 'Exactly. That is exactly what I'm talking about. Good analogy, April.'

She beams, as though this is the nicest thing anyone's ever said to her. I've never seen such a transparent desire for positive reinforcement. Zero takes a long drink of soda using one of those tuba-twisted plastic straws. He carries it everywhere with him. An attempt to extend the childhood he never had.

April is now entirely at ease and Zero has fallen so deeply into his subject that I suspect he is about to cease to communicate in any known earthly language. Sure enough, he throws back his head and neighs like a horse. I have no idea what he is trying to get across, but April appears to have an inkling. She pushes back her chair and goes, 'Mooooo.' All those years out in farm country have given her a certain authenticity. The other patrons turn to stare. Then they start to join in. The man with the love of Danish goes, 'Baaa.' A boy with a laptop starts to bark like a dog. An old lady in a beret clucks like a chicken. Everyone seems to know what's going on but me. I am torn between fury at feeling left out of what seems to be some kind of cosmic bonding experience, and wanting to fall into the floor.

'Oh, Zero,' giggles April, 'you're crazy.'

No one has ever told him that to his face before – except his dad, who beat him, gave his hamsters to a medical lab, and sent him away to boarding school when he was seven. I watch his face apprehensively, await a bad reaction. But he just ducks his head bashfully. Looks flattered.

April cosies up to him, balancing on delicate elbows. 'I don't know why but I feel so *good* all of a sudden, like everything is going to be okay.'

Dream on, sweetheart. You're in the wrong fairy tale. Fee fie foe fum . . .

'Let there be music!' says Zero. 'Gimme a quarter, Ellen.'

'There's a jukebox?'

'Sure. They salvaged it from the local diner.'

'All right,' I say grumpily. Dig in my pocket. 'But you are absolutely *forbidden* to play Devo.'

'No way, Ellen. Devo rules.' He wanders off, singing, 'We are *De*-vo. D-E-*V*-O . . .'

'Devolution is action,' I say, nodding in his direction. 'We're all going backwards. Fast.'

She stares at me uncomprehendingly, then says:

'Maybe Zero's not so bad.'

We sit in silence for a moment. I have no desire to make polite conversation.

'Um, Ellen,' says April in a low voice, 'have you had a chance

151

to talk to James yet? About Courtney? I only ask because . . . well, I have a feeling she might show up and I . . .'

'I'm sure that's not going to happen,' I reply smoothly. It is, actually. I called Zero yesterday and orally pounded his head into the floor. Told him to get her to come and swore him to secrecy. Threatened to kill him if he didn't keep his mouth shut.

'But did you find out anything?' she asks anxiously. 'I mean, does he *like* her?'

I shrug non-committally. 'He *seems* to like her.'

'But how much?'

'Well . . . it's hard to tell.'

This is not *exactly* a lie. He didn't express a complete aversion to her or anything. I am about to detail James's discreet but impossible-to-conceal admiration of the girl when Frederick enters the café. I choke on my cappuccino.

April was exaggerating a *bit* when she said he looks like a Nazi. It's true that he's blond and does a lot of heel-clicking but it's not his fault. In his family, that's just normal. Rumours that his grandfather was in the SS are strictly untrue. He stands in the doorway, glistening in that golden way that drives women to commit emotional suttee. Temptation, trouble, call him what you will, to crave him is to risk self-destruction. The road behind him is littered with corpses. He is up to his hips in blood.

Beside him is James, who is dressed, I am relieved to note, in his usual normal clothes. None of the tunics and tie-dyes he's been trying to carry off, just a cotton button-down shirt and jeans that show off his nice firm thighs. They come over to our table, James with arms outstretched, Frederick taking long military strides, hands held behind his back as though concealing a bullwhip. Hugs and exclamations follow. April is kissed and squeezed. Zero starts hopping up and down excitedly. James goes over to him and grips his shoulder, a kind of Vulcan hold that calms him down. I smile hopefully at Frederick, who is wearing steel-rimmed glasses in the shape of a lazy eight. He raises his eyebrows.

'You guys okay for drinks?' asks James.

'I wouldn't mind a refill,' says April. She is enjoying her latte after all.

'Me, too,' I say. 'And Zero looks like he could use another soda.'

'What are you drinking, my friend?' says James.

'Dr Pepper,' says Zero. 'But, look, they don't sell it over the counter. There's a kind of pirate operation going on in that corner over there. Use the code word "pop" and try not to draw attention to yourself.'

Thirty different varieties of Italian soda and Zero wants an ordinary soft drink. 'He likes the name,' James explains. 'His ambition is to have a cola named after him. The ultimate popular accolade.'

'Zero wants to be a nerd of the people,' I say.

'Well, look at Hawking,' says Zero. 'He's popular, and look at the benefits he reaps. You know, a lot of women find him very attractive.'

Frederick hasn't said anything yet. He looks bored, but then, he usually does. He and James go back to Philmont Elementary, where a history project on World War II put him in a special school for six months. They kept him under close observation (surveillance might be a better word). His muscular forearms are glinting. I am reminded of the time when I was nine (he seemed to like me a lot more back then) and he picked me up and sat me on top of a stone wall so that we were face to face.

'Are you familiar with the facts of life, Ellen?' he said. 'No? I didn't think so. Now, do you know what a penis is?'

James appeared from nowhere and hustled me away. I later saw him speaking heatedly with Frederick and making violent gestures. Shortly thereafter, I learned what a penis was. I didn't understand what all the fuss was about. From that point onwards, Frederick was my fantasy figure. I loved it when he teased me, pulled my panties down or threw me over his shoulder. Asked me what I was learning in school, filling in certain facts my history teachers had neglected to include. When I was twelve, he offered James a hundred dollars for my maidenhead. 'I'm willing to wait a year or so,' he said. 'I'm just placing a reservation.' It was the only time I ever saw James angry.

I moved on but I never forgot him. Boys came and went, but he was always there in the back of my head. He made everyone

153

else – except James – seem dull. No matter who else caught my eye, Frederick remained the yardstick.

'Rumour has it,' I whisper to April, 'that going to bed with Frederick is like spending the night with Satan.'

Her eyes widen. 'No.'

'Yes. He makes you do everything, and I mean *everything*, you swore to yourself you'd never do, even in your darkest thoughts. He has a way of figuring out what you want and then using it to humiliate you.'

'Gee.' She looks at Frederick with new fear. He is leaning on the counter by the espresso machine, riffling through his wallet. Offers the barista a hundred-dollar banknote between two fingers, and looks at him with mild contempt when it is suggested that he might have something smaller.

'You know,' April whispers, 'from this angle, he even *looks* like Satan. See those two little things on his head? Like horns?'

'That's his cowlick,' I explain. The one thing I know for a fact he despises about himself.

'Why does he keep clicking his heels?'

I shrug. 'Nobody knows.'

Poor April. I sense that she's completely bewildered. With the hugs and kisses over and the drinks on their way, it is dawning on her that she is going to have to come up with something to say. Conversation – for a self-conscious person, the ultimate terror. She cranes her neck in James's direction and fixes her gaze on his face, as though trying to extract some kind of emotional anti-freeze. No luck. Oblivious to her dilemma, he doesn't notice. He is in his element. Totally at ease.

'James looks great,' I remark.

'He always looks great,' she snaps. Bites her lip. In the absence of anything else, she's slipped up, defaulted to anger and hostility. Oh, April, nothing can save you now. You don't know it but you are totally alone, adrift on a raft in a merciless ocean, scanning the horizon for a no-show rescue.

'Well, I'll be darned,' I say. 'Check it out – over there, in the doorway. Isn't that Courtney?'

Yes, there she is, posing in all her glory. She is just as I remember her. Hasn't changed a bit, except maybe her boobs are bigger. She stands, a blueblood warrior, legs slender but muscular, gaze level, head high. Her hair, white blonde, is marginally darker at the roots, and cascades down from a perfect forehead. She's confident, isn't looking for answers, trying to light up the dark side of the moon with inadequate candles. Has always known what she wanted, gotten her own way. I detect nothing of the road not taken. She is conscious of her own attractions and likes to go in for the kill.

'Yo, Courtney. Over here,' calls Zero.

Slowly, as though she can hardly be bothered, she moves her head in our direction. Lets us gradually come into focus, enter her consciousness while she decides whether or not we are worthy of her attention. Then she smiles, a big smile, full lips over straight teeth that no doubt looked as ravishing in braces as they do now. She does not come over immediately, but looks away again, still smiling, as though she can't get over just how nice it is to see us, and after she has drawn sufficient attention to herself she starts to move, placing one leg in front of the other, step step step like a show horse performing dressage. I glance at April, who is trying to look eager, stay calm. I notice her teeth, the shabby half-hearted crookedness of poverty, of parents who cannot afford the rich orthodontic trappings of girls like Courtney. And me.

April. I can hear her thinking.

Help.

'Hi,' says Courtney, kissing everybody on both cheeks – except April and me, of course, and Zero, around whom she makes a wide detour. 'Hi, everybody. Sorry I'm late. Shall we move to that table over there? There's more room.'

For her ego, no doubt. We shift, en masse, and begin a subtle but combative game of musical chairs. Zero wants to be on the end where he can get a good look at the female patrons, but Frederick grabs this prime spot. I want to be between James and Frederick but so does Courtney. April wants to be between me and James but I want to be as far away from her as possible. In an instant, somehow, everything is settled. On one side of the table, Frederick, Courtney and James. On the other, lined up like three monkeys or pieces of fruit, Zero, April and me. Courtney the cat is lapping the full saucerful. Somehow I know, I just *know* that she gives one hell of a blow job.

155

'Well,' says James, clearly somewhat alarmed by her closeness. 'Courtney.'

'James. What a pleasure,' she says, fluttering her eyelashes. His face softens slightly. In amusement? Or is it that he can't resist her charms?

'I brought along those photos I told you about,' she says. 'The ones from the last ball at the Philmont Hunt Club. I thought you might like to see them.'

I'll bet you did. Any excuse to let him see you in a low-cut evening gown.

'It was a charity event, of course,' she continues. 'We raised a lot of money for a really good cause.'

Sure – yourself. What a *slime*. She's almost as bad as April.

'I've also got some pictures of my dog Blossom.' She slips a hand into her purse. I wonder how often she masturbates. 'A shih-tzu. She's adorable.'

'I have a dog,' April blurts out. Bites her lip. Looks agonized.

'You mean Puddles?' I say.

'No. Innertube. Remember?'

'That's a funny name for a dog,' says Courtney. 'What kind is it?'

'The short-haired kind.'

Courtney rolls her eyes to heaven. 'I mean what *breed*?'

'Um, I'm not sure.'

'Don't you have papers?'

Tartly: 'No.'

Courtney nibbles one of the rock-hard biscuits – she's the type that can bite through them, no problem. 'I love mongrels but my father doesn't think they're hygienic. One followed me home once but he had it put to sleep. I was kind of upset so he bought me Blossom and she's been an absolute darling.'

Wow. Talk about cut to the thrust. April looks positively faint.

'Hawking claims that in practice human actions are impossible to predict even if we know the governing equation,' says Zero, as though we've been discussing this the whole time.

'Zero, *what are you talking about*?' demands Courtney through clenched teeth.

'Chaos theory,' he replies cheerfully, oblivious to her irritation.

'You know. Deterministic laws, changes in initial conditions. Unpredictable behaviour. Variables.'

'*What?*'

'It's like this,' he says. 'The more order you impose, the more chaos you create. There. Isn't it beautiful?'

'In other words,' says James, 'trying to lead a normal life is a losing battle . . .'

'. . . so fight fire with fire,' says Zero. 'Rather than try to control your environment, court chaos. Work *with* the rogue variable. It's a very exciting concept. It means anything can happen, whatever the starting point – which is great for someone like me, who lives in hope of getting a date some day.'

'Oh, you'll get a date some day, Zero,' says April encouragingly.

'No, you won't,' Courtney automatically replies.

'What if your universe has too many variables in it already?' I ask.

'Then you're very lucky,' he says. 'Or unlucky. Could go either way.'

Courtney is looking impatient. Of course. Our mistake. The conversation has shifted away from *her* for a moment. Let's all start talking about her again, immediately.

'How's life in the field of contemporary art, Courtney?' I say. Might as well seize the opportunity to get her and James hooked on a subject of mutual interest. I remember all those volumes of nudes in his bedroom. If this doesn't do it, I don't know what will.

'Excellent – everything's totally falling into place,' she replies. 'I had an interview at a gallery the other day, and it seems the job's mine if I want it.'

'That's really great,' I say. 'My mother is very interested in art.'

'Really?' says Courtney, turning to James, as though it is he who has spoken.

'Now that you mention it, yes,' he says. 'She does have a thing for Georgia O'Keeffe.'

'Oh, I *love* Georgia O'Keeffe. Is she looking forward to the exhibition at MOMA?'

'I think she mentioned it – though she probably won't bother to go.'

'Well, we'll have to persuade her,' says Courtney. 'Maybe the three of us could go together.'

This is going even better than I expected. Not that Courtney needs much of a nudge. But what I need to do now is draw out her 'caring, sharing' side, as James still looks slightly intimidated. 'I understand your family is involved in a variety of philanthropic activities,' I say.

She nods solemnly, as though she's been asked to step up on stage. 'If you've been blessed with a good home and a loving family, I think it's really, really important to give something back to the world. Because not everyone is so lucky.'

James falls for this. 'Which causes are you involved in?'

'There are so many, I wouldn't know where to begin. But my personal favourite is "Fashion for Famine". It's really beautiful. Everyone – including at least one leading designer – fasts all day and contributes the money they would have spent on food to Third World famine zones. Then we wrap the whole thing up with dinner and a fashion show.'

Good God. Couldn't she have picked a better example? James, however, seems familiar with the event. 'It was Ethiopia a few years ago, wasn't it?'

'Yes. That was totally, totally sad.'

He nods in agreement. Looks bemused.

'Congratulations on your job, Courtney,' April pipes up, determined to make her presence known.

Courtney gives her the teeth, probes her critically, scans her soul in search of that emotional treasure trove, tarnished self-esteem. 'Thanks, April.' The way she says 'April' equates it to the name of some cherished maid. 'It's great to see you again. We didn't get much of a chance to talk last time. You were really quiet.' Chummy hand on the arm; quickly withdrawn. 'How have you been?'

'Fine,' April replies, in a voice at once strained and defiant.

As though satisfied that she has performed her social duty, Courtney turns away. She is the type who can make other people invisible simply by virtue of ignoring them, refusing to acknowledge their presence save by occasional darts of interest thrown out more to patronize than pay tribute. April, probably used to being put down but not so blatantly or rudely, looks

158

stung. Tries to catch James's eye, but he's still contemplating famine.

'Of course, the notion of intransitive systems would account for a lot.' Zero has fashioned a pendulum from paper napkins and a sugar cube and is observing it at eye level.

'That's not terribly significant, though, is it, Zero?' asks James, abruptly re-entering reality. 'It just means that if you give a man a kick in the pants, he walks in a different direction.'

'Are you kidding? It could explain away the Ice Ages.'

'James, do you have any interest in contemporary art?' says Courtney loudly. 'Because I've got a couple of tickets to a gallery opening and I wondered if you'd like to go.'

'Great.' He turns to April. 'How would you like that, darling?'

April licks her lips nervously. 'Um . . .'

Frederick hasn't said anything. He's taken out a paperback copy of Machiavelli's *The Prince* and is reading. I love the way he doesn't even bother to be polite. He reaches out and takes a sip of Courtney's 'fruit smoothie'. Eyes glued to the page.

'By the way, James, I got those footie pyjamas I was telling you about,' says Courtney, before April can reply. 'The ones from Bloomie's. I thought I'd have a slumber party – to which you've invited, of course.'

Allow her to run rampant and she will instigate a game of 'Truth or Dare' for the sole purpose of removing her clothes. I've got to get her off this sex kick; this is what's putting him off. If I can only get her to stick to the life of the mind . . .

'So, Courtney,' I say. 'How do you feel about Plato?'

She looks at me like I've asked her to dance without an introduction. *'Plato?'*

James chuckles. 'My little sister is always trying to make new friends on my behalf. She knows how hard it is to find someone who even knows who Xenophanes is.'

'Oh, I *love* the writings of Xenophanes,' she says, sliding smoothly into the little groove I've provided for her. 'I did tons of reading in philosophy at Bennington. It just totally, totally fascinated me.'

'Really?' James looks at her as though seeing her for the first time.

'Yes. I took a few courses. What was your specialty?'

159

'Ethics, actually.'

'Oh, that was absolutely my favourite . . .'

She's probably never given ethics a second thought in her life. But I have to hand it to her – she knows how to carry it off. April is trying to cope with the fact that she is being excluded from the conversation. Doesn't know what they're talking about. And even if she did, Courtney has thrown up an iron curtain and is not about to let anyone in.

Everything is going well but there is something bothering me, niggling, and I can't quite put my finger on it. I look around and catch Frederick examining Courtney with interest. God damn. Of course. I should have thought – they are two of a kind. By chance, she glances his way. He catches her eye and smiles. She colours. Uh, oh. She's been tied to the stake, chained to the wall. Frederick wants her. Oh, hell.

While 'beautiful' is a word I am loath to use to describe Courtney, the fact remains that she is. However, her face is slightly peculiar. She has what you might call 'good bones' – high cheekbones and all that – but her features, though fine, have a slightly cramped quality, as though her conceit is so potent and condensed that it mildly distorts her face. Frederick has nevertheless zeroed in on her. Whether or not he will follow through, I don't know. But we are displeased.

I'm beginning to think that I may be in a worse position than before. She wants James. Frederick wants her. Nobody wants me, as usual. Even Zero seems to have got lucky; he's cornered a woman by the restrooms. Granted, she looks like she's trying to get away. But still . . .

The problem is, if Courtney triumphs, she will be around for the rest of my life. I haven't even decided whether or not I could put up with her for a day – I'm beginning to think that she may be worse than April. She and James are off in a world of their own, the kind of kingdom only people with a shared passion can inhabit. She may not be an expert in the field of ethics, but she will say anything she has to in order to claim him as her own. There is no doubt in my mind that she wants him very badly. And who wouldn't? Guys fall into two categories, 'boyfriend material' and 'fling material'. Frederick is classic 'fling material', dangerous and thrilling, if you're willing to pay the price. James is ideal 'boyfriend material', being handsome yet modest, desirable yet faithful, strong yet sensitive, romantic yet not ridiculous. High potential earning power. Fiscally responsible, yet generous when it comes to major gift-giving occasions. A status symbol, a trophy husband, the kind you hang on to at all costs. Courtney loves a fling, that's clear, but as a successful career girl she requires a mate.

While getting rid of April is proving difficult, exterminating Courtney would be impossible, I suspect. I may have an even bigger problem on my hands. She's like a cockroach. Moves swiftly. Is fast, hard-shelled, cunning, indestructible. And talk about being frozen out – Courtney probably wouldn't let me back into the house. Would have the locks changed again and again, until I got the message. As for April, she would be well and truly banished. No solar system could tolerate two suns.

If I think *I'm* in a mess, all I have to do is look at April. Staring hard at James, willing him to look her way. It's not that he's ignoring her. It's that Courtney is singing her song, drawing him into the water. He has no choice but to obey.

'Why don't you tell everyone about your new job, James?' April says with a tight smile. Smart – I have to hand it to her. She knows Courtney will find it off-putting. Except that Courtney is even more clever than that. She will retaliate with a quizzical smile, get James to explain himself, have him back in Berkeley so fast it would make your head swim. Never underestimate your enemy.

James laughs. 'I'm working for the township.' *He* doesn't have a problem with being a 'garbage guy', of course. 'I'm –'

'Saw a great show on TV last night.' I have to cut him off, spin things around in a different direction. '"Real-Life Animal Rescue Stories". Anyone else catch it?'

'What exactly do *you* do?' asks Courtney, peering at April as though she is slightly peculiar.

April blushes. 'I –'

James interrupts: 'She makes jewellery.' Saves her from humiliation like a knight in shining armour. But April looks indignant, as though she's been betrayed. If only she knew what Courtney would have done with a choice tidbit like HerbElixir.

'Oh, jewellery,' says Courtney boredly, as though she's about

161

to call it a day. 'I love jewellery. You'll have to show me some of your stuff.'

Frederick is getting restless. I suspect he's sliding his hand up Courtney's thigh. I consider plunging a fork into his forearm. But this would not be politic.

'I have an idea,' says James, to April and Courtney. You can almost see the light bulb. 'Why don't the two of you get together sometime? April has expressed an interest in art history . . .' She has? '. . . and Courtney, you love design. April's handiwork is very interesting. She studied with the Abudabu Indians and I think you can clearly see their influence on her work.'

Dear God – he's decided that they ought to be friends. His logic dawns on me. Another protector for April. He's recruited me, now he's recruiting Courtney – a whole group of educated chaperones for his girl. Typical James, delegating responsibility. When is he going to learn?

Courtney nods graciously, all smiles and *noblesse oblige*. I have to make a decision. If I get rid of April, Courtney stays. If I get rid of Courtney, April stays. Now I'm *really* screwed. What am I to do? Lock them in a room together and see if they destroy each other? Think of some grand scheme to get rid of both of them at once? No. I can't take any chances. It's going to have to be one at a time. Courtney is the mightier foe – that much is obvious. She's the one who's got to go. As for April, I'll think of something. Later.

'Tell you what, Courtney,' says James. 'We're planning a trip to the Art Museum this Sunday. We'll probably get there about ten and begin with the Middle Ages. It's sort of a family excursion, but you'd be welcome to come along.'

This is even more extreme than I thought. If I'm not mistaken, he's beginning to see her as some kind of mentor for the girl. Is he totally clueless? Does he have any idea what is really going on?

'I'll think about it,' says Courtney, playing hard to get. April looks sick – her wonderful idea has been ruined. And I'm doomed. Somehow I know, I just know, that Courtney will show up. And what hope do I have against Lucrezia Borgia?

'Well, I'd love to stick around,' says Courtney, 'but I have to get going. I play the cello and I'm taking some master classes.'

162

James sits up straighter; he loves the cello. 'With whom?'

'Antonio Sartorietti.'

James looks impressed. *'Really.'*

'Yes. He's in town for a few days. I also play piano and guitar.'

'Ukelele, harpsichord, didjeridoo,' says James. I'd say he was smitten. 'Plus I dabble in French horn and African thumb piano.'

'Xylophone, me,' says Zero. 'And air guitar.'

'I played the flute.'

April has spoken. Five heads turn.

'Classical?' asks Courtney, feigning interest.

Embarrassed, April says, 'I don't know. They gave us all kinds of music to learn. I was in the school band –'

Amused look from Courtney, subtle tap on the table. April blushes. Then . . .

Frederick speaks. 'You mean, you marched?'

'Played and marched, marched and played. It was pretty dumb, I guess. We had to stomp around in patterns at football games but we sucked, we always came in last at competitions. The cheerleaders got all the attention –'

'I was a cheerleader,' says Courtney, interrupting. You were *not*. You *lie*. Will she stop at nothing?

'I love marching,' says Frederick, suddenly animated and alive, taking more interest in her than he has in anyone all afternoon. 'Tell me – how would you describe your uniforms?'

'Well –' April is flustered. 'They were kind of dorky, to tell you the truth. Green with an orange stripe down the side of the pants and big fuzzy hats like those things you clean your ears with –'

'Will you go to bed with me?' says Frederick. April gasps. Courtney slams her glass down. James whips around, stands, sits, knocks his drink off the table. I bury my head in my hands.

'Um, thanks, Frederick, I'm really flattered but James and I are –' April turns to me, alarmed.

'Don't mind Freddie,' I say. 'He has a little fetish about military history.'

'You and James are what?' Courtney demands. Frederick (her back-up) has been diverted, and now she is about to be informed that James is unavailable, wrested away from his own by a lower-class girl who is only there by consent.

'We're –'

'*What?*'

'We're going to have a baby.'

The way she says it, I know she is telling the truth. Courtney's face fills with horror and disgust. James, white-faced, turns to the mother of his future child with trembling courtesy and terror.

April sees his expression and does not seem to know what to say. And, as in most cases where a person does not know what to say, she says the wrong thing entirely.

'Surprise, honey.'

Wrong place, wrong time. Couldn't be wronger. James is reeling, falling, clutching at the sides of the hole he has dug for himself.

'And James –' April is starting to babble. 'James is working for the township as a garbage collector and I figure with a steady job we can get a mortgage and buy our own little home and raise a family. I've really enjoyed spending time with all of you but we've got to save money so we're not going to be going out much in future! I don't want to be a working mom, I want to be like James's mom and stay home and raise the kids – I think they turn out so much better that way, don't you? Ha, ha! James's mom will be around to help us out of course and so will mine, some of the time, because although she's really busy and lives far away she's going to want to be really, really involved with her grandchildren. And there'll be pre-natal classes and post-natal classes and who knows, I might even have twins. My mother had twins. The other ran away. Sometimes I dream of finding her . . .'

Courtney looks as though she thinks girls like April ought to be sterilized. Frederick is picking his nails and Zero is already shaking hands: 'Hey, congratulations, you two. Way to go. James – you sly devil.'

As for James . . . I don't like the expression on his face at all. He is calm. As though he's already decided, on some level, that this is not his problem.

Poor April. Victim of her fear of saying the wrong thing.

Devo is once again on the jukebox. Zero is back to being Zero, singing along, accompanying himself on the air guitar. ' "We're though – *being cool banananana*, we're through – *being cool banananana* –" '

164

'Zero, you're completely retarded,' says Courtney. This insult is produced like a sweet poisonous fig. He looks hurt.

I wonder what is going through her head. I suspect nasty visions of scalpels and suction. No doubt she sees April as responsible for this little hitch in James's rise to the top and will take it upon herself to put things right. I would guess that she imagines it her duty to save him. She's sunk her claws in and doesn't intend letting go. I'm doomed. So is April. And everything inside her.

9

'A *baby?*' shouts James. 'You're *twenty-three.*'

'Don't make me sound like some kind of pregnant teenager,' says April indignantly. 'And I'm not deaf. Yes, I'm going to have a baby.'

I am in my bedroom with my door slightly ajar, listening to James and April. They don't know I'm there.

'But how did it happen?' he says. I can't tell whether he sounds more outraged or baffled. 'I thought you were on the –'

'No, no, I ran out, remember? I was using one of those great big spongy things so you wouldn't have to use a condom. They're not one hundred per cent effective, you know. Didn't you read the leaflet?'

'Keep your voice down,' James hisses. 'I don't think my mother needs to find out this way.'

He's acting like a dick, I have to admit. But what can you do? Guys will be guys.

'Stop treating me like I've shamed you,' says April hotly. 'This is not the Fifties. I'm going to have a baby. It's a beautiful –'

'It's not "beautiful", April, it's stupid.' He sounds incredulous. 'I've always credited you with a considerable amount of intelligence, but perhaps I've been overly generous.'

He's really changed his colours. I cannot quite believe my ears. He's saying just about the worst thing he could say to her – that he doubts her mental capacity.

'You're trying to make out like this is all my fault,' says April. 'You think I got pregnant on purpose.'

'Well, maybe you did.'

'Oh, yes, that must be it – "girl gets pregnant to catch a man".

166

Do you really think I'm that dumb? How could you say such a thing? Anyway, you must have known that I was using birth control – that thing was as big as a doughnut.'

She has a point, I have to admit. It's interesting how the guy always manages to blame the girl. I consider the boys I've known, and I think I can guess what is going through James's head: go away/I can't deal with this/it's nothing to do with me. It's disappointing that he's behaving in such a predictable manner, but then, he's only human. Surely he's entitled to save himself. To act in the interests of self-preservation.

'There is nothing wrong with getting pregnant, April.' His voice is low and patient, tightly controlled. 'It's just that it's dismal timing.'

'But why?' she demands.

'Because we don't have any money,' he says, as though speaking to an imbecile.

'You have a job.'

'It pays *minimum wage*. Anyway, I think it's only fair to tell you that I'm not quite so enamoured of it now.'

'But you said you enjoyed it.'

'It had novelty value.'

You were slumming, you mean. Admit it, James – it was a trip to the Cotton Club.

'I was thinking maybe your parents could help us out,' suggests April.

'Why should they help us out?' he says. 'I love this breathtaking assumption that people are going to "help" us. I guess this is what they refer to as the welfare mentality.' This from James, who used to call himself a Communist.

'I've never been on welfare in my life,' she says. 'I've worked for every penny I've ever had and so have my parents. I was talking about a loan.'

He ignores her. 'What's more, my mother is going to be less than thrilled about being roped into babysitting duties. She's talking about going back to finish her degree – which she had to suspend when she became pregnant with me, incidentally. And Dad isn't going to be overly happy, either. He works hard, and the last thing he needs to hear in the evening is a baby wailing.'

'You're clutching at straws, Jimmy,' says April. She sounds

close to tears. 'You're trying to make it sound like I've done something wrong.'

'Oh, well, fine,' he says. 'Have the baby. It'll work out just great. I'll moonlight as a janitor, you can play the happy housewife . . .'

I'm beginning to get a bit bored with this. I have a feeling it will continue in the same vein for quite some time. Doesn't sound like I have much to worry about, actually – James sounds sufficiently outraged. Maybe it's time to slip out and get a burger.

'You know, April . . .' He sounds tired and resigned. 'I don't think there was ever really anything between us. We never had a future. It was just wishful thinking on my part. Maybe we should cut our losses –'

'Okay,' she says brightly, 'let's do that.' I hear footsteps. The sound of drawers being yanked open. 'Take that, and that, and that.' Items are being hurled; I hear the 'plop' as they hit human flesh. 'Take all those crappy gifts you gave me. They meant a lot to me at first. You made me feel like I was worth something, but it was all false, wasn't it, Jimmy? Gifts are easy to give – anyone with money can do that. But you never gave of yourself.'

'I did love you,' he says, 'in my way.'

'Well, hell, Jimmy, anyone can love the way you do – you just *stop* when the going gets tough. I should have known better, I really should have known . . .'

Puddles has crept in and is trying to climb up into my lap. I push her away but she's persistent. It's like she's trying to tell me something. Starts to whimper. Oh, no. I try to shoosh her, muzzle her with my hand. This is all I need.

'Look, you're right,' says James – sounding frighteningly like Dad when he's about to make a concession that will be to his advantage. 'This is all my fault. You deserve better than me. Maybe you should just go back to your parents and –'

'Oh, you *wish*,' says April. 'Nice try, but it isn't going to work. Don't give me that I'm-not-worthy-of-you crap. By the time I'm through with you, by God, you're going to know yourself a whole lot better than you do now. You need to take a good hard look at yourself, because you are well and truly screwed up. It's time you learned to love, Jimmy. What are you so afraid of?'

'I think it might be best if you went home,' says James. 'I'll give you some money – '

'*What* home, Jimmy? You know what my "home" is like. I'd sleep on the street rather than go back there.'

'It would be a stepping stone.'

'*I am carrying your child.*'

Judging from the stunned silence, I think she may have finally gotten through to him.

'What's more,' she adds, 'I think you really want this baby.'

'You give me too much credit,' he says flatly. 'I don't.'

I hate to say it, but even I don't believe him. I remember him saying that he'd love to be a dad. I can't figure out *what* is going through his head – and neither, it seems, can April. She has no leverage, no trump card to pull. Finally, she says, 'I thought you were different. I honestly thought you were caring.'

'Well, maybe I'm not who you think I am,' he says. 'Perhaps you had it wrong all along.'

This stops her short. She starts to speak, stutters, trips over her words. 'You're trying to turn everything around, Jimmy, make me feel like I've been living in some kind of fairy tale. Well, I may not have had an expensive education, but I'm not afraid to say what I think, and I think you ought to know that *I can see right through you.* You made up the fairy tale, not me. Rescued me, painted a picture of your perfect home, promised to whisk me away to paradise. You wanted to play the good guy, Mr Ethics, because the people at the soup kitchen thought you had a rod up your butt and you had to prove them wrong. You can't just throw me away, pretend that I'm the self-deluded one. I'm not going to let you. *For your own good . . .* '

'Let me decide what's good for me, April, will you?' says James. 'Because at the very least, I think you've demonstrated extremely bad judgement, and I don't think you're in any position to save my soul.'

He's being really hard on her – even *I'm* having difficulty listening. It clashes with my image of him as honourable and good. I wonder what the porcelain Jesuses are making of all this. Puddles squirms. I can smell something cooking. My mother must be downstairs.

'Becoming a father would be good for you,' April maintains. 'You'd grow up real fast, let me tell you.'

'You mean, like *your* dad?' he says with a kind of false admiration.

'Yeah. Like my dad. And my mom.'

'Okay, let's go over a few things about your family.' He speaks as though ticking facts off on his fingers. 'Dad's a mechanic, Mom's a drunk, you were an accident –'

'Stop it –'

'– and if I recall correctly,' he continues, 'you were born in the family car on the way to the hospital, which is just as well because your mother didn't have health insurance and they probably wouldn't have let her in, anyway. Am I right? Does this ring a bell?'

Judging from April's tone of voice, James has touched a nerve. 'Don't act like they did something wrong.'

This doesn't stop him. 'The pressure drove your mother to attempt suicide – one of many attempts over the years, I believe – and your father to give the landlord a crack in the mouth, an act which culminated in an eviction notice. They took very good care of you, didn't they?'

'Hey – they may not have had an easy life or a lot of money, but they did the best they could, which is more than I can say for people like you.'

'Excuse me?'

'Oh, you know what I mean. Look at Zero. His father is an astro-physicist and hates him. Frederick's dad produced a little fascist. Your father worked all the time when he didn't have to, he never even *played* with you –'

'You don't know anything about my family.'

'The hell I don't. It's time you faced some home truths, James. My parents may have problems but at least they can admit to them.'

'Sure they do. Communication is their strong point. As I understand it, they yell at each other all the time –'

'*Yes* – they do. And you know what? I respect that. It's honest. They may argue, but at least they don't try to pretend that everything's all right.'

'Anyone can let it all hang out – that's easy.'

'No, Jimmy, it takes courage to be able to say something's wrong. They've been through stuff your parents probably think only happens in Third World countries but when the going got tough they struggled, *fought the good fight* under circumstances that would destroy most people and by God I bet that's more than your parents would do.'

'My parents would do whatever was necessary to protect us –'

'Oh, would they? Let me tell you, James, I'm less than impressed with your family life. It seemed perfect at first but after a while I started to notice that things weren't all they seemed. The packaging was nice, everyone was very polite, but on the inside something was rotting and I was the only one who seemed to notice the smell. Like your mother. Nobody seemed to realize she was unhappy – or if they did, they didn't bother to find out why. And your dad – he's miserable. He tells those silly jokes to try and hold his life together. Neither one of them has ever achieved a single dream, not one. Even their marriage has turned into a ghost. As for you, you let them bully you into being an academic. Why do you think they did that? Because they loved you? *I* think they wanted to be able to say, "We have a son at Princeton or Harvard or Yale" in an effort to fill the hole in their *own* lives. You didn't have the guts to stand up to them, to think for yourself –'

'April.'

'And your little brother is a mole, he never comes out of the basement, he's completely demented, he doesn't have any friends . . . To be perfectly frank, the only normal member of this household is Ellen.'

'Ellen?'

I do not appreciate his you-must-be-joking tone of voice.

'Yes, *Ellen*. She's the only one I feel comfortable with – the only one who really listens, who doesn't try to get me to live up to some improved, ideal version of myself. It's called *unconditional love*, James, and I love her right back. With the rest of you I end up feeling like there's something wrong with me . . .'

Unconditional love.

She loves me unconditionally.

No one has ever loved me . . . in spite of everything.

171

'The only thing I regret,' says April, 'is that I haven't been able to do as much for her as she's done for me.'

This knowledge hits me in the head like an anvil. If what she says is true, she never wanted me out at all – quite the contrary. My image of April as usurper has just been shattered. I feel like I'm being sucked backwards into a hole. My head is spinning. I've made a grave error. Alarm bells are going off.

'Maybe we ought to discuss what we're going to do,' says James.

'What do you mean, "do"?' asks April.

'It doesn't have to be this way,' says James. 'I think it's important to point out the alternatives.'

'Like what?'

There is a short, painful silence. 'Well . . .' He clears his throat. 'There's a clinic – a very highly regarded one – just on the other side of town.'

The clinic. I've seen the place – and the two dozen or so protestors who stand around impaling people on picket signs.

'Oh, I see, a mercy killing,' says April. 'Keep the race pure.'

'That's not what I meant.'

'After all,' she continues, 'it'll be a half-breed. Part you, part me – and we can't have that.'

'Look, April, I know your religious convictions may –'

'My religious convictions have nothing to do with it. You people don't have feelings. Oh, you're willing to take responsibility if you're forced to, but if you can wiggle out of it –'

'It's a question of *timing*,' he says.

'Well, I'm sorry if it's inconvenient. You know, I can have this baby with or without you, so why don't I just go? Then you'll be free to do what you want. Screw Courtney, maybe. *That's* what you want, isn't it? I showed you what to do and now you want somebody better. I was something to practise on.'

'I only want you to know all your options.'

'Oh, I get it – you were doing me a favour. Well, let me tell you a little story about that particular option. My parents were hard-working people. They had dreams, like anyone else, but Fate had a hand against them. No matter how hard they tried, everything they ever attempted went wrong. The trucking business they tried to start, the farm they invested in . . . they'd

172

begin all hopeful and optimistic only to be slapped in the face. Anyway, they ended up broke because my dad had quit his job and they'd used up all their savings. And Mom was pregnant.'

'I'm sorry, April,' says James. 'I can only imagine –'

'I haven't finished,' she says abruptly. 'When my dad found out she was going to have a baby, do you know what he did? I'll tell you. He went straight back to his old bully boss – the one who'd treated him like dirt, the one he'd told to go to hell *and he asked for his old job back.* It was his dream to be his own boss, but he gave it up. For my mother and me. He didn't run away. He chose love.'

'Like I said, April –'

'The problem,' April continues, 'was that my mother chose love, too. She didn't want him to give up his dream, so she decided to get rid of the baby. Soon, before they had time to get attached to it. She had no money, not even the bus fare. So she did it herself.'

Dear God.

'While he was at work . . .'

No one should have to make choices like that. It never occurred to me . . .

Of course it didn't. These things happen elsewhere.

'. . . she took care of it.'

I'm part of it, that's the worst thing. I've wounded the vulnerable. Better Courtney with her twisted patronage than me.

I have committed a crime against humanity.

'What my mother didn't know,' says April, 'was that she was still pregnant.'

The twins. She'd mentioned that her mother had had twins.

'In other words,' she says, 'she goofed – got one but not the other. She's tall and big-boned, so she just thought she was getting fatter. When her periods stopped, she figured it was because she'd screwed up her insides. A few months later, she went into labour.'

I suddenly recall a small snapshot of my mother inside a hospital, holding me in her arms. Beaming, doctors hovering. My father nearby, clowning around with a cigar.

'So that's me, James,' April says, as though she's finished a

173

sandwich and is licking her fingers. 'The product of a botched abortion.'

There is a long pause. 'I suppose she told you this when she was drunk,' James remarks.

April carries on, almost to herself. 'I used to think that when it happened, the *termination*, the soul of my dead sister went into me – that I was born with two souls, like some people have a third thumb or six toes. But then I got to thinking that maybe her soul was given to someone else, a stranger, born at roughly the same time as she passed on. That's why I started travelling around the country. It wasn't just to get away from home. I figured if I went down the road and had faith, I would find her. My sister. The spirit of my twin.'

Oh, April. What a strange grail you seek.

'Sometimes,' she says, 'I felt like I could hear her talking to me. Leading me onwards, you know, giving me clues. When I ended up in California, homeless and broke, I thought, "That's okay – it's meant to be." Then I met you, and when you offered to take me home, I figured this must be it, the home stretch. My search is almost over.'

'April,' says James, 'I wish you'd told me all this before –'

Shut up, James.

'You were my guardian angel,' she says, 'but it was Ellen who clinched it for me. I felt like I *knew* her – I could almost hear her thoughts. There was this strange connection between us that I couldn't really account for. You probably think I'm some kind of flake-case, but I swear to God I believed this was why I'd been brought here – that this was my destiny and that Ellen was my twin.'

A few days ago, I would have regarded this as the ultimate insult. Now all I want is to collect broken glass with my bare fingers. I've got to undo the damage that I've done, but how?

'I never believed my mother really wanted me,' she says. 'It's awful growing up thinking you were a mistake. You have to understand, this is why I joined the church. I wanted to be born again. *Born again.* What a wonderful phrase. I wasn't supposed to be born at all, you see. I was given a second chance.'

The silence emanating from that room is as tranquil as a funeral

174

parlour. A moment later I hear James stumble downstairs, muttering, banging his head against the wall.

My opinion of him has plummeted. I wouldn't have thought he was capable of sounding so incredibly self-righteous and hard. It seems so out of character. But then, did I ever really know him? James and his cereal boxes. Christ. Poor guy. The victim of his own dwarfed capacity for love. Instead of cultivating it, he tried to uproot it and it backfired. There are some things you can't get rid of, and if you try, you pay the price.

I wonder if I should go in to see her, let her know I'm there if she needs me. But what right do I have to think that I might offer comfort? And what on earth could I possibly say?

That old saying comes back to me: be careful what you ask for . . .

Wise words.

I need a systematic plan.

'Jesus.'

The word startles me out of my deliberations.

'He knows not what he does,' says April. She is praying aloud. 'He's so smart, so gifted . . . I don't think he's in his right mind. It hurts so much to see him like this. I can hardly bear to watch –' Her voice catches, trembles. 'It's not his fault.'

I don't believe this. She actually feels sorry for him.

'Please, Lord,' she says, 'if there's anything I can do to make it better for him, help me do it. Please help me to help him. Even if it means I have to sin.'

Sin? As if she could possibly . . .

What might she have in mind?

I'm beginning to realize what James is afraid of. Once you love someone, you risk losing them – there is suddenly something at stake. Thereafter, you live your life in fear. You never stop suffering.

James is cracking, that's for sure, but that doesn't mean he can't be saved. It's a big job, though – I'm going to need back-up. There's only one thing to do. Recruit.

I follow the aroma of baking. 'Mom?'

She comes out of the kitchen, wiping her hands. Her spectacles are all steamed up. 'Hello, Ellen.'

'Hi. Listen, I've got to talk to you. Re: James. I wanted to ask – has he seemed okay to you lately? I mean, normal?'

She gives me her most tactful look. 'Normal? Oh, Ellen. He's never been *normal.*'

I'd forgotten that in my mother's book, being normal is a *bad* thing. 'Normal in terms of behaviour, I mean.'

'In what sense?'

'In –' For God's sake. '*Normal*. You know. Just normal.'

'Well, yes, I think so.'

She's wearing one of her own knitwear creations. It's got two extra sleeves flopping around the back. I indicate them. 'Are those for the two extra arms you claim you're expected to have?' She looks at me quizzically, but she's pulled that one before. I don't fall for it. 'Seriously, Mom. I'm worried about him.'

'Does this concern April?'

'No. Not exactly. He's just been acting a bit . . . moody.'

'Ah.' She nods sagely. 'The Family Melancholia.'

'*What?*'

'It hasn't re-surfaced for several generations.' She begins folding freshly laundered clothes and putting them into a basket. 'It was bound to pop up sooner or later. I wouldn't worry about it, Ellen. It's perfectly harmless.'

'It's not melancholia, it's schizophrenia. He's banging his head against the wall.'

'Oh, Ellen. He's just brooding.'

'Yes, I *know* he's brooding – that's the problem.' I don't seem to be getting through to her. 'Okay. Look. April. He feels very strongly about her. He's not used to that so he's suppressing it and it's re-entering his system and clogging it up. Like the carbon monoxide when the chimney got blocked. We almost died. Remember?'

'I think you've watched too many episodes of "This Old House".'

She's humouring me. I give up. Clearly her newly awakened rapport with her husband has not affected her policy towards her eldest son. But maybe she's just afraid of changing the status quo – after all, it's worked up until now. 'Fine. Forget it. Forget I said anything.'

She picks up the basket of laundry. 'Ellen, seriously. Leave it alone, whatever it is. If you're really worried about him, try to get him to do something. Engage him in some useful activity.'

Useful activity. My mother's solution to everything. Wait till she learns about the baby. Plenty of opportunity for 'activity' there. 'Couldn't you just have a word with him? Ask him if everything's all right?'

At that moment, April appears. Her hair has been brushed but her eyes are swollen. I fleetingly glimpse a resemblance to her mother. 'Hi, guys. What's up?'

'You don't have to explain,' I blurt out. 'I know all about it. I overheard.'

She looks at me as though she doesn't know what I'm talking about. 'I'm going roller-skating,' she whispers, 'with some people from the church.'

'Oh.' I don't believe for one minute that she's in the mood for roller-skating. 'Can I tag along?'

'I don't think so, Ellen. They've all been "Born Again" and I don't think you'd get along.'

Yeah, right. She's up to something, and I need to find out what it is. 'I don't suppose you have time for a cup of Java?'

'No. I'm late.' With a small smile, she slips out the door.

I turn to my mother. Tense every muscle, grit my teeth: *'Mom.'*

'She's a bit tired, Ellen. That doesn't mean anything.'

I am tempted to reveal the pregnancy but it's not my news to tell. 'You've got to talk to James.'

'I don't think that would be a good idea. You know I've always believed in letting my children lead their own lives.'

'Yes, but I'm concerned he's leading his own and several others, too.'

'He'll be all right. James always is.'

'Not this time, Mom. I'm telling you, he's having trouble expressing his feelings. That's not healthy, you know. I think we're witnessing the fruits of years of pent-up emotions, the by-products of repression. He could become downright dangerous.'

'Now you're being absurd, Ellen. If he wants to talk, he'll do it of his own accord. I think he should act of his own free will, don't you?'

'Yes, but I'd like him to open up before we have to have him committed, ideally.'

She laughs, hands me the laundry basket. 'Take that upstairs, would you?'

This is clearly not going to work. What am I going to do? My considerable mental resources have deserted me. I feel a small head ramming itself into my ankles. It is Puddles, trying to get my attention again. There is a piece of paper sticking out of her collar. I pull it out and unfold it.

A message is written in green ink. 'Follow her,' it reads.

Follow her. Of course. Why didn't I think of that? I don't stop to speculate upon the sender. I am out the door in two seconds, hot on her trail. It's probably not too late to catch her if I hurry.

The Philmont Roller Rink is located on the outskirts of town and is kind of an oasis of sleaze. It stands, in all its neon-lit glory, in the middle of a gravelly wasteland littered with crumpled pizza boxes and empty soda cans. Groups that make use of the facility tend to fall into identifiable categories – sales reps, nurses, paralegals, members of all the local evangelical Christian churches – the sort of people who travel in packs, all in search of a good time. It's about a mile from our house. The quickest route is through a series of shabby back streets dotted with shrubbery and downmarket cars, so it should be easy to trail her without being seen.

But who should I see padding in my direction at a frantic pace but Puddles, little Puddles, determined not to be left behind. 'For God's sake,' I growl, and lift her to eye level.

'Listen,' I hiss. 'You're going to ruin everything. I have work to do, so make like an egg. Understand?'

I put her down. Predictably, my words have no effect whatsoever. She immediately tries to follow. I shoo her away but she won't go. I give up, and continue on my way, Puddles trailing so close to my feet that I trip over her several times.

It's disconcerting to be walking through one of the less salubrious parts of town. The houses are small and mostly semi-detached, with that look of decay you find in neighbourhoods where people live from pay cheque to pay cheque like acrobats who take a leap of faith every time they let go of one rope to grab another. I spot April ahead of me, walking slowly, glancing occasionally from side to side. Puddles, unfortunately, has spotted her too and gets rather excited – April is, after all, her saviour. I scoop her up, clamp my hand around her little nose and mouth, and proceed, ducking behind the occasional car.

April, from the back, looks sad and doubtful, reluctant and weary. She's certainly not in any hurry to get where she's going. Every so often, she sort of sprints forward a few yards as though she's given herself a kick in the pants. Then she stops and catches her breath, as though she can hardly bear to go any further. At one point, she stumbles. Looks so dejected that it is all I can do to refrain from running out and picking her up.

We reach the turnpike, a wide stretch of highway that leads out of town. It's a bit ghoulish – smooth surface, bright green grass on either side. A phone booth appears in the distance, one I can't recall having noticed before. April makes her way towards it, trudging up a slight hill.

Who could she possibly be calling? And why would she call from a booth rather than from the comfort of home? I creep around to the side and hide behind a tree, observe her thumbing coins into the slot. She punches in eleven numbers. I can see her profile. The tip-tilted nose, the pert little chin. A lift of her head indicates that she's made her connection.

It soon becomes clear that something is wrong. Her manner is forced. She is trying too hard. A kind of hyper-realism has set in. As words are exchanged, her shoulders rise. She clutches the receiver harder and harder. Continues trying to smile, keeps failing, until she looks nothing short of desperate. She stands very still for a moment, then runs out of the booth. The receiver dangles behind her.

Now's my chance. I approach the telephone. Hear a voice, a woman's, with a strong regional twang. She is screaming. Irrational. Out of control.

'I know you're there. Don't walk away from me, you slut. Who the hell do you think you are?'

I feel cold, as though I've walked into a freezer and know the door is going to shut behind me.

'You thought you could run away. Everything that's happened

179

to you serves you right. Thought you were too good for us, didn't you? *Listen to me when I'm talking to you.*'

This last line is shrieked. I back away, unnerved, as though I've just encountered something evil.

Puddles hops around, whimpering, then runs ahead as though trying to lead me on. I follow, with that fast walk you use when you're desperate to go to the toilet. She flies on, looking back occasionally to make sure that I am right behind her.

Inside, the rink is dimly lit. The floor is grimily tiled and the walls are of cheap wood panelling that clearly hasn't been replaced in a very long time. There is a sense of shuffling and milling and a smell of locker room. I look around for April – maybe she really is meeting somebody. I spot-check the most likely crowds, examining one in particular that consists mainly of fresh-faced youths wearing tee-shirts covered with big bloody nails and quotes such as, 'Do it through your deeds'. But no cigar.

Then I spot her. I try to get through to her, sensing that she is in real distress, but there are hordes of paralegals in the way, swarming around as though deliberately trying to block my path. One of them is balancing a Styrofoam cup of hot chocolate on his forehead: 'Hey, guys, check this out.' Another is attempting to climb up on to a colleague's shoulders. In the meantime, April is entering the rink. I try to get in without skates, only to be stopped by a pompous self-appointed watchdog. 'S'not allowed,' he says. I start to claw my way through to the 'Skate Rental' counter, only to discover that he's following me, smitten, and has decided to make himself indispensable.

'I can get you roller skates for free,' he brags.

'Piss off,' I say. There is a roaring in my ears. The paralegals are cheering as one of their party performs a striptease up on one of the benches. One of the senior citizen crowd starts talking to me about the great time she had last night with some guy, and won't shut up. The man behind the counter seems to sense that I need help – holds up a pair of skates with a questioning look. I nod. He tosses them over.

I find myself on a large polished floor where people are whizzing round and round. April is circling the core. Her skating is concentrated, frenzied, almost as though she is trying to destroy herself. I've got to save her, stop her before she self-destructs.

The Big Friendly Guy is after me again. He's light on his feet, I have to admit. 'I wouldn't get too close,' he says. Makes a grab for me.

'Let go,' I shout. We struggle. By now, April is suicide-skating, working her way closer and closer to the middle. I pull away and take my skates off, make my way towards her. She's spinning fast, dead centre, face serene, as though this is the moment of truth.

Then she falls.

The skaters who'd cleared away to make room for her gather round. The Big Friendly Guy steps in; I give him a kick that sends him flying. Loop April's arm around my shoulder, help her out to the rest area. She sits there, staring straight ahead, her face immobile, frozen, like a mermaid trapped in ice.

'It hurts,' she says.

'What, your ankle?'

'Being alive. It's like walking on knives.'

I fidget. Twist around. Rack my brains for a reply. Scrutinize the noticeboard as though it might provide me with the right words.

'Jimmy doesn't love me, does he,' she says.

What should I say what should I say what should I say –

'It's all right,' she says. 'Don't worry about it.'

He loves her so much he's about to self-destruct. 'April, no. You don't know him as well as I do. He's just –'

'I thought I could lose it,' she says. 'The baby. Lose it . . . naturally, you know. I figured it would solve everyone's problems.'

She'd been trying to . . . oh. I shiver.

'I tried calling my mother,' says April, 'to see if I could go home for a while, but she didn't seem too happy to hear from me. I wish I could undo the past, Ellen. My life's been one long series of errors . . .'

The ice cracks, shatters. The tears rise out of her skin like beads of blood. ›

And strangely, unexpectedly, like rusty water from an unused tap, it comes. From me. Sympathy.

April doesn't seem to want to be touched. I limp to the counter and get her a cup of tea. It comes in one of those chewy Styrofoam cups. I add milk and sugar, stir it with a plastic stick. Hand it to her. Awkwardly.

'When I told her about the baby,' says April, 'she didn't handle it very well. I guess it took her by surprise. I should have prepared her a little bit beforehand. She . . . I don't know . . . she sees it as some sort of abandonment. Of her. She sees everything that way.'

She is starting to shake. Now is the moment. *Do it.* I take her hand. Her fingers, trembling like a crab that knows its claws are about to be torn off, close around mine.

'I don't blame her, you know.' April wipes her eyes. 'If you knew her, you'd understand. She has problems.'

Problems? She has a personality disorder. My mother may be deranged but at least she manages to keep it within certain parameters.

'I want it desperately, this baby,' says April, 'and what's more, I know Jimmy wants it, too. He reacted badly, but that was just shock. I shouldn't have sprung it on him like that. My mouth took on a life of its own.'

'That Courtney is truly repulsive,' I say.

April manages a thin giggle. 'Do you think he likes her?'

'No.'

She digests this. I don't think she altogether believes me, but I feel confident that it's true. What would he see in someone like that? She's the sort of person we used to laugh about together. This doesn't stop me from being disgusted with his behaviour, though. How could he have acted the way he did? I'd chalked it up to temporary insanity, but maybe that's giving him too much credit. Maybe he really is a jerk.

'Look, April,' I say. 'I'm going to be getting a heap of dough . . . hopefully . . . for this article I'm writing –'

'How's that going, by the way?' she says.

'Fine. But it means I'll be able to help you out financially. If you want to start over again somewhere, I mean . . .' I falter. What if she thinks I'm trying to get rid of her?

But she seems to sense my good intentions. 'That's okay, Ellen. You know, I don't think that's the solution. That thing I tried to pull just now? It was the easy way out. I'm going to stick around, Ellen, lean into it. That's God's will. It isn't just the baby. You'll think this is crazy but . . . I think He wants me to save James.'

Tall order, that. I consider trying to dissuade her, but I take one look at the expression on her face and I know that I cannot change her mind. I watch the crowds go by for a while. 'I hate the sort of people who have to be in a group to have a good time,' I remark. 'How did you become such a good skater, anyway?'

'I used to go with a church club. I remember the last time I went, just before I left home. I was so happy that day. We had such fun. Then I went home to find my mother drunk, and her and my dad throwing things at each other. They broke all the glasses. We had to drink out of plastic cups after that.'

'Oh.'

We sit silently for a moment.

'Is everything all right, Ellen?'

'Absolutely.'

I hope she doesn't take this as a brush-off. I don't want to burden her with my problems. A part of me senses that she'd like me to, but it's too late now. The moment has passed. I only hope it isn't too late for everything else.

A throng of well-dressed middle-aged women pass in front of us. The librarians. I think one of them recognizes me. She nudges a colleague. Points.

'Let's get out of here,' I say. We head for the door. Outside, Puddles is waiting. Panting lightly, hoping for praise. I sigh, stoop down, and collect her. On the way home, I try to think of various ways I can become a better person. I come up with quite a few. The good news is, none of them involve giving up sex or heavy drinking.

'Ellen?' April asks. 'How did you know? That I needed you?'

I chicken out, backpedal, unused to feelings of affinity. 'Must be that psychic connection,' I joke.

'Thank you,' she says simply.

I shove my hands in my pockets. ' 'Twarn't nothin', ma'am,' I reply. And keep walking.

It's about three o'clock in the morning and I cannot get to sleep – too many things are going through my head. Will April 'save' James? What will he do about the baby? What is going to happen

183

when we go to the museum? And who is leaving the notes?

Answers are not forthcoming and I have no oracle to consult. One thing I know for sure is that I've got to get back to work. I look at the nearly blank page in the typewriter every day. I keep hoping that whoever is leaving the messages will turn up and finish the article for me, but this is clearly not about to happen. I try writing by hand but it doesn't help. The problem is, I still don't have the necessary information. I am having bad dreams about Tyler Spee, looming large and laughing loudly. I fall asleep with my head on my typewriter sometimes, and wake up with 'IBM' stamped across my forehead.

Tonight is no exception. I have picked myself up and crawled into bed, only to be stymied by insomnia. Then, just as I drift off, I hear, 'Ellen? Can I talk to you?'

Echoes of April, but the voice is deeper, less plaintive. It is James, squatting, his face level with mine.

'Big brother.' I half-sit up. 'What on earth are you doing up at this hour?'

'I've got to talk to you.'

'Really? Well, I'd love to chat, but Keanu Reeves is waiting for me in Candyland. Couldn't it wait until morning?'

The fact is, he's scaring me. There's something not quite normal in his mien. He smells really strongly of cinnamon, as he always does when he's been lying in bed, but this time around I'm finding it the tiniest bit off-putting. 'What about?'

James lifts the covers and gets in beside me. Interesting – it is usually the other way around. He's wearing polka-dot boxer shorts. 'Do you know,' I say, 'that if you'd been wearing Y-fronts for the past fifteen years, you probably wouldn't even have a sperm count?'

'Then you know how I feel about it.'

'Uh huh.'

'What has she said?'

If he reckons I'm going to tell him, he can think again. 'Nothing much. I just concluded for myself that you're acting like a *guy*.'

He seems to find this very amusing. Doesn't realize that I'm not joking. 'Oh, Ellen, I knew I could count on you.'

'To what?'

184

'Oh, you know – to make me laugh. To put things in perspective. To help me.'

Uh oh. I should have known. 'Help you with what?'

'Ellen, I'm not ready to be a dad.'

So that's it. 'Well, you should have read the leaflet, James.' I shift around. He's lying really close to me.

'I'm serious,' he says. 'There's no way I can do this. I'm just not cut out for it.'

'Oh, I don't know, James. It doesn't have to be a complete disaster. You can get married, get a better job, buy a house with aluminium siding, engage in almost constant sexual relations –'

He slaps me. Not hard, but not playfully, as he used to. 'I mean it, Ellen.'

I'm not going to let him off the hook. 'Why don't you tell her that you love her and be happy, you idiot?'

'Because someone cut my tongue out a long time ago.'

'Speaking of which, do you remember that French kiss you gave me one New Year's Eve? You were really drunk and I told you I'd never let you forget it.'

'Are you suggesting that you're going to blackmail me?'

'Oh, for goodness' sake, James, I'm joking.' He's really becoming tiresome. 'Go back to sleep. It'll all look better in the morning.'

He seems to relax a bit. 'Christ,' he says. 'Sponges.'

'Well, what do you expect from a contraceptive that looks like dim sum?'

He twitches. Suddenly turns to me. 'It's no good. I need you.' Puts his hand over my mouth as though anticipating my refusal. 'Just listen. I suggested she kill the baby, Ellen.' I try to speak. He tightens his hand. 'I told her to murder our child. I studied ethics, Ellen. I raised money for starving refugees. What is happening to me?'

Couldn't tell you, I want to say, but I'm having trouble breathing.

'I think I'm reaching a point where I can't be held accountable for my own actions,' he says. 'I was in the bathroom earlier this evening, saying to myself, "If I give her a few too many aspirin then maybe, just maybe . . ."' He jerks, as though wrestling with

185

an inner demon. 'Just look after her for me, will you? Promise that you'll be there for her if anything happens to me. Because I'm losing it, Ellen. I honestly think I'm cracking.'

All this Dr Jekyll/Mr Hyde business has got to go. I'm sick of making excuses for him. I don't believe for a minute that he's going mad. He's still capable of reason and responsibility, and I don't think it's a good idea to let him believe otherwise. I try to pull his hand away from my mouth. He takes hold of my wrist. Pins it down.

'Promise,' he says.

I have no intention . . .

I'm scared.

He crawls on top of me, crushing me. 'Promise.'

I nod. One small shake of the head. He relaxes his grip. Rolls off.

'You're the one person I can count on to do the right thing,' he says. 'I knew you'd come through for me.'

This is a side of him I've never seen. He's always protected me, never made me feel threatened or unsafe. What might he have done had I not agreed?

He gets up to go. Squints. Frowns. Rubs the back of his head as though he's not sure what just happened. Moonlight streams in behind him. Then, almost as an afterthought: 'Sleep tight.'

The bastard. He has managed to offload responsibility once again. Now I am well and truly screwed. How am I supposed to save April from being hurt by the one man she truly loves?

I don't know. But I know where to go to find out. There is one sure source of answers. Mr Last Resort himself.

'What do you think?' asks Matthew. He is holding up something brown and spongy. 'It's my latest invention. The Caffeine Sandwich, soon to be known as the Caffwich.'

The disgusting little rodent has mixed instant coffee with hot water, stirred it up with peanut butter, and spread it between two slices of bread.

'Potentially endless flavour variations and highly marketable,' says Matthew. 'Best of all, now nobody has to sleep. And who wants to sleep?'

'Matthew,' I say. 'Who would eat something like that?'

'All sorts of people. Look at that caffeinated water they came up with. Just make it fashionable and people will go for it. Create a national trend.'

'And how is a nerdy eleven-year-old going to create a national trend?'

'On the Internet. Spark a media frenzy. *Newsweek* is already interested.'

His basement, unnervingly, is almost bare. The sinister light fixtures have been removed, as has everything else except the computer, which still flickers in the middle of the room. On one wall hangs a colourful poster featuring a happy executive consuming a large roll. 'The Caffwich,' it reads. 'The Ultimate Power Food.'

'That's pathetic,' I say. 'Coffee is a drink, not a solution.'

'Coffee is the elixir vitae,' he replies. 'Beloved of CEOs, artistes, graduate students and other tired mortals. And I'm a geek, not a nerd.'

'You're a pathetic no-life.'

'Speak for yourself.'

The computer, I notice, is particularly active today. Its screen is purple and resembles a face about to explode. Every so often, hieroglyphics or a diagrammatic picture appear, scroll down rapidly and vanish. The hum seems louder than usual.

'Is that thing okay?' I ask. 'It's not going to blow up or anything, is it?'

'No. But don't get too close.'

I can't tell whether he means it or not. With Matthew, you never know. I have to say, even he looks a bit wary of it. Well, not wary, maybe, but . . . speculative. Concerned.

'Can that thing understand what I'm saying?' I joke.

'Yes.'

I guffaw loudly, in the style of Dad. It's important to believe that he's kidding. He looks hard at me, stony-faced. I stop laughing. 'You're serious, aren't you?'

Matthew doesn't answer. I guess he figures he doesn't have to, being a man with a vision and all. Or else he doesn't want to. It's funny – ordinarily he enjoys unnerving me. But he seems to have other things on his mind.

187

'So what's up, Short-and-Stupid?'

'You know, Ellen, when you set something in motion, it becomes your responsibility. Yours and yours alone, no matter what it leads anybody else to do. You're the head honcho, *ad infinitum*.'

He's examining the screen. For a moment, I think I see the keyboard working like a player piano with no help from human hands. I shake my head, rub my eyes. Look again. It must have been a trick of the light. The computer has thrown up a picture of a sunflower.

'I seem to have come at a difficult time,' I say. 'I don't want to interrupt if you're having relationship problems.'

'Ellen, I can't help you. Whatever it is, I –'

'Sure, you can,' I say. 'It concerns Life Upstairs. Remember? The one you were part of before you descended to the netherworld?'

'It's April, isn't it.'

'Yes.'

'She's pregnant.'

'Uh huh.'

'And James is acting like a jerk.'

'That's right.' I am impressed. 'Did you get all that from Deep Blue?'

'Ellen, if you go on calling him Deep Blue, you're going to hurt his feelings. I just made an educated guess. The kind any damned fool could come up with.'

'Good. Then you're willing to help me.'

'Sorry – it's beyond my control.'

'Matthew, that is just the sort of attitude that allowed fascism to flourish: "Nothing *I* can do about it, might as well turn a blind eye. Hail Vichy . . ." Is that the way you want to be?'

'Ellen, I honestly don't think interference would do any good.'

I seat myself on the edge of the table. 'Oh, no? It might do quite a lot of good, actually. When in doubt, meddle.' I turn to the computer. 'What do you think?'

'So what do you want from me?' asks Matthew.

'Information,' I say. 'I want to know what's going to happen so that I can plan. So could you tell me? *Can* you tell me?'

'No.'

'You mean, you could but you won't.'

'No, I mean I would but I can't. I'm not a fortune-teller. And it's just as well – can you imagine the state we'd be in if we all knew exactly what was going to happen?'

'You'd know whether or not to take an umbrella to work.'

'Ellen, you want everything to be easy – you always have. You've got to accept that sometimes things are going to be difficult, and that you're simply going to have to use your best judgement.'

'My best judgement isn't up to much. I'd like to take advantage of your mighty intellect and superior decision-making skills.'

'I hate to disappoint you, Ellen, but there are some things we're not meant to know. You might call it the perpetual blank card in the tarot.'

'That's awfully mystical for you, Matthew. You might be more inclined to help me if you were a little less out of touch.'

'Ellen, there isn't a thing you could tell me about this family that I don't already know. In fact, there are things I could tell you that would make your sideburns curl. You want information? I'll give you information. Ever wondered why our parents had me screened for all sorts of genetic diseases? Or why they pretend they've lost my birth certificate? Or why I don't look anything like either one of them?'

It takes me a moment to figure out what he's getting at. 'Are you trying to tell me you're *adopted*?'

'You are singularly gifted, Ellen, at putting two and two together.'

'But Mom was pregnant. I remember.'

'Are you familiar with the term "hysterical pregnancy"? It was a phantom foetus. She had her tubes tied after she had you but years later wanted a third child so much that she sort of willed herself into an apparent medical miracle. Turned out to be phoney and she freaked out, so Dad pulled some strings and got her me.'

'You mean, you and I aren't even related?'

'Nope.'

189

'Boy. Forgive me if I say that this is kind of a relief.' This accounts for a lot, actually. 'So who's your real mom?'

'Don't know.'

'Are you telling me you haven't even tried to find out?'

'Sure I have,' he says. 'But like I said, there are some things we're not meant to know. Not yet, anyway – maybe later. In the right place, at the right time.'

What right time? Judgement Day? He's way too mature for an eleven-year-old. 'I don't get it. I would have thought you could lay your hands on any information you wanted.'

'Yes, but not the really important stuff. I have access to every government secret from the name of the latest Defense Department radar-evading aircraft – "Lurker", if you're interested – to the President's ATM code, but some data is inaccessible. It's just as well, really. I have two parents too many as it is.'

'Gee, I feel like I should introduce myself,' I say. The news is still hitting me. 'Do I know you?'

'Ellen,' Matthew says, 'even if I could help you, I wouldn't. It's time you learned to accept the consequences of your actions.'

'But I have,' I protest. 'I've made great moral strides in the past twenty-four hours.'

'It's not enough. You have to learn to make the right choices. *Before* things start to go badly wrong.'

It's as though he knows everything that's happened. Sneaky little devil. There is something he's not telling me. 'You're holding back on me, Matthew.'

'All I can say is, you may have another chance to do the right thing. So don't screw it up.'

'Thank you for having so much faith in me.'

'This is based on an in-depth knowledge of your character.'

'Question.'

'Proceed.'

'Does refraining from action constitute a choice?'

'Nice try, Ellen. You're going to have to figure that one out for yourself.'

It's a great closing line, like something out of a TV movie. If I didn't know better I'd think he was about to leave, soon and for good. But he's only eleven.

'What about you?' I ask. 'What does your future hold?'

'Me? I'm clearing out.'

'What do you mean?'

'Vamoosing. Getting out before the proverbial shit hits the fan.'

He hands me a brochure. *The Cromwell School for Exceptional Children*. Oh, this is totally grotesque. It's one of those boy-wonder schools where they let you play ping-pong and read Dostoyevsky all day. I notice a little suitcase in the corner filled with tiny pairs of underwear and small striped shirts.

'You can't just send yourself to boarding school.'

'Yes, I can. I already have.'

'Mom and Dad won't let you go.'

'They will when they realize I'm making an important contribution to humanity,' he says. 'And that I'll be safer there.'

'But what about money? How will you pay the tuition?'

'The Caffwich, sis'. Its time has come. Face it, Ellen – you and James are the ones having problems, not me. It's my generation that's going to take over and, believe it or not, we know exactly what we're doing.'

I feel a genuine sense of panic. The only truly rational member of the family is about to take off, probably forever, before I've even had the chance to get to know him.

'But Matthew, you can't leave. We need you. *I* need you.'

'Ellen, you came to me for information. I've given you something infinitely more satisfying. Morality.'

I'm twelve years older than he is. I'm supposed to have formed *his* character. *Exceptional Children*. The patronizing little shit.

'One question, Matthew. Why? Why bother?'

'Because I love you.'

'You *love* me?'

'Over and out.'

'Are you sure?'

He looks away (embarrassed?) and indicates the computer. 'Ask him.'

'You really are twisted.'

'Speak for yourself, big sis'.'

My kid brother is disappearing. I can still see him but I know that he is gone. Maybe I shouldn't have asked so much of him. Should have just left him alone to follow the virtual path he's exploring on behalf of all humanity. A pilgrim trying to find his way, clicking his mouse, boldly going where the rest of us are too ignorant or afraid to go.

The computer is throwing up hearts. They float across the screen like little balloons. 'Affectionate, isn't he?' I say.

'Yeah. I think he likes you.'

'Does he have a brain?' I ask.

'No,' he says, 'but then neither did the scarecrow in "The Wizard of Oz".'

'There is one thing I could really use a hand on,' I say. 'The article. I guess I'm crap at what I do, but I can't seem to get the answers I need, the proof. If I could just get a little bit closer to Mr Grosworthy himself, I think I might stand a better chance.'

'I'll see what I can do.'

It's time to go. I mount the stairs. Turn back. 'If his name isn't Deep Blue, then what is it?'

'Bob.'

I stare at him incredulously. *Bob?*

He shrugs. 'Bob.'

I turn away again.

'Hey, Ellen,' Matthew says.

'What?'

'Don't panic.'

When I next look in, he has vanished.

My little brother is gone. Or is he? Do I detect his cyber-shadow? A little trace of Matthew-essence that will linger in the basement? Perhaps I'm sensing the Phantom Foetus – forgotten, forsaken, desperate for attention. I find myself wishing I could hold it, cradle it, sing it a lullaby.

Matthew. What am I going to do without him? Well, maybe it's time we were all on our own. It's not fair to expect an eleven-year-old to keep a household functioning smoothly.

Three days later, a package arrives by special delivery, tied with a big pink bow. Inside is a case, a sort of beat-up flaking leather carry-case that opens to reveal, wrapped in a copy of *The Philmont Organ*, a miniature tape recorder and a bulletproof vest.

There is no note, but I recognize Matthew's unmistakable style.

Goodbye, Doktorlogik.

I miss him already.

10

'Is this it?' April says. 'It's not like the picture.'

'We usually park around back,' says my dad. 'It's free, and you don't have to walk up three hundred goddamn steps and listen to jerkoffs singing the theme tune from "Rocky".'

'I must admit, I am very glad they removed the Rocky statue,' says my mother. 'In spite of my belief in popular and accessible art, I'm very glad they removed the Rocky statue.'

April is looking at the back end of the Philadelphia Museum of Art as though she's not quite sure she believes it's what we say it is. James is staring out the other window, acting as though she hasn't spoken.

I am seated between them. 'Well, here we are,' I say heartily. Things are going badly already.

We climb out of the car, stretch our legs, pretend we're all remaining silent deliberately. Nobody seems to know what to do next. I am wondering how to ditch the parents. It shouldn't be difficult – they're completely out of it. I'd expected them to be upset by the departure of Matthew, but they don't appear to have noticed he's missing. In fact, they seem to be under the impression he's come along.

'Hey, hon – remember that time we jumped into the fountain and almost got arrested?' says my dad.

'I certainly do.' My mother gazes into his eyes, grabs his hand. They race towards the front of the building, my mother calling out behind her, 'Meet you at the East Entrance in two hours. Make sure you go to the Impressionist gallery, it's all been re-hung, don't go straight to the cafeteria and don't try to fool me because *I will know.*'

'Well, that was easy,' I remark. No one laughs. 'Guess I've inherited Dad's sense of humour, huh. You guys suck, you know that? Hey, let's party.' I grab James's arm and start to drag him bodily up the stairs. Catch April's eye and jerk my head towards the doors. 'Let's get this show on the *road*.' My idea is to get it over with quickly. We go in, we go out, nobody gets hurt. I'd tried to talk April out of it, but no cigar.

'Your mom would be disappointed,' she'd said.

'She'll live.' I'd attempted to forcibly remove her jacket and sit her down. 'It's time she learned that she can't bully people into being refined.'

'Ellen, I know what you're trying to do.'

I'd succeeded in getting the sleeve off. 'I'm not trying to do anything.'

'You want to protect me from Courtney, and keep her and James apart.'

'Don't be silly. I'm trying to protect you from something worse – my mother.'

'Ellen, I need to prove to myself that I'm not afraid.'

'Of what? Who? What are you talking about?'

'You *know* what I'm talking about.'

'Look,' I'd begged, 'don't go. Trust me on this.'

'I'm going, you're going, we're all going – and what's more, we're going to have a good time.' She'd jerked her jacket back over her shoulders. 'This is important to me. Just come with me, that's all I ask. Be there for me and I'll be okay.'

I'd thought maybe James would try to back out of it, but I'd caught him in the bathroom, shaving and applying a nice cologne. 'You're a bastard,' I'd said. He'd grabbed me and started tickling me. I'd had to beat him off with a backscrubber.

'I hate museums,' I remark.

James is walking towards the entrance as though he's got prosthetic legs. I assume it's a kind of feigned reluctance. He knows perfectly well that there is a luscious blonde bombshell waiting for him inside. I'm going to do everything I can to screw it up for him. He doesn't know what I'm capable of – yet.

Poor April. I know how hard this must be for her. She's looking sort of petrified, actually. I get behind her and start pushing her towards the building.

195

'Ellen, it's okay,' she insists. 'I just want to take it in from the outside first.'

Perhaps she's simply overawed. Even from the back, it's impressive. A big, honey-coloured, neoclassical sort of thing. Very appropriate. None of your Pompidou Centre nonsense – no pipes or primary colours.

'It's beautiful,' she says shyly, as though it's a present from me personally.

I observe James enter. Grab her arm. 'All right, let's *go*.' Start running. Whip through the revolving doors and into the West Entrance lobby.

'Big brother,' I say, 'where do you think you're going?'

He's trying to sneak off. 'I wanted to check my coat.'

'Bullshit. You stick with me. We get through this together or not at all.'

'Ellen, it's warm in here. I don't want to have to carry –'

'Freeze.'

He halts, mid-step.

'Right,' I say, placing my face close to his. 'You follow *my* lead, understand?'

'I think,' he says, through gritted teeth, 'that we should take our cue from April – do what *she* wants to do. This is her first visit, remember? I don't think you're being very considerate.'

I glower. This is rich, really rich. 'Impressionists, cafeteria, gift shop, in that order or you're dead.'

I brace myself for his objection, but he just kisses me on the cheek and says, 'Whatever you say, little sis'.'

He's got something up his sleeve. Maybe he and Courtney have arranged a rendezvous. I am not going to let him out of my sight, if I have to trail him into the men's room. I smile ghoulishly. 'You won't mind skipping the Middle Ages, then.'

'*I'd* like to see the Middle Ages,' says April, tentatively.

'There. See?' says James. 'Stop setting the agenda.'

I look at her, glare at James, look at her again. 'Okay. We do a quick whip round and then we go. Understand?'

All kinds of people are milling about. Art students, old people, couples, packs of kids. It's free on Sunday mornings. The rest of the week, you have to pay. One disgruntled man is trudging by

196

with his wife. 'My feet hurt,' he complains. 'I can't walk no more.'

'We haven't seen the Picassos yet,' says his wife. 'Keep going.'

I tear up the stairs, two at a time. 'Take it easy, Ellen,' says James. 'Slow down. April's not used to this. You have to get used to whole new time-space dimensions here.'

'So take her arm,' I say. 'Medieval art. Over there. *Let's go, people.*'

Medieval art, or MA, is full of bright biblical paintings and macabre reliquaries embellished with enough blood, guts, bones, scabs and arrows for any gore fiend's picnic. Bearing in mind her whitewashed Christianity, I am concerned as to what April's reaction will be. Then I remember the tee-shirt with the three bloody nails. This stuff is business as usual for them. I doubt if it will faze her in the slightest.

We stop in front of a picture of the Virgin and Child. James gazes at it reverently. 'Isn't it exquisite.'

'Yeah,' I say. 'I like the way He's sort of looking in the other direction. Ever notice that? He treats her like she isn't even there. Men are like that.'

'Ellen,' he says.

'Actually, I like it better than the implication that they had this perfect mother-child thing going. No one's going to tell me that they weren't a little dysfunctional.'

'*Ellen,*' says James. 'I think you might be offending April.'

'It's all right,' says April. 'I'm not offended.'

'See anything you like?' James asks her.

'Yes, everything,' she says wretchedly. As in the café, her voice sounds strained and higher than usual. Defensively: 'Well, they all look kind of alike, don't they?'

He takes a deep breath. As though she's uttered something sacrilegious: 'Oh, they do, do they?'

'Sure they do,' I say. 'Once you've seen one virgin, you've seen them all. I'm *really hungry*. What do you say, James? Cafeteria?'

'April is our guest,' says James. 'She wanted to do MA, so we're going to do MA and do it properly. Get your priorities straight, Ellen – you're being really selfish.'

There he goes again, trying to make me feel guilty. I cannot believe how manipulative he is. He freaks out on me in the middle

197

of the night, babbles on about aborticide, deputizes me against my will and then paints himself as Mr Considerate. *I'm* the one practically holding her hand. We both turn to April, who doesn't seem at all well.

'Whatever's fine with you guys,' she says weakly.

'She needs a cup of tea,' I say to James.

He pretends not to hear me. 'Well, look what we have here – the Lorenzetti altarpiece.' He speaks as though he's just bumped into an old friend. 'Fourteenth century. Pay close attention, April. Note how he manages to create the impression of depth and three-dimensionality in such a way that the viewer feels that he or she is looking through a window into another world . . .'

I let his voice fade into the background. 'Are you all right?' I ask April, who is looking really ill.

'I sure am,' she says. 'Don't get me wrong, Ellen. I love these pictures. I want to see them all. It's just –'

'Note the cunning use of detail,' James drones. 'The fringe on the Virgin's robe, for instance . . .'

'The baby Jesus looks like he's about to spit up,' I observe. 'Mary doesn't look too happy, either. But I guess I'd be pretty pissed off too if I'd found myself with child and I'd never even had sex . . .'

'Yeah,' says April wistfully. 'Giving birth must be scary enough if you're *used* to things going in and out of –'

'Say, do you think she had any kind of pre-natal training?'

'That's enough, Ellen,' says James.

'I would have asked for an epidural,' says April.

'She would have needed it,' I say. 'Look at the *size* of him.'

James is beginning to look like the victim of some kind of conspiracy. Serves him right. He makes one more attempt to get away. I go up behind him and collar him. 'Nice try.'

'Hey,' he protests. 'I just want to –'

'This isn't about what *you* want to do. It's about what –'

'Look over there.' He points. 'Isn't that Frederick and Courtney?'

And so it is. There they are, the Gruesome Twosome, standing around like a couple of arrogant Michelangelos. Great. This is all I need. I wave. Courtney shoots me a look of pure disgust, then spots James and brightens. Frederick looks as though he's found himself in the wrong gallery. Yawns. Stares at a painting of the Archangel Michael as though he'd like to pick a fight.

'Are you all right, Ellen?' says James, startling me.

'Never felt better.' Best to get this over with. 'Let's go over and say hi.'

'Ellen,' whispers April, tugging my sleeve. 'Do you think Courtney and Frederick are *doing it?*'

Good question. I examine them for telltale signs of two people who have fornicated. Prickly body language? No. Out-and-out disgust? Not a trace. Nor is Frederick lording it over her as he would be if he'd already mounted her. The balance of power seems about equal.

'I don't think so,' I reply.

'Then I'm in trouble,' she says. 'She must be saving herself for James.'

It's true, she's switched on the teeth. Any hopes that she might turn up looking like hell are shot to shit. Her face seems less squashed than usual. She's pulling her best debutante, all winsome and Vanderbilt-Whitney, acting as though the Art Museum is her second home. James has sauntered over to her, every inch the gentleman. I overhear bits of the conversation. Gather that she did a summer internship here when she was twelve, and that her mother knows all the trustees.

'Professionally, I focus on contemporary work,' she says, 'but I have to admit, the Middle Ages are really close to my heart.'

I'll bet they are. She's the original Iron Maiden. James is staring at her collarbone and enquiring after her health. April is hanging back like the child who stands around at parties, left out, overlooked, plate of cake in hand. Apparently she isn't even worth hating, as far as Courtney is concerned. No, she seems to have bestowed that especial favour on me. She isn't subtle about it, either. I guess she figures she doesn't have to be. Turning briefly away from the others, she leans towards me in a friendly manner.

'I hate you,' she says quietly, through the teeth.

She's deranged. It's funny – she doesn't *appear* psychotic. But then, how many psychotics can afford designer dresses? Hers is sheer but not transparent, the kind of trendy garment that reveals all by leaving most to the imagination. I try to gauge how much James really *likes* her but it's hard. As usual, his manner is cordial and amused. Frederick takes no notice of me, but then I expected that. I am trying to devise a way out of this mess.

'Where's Zero?' April asks. Her champion, her quantum hero.

Courtney rolls her eyes. 'Zero's sweet but he's such a dork. He wears sandals and picks at his underpants. It's embarrassing to go out with him.'

'I liked him,' says April, but of course she is ignored.

'Did you enjoy the Truffaut the other night?' James asks.

'I enjoyed it very much, thank you,' says Courtney. 'What an extraordinary director. I have season tickets for the next film festival – perhaps you'd like to come along.'

'I just might take you up on that.'

What Truffaut? And how did he know? Did he call her? April looks like she's about to cry. A game is being played that she has no chance of winning. James, sensing that she is hurt, puts an arm around her shoulder, but this doesn't faze Courtney in the slightest. Quite the contrary. She is as touched as she would be watching a nun caress a leper. As soon as she's given this little scenario her stamp of approval, she sort of pony-trots over to Frederick, whispers something in his ear, then comes back to James and announces, 'We're going to wander through the Renaissance, then go down to the restaurant and drink champagne. Would you care to join us?'

Wander through the Renaissance. Spare us. The invitation clearly excludes April and me. Well, we'll see about that.

'I'd *adore* to,' I say. 'What do you say, April? Check out a few da Vincis and then get drunk?'

'Actually,' says Courtney, 'there is something I'd like to talk to James about *privately*. We're introducing a series of lectures at the gallery and I think he'd make a wonderful speaker.'

'He would,' I enthuse. 'Don't see anything private about that, though. Do you, James? Hey, everybody.' I flag the attention of passing visitors. 'My brother here is going to be a lecturer. What do you think?'

'I'd buy tickets,' says a Caribbean woman in a tiger-striped dress. 'Me, too,' adds another, 'if he talks as good as he looks.'

'Hear that?' I say. 'We need a group opinion.'

I've almost defeated Courtney – temporarily, at least. She slumps and looks moody. 'Fine,' she says. 'Let's –'

'I'd really like to walk around with Ellen, actually,' says April. 'You would?' I ask stupidly.

'Sure.' Unbelievable – she sounds totally self-assured. April has found her voice. 'James, why don't you go off with Courtney and Frederick? Ellen and I will catch up with you later.'

Is she crazy? We're talking recipe for disaster. As for Frederick, I can't imagine a more inappropriate chaperone. 'No way,' I say.

'Yes way,' she breezily replies.

'Are you sure?' says James, astonished.

'Absolutely,' says April. 'It will give me and Ellen a chance to spend some quality time together.'

I glance at her in alarm, realize that she is teasing. It strikes me that she's witty when you give her half a chance.

'Well, okay,' says James with manufactured regret. 'Are you sure you'll be all right?'

'Of course. I'll be with Ellen, after all.'

Frederick is lounging against the wall by a statue of the Virgin Mary – trying to chat her up, it seems. Courtney looks as though she's about had it with all of us. April throws up her chin and takes off. I am flabbergasted, momentarily rooted to the spot.

'Hey,' I say, running to catch up. 'Is this a good idea?'

'I'll explain in a minute,' she hisses, walking quickly. I have no choice but to follow. I catch fragments of conversation as we move through the crowds, the voices nasal, vowels pressed into the upper palate and squeezed out.

'Slow down, ladies,' says a guard. 'You trying to steal a Van Gogh?'

The wheelchair contingent is out in full force. There doesn't seem to be any speed limit on them. One goes racing by so fast that I have to jump out of the way.

We find ourselves in Arms and Armour. Ancient swords and helmets surround us. April pulls to a stop. Looks puzzled. 'They didn't have very big heads.'

I fall against the wall, panting. Nearly collide with a five-hundred-year-old full metal jacket. 'April, *what* the *hell?*'

'Sorry,' she says. 'I wanted to let you know what I was doing, but I couldn't explain right then and there.'

I place my hand on a steel shoulder-plate in an effort to steady myself. A guard gives me the evil eye. The man with the sore feet limps by. 'My *feet* hurt,' he insists.

The woman looks belligerent. 'We have two more centuries to get through. Shut up and walk.'

'I am mighty confused,' I say to April. 'Why did you just take off like that?'

'Because this is my big opportunity to show James that I'm not clingy.' She is determined, almost fevered. 'I'm going to show him that I've changed my colours. It's like you said – if you love someone, set him free. That's what I'm going to do.'

Uh, oh. She's taken my advice – always a bad idea. 'Look,' I blurt out, 'I hate to be blunt, but at this rate I'm going to end up with Courtney as a sister-in-law. I was wrong –'

'No, you weren't. Oh, Ellen, don't you see? I was so possessive. That's why I wanted him to get a crap job, stay away from his friends. But that was unfair and insecure. I'm not like that any more. I'll show him that I don't mind his going off with Courtney – or anyone. It will be liberating. For him, for me. And anyway, I trust him.'

Trust. It's a relative term. She's been hanging out with Jesus too long. Always said that boy was a bad influence. Someone needs to teach her a bit about the complexities of human nature. Judging from her expression, though, there's something more she hasn't told me.

'There's another reason,' she says, 'that I wanted to get away. A more selfish one.'

'What's that?'

She fades in and out for a moment, as though willing herself to disappear. 'Oh, Ellen, can't you tell? Isn't it obvious?'

'You've lost me.'

'I'm *stupid*.'

April speaks as though revealing her deepest, darkest secret. Her voice is defiant, her face suffused with self-loathing and shame. 'Uneducated,' she says. 'Dumb.'

Oh, no. Please, no. Not this. What the hell are you doing up there, God? 'April, don't be silly. Remember what Zero said –'

'No, it's true. You don't understand.' She shakes her head, as though trying to throw off her fears long enough to confront

202

them. 'Every time James opens his mouth, I feel like I've been stabbed. It's like someone has slammed a door in my face. And when someone like Courtney's around, it's worse. She doesn't seem to be paying attention, but I know she's laughing at me.'

'April, don't let Courtney get to you. She's a phoney. I don't think she's even very bright. She just regurgitates things she's read in film catalogues and capsule reviews in *Cosmopolitan*. Her parents bought her an education, and she wears it around her neck like some kind of add-a-pearl necklace.'

'But don't you see? That's everything. She knows all the words, all the right things to say.'

'But that's just a *language*. It can be learned.'

'She has confidence and opinions,' she says flatly. 'Those can't.'

I sigh. 'Don't be ridiculous. You're brilliant. You're –'

'Don't patronize me.'

She trembles with the intensity of her feeling. 'I thought you, at least, would be straight with me. You're the *one person* –'

'Look,' I say, as patiently as I can, 'if someone like *Courtney* can masquerade as an intellectual –'

'But I don't want to masquerade. I want it to be real – and you have to grow up with it or it's no good. Facts can be learned, but not confidence and opinions. Face it, Ellen, it's too late for me.'

'Now you really *are* being stupid.'

'Oh, shut up, Ellen.' She turns on me, suddenly furious. 'What do you know? You've never had any problems. You have a beautiful home, plenty of money, an education half the world would kill for –'

'I didn't ask for it.'

'It doesn't matter. You don't realize how lucky you are. Do you know what my school was like? Crowded classes, no extras, no music or art. The bright kids got saved – were siphoned off. Most of the others didn't give a damn, treated the whole thing like one big joke.'

'You should have been siphoned.'

She shrugs. 'Well, I wasn't.'

I can imagine April frantically waving her hand, trying to get the teacher's attention. Farm girl, they would have thought.

Mechanic's daughter. 'They must have noticed how intelligent you were.'

'Sure – I was the smart one in an average class. But not one of the special ones, one of the Courtneys. Just once, I wanted to be singled out. To be special, like you, Ellen – that would have meant more to me than anything else in the world.'

She starts weaving through the Armoury. Black knights hover above us, charge along on model horses. I trail her closely, fearful that she might fall. I try to get her to sit down, but she seems to feel the need to push herself to the limit.

'Special is one thing I'm not,' I say.

'Yes, you are. Even your bedroom, Ellen. To you, it's just a place to sleep, but to me it was heaven – the real thing, not the stupid mock-up I made out of plastic flowers and paint.'

'If you liked it so much,' I say, 'why did you change it? Why did you take everything down?'

'Because I felt like a fraud. It was your world, not mine. I could just picture James walking in and asking me what I thought of Kandinsky. And you. I was terrified of you – scared you might come back one day and show me up for what I was. I thought you might turn out to be Courtney – someone too indescribably perfect to have anything to do with me.'

Not so long ago, I would have found this gratifying, but now I just feel like an idiot. 'As you can see,' I say glumly, 'you had nothing to worry about.'

I turn and start walking away. Wheelchairs are whizzing all around me. A woman rolls by, eating a ham sandwich. The guard doesn't seem to care – in fact, he high-fives her as she leaves the gallery.

Now it's April's turn to catch up. 'You can't run away from it, Ellen,' she says. 'There are certain things you ought to know.'

'Like what?'

'Like how much your mother missed you.' April grabs me by the shoulder. 'She's looking for you, Ellen. Looking everywhere.'

'I'm right here,' I say.

'No, you're not. Nobody knows *where* you are. It's like you're off in some crazy world where you think everyone is against you. You make her so sad, Ellen. She's always talking about you. She does nice things for you and you don't even notice. All those chocolate cakes she's been baking? They're for you. Not me. You.'

The chocolate cakes. Baked with sugar.

'But I thought –' I'm confused. 'She's been acting screwy since I got home, but *I* thought . . .'

'That she'd replaced you with me?' says April.

'Uh huh.'

'Fat chance. She'd sacrifice anything for you. She'd pierce her own breast to feed her children, Ellen.'

'Well, how was I supposed to know?'

'It's so obvious.' Exasperated. 'How could you not notice? She'd die for you, Ellen. Have you ever stopped to consider that?'

April's talking about maternal love as though it's something my mother invented. 'If that's true, she's been real subtle about it.'

'She's afraid.'

'Well, one of these days she'll get a life.'

'You *are* her life.'

'Well, I didn't ask her to be that way,' I snap. 'I didn't ask Christ to die for my sins, but he went right ahead and did it. Thanks but no thanks. When I want a favour, I'll ask.'

April stops, digs furiously in her pocket. Pulls out a crumpled photograph. 'I carry this everywhere with me. See?'

A faded picture of a strong-jawed woman. Guarded smile. 'That's my mom,' says April. 'Don't you get it? She screamed at me for things that weren't my fault, lashed out at me when her life took a nose dive. But it doesn't matter, Ellen, because she loved me.'

'I don't have a snapshot of my mom,' I say stupidly.

'It's *here*,' says April, smacking my forehead. Hard. I reel backwards. 'It's in your head. You carry it everywhere with you, and you don't even bother to look at it. Do you know what she told me? That she walks around town sometimes, hoping she'll run into you – did it even while you were gone. Used to go into town, pretending she might find you there. Did you know that?'

'I didn't mean to –'

'You couldn't even bother to send her a *postcard*. You really are *pathetic*, Ellen.'

She is panting, exhausted by the force of her emotions. Can hardly stand up.

'You'd better sit down,' I say.

'No. I am going to get through to you once and for all. You don't know how lucky you are. You don't know –'

Her legs buckle. She faints, eyes closing, head lolling back. A fan of golden hair on the floor. A security guard comes running, speaking into her walkie-talkie.

'It's all right,' April murmurs, coming to. 'I'm fine.'

'You pregnant, honey?' asks the guard sympathetically. 'I can tell. I've got three of my own.'

I say nothing. Scan the area for James. April is already trying to stand, forehead stubborn, shapely arms showing their muscle.

'Will she be all right?' says the guard.

'I'll take care of her,' I say. But April is already stumbling off on her own, as though driven by holy rocket fuel. I catch up, tug her sleeve. 'April. I think it's time to go find James.'

'No.' She is adamant. 'We're going to go look at some art.'

'Art?' I say blankly.

'Yes. That's what we came for, isn't it? Paintings? Sculpture? Statues of naked men?'

'April, I've got to level with you.' The least I can do is be honest with her. 'It's not just Courtney who's not to be trusted. It's James. He came to me the other night –' I see her wince. I take a deep breath and proceed. 'He was acting really funny. He's not what he seems, not entirely – I'm only just beginning to discover this myself. He's never had to make any difficult choices –'

'I don't care,' she says evenly. 'My life is my own responsibility now. I choose to do what we came for.'

I have to tell her the full story. 'April, that day in the café . . . when Courtney showed up . . .' This is hard to say. She'll hate me now. 'It wasn't an accident. I'd called Zero –'

'I know,' she says simply.

'How?' I say stupidly.

'Same way I know everything.' She points up.

Of course. 'God told you.'

'No. I heard through the walls – your voice really carries. It's

206

all right, I understood. Things happen for a reason. I needed to face my fears, Ellen. You sensed that somehow, and helped me out.'

'I wanted you to leave.'

'You only thought you did.'

And then I realize she's right – I've liked her all along. I'd been too busy trying to protect my position to recognize an ally. She's on my side, knows me better than I know myself. How could I have been so blind?

'Are you sure you feel up to it?' I ask.

'You bet.'

'Great. How do you feel about Buddhism?'

We set off, claim the corridors with eager strides, and find ourselves in Asian Art. A sign by the entrance reads, 'Guest exhibition of Korean art sponsored by LandDevel.' I stop short, jab the sign with my finger.

'This is a set-up,' I hiss. 'They're out to get me.'

'It's just a coincidence.'

'There are no coincidences. A statue's going to fall on my head. They're in there somewhere, waiting for me.'

April drags me in. 'Then this is your big opportunity.'

But the displays tell me nothing. Wine pots and incense burners, funeral urns and shrines, enormous Buddhas with those irritating benevolent smiles. 'I prefer Hinduism,' I say. 'Did you see that terrific statue of elephants copulating? It's one of my favourites.'

April laughs. 'James was right – you're sex-obsessed.'

He *said* that? Well, James is full of surprises. What else did he say, I wonder. What other unpleasant discoveries will I make about his character before all this is over?

'I like that one a lot,' she says, peering into a small glass case. 'That guy with four arms.'

'That's Shiva, god of creation and . . . something else. I can't remember.'

I try to concentrate but my mind keeps defaulting to James. He's practically left her at the altar. Maybe I'm being paranoid. Perhaps he's just sick of the Philadelphia Museum of Art. Or maybe he wanted me and April to be alone, rub off on each other, each adopt some of the other's qualities so that together we'd be one perfect girl, the union of two people for whom he feels a highly conditional love . . .

No. I'm being way too generous. 'James is a lying shit and we've got to find him,' I say. 'Here's what we do. We check out the Renaissance, then head for the restaurant. If we don't find him, we'll try the gift shop and if he isn't there *by God I'll tear this building apart brick by brick —*'

'Relax, Ellen.' She's taken my arm. Is leading me around as though we are an old married couple enjoying a day out. 'Oh, how beautiful,' she breathes. 'Just look at that face.'

She is gazing up at a tall stone statue of a god. It's giving me one of those supercilious smiles. A tiny Buddha nestles in its hairdo and a kind of towel is wrapped around its waist. I squirm. It's making me feel really uncomfortable.

'Let's get out of here,' I say.

'"*Avalokiteshvara*",' April reads. '"Saintlike being of compassion".'

'I don't like it,' I say. Try to drag her away. 'Let's go.'

'Not yet,' says April. 'I'm getting really good vibes.'

'Isn't Jesus going to kick you out of the club for this? Or are they all part of the same spiritual mafia?'

She doesn't reply. Her eyes are shut and she appears to be in prayer. I scan the room uneasily, as though James and Courtney might be tucked away in a corner somewhere.

'A girl,' says April, out of the blue.

'Huh?'

'The baby. It's going to be a girl.'

She seems quite certain, all of a sudden. 'What is this?' I demand. 'Some kind of celestial ultrasound?'

'I think it might be. Ellen?'

'What?'

'I want you to be godmother.'

I am silent for a moment.

'Godmother,' I say. 'Me?'

'Yes.'

'Are you sure?'

'Yes. Will you?'

'Yes.'

We conclude this conversation quickly – as though I am embarrassed and she is afraid of a no. She should know that I'd never refuse her. Oh, April, my one true friend. I will protect you, I promise, whatever happens. I will never let you down.

The *Avalokiteshvara* smiles down on us.

'I love the museum, Ellen,' says April. Her eyes are shining as though a whole new universe has opened up, a window to a world she thought she'd never be able to call her own. But a slight discomfort in her posture betrays her sense of an invisible barrier that will always prevent her from being more than an outsider looking in. She is still diffident, still fragile. How can I reassure her?

'Hey, April, this is only the beginning. I was thinking, there's no reason why you couldn't go to college.' I recall our visit to the LandDevel house. 'You mentioned wanting to be a journalist –'

'This has been the best day of my life,' she says rapidly, as though short of time. 'I haven't been able to tell anyone, but I've been so excited about today. Even with Courtney showing up, it's been great, and it's all thanks to you, Ellen.'

Thanking me for her own execution. I've betrayed her over and over. Now James is off with a certified man-eater. What kind of a friend am I? I feel a sickening lurch in my stomach. My instinct is telling me that we must get to him, and fast. 'Look, I'm starving. Why don't we nip down to the –'

And then I spot him. From behind. Those unmistakable tufts of hair.

Frederick.

I feel that thunderbolt of recognition that goes hand in hand with unsatisfied lust. I wonder if he knows I'm there. Wishful thinking on my part. Like he'd care. He is staring at a *surasundari*, one of those sexy statues they stick on the front of Hindu temples to get men to come in and say their prayers. She's giving him the old sock-it-to-me-big-boy, which I wouldn't have thought he'd fall for. Her hip is thrown way out and her earrings are bigger than her ears. She's even wearing a garter belt, or something very like it. I examine my reflection in a glass case; I look like hell. My hair is frenzied and my face is pure '*Les Demoiselles d'Avignon*'. What am I to do?

As though someone is directing my hand, my fingers close around an object in my pocket, something cool and plastic. Of course. It's the necklace April gave me, the black choker that transformed me so completely. Too completely. Scarily so. Would it be bad luck to put it on?

I look to my side, behold without surprise April's reassuring nod. I don the choker, feel as though I have been blessed. Wonder if a price will be exacted.

Frederick turns around, casts a mild glance in my direction, looks back at the *surasundari*, then walks over to me. Stops and slowly, slowly leans towards me until his lips are almost touching my ear.

'My God, you have nice tits.'

??????

'I was hoping I'd run into you,' he says. 'J and C are being *such* art snobs. If I wanted to look at paintings, I'd study the ones my ancestors stole.'

Is he talking to me?

'You've turned out well, Ellen. I hadn't really noticed. I don't think I've ever realized just how lovely you are.'

This is too good to be true. But it *is* true. Isn't it?

'Why don't you and I go and have some fun?' he suggests.

Oh, no. No way. *That* is out of the question. April is standing only a few feet away, vulnerable and alone. She needs me by her side to catch her if she falls.

'I want you,' he murmurs.

Unfortunately, I have never been able to resist being wanted.

I wander over towards April, dazed. She beams happily, knows what's happening. 'You go on, Ellen. I'll be fine on my own. I'm beginning to feel like I could conquer the world.'

She sounds confident and bold, ready to strike out on her own. But do I detect, in her eyes, a little flicker of residual fear?

'Don't do it,' says a voice. An old white-haired security guard. He looks familiar, but he's not looking at me. He must have been talking to himself.

Frederick is studying the exit; he has such a short attention span. I'm losing him . . .

'I won't be long,' I tell her in a stage whisper. 'I'll meet you in the Great Stair Hall in fifteen minutes.'

Fifteen minutes? What I am expecting to accomplish in fifteen minutes? Frederick pulls me away, a jailer leading an unwilling

210

favourite to his quarters. I can feel April behind me, soldiering on. I am abandoning her, but only temporarily. Surely nothing bad can happen in a quarter of an hour.

Lifetimes have been undone in less time than that, of course. Atlantis slid into the sea. Mount Vesuvius turned a town into a tourist attraction.

But I keep walking.

Inside the ladies' room are three stalls, two sinks and a poster advertising the Impressionists. Frederick props himself up against the sink, facing me, and asks, with disarming frankness, 'Ellen, who took your virginity?'

'None of your business.'

'I lobbied for it but James refused.'

'Can we talk about something else?'

'Was it James?'

'Don't be disgusting.'

'Defensive reaction, Ellen. That's as good as a yes.'

He's making my skin crawl. I'm having second thoughts. 'Maybe this isn't such a good idea, Freddy.'

'Of course it is. Don't be silly. I know you, Ellen, better than you think. Precocious Ellen. Take your shirt off.'

He turns me around and presses me up against the wall. Holds my wrists together. 'How's your vocabulary, Ellen?' Lifts my arms slightly. I wince.

'Forgive me for saying so, but this is a funny time for a spelling bee.'

'Answer the question.'

I think he's dislocated my arm. 'Not so hot, actually.'

'Give me the definition of "concupiscence".'

'What?'

'Give it to me.'

'I don't *know*.'

He slips his hand down the front of my trousers. '"Sexual lust". Can you imagine what a thrill that gave the lexicographer? "Orgasm." Definition. Go on.'

'For God's sake, Frederick, how am I –'

I can feel him unbuckling his black leather belt. '"A paroxysm of desire or rage". Come on. You're not trying. "Fellatio".'

Dream on, Frederick. I'm not enjoying this. Moreover, I'm worried about April. I try to wiggle free. Hear a noise. We both freeze.

'They've probably got a camera in here,' I hiss. 'We're going to get caught. They'll never let us into the museum again and then what'll I tell my mother?'

'Calm down, Ellen.' He's strong-arming me into one of the stalls, the extra-wide one designed for the handicapped. Someone has thrust a *Guide to the Museum Collections* into the sanitary napkin disposal. Frederick grabs me and kisses me, parting my lips, easing his tongue over mine. I'm helpless. It's no good. I can't resist him.

'Now, where were we?' he says. 'Oh, yes. "Fellatio".' One hand caresses the small of my back. 'Define.'

'I have no idea.' Against my will, I am liquefying. 'Enlighten me.'

'"Stimulation of the penis by sucking". Say it.'

'"Stimulation of the . . ."' My face grows hot. 'I can't.'

'Yes, you can. Remember how you used to try to impress me with big words, when you were a little girl?'

This is so embarrassing. 'Rings a bell.'

'Then say it.'

'"Stimulation of the penis by sucking".'

'Good. Now say it like you mean it.'

'I'm sorry?'

'Once more, with feeling. Do as you're told.'

'"Stimulation . . ."' It's no use. I cannot choke the words out.

'You're a little bit slow, aren't you?' he says tenderly, as though he understands. 'I think I'd better give you an example of every-day usage.'

'What do you mean?'

'I mean I'm going to make sure you never forget it.'

He is easing his trousers down with one hand. Crisp white shirttails flank his cock which I already know, from judicious spying when I was a child, is surrounded by glistening golden hair. He places my hand on it, shows me what to do, as though I'm still his prepubescent admirer.

'Very good,' he says. 'Now on your knees, my dear.'

212

I'm changing my mind all over the place. Voices are shouting inside my head. The security guard, warning me. Tyler Spee: 'Probe, Ellen, probe.' James's yodelling, Puddles's yapping, all blended together into one great cacophony of alarm. Something tells me I must get back to April on the double, but I'm not sure how to extricate myself. Frederick's got me by the scruff of the neck, and is not taking 'no' for an answer.

'Try, Ellen,' he murmurs. 'Just try.'

Oh, dear . . .

'I want you *so much*.'

What can I do? My impossible dream is coming true . . . sort of . . .

'Not bad,' he breathes. 'Not bad.'

I have to trust providence, don't I?

'Take your time . . .'

The Lord will provide.

Suddenly, the door to the ladies' room is thrown open. I hear a female voice, accompanied by a lower one, gruff and authoritative, and the unmistakable, inexorable grinding of a wheelchair.

'Feet,' the woman screams. 'I see feet.'

There is a banging on the door of the stall. 'All right,' says the male voice, half-menacingly, half-reassuringly. 'You come on out, now.'

'*Two* sets of feet. There are *two* of them, officer. Arrest them at once.'

'Now, ma'am, I am not an officer of the police, just a five-dollar-an-hour security guard. I have no powers of arrest –'

'I'll do it myself then.' More banging. '*Open up in the name of the law.*'

'I think she's one of those new wheelchair cops,' I whisper. 'We'd better do what she says.'

'*Finish,*' orders Frederick. The extra tension seems to be turning him on.

The woman is ramming the dread wheelchair into the door: '*Open up, open up.*' The guard is trying to subdue her. A cry of pain; she's decked him one.

Frederick isn't letting me stand. 'Don't stop, Ellen, don't stop.'

The lock finally gives way. I turn. A monumental woman in

a wheelchair is seated before us, her eyes flashing with righteous anger. The guard is doubled up behind her, rolling his eyes towards the door. 'There they are,' she yells triumphantly. 'I caught a glimpse of them earlier. You can tell just by looking at them that they are exactly the sort of people to take advantage of *handicapped facilities.*'

She lunges towards us. The differently abled? Don't underestimate them. Frederick – unsatisfied, irate – pulls up his trousers and grabs my hand. We run . . .

. . . to the door, the East Entrance, the cavernous lobby, where at the top of a massive flight of stairs April stands ecstatic, filled with new confidence and hope, having touched upon *her* impossible dream. Her eyes search the Great Hall, looking for me, for James, eager to share her discovery that she has as much right to walk this earth as anyone. She starts running down the stairs, sure-footed at first . . .

. . . then her eyes and mine simultaneously alight on the sight of James and Courtney embracing at the bottom of the staircase, intertwined like Hindu statues. April pauses in mid-air for a moment like an angel slapped in the face by God, then falls, a violent, humiliating fall, down the Great Staircase, stumbling, clutching, gasping for help, with no one to catch her and no handrail to grab. Her cry of pain when she reaches the bottom rips across the uppermost reaches of the Hall, silencing the hum of voices. She tries to rise. Fails.

With a kind of tranquil guilt, James breaks away from Courtney. 'There's Mom and Dad,' he says. The last words I hear him say before he vanishes.

April is clearly in terrible pain, has curled up like a crayfish being prodded with a stick. Courtney runs up to my parents like a prom queen in distress, the delighted bearer of bad tidings. Frederick, to my very great surprise, is still present. He kneels beside April. Takes her pulse, checks her eyes. Mouth-to-mouths her with a precision far more urgent than that which he used on me. But even the kiss of life can't revive her. She lies there, motionless.

April has been singled out for the worst of all possible reasons. Clumsiness, not cleverness. She has achieved the cruel inverse of her dream. To look foolish, especially in front of a girl like Court-

214

ney, is what she dreads most in the world. A crowd gathers around, sympathetically but hungrily. Someone calls for an ambulance. I feel useless. Hold her hand.

'Ellen,' she whispers. 'Where is James?'

I look down at her, unable to cover up the fact that he is nowhere to be seen. Or that I am to blame for . . . everything.

She appears to be slipping out of consciousness. 'Thanks for looking out for me, Ellen,' she whispers and I know that she means it with all her heart. 'You're a real friend.' She shuts her eyes. Someone lays a jacket over her.

Now I know why we can hear each other's thoughts. We're two halves of the same person. Creator. And destroyer.

11

As hospitals go, it's all right, in a sick Welcome Wagon sort of way. Attempts at hominess set uneasily against the atmosphere of death and sterility that never deserts the place. I have been here three times: for removal of my wisdom teeth, tonsils and appendix – none of which, they assured me, I really needed. As a result, I'm inclined to think of it as a place where pieces of my body are systematically removed. A tea and coffee cart stands in one corner beneath a 'Thank You for Not Smoking' sign and a poster showing a pair of bisected black lungs. Crocheted afghans lie complacently against mustard-yellow vinyl couches, the kind that tear your skin off when you stand. On imitation teak tables are stacks of magazines, everything from *Family Circle* to *Dementia and You*. Flowers are sold from a chilled glass case. A nearby gift shop offers satin baby bootees, goo-filled chocolates in decorative boxes, stuffed animals, mugs bearing inspirational messages and stationery embellished with butterflies. Just the sort of thing you'd take to a woman suffering from heart disease or a man dying of prostate cancer.

'If I were a terminally ill patient,' says my dad, 'I'd welcome a small bottle of liquid cyanide. Or a copy of *The Tibetan Book of the Dead*.'

'Hush,' says my mother.

'Sorry, I didn't think,' he says. Indicates the near-empty room. 'All these people might hear us.'

He's being sarcastic, but he's already grabbed an issue of *Life Magazine* and is tearing it to shreds. My mother is picking at her handkerchief, eyes darting around as though searching for someone to spit-wash.

216

'When do you think they'll let us see her?' she whispers.

A young doctor wearing a surgical cap and gown enters; sees us and does an almost imperceptible double-take, as though he's just remembered that we're the reason he's wandered in. 'Parents of April Merryweather?'

My parents exchange glances. 'Guardians,' says my mother.

'Mr and Mrs Klapman.'

'*Kaplan*.' Dad is losing it.

'Ah.' The doctor looks at his clipboard as though he's only just noticed it's there. 'Miscarriage, no complications, we suctioned up her insides, she should be all right. Sprained ankle, mild concussion, we'll keep her in for observation tonight in case of haemorrhaging, infection or liquid on the brain and you should be able to pick her up tomorrow at noon.'

'Did the operation . . . go well?' my mother asks.

'Sure,' he says boredly. 'I've done hundreds of these things.' Takes out a cigarette; stops, holds it out between thumb and forefinger. 'Do you mind? I hate surgery.'

My mother, tentatively: 'Isn't that a "No Smoking" sign over there?'

He examines it. 'So it is.' Laughs appreciatively, as though we've all shared an in-joke, and lights up.

'I'd like to know the long-term implications of this,' says my father. 'I mean, will she still be able to have children?'

'Oh, yes. Yes yes yes. Though I'd wait a while, first. Tell the husband or father or whatever he is to tread lightly for the time being. Come with me. I'll take you in to see her.'

He's probably the only doctor to wear alpha and omega dog-tags around his neck. Catches me looking and flicks them up between his fingers, absently: 'Reassures the patients.' Grins without moving his mouth.

'*Where is James?*' asks my mother as we walk along, though we all know that no one has an answer to this question.

April is half-propped-up in bed and smiles faintly but eagerly at our entrance. 'Hi everybody.' She seems slightly giddy, as though unaware she's lost the baby. 'Have you come to get me?'

'We can't take you home quite yet, dear,' says my mother, 'but we spoke to the doctor and he says you're going to be just fine.'

'You mean, I have to stay here?'

'Only for one night. Now, I would like to give your parents a call.'

'No,' says April, quickly.

'I think they ought to know what's going on –'

'Please don't.' Her tone is emphatic; this sentence exhausts her.

My mother nods in reluctant agreement. Looks thoughtful.

'Ellen.' April turns to me. Her eyes are half-closed but sparkling. 'We had such a great time, didn't we? At the museum?'

'Yeah.'

'We can go back, can't we?'

'Sure.'

'Is James here?'

'He's . . .'

Mercifully, her eyes are shutting. Clearly, she hasn't remembered everything yet.

There is silence in the car on the way home. My mother is upset and stares out the window. My father drives grimly as though he's headed straight for Hades, determined to hold someone accountable.

'You okay back there, Ellen?' he says.

'Fine,' I answer. Though I'm not.

All three of us are quiet for a while.

'Do you think they'll let her keep it?' says my mother, suddenly.

'Keep what?' says my dad.

'The foetus. I've read that sometimes they let you take it away in a box and bury it. We could have a little ceremony and put it with the kittens out in the back.'

He takes her hand, which is shaking. Ordinarily, she would tell him to keep both hands on the wheel, but this time, she's still. The interior of the car is strangely dark and flat, as though a vital flame has gone out, a light so subtle and delicate that, until tonight, it flickered almost unnoticed. Now it's gone. Something is missing. The soft illumination that has become as necessary as breathing is no longer there.

I can feel her absence closing in on me. Oh, April, I miss you so. Surely something can be done . . .

* * *

I am determined that April will recover – so much so that her convalescence starts to consume my every thought. Regrettably, I can't come up with a single idea. The only real restorative would be James.

My first impulse is to track him down. Perhaps he's holed up with one of his cronies. But phone calls yield no results. Zero claims he hadn't even known he was missing, and that Courtney is out of town. I call Frederick, heart thumping, and get broken English from a Polish servant, who I know for a fact speaks perfectly except when screening calls for his master. Kermit, the creepy little slime, hangs up on me. Conspiracy? Mere shyness?

It's no use. James is determined not to be found. Maybe there is something else that would cheer April, keep her spirits up. A treat of some sort? A surprise? Perhaps a loving message from her family. I know she specified that we were not to get in touch, but still . . . if I were able to tell her that they'd said, 'Get well soon,' it might help. She seems to think that they don't love her.

Their details are bound to be among her personal belongings. I feel justified in rooting through her room. It's not like I haven't done it before, I reason, and surely it's not any more immoral to do it twice. A cursory inspection reveals a brownish lipstick with which she'd been experimenting. A little cut-out birthday card she'd been making for James. A slip of paper on which she'd been trying to keep track of her weight and measurements, covered with angry black 'X's, all disheartenment and failure. A compact, engraved, 'To April from Jimmy'. And a book, of all things, with her name inside the front cover. *An Introduction to Journalism*, from the Zenith Central Correspondence College. And a letter, explaining that she'd been dropped from the course due to failure to pay the fees.

I put the letter back slowly. There is no evidence of an address. The porcelain Jesuses are standing around as though preparing to pass judgement. Hardly a jury of my peers, but still. I trip over the rug as I leave, fall flat on my face. The pain is justified and welcome.

I never venture into the Morgue unless I have to, but this is one of those occasions that calls for extreme measures. I am changing

219

tactics. I'm in search of something fun, a plaything, some silly item that might cheer her.

I'm assuming this is where they've put my toys, as I can't seem to find them anywhere else. I have to admit, they're worth hiding. Mostly ordered by my parents from various mail order catalogues. An anatomically correct cadaver from a Swedish educational institute, complete with scalpel and guidebook, *How to Perform an Autopsy on Your Pet*. A game called 'Earthquake' in which you have thirty seconds to evacuate a building before it collapses, and a corresponding game called 'Search and Rescue', which comes with miniature victim recovery equipment and sniffer dogs. I'd been given a chemistry set, Monopoly, a plastic model UN. And instead of a Barbie Doll I'd had a 'Bardie doll', a tiny Shakespeare which came with children's versions of *Julius Caesar* and *Macbeth*.

None of these are suitable for April. I'd wanted something light and amusing. Even my Jack-in-the-box is out of the question; it's a particularly sinister version that cranks up to play a short weird tune and out of which springs a truly hideous Jack which, now that I think of it, bears a striking resemblance to James.

This is pathetic. Even I can hardly bear to look at the stuff. I dig through a few more boxes, but can find nothing more of mine. Just family photo albums. Embarrassing clothes. A lot of old letters and documents. I open one or two, wondering if they contain anything I should know.

It strikes me that I don't know much about why I turned out the way I did. Had I been given a choice, it's certainly not the prototype I would have chosen. I have no atavistic impulse, no desire to discover my roots, and in fact have nothing but contempt for people who trace their genealogy or indulge in past-life regression in hopes that they'll turn out to have been someone interesting (which, funnily enough, they almost invariably do). Yet suddenly I understand the desire to figure it all out, untangle the string by tracing it back to the original knot. So I shuffle around in the boxes some more.

I come across a yearbook, crammed full of photographs and papers, which look as though they'd been hastily stashed there when more pressing things took over. Mom at Barnard, looking bored. A photograph of her girlish self, scowling for the camera.

220

Then a newspaper clipping. Same old Mom – except she's wearing hippie clothes and is hurling paint bombs at a politician, her mouth open, twice as big as usual, a great black kidney, like Lucy yelling at Charlie Brown.

I slam it shut. Christ. Open it again. There she is, shaking Abbie Hoffman's hand and grinning. I learn that my mother subscribed to *Freedom Fighter Weekly*; partook of various mind-expanding drugs; occupied a local military compound; organized Anti-Imperialist Pot-Luck Dinners. Demonstrated against all the usual things – censorship, nuclear weapons, racism, patriarchy. Wore tie-dyes. Ate yoghurt. Was arrested two times. This is a revelation. My mother has a rich past of which I have been previously unaware. Why hadn't she told me all this before? She probably had, but I hadn't been listening.

'Snooping, Ellen?' My mother appears, as though she's just popped out of the pages of the book. Leans against the door-frame, expression arch, arms crossed.

'Would *I* do that, Miss . . .' I consult an article. '. . . Can-Crack-Anything-Classified 1965?'

'*Touché.*'

'Why didn't you *tell* me you had a criminal record? Do you know how much clout that would have given me at school?'

'It never came up in conversation.'

'I understand you were also the Paint Bomb Queen.'

'Didn't you wonder why I gave you balloons and all that poster paint when you were a child? I was hoping you'd follow in my footsteps.'

'My generation wasn't into that. We decided that it wasn't worth the trouble.'

She is wearing a silk blouse and beige skirt, an outfit so at odds with her lunatic mind-set that you wonder if she isn't as schizophrenic as James. Her gaze sweeps over the clippings – pleased, nostalgic. All at once I understand the origins of my mother's 'practicals'. They're scaled-down versions of the things she did as a young adult, signifiers to herself and everyone that she had a life before she was a wife and mother. She sits down next to me, as though sensing that I would like further clarification of what is essentially her secret history – a way of life that perhaps she wishes she'd never abandoned.

221

'I am content, you know,' she says. 'When I married, I acted out of choice. But sometimes I need to look back and remember. It was all so wonderful. We felt so essential, so alive.'

'As opposed to bloated and apathetic, like us.'

'In a way,' she continues, 'motherhood was an extension of radical politics for me. A need to feel needed, to change the world. To make a difference in people's lives.'

'So you gave birth to your own little subculture. Very clever.'

She casts me an amused look. 'You and James and Matthew hardly constitute a subculture.'

'I don't know. I think we qualify. The kind that grows in a Petri dish, maybe . . .'

My mother's leafing through the yearbook, examining faces. 'Sometimes I wonder what happened to my old friends.'

'You had friends?' This is news. She never even seems to crave company. The area is full of old hippies she could hang out with, liberals who opposed the establishment in the Sixties, then inherited all their parents' money. You see them around. They have long hair. Belong to Greenpeace. Do macramé. Send their kids to Quaker schools. So why . . .

'Of course, I had friends,' she says. 'What did you think I was, some kind of pariah?'

I suppose she had been a bit of a party animal, even when she was first married. I have a vague memory of a bash she threw when I was young. Loads of booze, a table heaving with exotic delicacies. Guests comprising at least twenty different nationalities. Loud music, red light bulbs. One man kept setting his fingers on fire – that was a big hit. The neighbours called the police who, as I recall, took off their hats and joined in the fun. One of them turned out to be particularly good at limbo. It didn't end until six o'clock in the morning; when I got out of bed, half the guests were still lying there, asleep.

'You should get in touch,' I say. 'Once a troublemaker, always a troublemaker.'

'Oh, I don't know,' she says. 'I expect they all got married and settled down. Might be a bit depressing.'

'That's true,' I agree. Get the impression I've said the wrong thing. April's words reverberate: 'Your mom . . . She's such an adventurous person.' She'd noticed. I hadn't. I'd only thought of my mother as peculiar.

Mom's rooting around in the box where I found the yearbook, as though motivated by a kind of perverse curiosity about her background, a desire to quantify how much she had lost. Pulls out a hood ornament shaped like a peace symbol. Some beady moccasins that I think may have been Dad's. A complicated water pipe with all sorts of nozzles protruding.

'Cool,' I say. 'Let me guess – a shower attachment.'

'Ellen, are you happy?' she asks abruptly.

I shrug. 'Sure.' The silence hangs. I'd never really thought about it. Not certain I want to start now.

'Because your happiness is more important to me than anything else in the world,' she adds.

'Oh.' This is news to me. I don't know what to say.

'I'd hoped to bring my children into a better world,' she says. 'When it looked like that wasn't going to work out –'

'Oh, give yourself some credit. It's marginally better. We've got microwaves, remote control TV.'

'– I decided the next best thing would be to devote myself to their happiness. Sometimes I feel as though I've failed.'

'Don't be silly,' I say awkwardly. 'You did a great job. Look at James and Matthew. Barely grown-up and they've already got responsible jobs.'

'I'm talking about *happiness*, Ellen. Real happiness – that feeling that makes you get out of bed in the morning.'

'I have the next best thing,' I joke. 'An addiction to hot coffee.' I wish she'd get off the meaning-of-life stuff. It's making me profoundly uncomfortable.

'What do you want the most, Ellen?'

'Dunno.' I start fooling around with the Swedish cadaver. 'Money.'

'I'm serious, Ellen.'

'So am I. Starting with three thousand bucks. Do you know, I've almost finished my article?' This is a lie but I am suddenly desperate for something to offer her. She doesn't look as though she believes me. 'Apart from that, nothing. I don't really want anything.'

'A home of your own?' she suggests. 'Children?'

'Uh, no.' I glance towards the door; escape is out of the question. 'Sorry to disappoint you. Maybe James will provide you with some grandkids.' I halt. Remember what's just happened. Until a few hours ago, she'd had a grandchild on the way. I clear my throat. 'Sorry.'

'That's all right.'

'I get my big mouth from you, you know. And the foot I put in it from Dad.'

'It's quite all right.'

Our conversations have always had a chilly quality, as though civility is to be prized above emotion. What had she been like in the Sixties, when passionate expression was the norm? I find myself wishing I'd known her then.

'Did you ever talk about it?' I ask. 'With April, I mean. Motherhood and all that.'

'We discussed it. Goodness knows she needed guidance. For someone who's been through such rough terrain, she's incredibly naive.'

'So she told you she wanted to have babies.'

'Yes, and I told her everything I wished people had told me. About the pain, the depression. The possible complications.'

'What sort of complications?' I ask.

'All sorts. I'd had more troubles than most.' My mother's face shifts, changes, as though she wants to tell me something and is trying to evaluate how I might react.

'Like what?' I am curious. Recall the Phantom Foetus.

She draws a deep breath. 'After James, they told me that I couldn't have any more children. My first pregnancy was difficult, very difficult. They advised against another. Said I might . . .'

She doesn't have to say it.

I try to imagine life without my mother. At one time, I would have claimed that it wouldn't have made any difference, but in fact it would have made all the difference in the world. There would have been no one to praise and protect me, make every pathetic attempt at glory seem accomplished. Poor mother – the educational toys had made little impact on me. It took awhile for my C's to turn into A's. She'd helped me with my homework, had encouraged me to do my best. When I got discouraged, reassured me, until I learned to believe in myself.

'But you went right ahead and did it, anyway,' I say.

'I wanted to have you,' she says.

I want to ask if I'd been worth it, but I'm afraid of what I'll hear. I remember the many times I'd rejected her, pushed her away. *I had my womb removed, did you know?* Her words come back to me. I cringe.

For years, I've watched her killing off a part of herself. It's probably too late to stop her now. But what if there was just the slightest chance that I could save her? By doing something as simple as reassuring her?

'Mom . . .'

'It's funny,' says my mother, wiping dust from her hands. 'Had April told me she was pregnant, I would have felt so excited. Almost as though it were me.'

But I can't give her what she really wants. A second chance. That's what Matthew had been – another shot at motherhood. An opportunity to get it right after I'd turned out to be a dud.

'I'd have thought, how wonderful – perhaps we'll get a little girl-child,' she says.

Jealousy wells up – I thought I'd banished it forever. *I'm* her girl-child. Me. Why haven't I ever been enough? Why does she keep looking for others to take my place?

'Such a shame, her losing the baby,' says my mother. 'It would have been such fun . . .'

'I'm glad,' I snap fiercely. 'I'm glad she lost her.'

Even as I speak, I know I don't mean what I say, but it's as though (not for the first time) my mouth has taken on a life of its own. 'I want things to be the way they were before she came. You found a replacement for me. Gave her my room, let her take my place. You weren't even glad to *see* me. I know I should have telephoned, but I wanted it to be a surprise.' I can feel my neck growing hot. I'm making a fool of myself – again. 'I was just never good enough, was I? Just never good enough . . .'

She is staring at me, open-mouthed. I don't wait for a further reaction, but leave. Once more, I've screwed up. The wrong words flew out like friendly fire.

Something tells me this is a runway nosedive – the end of something that never even got off the ground. I'm already wishing I could eat my words. I've betrayed my mother, April, and my own godchild-to-be. But apology would lead to reconciliation and this is more than I deserve. Family is for others, not me.

April has returned and is sleeping in my room. My idea. She had happy memories of being there, and I am hoping against all odds that it will make her feel better. Also, I am afraid the room she shared with James will remind her of his absence. He still hasn't come home.

'Where *is* he?' asks my father.

'This is so unlike him,' says my mother.

Doctor Dogtag has prescribed some tranquillizers for April. It seems the night after we left, she got rather upset and had to be sedated. She dozes continuously, less Goldilocks than Sleeping Beauty, waiting for a Prince Charming who isn't going to show. Her body hardly moves but her mind is furiously at work; her eyes dart back and forth, as though watching some kind of debate taking place on her behalf. I sit by her bedside and try to think of ways to rouse her, wake her up before she comes to any unwise conclusions.

I try talking to her. 'Hey, April – when you decide to get your butt out of bed, we can sign up for an art course. A life drawing class, maybe. Check out some naked men.' I hold the talking Jesus doll by her ear, pull the string in his back: 'Jesus loves youwwww . . .' Nothing.

Periodically, my mother brings up some cream of wheat, tries to spoon it into her mouth and fails. My dad tries telling her jokes. No response.

Then one morning, while we're sitting in the living room, she appears, tired and dishevelled, as though she's been through a terrible ordeal.

'Hi, guys,' she says. 'Any more coffee?'

'Yes. Let me.' I leap to attention.

'No,' she says, stopping me. 'Thanks, Ellen, but I'll get it myself.'

In spite of appearances, she seems lucid and resolved. We treat her delicately, carefully, but she won't accept any help. She fixes her own drinks, makes her own meals. Limps around doing her own laundry until I want to tear it out of her arms. She's determined to accept no assistance, to become entirely self-reliant.

Doesn't ask about James, as though she senses that there is no answer we can give.

Once, late at night, I hear her talking on the phone. She sounds distressed. I try to eavesdrop, but the only word I catch is, 'Don't . . .', whispered over and over and over.

At first, I try to act as though nothing is wrong, but as I watch her sink deeper and deeper into herself, I decide that drastic measures are called for. She's planning something, that's for sure, and I must do everything in my power to prevent it.

I will persuade her that I require her help. She won't leave if she thinks somebody needs her. Hadn't she offered to help me with my story early on? 'Hey, April,' I say to her one day when she's in the kitchen. 'Could I have a word with you?'

She nods. Lays a thin slice of tomato on a piece of dry toast. This is further cause for concern. She seems to have put herself on a starvation diet, as though her sole desire is to fade away.

'It's kind of embarrassing,' I say apologetically. 'I have to eat my pride here. Basically, I'm stuck. On the Grosworthy article. I can't get the information I need, and I wondered if you could help me.'

'Sure.' Her tone is listless, as though she's reciting from a script.

'I got this tape recorder here. Gift from Matthew.' I present it in all its high-tech glory. 'Not bad, eh? Pulitzer, here I come. It might be just the thing. Whatever Grosworthy says, I tape. Gunshots, insults, it could all come in handy. People come out with all sorts of things when they're irate. I've even got a bullet-proof vest. You could wear that. I'll just don my old fisherman's sweater . . .'

'It's full of wild animals,' she says. 'Big cats. They bite and scratch.'

'Ah, well, that's where you come in,' I explain, improvising. 'I figure one of us can hold the tape recorder, and the other can carry the stun-gun.'

'Where are you going to get a stun-gun?'

'I hadn't got that far, actually.'

'I'd love to help, Ellen, but I don't think I'm up to the legwork.'

'Right. Your ankle. Well, it's healed up a good bit, hasn't it?'

'Not really.'

'Oh, go on. Be good experience for you, if you want to be a journalist.'

'I don't.'

This is proving more of a struggle than I thought. I have a strong feeling that April is planning to leave, and it's up to me to make sure she sticks around, at least until James returns. He owes her an explanation, and hearing it will help her to move on. They say it's impossible to accept a loved one's death until you view the body, and I figure pretty much the same logic can be employed. One glimpse and she can go, if she likes. But not yet.

Though she tries to pretend otherwise, James is omnipresent in her thoughts. Her show of independence might fool others but not me. April is bleeding on the inside where she thinks it doesn't show, but she forgets how well I know her and I know she's in distress. She spends the evenings in her bedroom, the one she shared with James. Keeps the blinds pulled down, as if to deny herself the slightest radiance, but leaves the window open, as though hoping her loved one will return. When night falls, her painted blue sky turns to black. The sun vanishes, the artificial flowers gasp.

One afternoon I walk in to find her sitting in the darkening room, wearing James's old coveralls.

'I'm garbage,' she states, matter-of-factly.

I take the letter she's holding out of her hand. 'Dear April,' it reads. 'It was worth a try but it was all a mistake. Please accept my deepest apologies. I've returned to Berkeley where I am going to try to take up where I left off. You will find some money enclosed . . .'

For a moment, I think she's cut her wrist, but it's only the way her arm is dangling.

'You're welcome to stay here as long as you like,' I say.

'Thanks,' she says, as though she doesn't believe me.

'I wish you would. Like I said, I could use your help.'

'Oh, Ellen. You don't need my help. People like you don't need anyone.'

If only she knew.

We sit there watching the light fade. Pretty soon, we can no longer see the rainbow, which strikes me as a particularly bad sign. No hope, no possibility of a pot of gold. Even if it's there, we won't be able to find it.

'I saw a real one in California,' says April. 'The first day I arrived. A rainbow. The biggest one I'd ever seen.'

And she'd probably figured it was an omen, a good one. So much for miracles and wonder.

'By the way,' she says. 'I may have a visitor arriving.'

'Great,' I say. Eager for any positive news.

'I've told her not to come, but she might come anyway. She's a bit . . . unpredictable.'

'Sounds good to me,' I enthuse. 'Any friend of yours is a friend of mine. Who is she?'

A wry look, a grim smile. 'Don't make further enquiries.'

Sudden change is close at hand. I can feel it as one can sense a storm drawing nearer on a hot summer's day. Someone has drawn the Death card, for which you can never prepare. A skeleton is dancing, waving a scythe, preparing to conclude the cycle.

12

She is blonde, big-boned, and is sitting on our front porch as though she owns it. Wears a tube top and is sweating, as though the fires of hell are too close for comfort. Her feet, clad in shabby Seventies boots of brown-orange leather, are up on one of the chairs. She doesn't look up.

'Excuse me,' I say. She lifts her head, slowly, as though she's been lying there for twenty years and I'm the one who's encroaching. Same pert nose, similar jaw, but she has more *face* somehow and it's bloated and puffy, no doubt the product of a permanent hangover. Wears a belt with the word 'Baby' burned into it repeatedly and a holster on the side for a gun. The woman smiles and says:

'I exercise my right to bear arms.'

There is a big handbag by her side, the kind that contains everything, which she appears to have unloaded on to the table in an attempt to make herself at home. A pack of cigarettes. A bottle of blended whiskey. A couple of tattered maps. A few fruit chews. A photograph of April.

'While you're up, I could use a glass and a couple of ice cubes,' she says, reaching for the bottle. I catch sight of a long black slash across her palm. She flashes it, a swift, decided gesture, almost a 'fear not'. 'I had it put there when I learned I was supposed to die young. Told the tattooist to give me one hell of a lifeline. It seems to have worked. Wish it hadn't. He also did a bullethole around my navel. Want to see?'

'I have a better idea,' I say. 'Why don't you go away *and not come back?*'

She laughs. I am tempted to laugh with her, give the impression of rapport, and then proceed to throw her off the premises. But something tells me she's not that easily discouraged, and that we're going to be locked in combat for some time. So I compromise, chuckle, slap my hand against my thigh and say, 'Let me get you that glass.'

No one is home, thank God. I don't know what my mother and father would make of all this, but I have a feeling they would handle it badly. This is a situation that calls for diplomacy and tact. I emerge with glasses, ice, and a bag of low-fat potato chips which the woman picks up and lazily examines.

'This what she's eating nowadays?' she says. 'Members of your socio-economic group are so health-conscious. She'll be thinking she's too good for the old neighbourhood.'

'Now, why would she think that?' I say. 'Don't be ridiculous.'

'She ever mention home?' she asks.

'No. That is . . . no.'

The woman pulls out her gun and shoots the cord holding up my mother's wind chimes. They fall to the ground with a discordant tinkle. She settles back and closes her eyes with a satisfied sigh.

'Would it be safe to assume that as long as you have something for target practice, you're happy?' I ask.

She lifts her head up slightly and opens one eye. 'No. I won't be happy 'til I get my girl back.'

'She's not your girl any more.'

'The hell she isn't.'

'She's her own person now.'

'Oh, is that what she's trying to pull? Well, I'll have you know she couldn't survive for five minutes without me. She's been calling me up. About time, too.'

There doesn't seem to be any point in arguing. She shuts both eyes again and sinks more deeply into the chair. Her face is oddly peaceful, as though she has finally come to the end of a long road.

'Tell you what,' she says. 'I'm going to go out for a while. Might as well do some shopping while I'm visiting this here fancy town. I'll be back later to pick up April. You'd better make sure she's here. I'm holding you personally responsible.'

She sweeps her belongings into her bag and saunters away,

231

turning her head from side to side as she goes, greeting bewildered neighbours with a cordial, 'What the hell are you staring at?'

April's visitor has arrived.

I've got to locate April, on the double. I have no intention of letting her mother destroy her all over again. Drag her back, tear her down. But where *is* she? I've no clue. Though I've tried to keep track of her, she's eluded my grasp. I search the house but no one's home. So I get in the car and drive.

Where might a girl like April go? There are only so many places she feels comfortable. She'd feel awkward asking for a room at the inn, even if one was available. I've got to find her before she heads home. I check the train station, the gift shop, the public park. Suddenly, it hits me. The most obvious sanctuary. The Church.

The House of Fishes and Loaves isn't a *terribly* well-known place of worship. You could safely say that it accommodates one of the more obscure denominations. They're Born Agains, that's all I know. I'm unlikely to find it on a road map. I careen around a corner or two, bark questions at passers-by. Then I spot him. My man Myron, trailing somebody carrying a twelve-foot cross.

I lean out the car window. '*Myron*. Nice one. Is this your latest assignment?'

'Piss off,' he shouts. He's limping along nicely.

'How's your boss? Sawed the other leg off yet? Hey, I need to locate a church.'

He jabs the air in front of him: 'Ask *him*.'

Bearded guy – but then, he would be. His hands are large and his skin is the colour of spring soil.

'Excuse me,' I shout. 'House of Fishes and Loaves?'

The man stops, leans the cross against a tree. Gestures. 'Three blocks down and take a right. You can't miss it.'

'Thanks. Hey, what's with the crucifix?'

'Jesus told me to carry it around the world.'

I suppose there are worse things Jesus could have told him to do – like burst into McDonalds with a semi-automatic. 'What's your name?'

'Bill.'

'Well, good luck to you, Bill.'

'Thanks. And you.'

I wave to Myron. 'Let me guess – your boss promised you a by-line. You should know better than to fall for that one.'

'Go ahead and laugh,' he snarls. 'I'll send you a postcard from Zimbabwe.'

I locate the building. Its plain exterior denotes a kind of frankness – what you see is what you get. The inside is simple: one long white hall trimmed in wood. Natural light ripples against the walls. On one side, a magnificent stained-glass window. On the other, a huge picture on brown paper of a goldfish and a loaf of sliced white bread.

'Sunday school project,' says a voice behind me. I turn. It's the minister. At least, I assume it is. You couldn't tell from his outfit. Call me old fashioned, but I don't think ministers should wear 'God is Love' tee-shirts. 'You know kids. But they managed to grasp the general idea.'

'I'm looking for a girl named April,' I say.

'Any luck?'

'No. I was hoping you could help me.'

'*I* can't.' He gestures towards a small statue of Jesus. 'But *He* can.'

Thanks – that's very helpful. 'I'm serious.'

'So am I. Seek and ye shall find.'

'Next you'll be suggesting I try moving in mysterious ways.'

He smiles and points up. 'That's His prerogative.' He is carrying a rag and appears to be dusting. Catches me staring: 'We're a bit short-staffed.'

'Underfunded.'

'That too.'

'So am I.' I hand him a buck.

'Is this for the poor?'

'No, it's a bribe.'

'Excellent.' He folds it up. 'I'll put it towards the Spring Fling.'

'Do you have any idea where April might be?'

'Probably in the last place you'd expect to find her.'

I think of home. 'I've already looked there.'

'Then maybe she doesn't want to be found.'

I give up. This is pointless. And I'm down a dollar, which I

233

can ill afford. He's taken up a broom and is starting to sweep, as though I've already gone.

'I never did get the bit about the fishes and loaves,' I say. 'If He could do it once, why couldn't He do it a hundred times? I mean, why not feed all those ghetto children instead of leaving it up to the Hare Krishnas?'

'Miracles make things too easy,' he says. 'Grace takes work.'

'Okay, but He could go to, say, the Third World once in a while and relieve the starving masses.'

'He does. Who do you think came up with the Red Cross?'

He's working his way towards the door. People just can't get away from me fast enough. I look up at the stained glass – modern, magnificent, almost incongruous in the unassuming setting. It twinkles. 'Gift of LandDevel', a plaque below it reads. I can't get away from these people. Is this man an agent of theirs, sent to thwart and frustrate me? It depicts Jesus with His legs crossed. Disciples sitting on what look like bean-bag chairs. There's a computer monitor in the background.

'I suppose that's what He'll use to let people know he's back,' I remark. 'Television. The Internet.'

'Maybe,' says the man. 'Though something tells me word of mouth will travel pretty quickly.'

'Well, thanks for all your help.' I am desperate, almost inclined to stop and say a prayer. But I've never prayed in my life.

'Ellen. When you love someone, everything you do to try to help them is a prayer.'

The minister hasn't spoken. He isn't even there. It's somebody else. A deep, gravelly voice. But there is no one in sight.

Then driving back through town, I spot him, sporting an uncharacteristic five o'clock shadow. Walking down the street, or rather skulking, with a sort of stubborn hunched-over lope that radiates go-away vibes.

'Yo, Hamlet,' I yell. 'Long time no see. How's it going? You've been sorely missed back at the castle.'

He ignores me. Picks up his pace. I follow, trailing him closely. 'What's all this about Berkeley? Unless Pennsylvania has turned into California this is just more of your crap. Where the hell have you been? *I want some answers, James.*'

'It's no use, Ellen,' he shouts. 'I have nothing to say.'

'Nice try, but it's not going to work.'

'Leave me alone.'

'You're being really selfish.'

'You just don't understand. I'm not who you think I am.'

'Don't give me that Jerusalem Fever bullshit. Get in the car.'

'No way.'

'But it's safe to come home now. Didn't you know? She's dead.'

I want the satisfaction of seeing his face turn white. But he only starts walking faster, turning into a side street. He's not going to get away with this – not if I have anything to do with it. Fortunately, Philmont is nothing if not salubrious; there are no dark and inaccessible back alleys. I veer sharply to the right, in hot pursuit. Start driving down the too-narrow road.

James halts, aghast. 'Ellen, this is a one-way street.'

I knew this would annoy him – the first-born always has an overdeveloped sense of law and order. I ram the car into a nearby 'Stop' sign several times. Passers-by start to look. I honk the horn, jump out onto the sidewalk, point to James: '*He* did it.'

'I've seen him before,' a woman comments. 'He hit that little old lady at the crossroads. Took her handbag.'

'Yeah,' says someone else. 'I recognize him.'

The crowd is baying for blood. 'Okay, Houdini,' I say to him. 'No more vanishing acts. I think it's time we had a little chat.'

'I *know* she's alive,' James hisses. 'I called the hospital.'

'Not April,' I say. 'The baby.'

Poor fool. He hadn't expected that. 'But I thought everything was fine.'

'Wrongsville.'

He's in a state of shock. 'I'm a bad man,' he whispers.

'True,' I say, 'but you don't have to be a coward. Come home.'

He shakes his head. 'Impossible.'

'You're taking the easy way out.'

'No, I'm not. Don't you think I want to see her?'

'Then what are you waiting for? Afraid the lovely Courtney will object?'

'For God's sake, Ellen. Don't you understand what that was

235

all about? It was the only way to set her free. April, I mean. I wanted her to hate me.'

'Boy, you're almost as much of a wuss as Dad. Do you know, he couldn't bring himself to propose to Mom? Had to pop the question through a fortune cookie. There's something I think you ought to know, James. April's mother is here. She's come to take her back. The least you could do is return and say goodbye.'

'It would only make the situation more painful.'

I'm losing patience. 'James, *what are you afraid of*?'

'Myself.'

So tall and strong and yet so full of self-doubt. Scared that the tight little knot that constitutes his world will unravel.

'Just get in the car,' I say.

'Can't do it, Ellen. I deserve to suffer. And the sooner I start, the better.'

I explode. 'Lose the hair shirt, James. All this *mea culpa* business has got to go. You need to persuade her that she hasn't done anything wrong. If you don't, she's going to keep blaming herself, and then you'll have to live with that, too.'

'*You* tell her.'

'I tried. Didn't work. You can't wiggle out of atonement.'

'Next you'll be telling me you've accepted Jesus Christ as your personal saviour.'

'And renounce the sins of the flesh? You know me better. Now, do me a favour. Come and claim her. Live happily ever after.'

He shakes his head. 'It would make me feel far too good.'

If it doesn't hurt, it doesn't work. Boy, is he screwed up. Poor Protestant. 'James, why do you make things so difficult for yourself?'

He shrugs. 'Stick with the devil you know.'

'So you're not coming?'

'No.'

I guess it's up to me, then.

My mother and father are sitting in the living room, talking to April's mother. Or rather, my mother is sitting, my father is standing, pipe in hand, by the fireplace in what I call the 'Danger Position' and April's mother is lounging across a couple of my

236

mother's Empire chairs, examining an antique Chinese vase that has been in my mother's family for generations.

'This is nice,' she says. 'They have the same one in pink at the Dollar Shop – but then, you wouldn't know what the Dollar Shop is, would you.' She spots me. 'Well, hello, Rich Girl.'

My mother is trying to prevent fireworks. Seems to realize she's met a looser cannon than herself. 'Hello, darling. We've just been talking to Mrs –'

'Goldie. Call me Goldie. As in Hawn, as in locks. There, you see? I'm not totally illiterate.'

'Gun,' I mouth to Dad, but he's looking out the window as though keeping an eye out for the sheriff.

'Would anyone like a drink?' I ask. 'Coffee? Tea?'

'Get me half a glass of your best filtered water.' Goldie holds her whiskey high above her head. I have to admire her style. It occurs to me that the police might be helpful in a situation like this, and I am trying to figure out how to get to the phone without –

'And don't even think about calling the cops,' she adds. Apparently, I have the same psychic connection with her that I do with April. 'Or I'll blow your head off.'

'Speaking of getting my head blown off,' I say, 'I've just had a very trying afternoon, so would you mind very much if we skipped the beverages –'

'Get the water.'

'Right!' I run for the kitchen.

'I think it's time you thought about leaving,' I hear my father say.

I race back in before she can pull the trigger. *'Water for everyone.'* Hand out glasses, a clean linen towel over my arm. 'Still? Sparkling?'

Then the door opens and April appears. Stops short at the sight of her mother, who rises.

'Come to take you home, babe,' she says briskly. Her tone is firm and does not allow for argument.

'Okay,' says April uncertainly.

'No,' I say. 'She's not going.'

April looks over at me helplessly. 'Don't think I don't

237

appreciate everything you've done for me, Ellen. The fact is, it couldn't last.'

'April, sit down,' says my father. 'Let's talk this over like rational human beings.'

'Isn't that what we're doing?' demands Goldie. 'Are you implying that April is acting like some kind of dumb animal?'

'Don't be absurd,' says my father.

'"Don't be absurd,"' she mimics, and looks away in disgust.

'Mom, these people have been really good to me,' April whispers. 'Please don't get angry.'

'Shut up, babe,' says Goldie.

'Mrs Merryweather.' Oh, no. My mother is taking the PTA approach. 'April has been very ill. If that is in any way our fault, we are very sorry. But I might point out that while we may not have made all the right decisions, our intention was always to take care of her.'

'You took care of her, all right,' says Goldie. 'You take her in, introduce her to a life where she feels like a freak, let your no-good son run away when it turns out he's knocked her up, then throw her out. Yes, you've taken *real* good care of her. Truth is, you're a bunch of upper-middle-class do-gooders who take people in and then chuck them out when they become inconvenient.'

'April is not an inconvenience,' says my mother, 'and she can stay as long as she likes.'

'Oh, and I suppose you don't realize she's the reason your precious son is staying away. Don't tell me the day isn't going to come real soon when you *gently* take her aside and suggest that it might be time for her to be moving on. *For her own good.*'

I look over at my mother. Of course this isn't true. But her expression is decidedly queer.

'You've already done it, haven't you,' says Goldie. 'You've already had that little chat, told her it might be a good idea if she moved out for a while, just until everything settles down, and of course afterwards she'll be welcome to come back *which you'd know in a million years she'd never do.*'

All at once, and with a kind of sick feeling, I recall the conversation with my mother: 'I want things to be the way they were before she came . . .'

My mother is doing this for me. I want to shout that I hadn't meant it, but everything I do or say seems to make things worse. In any case, the 'way things were' had been largely an illusion. Nothing had revolved around me – I'd only imagined that it did. Now I'm paying the price for my wishful thinking. And so is April.

'Only as a temporary measure,' says my mother. 'Just until we find out what's happening to James.'

'Oh, yes,' says Goldie. 'James. Your globe-trotting, Harvard-going, champagne-swilling, Plato-quoting, spineless goddamn sonuvabitch son *James.*'

'Don't call him names,' says April. 'Stop right now, Mom. These are good people, and James is a good man.'

'Don't you get it, honey? James didn't really love you. You were entertaining white trash to him. His little redneck darling.'

'That's not true,' she says hotly, more in James's defence than her own.

'Oh, yeah? Look me in the eye and tell me he loves you. That you know for a *fact* that he loves you.'

April turns away. Her cheeks are flushed and her eyes are open very wide, as though she's holding in her tears by a massive effort of will. 'If he doesn't love me,' she says, 'it's not his fault. He tried. You can't make yourself fall in love. Or out.'

What could I tell her? That he's punishing himself? That he loves her but is refusing to drop by? She's lost all confidence. It's terrible to see. What's worse, I cannot find the words to reassure her. She leaves the room briefly and returns with a bag. Must have anticipated this and wanted to make it as easy on everyone as possible. Awkwardly, she faces my mother and father.

'Thanks for everything,' she says. 'I mean it. I'll never forget everything you did for me.' She turns to me. Then away. Out the door.

Five minutes of silence follow.

'Well,' says my father, 'maybe it's all for the best.'

My mother doesn't contradict him.

I go to bed early. April has cleared away every trace of her presence – her make-up, her clothing, her photograph album, her

239

book. The only thing she has left behind is her porcelain Jesus collection.

I pick up the Middle Eastern-looking one with the big gnarled feet and hold it up against my cheek. It doesn't do anything for me. I feel cold and shivery but cannot bring myself to seek comfort from the usual outlets. Even if sex and liquor were available, I don't think I'd have the heart. I slide between chilly sheets and shake. After several hours of fitful sleep, I awaken to find a warm weight on my feet. A well-deserved demon? An avenging incubus come to torment me for my sins?

It is Puddles, anxious, but cheerful and panting, fur straggly and tangled and damp. I tuck her under my ear. 'Am I ever glad to see you.'

It's cool and the moon is bright. I know that further sleep will be impossible.

'What should I do, Puddles?'

She wiggles out of my grasp with fresh intelligence and looks up at me excitedly. Then runs a few steps towards the door. Stops. Looks back at me.

Of course. She knows exactly where her saviour is. The sky is clear enough to see the stars. Puddles will lead the way.

I've got to get to April. I'm not quite sure what I'm going to do when I find her. All I know is that I've got to try to do the right thing.

13

Suburbia at night. The cease-fire begins. For eight hours or so, no more tedium and routine – or loss or pain or any of the other unacceptable emotions everyone refuses to acknowledge. Judging from the blacked-out windows, I am the only one awake. The moon has turned the road into a lunar river. Puddles, leading the way, is luminous.

The centre of town is dead, even for Philmont. The upmarket boutiques are lifeless and dark save for dim spotlights which only serve to highlight the fact that no one is there. All the precious stones have been taken out of the jeweller's window. The movie theatre looms ominously. The bank's digital clock, like an out-station in space, alerts an empty street to the time and temperature. The church bells strike four.

'I wish I knew where you were going,' I whisper to Puddles. I try to figure out where she might be headed. For all I know, she could be taking me all the way out to the Midwest. I get to thinking about those weird murders that occur in the area about every five years – head in one district, torso in another – and become keenly conscious of the absence of people. Whistling doesn't help. Neither does assertive body language. In the distance, I hear the siren of an emergency vehicle. Ambulance, fire engine, I always forget which is which.

We head east down the turnpike. I try to pick up a cup of hot coffee at the all-night mini-market, but Puddles jumps up and down impatiently. We pass car dealers, supermarkets, veterinarians, condominiums, dentists' offices, small advertising agencies and banks. And then I see it. The Philmont Happy Motel. Of course. I should have known. Where else could they afford to go?

The Philmont Happy Motel is one of those long two-storey buildings with a large bar and a pool, where the more pitiful local business conferences are held and second-rate Pooh-Bah lodges throw their annual Christmas parties. It's surrounded by three giant mirrored monoliths that represent the interests of several mysterious corporations, and from which I have never seen anyone come or go. I went to 'The Happy' once with a guy, intending to fool around, and ended up shooting pool with a legionnaire while my intended played twenty-five rounds of Pac-man.

I bang on the glass door, but the night clerk, with the excessive authority of the uniformed and badly paid, smiles primly, disapprovingly, and indicates that they are closed. I wave my hands, pantomiming emergency. He turns back to his newspaper.

Puddles is leaping around excitedly. Leads me to an open side window.

'It's called *trespassing*,' I hiss. 'It's illegal. Do you want me to end up in Sing Sing?'

Thirty seconds later I'm shoving her through, and hauling myself up behind her. I find myself at the meeting point of two long corridors lined with doors. Against one wall stand two vending machines, one for snacks and one for sodas, and a box full of books – dirty paperbacks and, oddly, a copy of *Mill on the Floss*. 'Book Swap' reads the sign. The walls are beige, the carpeting brown vomit. The light, though harsh, fails to illuminate anything.

Puddles is already sniffing around the doors with concentrated professionalism. All at once, she takes off, and I follow. Scratch and whine, scratch and whine. She has stopped in front of a door. I knock.

A strange man appears. He's grey, fat, has lips like a couple of slabs of liver. Needs a shave. We look at each other.

'This must be my lucky night,' he says.

'Or maybe not,' I say.

Then the door across the hall opens and there stands April.

* * *

242

The room is small and gives the impression of a great density of darkness, relieved only by the glare of the television, which is tuned into some sort of spooky sci-fi movie, and the bare bulb of the damp and clammy bathroom.

I hear Goldie's voice: 'Let's have some more light in here, babe.'

On goes a lamp, which irradiates an extraordinary array of beer cans, cheesesteak wrappers, boxes of doughnuts, cigarette packets and empty pizza boxes. Smoke clouds the room like dry ice. It appears to be emanating from some kind of hookah. I trace the long plastic tube to a mouth, which is attached to a woman. Goldie. Who is sprawled across the bed, evidently much pleased with her purchases, situation and general surroundings. If I hadn't known better, I might have even thought she was glad to see me. She isn't, of course. Grins hello and throws a lit cigarette in the direction of my face.

'Hello, Rich Girl,' she says. 'Like a beer? Help yourself. Only stick to the Budweiser, because I'm taking the ones with the Revolutionary War hero on the label home as souvenirs. Local brewery. Very historical. Probably be collector's items one day.'

'Glad you've found time to do some sightseeing,' I say.

There is one double bed. Also a cot, provided by the management and on which April is sitting. Beside Goldie are several candy wrappers filled with half-eaten bars of sugary coconut covered with that artificial chocolate coating that tastes like wax. Goldie is smoking, eating, drinking, reading *The National Enquirer*, watching television and talking, all at the same time. Like April, she seems to have multiple arms, though she is putting them to much more degenerate use.

She puts aside *The National Enquirer*. 'How rude of me to keep my nose buried in that paper. Usually, of course, I read something more intellectual – like the *Weekly World News*.'

'One of my favourites, too,' I say. 'Say – is that an *authentic* pair of cork wedgies?'

She is wearing an open robe over a swimsuit. 'I figure this is kind of a vacation for me,' she says, by way of explanation. 'Haven't had one for years. Look out the window and check out that pool.'

243

I obey. Do I have any choice? It looks like something out of *Psycho*. 'Nice.'

'By the way, what the hell are you doing here?' asks Goldie.

'I think we have some unfinished business.'

'The guy at the front desk didn't let you in, did he?' she says. 'Because I specifically told him, no visitors, and I can't be bothered to punish him. I'll bet you snuck in. I'd be perfectly justified in blowing your head off in self-defence.'

'Let's make a deal,' I say. 'You give me April and in exchange I won't go over to the police station across the way and inform them that an out-of-town alcoholic has just threatened me with a gun.'

'Guys,' says April tiredly, 'cut it out. You'd better go, Ellen. I know you're just trying to help but you can't. Really – there's nothing you can do.'

Her skin is dry and drawn, and she has bags under her eyes. Presumably, her mother's feverish enjoyment of her 'vacation' is keeping her awake. She's still in her day clothes. Puddles tries to crawl up into her lap, but for once April doesn't seem to notice her. She looks over at her mother and says, 'If we want to make an early start, maybe we should go to bed.'

'Honey,' says Goldie, waving a cigarette, 'the whole point of staying up all night is that you don't have to wake up in the morning.'

'Excuse me,' I say, 'but April looks as though she could use some sleep.'

'Nothing's keeping her up.'

'Except the television and the very real possibility that you're going to set the bed on fire.'

Goldie ignores me – which is kind of a disappointment, as I'd felt we were developing a real bond. I pick up a bag and start to load it up with anything that looks as though it might belong to April.

'What are you doing?' demands Goldie.

'Well, I'm not cleaning up the empty pizza wrappers.' I carry on. Can sense Goldie poised above me, like a rattlesnake ready to strike. I go about my business, then look up calmly, prepared for whatever she has in mind, only to see her relax and pick up the phone.

244

'I'm going to call Security,' she says.

'Mom, don't,' says April.

'Keep still.' Goldie presses a couple of buttons.

'Stop!'

Her mother hangs up, infuriated. *'Don't tell me what to do.'*

'Hey, April,' I say, picking a doll off the floor, 'is this hacked-up Barbie yours?'

'It's perfume,' says April. 'Mom got it for me as a gift.'

'Oh, I see, her neck is the opening of the bottle. Just out of curiosity, where's the head?'

'I think I lost it,' says April guiltily. More likely her mother had a fit of some sort and threw it in the trash.

Goldie looks at April for a moment with repressed fury, then reaches over and turns on the radio; it emits the raw sounds of Fifties rock'n'roll. The television is still on. She leans back and closes her eyes as though she finds this racket soothing. Through the smoke, I note that her bottle of whiskey is almost empty.

'She isn't driving tomorrow, is she?' I whisper.

April nods miserably.

'She'll get arrested,' I say. 'Can't you keep her here for another day?'

'No. She's determined to get going. Anyway, she'd just keep drinking. I want to get her out of here, actually. She kept making friends at the bar. It was really embarrassing.'

'Let's dance,' says Goldie suddenly, her eyelids flying open like a resuscitated mummy. She rolls over, rises, stumbles over to April, seizes her hands and starts jitterbugging, whooping occasionally. April, agonized, responds with token movements. Goldie is in an ecstasy of motion, possessed by jerks and tremors as though in the frenzies of a holy dance. Nudges her daughter periodically, encouraging her to show some enthusiasm. I suspect that this kind of behaviour has been going on all evening. It shows on April's face.

I finish packing. 'April, let's go. Come on, let's *move.*'

'I can't.'

'Face it, Rich Girl,' Goldie says, 'she wants to stay with me. She wants *me*, not you, do you understand?'

'April,' I plead, 'you can't give up. You can't keep running away.'

'Ellen, I want to go with you but I *can't.*'

Her cry is full of sorrow. Her mother stops dancing, looks hard at her, leans back and raises her hand as if to strike. I catch a glimpse of the tattooed lifeline as her palm moves through the air. I reach over and grab it.

'You don't want to do that,' I say. 'You'll regret it, just like you regret everything else.'

She smiles wetly and struggles, as though we are playing a game. 'April, get out,' I say. 'Take that bag and meet me outside.'

April makes a move. Her mother lunges for her. *'Stop right there,'* she screams. 'You worthless brat.' Shakes her. April tenses up, frightened, then tries to pull free. Her mother's eyes are wild, filled with vengeance, with a lifetime of discouragement and struggle.

'This is all your fault,' says Goldie.

'Mom, I haven't done anything wrong.'

'Thought you could escape, did you? Well, why the hell should *you* be allowed to get away? *I* couldn't.'

April has broken free, is backing her way around the room. Goldie is slowly staggering towards her.

'You know I'd do anything to make your life better,' says April. 'Why do you think I'm here?'

'Don't act like you're doing me a favour.'

'If you'd just give me another chance –'

'I don't think you deserve a second chance, do you, honey?'

'Mom, whatever I've done wrong, I'll make it up to you –'

'You can never make it up to me. Don't you understand? Nothing you can do will ever, ever make it up to me. You just couldn't wait to get away from us, could you? Ran away at the first opportunity. Well, maybe I'd have been a better mother if you hadn't been such a superior little princess, did you ever consider that?' She is gaining momentum. April is sliding backwards like a terrified desert lizard trying to blend into the sand. 'Your father and I sacrificed everything for you and you turned your back on us. Worked sixteen, eighteen hours a day and you deserted us.' She grabs April. Her tone is rising. 'Well, what are you going to do about it, huh? How are you going to pay us back for everything we've done for you? *What are you going to do to make it up to us?*'

246

'I love you, Mom,' says April desperately. 'I love you, I love you, please listen, Mom, I love you. Please listen to me –'

'It's all your fault, the way things have turned out. All your fault, all your fault –'

April continues, as though reciting a sacred chant. 'I love you, Mom, please listen, forgive me. Forgive me for being born.'

But too low, too late – these last words are whispered. Goldie screams:

'I should have got rid of you with the other one.'

April jerks away, juddering, as though she's been injected with a poison that causes loss of bodily control. I become irrationally afraid that she will throw up or wet her pants. This is the end. She was hanging on by a thread. Her mother collapses, sobbing, and says, 'Why did you run away from me?'

April creeps up, a cub who's been cuffed one time too many. Places a terrified paw on her mother's shoulder. Goldie jerks her arm away.

And April turns.

'You killed my twin,' she says. 'You killed my sister and you would have killed me, too, if you'd known.'

'Yes,' Goldie hisses. *'Yes.'*

'But I survived, didn't I? And that pissed you off. Then I found someone who cared about me, James, and you couldn't stand that, either. You were delighted when everything went wrong. Couldn't wait to get up here and start ruining my life again. You can't stop clawing me back, can you? You can't bear the thought of my being happy.'

Goldie is gleeful, triumphant. 'Yes, yes.'

'You hated me,' continues April, her tone intent. 'You just couldn't punish me enough. So I popped out one day and ruined your life? That's crap. Your life is not my fault.'

'Nobody ever said it was,' says Goldie.

'You *did*. You blame me for everything – you always have. I could never do anything right. Of course I wanted to move out, run away. I thought I was going to go insane. I tried to go to college, saved up enough for one semester, and the two of you just had to go and screw it all up by starting another stupid business and getting into debt.'

'Yes,' says Goldie, 'that's right. That's exactly what happened.

We did it on purpose. You deserved it and *I'll never regret it.*'

And then it hits me what she is trying to do. She is making the ultimate sacrifice. If you love someone, set her free. *This* is Goldie's agenda. To liberate her daughter by pretending to hate her. To release her forever by giving her up. She knows extreme measures are called for to crush April's love – and if this doesn't work, she will destroy herself, disappear, whatever it takes to cut the cord. I suddenly see her in a whole new light. Don't do it, Goldie, I want to shout. It doesn't have to be this way . . .

'You enjoy making my life hell, don't you?' says April.

Goldie smiles darkly, does not reply. Knows that April will hold on until emancipated by force, hurled into the heavens where she will finally be free. Free of suffering and bad memories, free of her past. Free of the mother who cannot bear to let her go.

My head is spinning. 'Wait,' I say, 'stop.'

'This is none of your business,' says Goldie, unable to tear her eyes away from April, as though she knows the hour of parting is at hand.

'It is her business,' says April, 'she's my friend.'

'Well, she'd better be,' says Goldie, 'because I never want to see you again.'

I hear a rushing in the room, as though the winds are mounting. It's just the tumult of the television but it feels like a tempest. The lights are flickering, the pressure building.

'She's lying, April,' I shout. 'She doesn't mean a word she says.'

'I know that,' says April. 'I know.'

She falls forward, forgets. Gives up, gives in. Her eyes shut and her body goes limp. Her mother catches her, rocks her back and forth. For a moment, I am once more convinced that she is dead – that Sleeping Beauty will never wake, that the Little Mermaid has finally frozen to death. But no. Her eyelids flutter, breath fogs a mirror. Air refreshes, ice melts. The kiss of life revives. Her mother has rescued her, brought her back from the dead. Accepted her forgiveness and surrender.

'I wanted to make you strong,' her mother whispers. 'This was just my backwards way of doing it. You're what's kept me going, don't you know that? The only thing I've never regretted.

248

You mean so much to me, so much. I wanted to save you so I tried to give you up. I couldn't even do that right. I'm sorry.'

But what has happened is that Goldie has given birth a second time. Has been granted mercy, offered another chance. This is more, far more, than she'd ever hoped for – her impossible dream has come true. As for April, she's been born again – for real. And is whole at last.

I want to stay just a moment more, try to soak up the radiance. Bear witness, burn this picture into my mind in the hopes that I, too, will someday be offered redemption. I've lost her. Oh, April, my heart is breaking. Our paths may never cross again. I will become a memory, as will this whole alchemistical time. You will move on to something greater than any of us could give you.

The sun is rising over the swimming pool, which shifts from grey to liquid blue. April is still cradled in her mother's arms. I get the feeling I'm not wanted, but then that's nothing new. Time to stage a tactful exit. I start inching my way towards the door.

'Hold it right there, little missy.'

I halt.

'I understand you've been real good to my baby.'

I shift awkwardly. Don't feel I can deny this, although it isn't true. 'It's been nice having her.'

'I want to break the cycle.'

I'm not sure what she means.

'I want her to stay here,' says Goldie. 'Start a new life. I don't want her to end up back where she started. It wouldn't be right.'

'She's welcome to live here as long as she likes.'

'Good.' She turns to April. 'I'm sorry about your baby, honey. Maybe it just wasn't the right time. I light candles to your little sister. Don't ever think I don't care.' Then to me. 'Something tells me we're going to get along real well.'

'I'm very relieved to hear that,' I say.

She seems satisfied. Heaves herself up. 'Well, get a move on, you two.' She gives us her angriest look. *'Go on.'*

'I've decided to stay with you,' says April.

'You can't,' says her mother.

'Says who? Aren't I allowed to make my own decisions?'

Goldie looks as though she can hardly believe her ears. 'Are you sure?'

'Yes, I swear. I miss you and Innertube and Dad. I'd love to. It's really important to me.' She seems adamant.

Goldie doesn't try to talk her out of it – where she comes from, you don't query good fortune. 'Your father will be awfully glad to see you, honey. He misses you like crazy.'

There is nothing more to say. Partings are always difficult. April is leaving. It's hard to believe that I will never see her again. I'm even going to miss Goldie who, for one extraordinary moment, resembles my own mother, almost as though one has been superimposed over the other. I clear my throat, try to think of an appropriate farewell. Anything I say will be wrong, as usual, but I can't just turn and walk out.

'Nice meeting you, Mrs Merryweather,' I say. 'Maybe you and I could hold up a mall together sometime.'

'I just might take you up on that.' She snorts, smiles. I get the impression that she likes me. 'Just one more thing, Rich Girl.'

'What's that?'

She points at me, her finger merciless and direct. 'Don't look back. Don't *ever* look back.'

Puddles is crawling in and around the pizza boxes. Clamps a lump of thick-sliced sausage in her jaws. Runs over to me, lays it at my feet. I pick her up. 'Can I keep her?'

'She's yours. Well, 'bye, Ellen,' says April. 'I'll give you a call.'

No, she won't, though she doesn't know it yet. As soon as she leaves, this part of her life will cease to be real. Her time has come to move on. 'Great,' I say. 'Then this isn't really goodbye.'

Sometimes you don't know what you have until it's taken away from you. I open the door. Raise a hand to Goldie, palm outward. She does the same. The lifeline flashes.

Fear not.

I leave the building. Start to shiver. There is a peculiar early-morning dampness in the air. The giant corporate monoliths are less prominent in the daylight. The grass looks too green to be real.

I half-expect my mother to be there, waiting for me, as she used to do, after school. But this is absurd – she doesn't even know where I am. I recall April's description of my mother's trips into town. Searching for me, hoping to find me even when I was in another country. If only I'd left a trail of flowers. If only . . .

I begin the long walk home, crippled by loneliness and regret. Red light slices the sky. Opens into piercing yellow. I turn my gaze downwards and proceed with reluctance. It occurs to me that I have nothing, absolutely nothing, to look forward to.

Then I hear footsteps behind me. April appears by my side.

'She insisted.' She is flushed, breathless. 'Says I can come home when I've . . . resolved everything here.'

I don't think I've ever been so happy to see anyone in my life. 'Are you sure about this?'

'Yes. Say, Ellen . . .' She looks embarrassed. Bites her lip. 'Do you think your parents would mind if I stayed on for a couple of days? Just until I get my act together?'

'Of course they wouldn't. You know my mother didn't mean all that crap she said. She . . . oh, I'll explain later.' I cast one more glance back at the motel. Pray that Goldie will make it back safely. Picture her loading up tiredly, wondering why every journey has to be so hard. I hope with all my heart that she'll be able to carry on. Something tells me not to worry. Everything is going to be all right. The crops may be a bit straggly this year, but they'll grow. And in time, maybe flourish.

April only hesitates once, when she sees a familiar car on the road. She shouts, waves, starts to run. Watches the car recede into the distance, wipes a tear away.

Godspeed, Goldie.

14

When we enter, it's silent – a haunted house that even the ghosts have abandoned. Countless windows or no, darkness predominates. Shadows hang in the corners like cobwebs.

The best lace tablecloth is looking more tattered than antique. The bittersweet china, dusty. The vase of roses in the middle, the worse for wear. The leaves have dried and are dropping off. Their heads are bowed, as though in mourning.

My home. Until so recently, the scene of seismic upheavals. Now all is quiet, deathly so, and I'm convinced it's all my fault. If I hadn't been so stupid as to expect an effortless apotheosis, none of this would have happened and we would all be better off. Or would we? Maybe changes had to be made. Sometimes you have to lose your way before you get back on the right track. Unfortunately, I think we may have taken a few too many wrong turns. I can feel the regret in the air, the sense of loss. I'm afraid to raise my voice, wake the dead.

'Anybody home?' April shouts.

'Oh my God oh my God oh my God oh my God *children.*' My mother comes running, legs whirling like a rotary beater. My father comes bounding down. My spirits lift; this is how they used to greet me when I came home from college. But it is mainly April they embrace and exclaim over, apologize to and hug. My dad is as pleased as if he'd just been made a father again. My mother has taken April's hands.

I stand to the side, waiting patiently for my turn, until it slowly dawns on me that my turn is never going to come. I had my chance and I blew it.

Light fills the whole downstairs, as though someone has waved a magic wand. The gloom lifts. Spring has arrived, after an unexpectedly long winter. My mother's plants seem to have grown several inches and my parents look ten years younger. The whole household is coming back to life, and April deserves credit for that. I should be happy for them, and I am, but I will never stop feeling excluded. Something tells me my days here are numbered, and that I should start preparing to leave.

But how to say goodbye, begin my new life with integrity? End on a good and honest note? It's time to lay the cards on the table, set the record straight, take the blame.

'The reason Mom asked to you leave, April,' I say, 'was because of me.'

Everyone turns. My mother stares. April looks slightly bewildered.

'I said some awful things,' I continue. 'Stuff I didn't mean. Mom asked you go because she thought I wanted you out. It's all my fault. I'm sorry.'

Says my mother, astonished, 'But, Ellen, that simply isn't true.'

'Yes, it is.'

'No, it isn't.'

'Yes, it is.'

'Five minutes in the kitchen, Ellen.' She exits.

The last words I hear are my father saying, 'Did I just hear Ellen *apologize?*'

My mother turns, faces me. Real showdown position. What's it going to be this time? An interrogation? A reprimand? But nothing could have prepared me for what I hear her say:

'Ellen, your father and I have decided to give you the money. Three thousand dollars. You can just take it and leave, as soon as you like. You don't have to write the article.'

I cannot quite believe my ears. 'Are you serious?'

'Yes,' she says. 'No catch, no strings, no conditions. So you are free to go, whenever you like. Your father will withdraw the money tomorrow in cash.'

I am completely dumbfounded. For a moment, I can't speak. 'When did the two of you decide this?'

'Last night. We had a long talk.'

I'll bet they did. This is their tactful way of letting me know

253

that they want me to make like an egg. They can't get rid of me fast enough. I'm being banished.

'Fine,' I say stiffly. 'I'll be out of here tomorrow.'

'Don't think we're trying to pressure you –'

'Of course not. It's about time I left. I should never have come back in the first place.'

'Ellen –'

'For the record, I did try to write that article. But I failed. Okay? I failed.'

'But, Ellen, that's not the –'

'Just call me Ellen "Incompetent" Kaplan – a complete failure at everything she does. An utter disgrace to her family. Look, I'm not surprised you want me to leave, but you could at least have the decency to be honest with me. I feel like my own parents are lying to me and it . . . it . . .'

Hurts.

It's becoming harder to talk. I turn. Face the sink. Will her to go away.

'Ellen,' says my mother.

I'm starting to cry. How humiliating. This is the last thing I need. And it's pointless. It's all over.

'Ellen, look at me.' I hear her footsteps, feel her hands on my shoulders. She tries to turn me around.

'Leave me alone.'

Immediately, I wish I hadn't raised my voice. I don't want the others to hear. Sound carries, I've discovered, whether you like it or not. Secrets rise to the surface, like steam.

'Ellen, you're just being silly.'

I whip around. 'Don't try to pretend this hasn't been coming for a long time.'

'What on earth are you talking about?'

'You *gave* her my *room*,' I cry. 'Replaced my photo with hers. You weren't even glad to *see* me. Call me paranoid, but I got the impression you were trying to freeze me out, a pretty clear indication that you wanted to see the back of me –'

'Ellen, when are you going to get it through your head that we *love* you?' my mother says. '*That's* why I took your picture down. I missed you so much, I could hardly bear to look at it. It's the very reason we're giving you the money. Because we believe in you, and we no longer want you to think that you have to live up to our expectations. You don't have to be a journalist. You can be anything you want. Be nothing at all – we don't care. We only want you to be happy.'

I can hardly believe what I'm hearing. Could they mean it?

'As for April,' she continues, 'I was only trying to care for her as I would want someone to take care of you, if you found yourself vulnerable and alone. I asked her to leave because I felt she needed to spend some time with her mother and resolve a few things. It was intended as a gentle nudge.'

'So you don't think I'm a monster?'

'Of course not. I know you didn't mean what you said. Don't you think I said similar things to my mother? I said worse.'

'Really?' I am impressed. 'Like what?'

'Never mind. It doesn't matter. The point is, she had one expectation of me – to "marry well". And when it emerged that I had no intention of doing so, she became angry and never forgave me, just as my father never forgave me for not being a boy.'

I remember all the times my mother gloated over me, the family 'girl-child'; maybe I'd been celebrated, after all. 'So what happened?'

'We never reconciled. She refused to accept me as is. I don't want to do the same to you.'

I wonder if April and Dad are eavesdropping. If I ever move out, it will be to a home where every room is sound-proof. 'Um, okay,' I mumble. I don't know what to say.

She peers at me. 'You do understand, don't you?'

'Yeah.'

'Good.' But she doesn't seem entirely convinced.

'Just one question,' I say. Now seems an appropriate moment to ask. 'Why weren't you glad to see me?'

She looks surprised. 'What, just now? But we were.'

'No. I mean, when I first arrived.'

'Ah.' A flicker of understanding in her eyes. 'Because it seemed too good to be true. I thought you might be a mirage. Also –'

'What?'

'You didn't seem particularly glad to see us.'

'I didn't?'

'No. You never do.'

'Oh.' Of course. She'd feared rejection – which is not surprising. 'I was, though. Happy to see you, that is.' Like a battered ship arriving in a safe haven. Or a prisoner of war returning at long last to native land.

'I'm glad to hear it,' my mother says. 'You were always so independent. Looking back, I can't help but feel as though I did something wrong. It shouldn't be that easy to leave home. Soon, you'll be off again, and suddenly, there's no more time. I've had my chance and now it's too late. I'm all out of time.'

I have a feeling she's not just talking about me. It's everything, her entire life. I grab the hourglass, the one my mother uses when Jehovah's Witnesses come to the door. Turn it upside down.

'There's plenty of time,' I say. 'I'm sticking around. And you haven't even clocked up half a century.'

Her eyes move towards the hourglass. She watches the grains slowly drain and settle.

'Well . . .' I clear my throat. 'It's not a *very* dramatic spectacle but you see my –'

She grabs it and hurls it to the floor.

'To hell with time,' she says.

Yes. To hell with time.

'I missed you, Mom,' I say.

'I missed you, too.'

She hugs me at great length. A lifetime's worth of hugs.

'I couldn't have been so independent if you hadn't done everything right,' I whisper. 'You never allowed me to think that anything I ever did would go wrong. You created my whole world, then let me believe I'd done it all by myself. That's why it was so easy to leave.'

I hadn't known all that until I said it. My mouth is acting of its own accord, but for once, I don't want to take anything back. We stand awkwardly for a few moments. Examine the linoleum on the floor.

'Maybe we should work out a system of semaphore,' I say. 'This talking business is rather difficult.'

'Perhaps we just need practice,' says my mother.

'I expect so.'

256

Another silence. There is much at stake. But room for mistakes.

Perhaps it's not so bad, having a mother who drops eyeballs into highballs. I'm beginning to think I'm very lucky, actually. Maybe she and I can hang out.

Suddenly, she lifts her head. 'Is that someone at the door?'

He stands in dishevelled splendour in the doorway where he once stood with a bouquet. James. Poor guy. He's reached a turning point, all right. He's a mess. Looks bone-tired. His hair is tangled, his clothes are torn. I wouldn't be surprised to hear that he'd crawled here on his hands and knees. He walks towards April. Lays himself at her feet.

'Save me,' he says.

She crosses her arms. 'Save yourself.'

He lifts his head, astonished. This was clearly not the reply he was expecting. 'Say what?'

'I am not your saviour, James.' She speaks slowly and clearly. 'If you want to be saved, you're going to have to do it yourself. Do the work, James – lean into it. Now get up. You're acting like an idiot.'

He looks as though she's just suggested he jerk off. Cannot bring himself to believe what he's heard. He stares at her for a moment, then rises to his feet.

'I was going to ask you to marry me,' he says.

'I'll bet you were,' April replies. Exits. Returns shortly with a cardboard box. 'Here.' Sets it down at his feet. It is the porcelain Jesus collection. 'Take it. It's yours. You need it more than I do.' And she walks out.

His stunned expression tells me that this was not supposed to happen. I suspect he is frantically trying to figure out where he went wrong. She's thrown him for a loop; it's caught him by the ankle. Now he's dangling upside down, completely helpless.

'Give it up, big brother,' I say cheerfully. 'She's trumped you.' I shouldn't be so mean – but then, it's so much fun. And he deserves it.

'I've been dumped,' he says wonderingly. 'I don't believe this.'

'Relax,' I say. 'It's not the end of the world. Just think – you and the Jesuses can rent a house on Cape May next summer. Just imagine all the great times you're going to have together.'

I trust April is unpacking her belongings. I'm going to have to shovel out the Morgue. I'll sleep there – she can have my room. It's hers now, really. She's earned it.

'I guess redemption isn't easy,' James says.

'Nope,' I say. 'It ain't.'

I leave him hanging. Go out to the little room where people hang their coats. There's a small padded bench there, where I encounter April.

'You bitch,' I say.

'It's kinder this way.' I notice she is trying not to laugh. 'God helps those that help themselves.' She loses it.

I'm confident now that she can look after herself, but that doesn't mean she isn't fragile. She's taking the first few tentative steps into the next stage of her life, and there are bound to be a few rocky patches. This time, though, I won't screw up. I'll be right by her side.

'James is a lucky guy,' I say, sitting down next to her. 'Those things will be collector's items one day.'

'Only the one from the Franklin Mint.'

'Won't you miss them? The Jesuses?'

'No. I was getting a bit tired of them, actually.'

There are a few more questions I have to ask. 'You haven't lost it, have you? Your faith, I mean?' I haven't *got religion* or anything like that but I have to admit, I would feel devastated if she lost hers.

'No,' she says. 'It's stronger than ever.'

'Can I ask you one more thing?'

'Sure.'

'How can you feel so passionately about someone you've never met?'

'What, you mean Jesus? I've met Him,' she says offhandedly, as though she meets superstars every day.

Wow – and I thought meeting Henry Kissinger was impressive. 'What's He like?'

'He's nice. He kind of likes to kid around. You know all that walking on water stuff? It started out as a joke, and sort of got out of hand. Scared them half to death. They almost wet their pants.'

'Is that when He said, "Don't be afraid, it's only me"?'

'Yeah. He was really reassuring.'

'Anything else you can tell me about the Son of God?'

'Only that He loves you.'

'Hm.' A few days ago I would have thought, well, at least *somebody* does. But maybe people have more love in their hearts than I thought. 'I think I'm more of a Buddhist, really.'

'That's okay, Ellen. There's room for everybody.'

We remain there companionably for a couple of minutes, giving James time to make a graceful exit. Now that April's been taken care of, I need to start thinking about myself. I have to decide what to do next.

'The money's mine if I want it,' I tell her. 'They're giving it to me right away.'

'You shouldn't accept it unless you've done the work,' says April blandly.

'Thanks, Sunshine – I'll bear that in mind.'

Suddenly, she stands. 'Let's go for it,' she says. 'Come on.'

'Right *now?*'

'Why not?' She throws my jacket at me. 'There's no time like the present.'

'But I'm exhausted,' I bleat. 'I hardly slept.'

'Stop complaining.' She drags me up. 'You're so lazy, Ellen. Let's get moving. Where's that tape recorder of yours?'

'I'll get it.'

Why not? I've nothing else planned for the day. April seems to have something specific in mind. I can't imagine what it is, but she seems to know what she's doing, so I guess I'll go with the flow. I run upstairs, grab tape recorder and notebook. Two pens. And my Swiss Army knife. Well, who knows? We could end up anywhere. It's a jungle out there. Be prepared.

'Here.' I hand her a pen. 'I dub thee journalist. And take this.' The tape recorder. 'I expect you're more proficient than me. Where are we going?'

She smiles. 'The Grosworthy Estate.'

'Oh, no.' I recall how I almost got shot. 'Tried that. Not a good idea. We'll die.'

'*Ellen*. It's time you got rid of that attitude. Just trust me.'

'Fine – let me get the bulletproof vest.'

'You won't need that thing – you'll only look stupid.'

259

'You're right,' I say unenthusiastically. 'Let's go.'

Ellen Kaplan, Ace Reporter, is on the job again.

We push the speed limit, as though time is of the essence. And in a sense, it is – I'm about to lose my nerve. The road is hilly and I start to feel sick. April is driving and refuses to slow down.

'This is great, Ellen,' she roars. 'We should do this more often.'

We pass a billboard along the way. 'Go Back,' it reads. There is a white cross on the road, supporting a skeleton. I briefly wonder if it could be Myron.

'I want to go home,' I state, clutching the dashboard.

'He's trying to scare you,' says April. 'Ignore it.'

We pull up, and help each other over a crumbling patch in the wall. Find ourselves in a kind of woodland.

'I smell smoke,' I say. 'Not the friendly wood-fire kind. The something's-just-been-detonated kind.'

'He sets things off all the time,' she says. 'Don't pay any attention. I think it's this way.'

She seems to know where she's going. Not only that, she's demonstrating a surprising lack of fear. I follow. Birds circle.

'That hawk almost flew into my head,' I yell. 'You want to get us killed?'

She ignores me. Perseveres. I have no choice but to carry on. I have the eerie feeling that someone is keeping track of our progress. I start worrying about booby traps and wonder if we'll end up in a hole in the ground, Grosworthy shovelling dirt over our heads. I turn around, try to run. April calmly grabs me.

'We're almost there,' she says. 'You can see the house.'

'Good. Then we can stop right here, say we tried, and go home.'

'It's no good, Ellen. We need an interview. What's that you called it?'

'The Duck.'

'Right. We've got to get the Duck.'

We start chanting, 'We've got to get the Duck. We've got to get the Duck.' April's fervour has overtaken me – I feel like I'm flying. *I am invincible*. I approach the building, panting, stumble up to a window and peer in, pen at the ready. Only to hear a voice behind me say:

'Hello, Ellen.'

I turn. And there he is, in all his white-haired glory. Grosworthy.

15

I cannot believe this. Here he is. Wearing no helmet and wielding no gun. I gaze at him stupidly for several seconds. 'Mr Grosworthy?'

'Please,' he says. 'Call me Eamon.'

April has appeared. 'Hi, everybody.'

'Hello, April,' he says. 'Glad you made it all right. And thank you for bringing your friend.'

I gesture, incredulously. 'You *know* this guy?'

April nods, slightly guiltily. 'He goes to my church.'

'The House of Fishes and Loaves?'

'Uh huh.'

I explode. *'Why didn't you tell me?'*

'I tried to,' she points out. 'Coming home from LandDevel, remember? I tried to get through to you, but you just didn't want to know. It seemed important to you to do it yourself, and I figured it was better that way. Anyway, Matthew told me not to.'

So that little slime was in on it. And all along . . . 'I feel like such an idiot,' I say.

'Hubris has been many a great man's downfall,' says Grosworthy. He's wearing what looks like a Boy Scout uniform and is carrying a pair of field glasses. 'And, not to be exclusionary, many a great woman's. Never be too arrogant to listen and learn, Ellen. I trust you've learned your lesson.'

I turn to him, irritated and momentarily free from fear. *'Fishes* and *Loaves?'*

'I like its lack of pretension,' he replies.

This is an outrage. 'Do you know how much trouble you've put me to?'

'Oh, yes.' He seems pleased with himself. Raises his binoculars. 'Look, a yellow speckled swallowtail.'

'How do you know who I am?' I say.

'I've been keeping track of your journey from the beginning.' A small bird comes and lands on his finger. 'And I know the editor of *The Philmont Organ* – though he doesn't know me. It all started when I made the acquaintance of April here . . .'

April is a few yards away, playing around with a lot of little Puddles look-alikes.

'. . . and we hit it off. When you returned home, she told me all about you. I wanted to make sure you were taking good care of her,' he says, 'because your brother certainly wasn't. I consider her a personal friend of mine, and I always look out for my friends. Speaking of which, meet Obadiah.'

A small monkey has appeared on his shoulder – the one from the library. Of course. It belongs to him. It's an arrogant little thing. Stares at me haughtily.

'He's my taster,' says Grosworthy. Hands him a cookie. 'Here – eat that. Also my messenger, spy, and general PA. He's a bit of a psychic, too, I think. Not to mention a dandy little companion.'

I am still getting over the shock. 'I don't believe this,' I say. 'I could have had access to you all along.' If I'd gone to *church*, of all places. I can see my epitaph now: Ellen Kaplan – she did it the hard way.

'Don't feel bad,' he says. 'You're only a rookie. I know all of this must seem a bit strange to you, Ellen, but you remind me of my younger self. Stubborn, but not without promise.'

'So,' I say glumly, 'just for the record, *are* you selling to LandDevel?'

'I *am* LandDevel.'

I stare at him. *'What?'*

'It's a front I put up,' he explains, 'to accomplish a couple of small tasks – one of which was to scare my neighbours, of course. The other was to test for corruption on the Township Zoning Hearing Board, perform a bit of a public service. See if applica-

263

tions were going through that shouldn't, find out if pockets were being greased.'

'And were they?'

'Absolutely chock *full* of lard. Ellen, I have a story for you that I think you've earned, one that will shock the town. Not only am I not selling to LandDevel . . .'

'You *are* LandDevel,' I say, 'and what's more, that little playground for the handicapped shouldn't have been sold . . .'

'. . . nor should the community arboretum. Exactly.'

'So the whole Willow Avenue development is just a sham.'

'Correct,' he affirms.

'You went to an awful lot of trouble, building all those houses.'

'I had to make it convincing. You did well, Ellen. I'm proud of you. Not everyone could have figured this out.'

'I didn't figure it out. You just told me.'

'Because you found me,' he says, 'and thus proved yourself worthy of the knowledge.'

Seek and ye shall find. Figures. 'So, can I tell my editor?'

'Tell everyone,' he says expansively. 'Tell the world.'

He looks even shorter than I last remember, as though he is shrinking, hoping eventually to become one with his own landscape. This man has the strangest agenda of all.

'One question,' I say. 'Why me? Why help *me* out?'

'Well,' he says, 'I guess I like you.'

'But you don't know me,' I point out.

'I know enough to know true grit when I see it.'

'I have no grit,' I say. 'I am without grit. I am utterly gritless.'

'Grit develops naturally. It starts with initiative. Going to visit LandDevel –'

'April's idea,' I say.

'But you went – I saw you. I'd installed a video camera in the Show Home. Word of advice, Ellen: learn to look up. Terrible disguise, by the way. And then there was the Residents' Association evening. I put up the flyer. You probably didn't notice, but I was the bartender they hired.'

'You were in the museum, too, weren't you?' I'd seen the uniform, not him. Everything is becoming clear to me now. 'And the church . . .'

'. . . dropping clues all along the way. Don't feel bad – they were fairly obscure. I have to admit, you disappointed me in the museum. You shouldn't have abandoned April, but I don't entirely blame you for that. The flesh is weak. I, of all people, should know that. Then there was the library.'

Where the technology had turned hostile on me. 'You were throwing up all those messages on the computer.'

'To discourage you – with Matthew's help. He and I met through April. I had to test your resolve, see if you'd persevere, and you did. Well done.'

Now I want *all* the answers. 'What about the notes? How did you manage to deliver those?'

'That was Obadiah's doing. He took the photos, too.'

The dirty photographs. 'Get out.'

'He did,' says Grosworthy. 'Camera in his collar. I have to confess, that was a red herring, designed to confuse you. I wanted to see what you'd do. I needed to make it difficult for you, Ellen – otherwise, you wouldn't grow.'

So he'd been deliberately trying to frustrate, exasperate, aggravate and enrage me – all in the name of my character and career. Well, what can I say? What a *pal*.

Chairs have been brought out by a manservant. Grosworthy strikes me as being the kind of guy who has a loyal following. We sit and watch the frolicking puppies and the play of light over the trees. It's not a bad set-up. I'm glad it's not going to be destroyed. 'So you won't be selling,' I say.

'No,' he says. 'I am, however, going to proceed with my little plan for a rehab centre on the grounds. The neighbours won't like it . . .'

'. . . but they may change their minds when they discover that their images are about to be downloaded on to the Internet.'

'It's a last resort, Ellen.' He chuckles. 'But it would be to benefit a greater good.'

Life is sweet. I observe April stroking the nose of a large dog. 'Wolfie's looking fat,' she yells. 'I think you'd better put him on a diet.'

'I'll need names,' I say. 'The Zoning Hearing Board members. And proof.'

'You'll get it,' he replies. 'Provided you stay for lunch.'

I have the feeling he likes playing games, an inclination which may or may not be healthy. 'Do you do this sort of thing often?' I ask. 'I mean, is it a sort of hobby of yours to re-direct people's lives?'

'I like to help out where I can,' he says.

'I thought you were supposed to be a misanthrope.'

'I was. Who could blame me? Everyone I ever cared about was killed. Thus I was motivated by a need to torment those who represented the worst in human nature. But somewhere along the way, it turned into the desire to do good. I wanted to do penance for my sins.'

'Which were?'

'Being alive. Surviving the war, while my comrades died. And shooting all those civilians. I was following orders, but that's no excuse – better to shoot yourself.'

'So I was one of your Sunday School projects,' I say.

'Just about.'

The smell of smoke has dissolved, leaving the scent of greenery and fresh air. 'Walk with me,' he says, and I do. He indicates the presidents on pedestals as we pass them. 'These men were my heroes, until one of them sent me into Korea. I was eighteen and so were my comrades. Sending children into war. Obscene.'

We pass a skeleton on patrol – propped up against a sort of headstone. I indicate it. 'What's with the bones?'

'Originally, my way of trying to hold on to those I love. Now, it functions as a kind of memento mori. I need it. It helps me to enjoy life more. Nothing like death to focus the mind.'

'Was he a friend of yours?' I ask.

'You bet – they all are. I have quite a few. His name was Monty – and you know what? He's still pretty good company. I'm having four others delivered tomorrow. A goodwill gesture, long overdue. Courtesy of the North Korean government.'

Is it my imagination, or do I hear the sound of drums and marching?

'I couldn't save my comrades, but by God I can bring them home.' He surveys his territory, in particular a small structure that I presume is destined to become the rehab centre. 'You know, I like it. Helping people. I'm starting to feel good.'

'What about that shot you fired at me?'

'A blank,' he says. 'Every shot I've fired since the war has been a blank.'

The sound of marching is getting louder. There's a small military contingent coming up the drive, carrying what look like coffins.

'They're here,' exclaims Grosworthy, delighted. 'A day earlier than expected. I must have got my dates mixed up. Excuse me, Ellen.'

A mix of Oriental and American faces. Impassive, solemn, they take measured steps, carrying four coffins draped with flags. Grosworthy bounds on ahead, exultant. 'My friends, my friends,' he crows. *'Welcome home.'*

April comes up to me. 'Isn't it great?'

'It's nice to see the guy so happy.' Best to pretend all this is normal. I turn to my right. Glance in the nearest window, only to see what look like acres of skeletons.

'He strips the flesh himself,' says April. 'At least, that's what he says. He's got a maggot farm out back –'

I don't think I want to know. I'm beginning to feel sick. 'Perhaps we should be moving on,' I suggest. 'Leave him alone with his old buddies.'

'Oh, no,' says April, aghast. 'We have to stay for lunch, or he'll be crushed.'

I guess I can bear it. Anyway, I'll need some names and numbers. The Zoning Hearing Board story is a good one all right – and this time I'll pursue plenty of sources. I should get in touch with Tyler Spee, show him what I've made of myself. Maybe make a move on him, at long last. Except he probably still thinks I'm an idiot.

He is nailing a sign to the door. The editor, that is – with a kind of resigned pounding, as though hammering nails into his own coffin.

'*The Philmont Organ* regretfully announces that after 120 successful years it has become necessary to cease publication. Many thanks to all our loyal readers. Queries re: outstanding debts should be directed to . . .'

So the Duck has spontaneously combusted. And just when I'd made my first kill. The competition must have got to them – that new colour paper, with the news that people actually want to read. It's a shame.

'I guess we just weren't sufficiently weird,' I say. 'Or something.'

He steps back. Doesn't seem surprised to see me. 'I knew this would happen,' he says affably. 'We never had a hope in hell.' He's wearing a prosthetic leg. Surprising – I didn't think that was quite his style. But then it hits me. His sidekick's gone. There's nobody to treat like an artificial limb.

'So where's Myron?' I ask.

'En route to Nepal. He should be in Egg Harbor by Tuesday.'

'He doesn't know the paper's folded, does he?'

'No.'

Well, that should be a bit of a surprise for him when he gets back – if he ever does.

'Grosworthy's not selling,' I say. 'I just found out. Not that it matters now.'

'Good job,' he says, boarding up the door – and just for the hell of it, breaking a few windows. 'I knew you'd come through. I always said I knew how to pick 'em.'

'Pick what?'

'Cubs. You were expendable, it's true, but I wouldn't have bothered sending you out if I hadn't thought you'd be able to do it.'

I'm almost afraid to believe what I'm hearing. 'So it was me specifically?'

'Let's put it this way – I know a wilder card than myself when I see one.'

So I *had* been special, after all. Or screwy, anyway. I'm grateful for the professional commendation, particularly from such a fine practitioner in the field.

'What about you?' I ask. 'What are you going to do?'

'Going to edit a paper out in Germany – get out of this goddamn country for a while.' He puts the hammer down, leans up against a railing. 'Could use an assistant, incidentally. You interested?'

I can't believe my ears. 'You're offering me a job?'

'Sure. Why not? Get out of this god-forsaken pseudo-democratic pit-hole they call the US of A.'

A couple of weeks ago, I would have called this the opportunity I was waiting for. But now, I'm not sure I want to go. I dig my hands into my pockets, finger the lint as though this is a form of divination that will provide me with the answers. Interesting prospect, but it would be too easy to run away. Fight or flight? I must choose wisely.

'Thanks,' I say, with genuine regret, 'but I've decided to stick around for a while. Don't know quite what I'm going to do but . . .'

The editor raises his hand, as though in benediction. 'Go to the new colour paper. With my blessing.'

That's what I was waiting to hear. 'Thanks.'

'Give them a call today, if possible – and make sure they give you a by-line.'

'Will do.'

'Incidentally,' he says, 'you know a guy named Tyler Spee?'

My heart thuds. 'Yeah. What of it?'

'Met him at a conference – your name came up. He said . . . let me see, now: "Ellen Kaplan couldn't shift her butt to avoid a bee sting in her backside."'

'I never told you my name.'

'It's a small town. Word gets around. You heard of Courtney Huffington?'

I cast one glance back at him as I walk away – a man who believes in what he does and will pursue it whatever the circumstances. He's starting to whistle. Shakes his phoney leg as though in time to a song. Doesn't seem too upset. Why should he be? He's a journalist down to the tips of his artificial toes, and what's more, he's handy with a hammer.

I return home to find my dad kicking a ball around the front yard. He's wearing a pair of suit trousers cut off at the knees. His hair is flopping all over his head. He's given his yarmulke

269

the day off, I observe. Either that or he's lost it. He's probably lost it. At least I'll know what to get him for Christmas.

'Hey, Dad,' I say. 'About the money. I appreciate the offer, but I've decided not to accept it. I'm going to try to get a job.' He continues to boot the ball around. 'I'm turning down money, Dad. Dad?'

'What? Oh, hi, Ellen.' He's wearing some old exercise shoes that he must have dug out of the Morgue. He kicks the ball up with one toe. Spins it on one finger and rolls it across his shoulders like one of those professional basketball players.

'So you can forget about it,' I say. 'The three thousand dollars.'

'Good, because I don't have it, anyway.' He whacks the ball with his head, Pele-style. It flies into the neighbour's front garden. 'Gave it all to Greenpeace. We're not going to have as much money as we used to, Ellen. I've quit the legal profession.'

'Oh,' I say. 'Well. Congratulations.'

'I told my boss that I'm through defending immoral sleaze-balls. I lose the salary and all the benefits but, hell, who cares? I'm free. You want to know how that makes me feel? I'll tell you how it makes me feel. Like this.' He crouches down and kisses the ground. 'It's heaven, Ellen, sheer heaven.'

My dad starts leaping around the yard, kicking his heels and yelling, 'I'm free, I'm free,' like a demented cartoon character. Mrs Tilty Tennis-Hips comes out and stands on her front porch, arms crossed, lips pursed. He gives her a wave. She throws up her arms and returns to her house. The old guard, unfortunately, is alive and well. Some things never change.

He's now a fully-fledged nutcase, all right, and pretty soon he's going to look around and realize that he doesn't have any health insurance. But so what? He's happy. The rest can be figured out later. Why rush? There's no hurry. We're all racing towards death too quickly.

Then abruptly, he stops.

'Hey, Ellen,' he says awkwardly. 'It's good to have you back.'

'Thanks, Dad.' I stand there for a moment, embarrassed. 'Good to be here.'

He seems satisfied with this. Resumes his dance, his lunatic ballet. I watch him cavort for a while.

'Hey,' I say. 'What if I decide to drop everything and embark on some kind of spiritual journey like everybody else around here seems to be doing?'

He stops and is, for a moment, the old Dad. The finger of authority comes down:

'Don't even *think* about it.'

My mother is seated in the dining room, sorting through old boxes. Throwing things out? Not on your life. Rather, she seems to be sorting out what's important from what's not. She looks up kindly when I enter.

'Hello, Ellen. Is everything all right?'

'Sure is. Whoa – check out those love beads.'

She puts them on. 'You know, I think I just might look up an old friend or two.'

'Go for it.' I make the old fist-and-forearm power-to-the-people sign.

I notice April and Zero talking quietly in the living room. He must have stopped by to see if James had returned, but James is nowhere to be seen. Their heads are bent over a book he is showing her; occasionally, they lift their faces and exchange observations. I am momentarily worried that he has cornered her and is boring her to death, but she is giving every appearance of enjoyment. They chat courteously, gently, as though they've known each other for centuries but have only just had the pleasure of meeting. It's almost as though they are courting.

There is a knock at the door. A dozen dark heads hover. I open it. A woman flashes ID: 'FBI.' They pile in, a flood of blue jackets, authoritative and efficient. Proceed to strip-search the house.

'Do you know the whereabouts of Matthew Kaplan?' one of them asks my mother.

She looks bewildered. 'Isn't he in the basement?'

My father runs in. Their eyes meet in alarm. 'Stash,' they mouth to each other. My mother and father have a stash? Already? What did they do, call Dial-a-Weed? They run upstairs, knock a

271

few things over. I hear the sound of something being flushed down the toilet.

I go down to the basement where several of the Federal agents are milling around. Find James huddled up in a corner, wrapped in a blanket. He's shaved his head.

'Are you okay?' I ask.

'Yes,' he gasps, dry-mouthed. 'I've decided to live in the basement.'

So this is his latest idea. To withdraw from the world, hole up like some kind of anchorite. 'You haven't taken any kind of vows, have you?' I say. 'Because poverty and obedience are pretty straightforward but I think you've overestimated your capacity for chastity . . .'

'Could you get me a soda?' he whispers hoarsely.

'A *soda*? Some monk you're going to make. You think St Benedict asked for a soda?'

'I'm just getting the hang of this,' he snaps.

'Give it up, James – you can't hide out here forever.'

But he seems determined to carry on with this course of action. Poor guy, he has such a long way to go. I used to believe he was an 'old soul' but I'm beginning to think he's recent issue. I remember Bill, carrying his cross – he's going to have an easier time than James here. All I can do is provide moral support until such time as he's ready to venture out. If I look closely, I can almost see the old Spock – the confidence, the restrained but kindly smile and good looks. It's funny to think that I used to consider him the ideal man; it was all just a kind of shell. He hadn't nourished his insides, his self – all he had was the exoskeleton. I wonder how many more of them are out there, walking around, waiting to be stepped on and cracked.

'Speaking of chastity,' I say, 'where did you leave things with Courtney?'

'Didn't you hear?' he says. 'She went on an art-buying tour of Central America and was captured and held hostage by freedom fighters. Apparently, she's joined the movement.'

I can picture that, actually – an outlet for all that sexual energy. Better revolution than fornication. I go back upstairs. The FBI are filing out. They've found nothing, of course – talk about artificial intelligence. One of them salutes me as he leaves. Straightens the picture by the door. Exits.

My father is standing in front of the television. Or rather, he is doing a little dance I call his 'victory jig', which he usually only does after winning cases.

'Get a load of this,' he says. 'The Grosworthy Estate is under siege.'

I am stunned. 'By whom?'

'The local Residents' Association. They knocked down the gate and now they're storming the premises. Want to know if he's going to leave his land to the mercy of developers and *he won't tell them*. Isn't it great?'

The screen shows a crowd of protestors snaking their way across the huge front lawn, waving signs, preceded by a tank. The beating of a helicopter obscures their roaring voices. Security guards have positioned themselves in the trenches and behind the topiary. Grosworthy is probably inside his house, hugging himself with glee and arranging for National Guard back-up.

My dad is clasping his fists above his head: 'I *love* this guy.'

'Excuse me,' I say. 'I have to make a phone call.' My story is better than good now – it's hot.

'And now for the rest of the day's news,' I overhear as I leave. 'Students at the exclusive Cromwell School have gone underground. They are believed to have tapped into top-secret government files and are rumoured to be developing a computer-human hybrid, previously only a product of speculation in fiction and popular films. The FBI is particularly anxious to track down one Matthew Kaplan, age eleven . . .'

I hear my dad drop the remote.

Frederick is lying on my bed. Hasn't removed his boots, the arrogant bastard. He looks at me tranquilly, as though he fully expects some form of sexual satisfaction within the hour.

Why am I always finding people in my bedroom? 'How did *you* get in?' I ask.

As though it ought to be obvious: 'I scaled the wall.'

'Well.' I sit down beside him. 'This is a surprise.'

273

'I would have arrived sooner, but I've been out of town.' The bastard is practically picking his teeth. He looks gorgeous, as usual – though I have to admit, his appeal is *slightly* tarnished by his demonstrated medical knowledge and expertise. I can't get over the sight of him acting the good guy in the art museum lobby – it makes him seem less *dangerous*, somehow.

'Frederick?' I say. 'How exactly is it that you know first aid?'

'I work for the Red Cross.'

This beats everything. 'The *Red Cross?*'

'Yes, Ellen. That's what I do.' He rattles off the names of half a dozen indigent countries and war zones. 'Why do you think I fly all over the world? For fun? I'm trying to atone for my ancestors.' He hands me something. 'Look, I've brought you a present. A Tangolian "luck doll". See? I had it custom-made – it looks just like you.'

'Oh, neat.' I take it, examine it closely. The resemblance really is astounding. 'Thanks.'

'I thought the great big feet were a nice touch.'

I hit him.

He takes it firmly out of my hand. Places it on the bedside table, and leans back on his elbows. I think I know what's coming.

'Time for lesson number two. Just do exactly as I say, and I will make you very happy in return. Forever,' he adds, 'if I don't get hit by crossfire.'

His wish is my command – in the bedroom, anyway. I climb on top of him. He smells like pine oil, my favourite scent. 'I think we make a good team, don't you?' he says, as I unbuckle his belt.

'Wait. There's one thing I've always wanted to do.' I lick my hand, lean over and flatten his cowlick. 'There.'

Now, we're even.

April is standing in the back garden as evening falls. Not wishing on a star but examining her galaxy, studying her universe more critically. Her whole life lies before her. She's made a fresh start. The wealth of possibility is great. Sleeping Beauty is on alert, wide awake. The ground beneath the kingdom is rumbling.

I go outside and join her, stand by her side. 'So,' I say, 'are you sorry you came?'

'It's a nice town, Philmont,' says April, 'but I have to admit, it's as full of screwed-up people as anywhere. They're just rich screwed-up people.'

'Yeah, that's for sure.'

Crickets and blackness. The cold smell of dusk. Most places look just about the same in the dark. Nightfall, the great leveller – the time at which you can't tell who's mowed their lawn and who hasn't, and when we're all equally vulnerable in our dreams.

April's hair lifts gently in the breeze. Her forearms look strong. Together, we could conquer the world, though I have to be honest with myself – she could probably do it single-handedly. For one awful moment, I wonder if she's stopped needing me. I've got to stop being so afraid. People move on, they develop, they grow, but that doesn't mean you have to lose them.

'Are you going to start college?' I ask.

'You bet. Might even convince my mom to quit drinking, get my dad to take some adult education classes. No reason life has to be as hard as it is. Got to make up for lost time.'

I envy her. It really does feel as though we've traded places. She has all the confidence I once imagined I felt. In the beginning, she'd seemed so destitute. Now I'm the one starting from scratch. Briefly, just briefly, I wonder if it has all been worth it. What if James had never brought April home . . .

We'd all be exactly where we started. Trapped in a perpetual game of statues, forever frozen in the same position, feet mired in unconsecrated ground.

I can't help but wonder if she has any vestigial feeling left for my big brother. I need to know. 'What do you think will become of James?' I say.

April looks as though she is trying very hard to remember something she is not sure really happened. 'Full mental breakdown?' she suggests.

'There is the family melancholia.'

'Well, there you go.' But she looks sad, as though recalling a happier, more light-hearted time. A period of loving someone,

275

and imagining that they were going to take care of you forever and ever and ever . . .

Suffer no longer, golden girl. Live happily ever after. For your sake, for mine. For the sake of all humanity.

'I love you, Ellen,' she says.

'I love you, too.'

And I do.

Good night, Philmont.

Good night, Matthew, wherever you are.

Good night, Mom, Dad, James, Puddles. And don't worry – it will all look better in the morning.